FIREWALL

Center Point
Large Print

Also by DiAnn Mills and available from
Center Point Large Print:

Pursuit of Justice
Attracted to Fire

**This Large Print Book carries the
Seal of Approval of N.A.V.H.**

FIREWALL

FBI : Houston

DiAnn Mills

CENTER POINT LARGE PRINT
THORNDIKE, MAINE

This Center Point Large Print edition is published
in the year 2014 by arrangement with
Tyndale House Publishers, Inc.

Firewall is a work of fiction. Where real people,
events, establishments, organizations, or locales appear,
they are used fictitiously. All other elements of the novel
are drawn from the author's imagination.

The text of this Large Print edition is unabridged.
In other aspects, this book may vary from the original edition.
Printed in the United States of America on permanent paper.
Set in 16-point Times New Roman type.

ISBN: 978-1-62899-176-5

Library of Congress Cataloging-in-Publication Data

Mills, DiAnn.
  Firewall / DiAnn Mills. — Center Point Large Print edition.
    pages ; cm
  Summary: "After an airport bomb interrupts her honeymoon departure,
Taryn awakes to find she and her missing husband are prime suspects.
FBI agent Grayson Hall will need to uncover the truth before he and
Taryn become two more casualties"—Provided by publisher.
  ISBN 978-1-62899-176-5 (library binding : alk. paper)
  1. Newlyweds—Fiction. 2. Honeymoon—Fiction.
    3. Terrorism investigation—Fiction. 4. Missing persons—Fiction.
    5. Large type books. I. Title.
  PS3613.I567F59 2014b
  813'.6—dc23
                                                    2014015606

This book is dedicated to the brave men
and women of the FBI.
Thank you for the sacrifices made to
keep our country safe.

Acknowledgments

I want to thank these amazing people for their assistance in helping me write *Firewall*. Your expertise has given this story life.

Don Anthis: I value your friendship and spin on characterization.

SA Shauna Dunlap, media coordinator, FBI Houston division: Thank you for catching my mistakes with FBI procedure and for answering my many questions.

Randal Dupre: I admire your skill of hapkido. Thanks for the help!

Lynette Eason and Julie Garmon: You are the best critique buds!

Beau Egert: Thank you for answering my questions about liquid natural gas.

Janet K. Grant: Thank you for your constant encouragement.

Karl Harroff: Thanks for sharing your knowledge of firearms and ammunition.

Rachel Hauck, Karen Young, and Debbie Macomber: Thank you for helping me brainstorm this story.

Dean Mills: No woman could ask for a more devoted husband. Thank you for believing in me.

Dane Money: The people of Houston rely on your skills and dedication as a police officer.

Thank you for helping me create a believable character.

Kerma Murray and Stella Riley: Thank you for reading my story and offering helpful comments.

Chapter 1

**Present Day
Mid-September
7:00 a.m. Monday**

Taryn's perfect day melted in the heat of an early morning bottleneck. Houston traffic was a war zone during rush hour. Six lanes of bumper-to-bumper vehicles slowed to a crawl with a road construction crew flashing warning lights ahead. Six lanes narrowed to five, then four, then three, then two.

Shep touched her arm, his gold-brown eyes expressing tenderness. "Babe, the driver will get us to the airport in plenty of time."

"I hate traffic." She pulled her iPad from her purse, a habit when she needed to keep her mind occupied.

"Taryn, our honeymoon starts today." He smiled. "Do your new husband a favor and put away your gadgets. Didn't the VP tell you to forget about work and concentrate on your husband?"

"He did, and you have all my attention."

"Better yet, let me have all your toys, and I'll keep them safe. The one thing I plan to do for the rest of my life is take care of you."

Oh, this wonderful man. And he was all hers.

"You're right. My life's no longer a solo project. I've been single for so long—"

"And a workaholic. Don't worry. I have room right here in my backpack." He chuckled, the rich sound reminding her of a thundering waterfall. "I'll keep them for you, Mrs. Shepherd. But I doubt you'll have time to use them."

She blushed, remembering last night. How could she argue with such devotion? "Can I at least keep my phone?"

"I suppose." He brushed a kiss across her lips. "I love the blush in your cheeks."

Would she always grow warm with his touch? "Comes with the hair."

"A gorgeous match." He twirled a tendril of her hair around his fingers and let it fall against her neck, causing a shiver from far too many sources.

Taryn knew what he was thinking, but she couldn't respond with the limo driver listening to every word. She handed Shep her iPad, hoping he understood that until she met him, her first love had been designing software. Now, with bittersweet regret, she watched him tuck her technological lifeline into his leather backpack.

"We'll be at the airport in twenty minutes." He took her hand into his. "Then we're off to our San Juan paradise. We might never come back. Live in Puerto Rico forever."

She snuggled close to him. For the first time in years, she wouldn't miss work—no software development projects or unrealistic deadlines. And to think she'd spend the rest of her life with this delicious man. Had it only been three months since they'd met and fallen in love? From the moment he walked into her life, he'd become her prince. They'd been inseparable, just the two of them, realizing they were meant for a lifetime. She'd dreamed of a man like Shep since she was a little girl, a man who wouldn't care that she kept her nose in books. His entrance into her heart was like a golden path to a fairy-tale future.

After checking in at the airport, she stared at her boarding pass and wished it held her married name: Mrs. Francis Shepherd. Their next trip would show them as husband and wife.

Security moved like the traffic they'd left behind. In the crowd, everyone's personal space was invaded, and some people responded with hostility. Taryn stepped into a long, winding line, and Shep wrapped an arm around her waist. Oh, she loved her new life. He blew her a kiss while loading his shoes and personal belongings into a bin. If cravings like these occupied her mind for the next fifty years, how would she ever get any work done again?

Once they walked through the body scanner and gathered their things, they wove through the crowd and on toward the gate. The predawn coffee caught up with her. With the urgency, she pointed to the women's restroom. "Do I have time for a quick stop?"

"Sure. My fault since I filled your cup twice to wake you. Let me have your carry-on, and I'll wait here." His smoldering look could have melted the wings off a jumbo jet.

"I'll hurry."

"No problem. The future's ours."

Rushing inside, she noted six women ahead of her, one with two children. Shep had a tendency to be impatient with time constraints, but she'd be miserable on the plane if she didn't wait her turn. Her iPhone notified her that she had fifteen minutes before boarding time.

Finally a stall opened and she hurried in. While she was drying her hands, a thunderous explosion shook the floor. A crack snaked up the wall. Then another. The mirror shattered, breaking her image into shards of glass.

She screamed and swung toward the entrance. Before she could take a step, the ceiling collapsed. Amid dirt and fallen tile, moans filled the air like a nightmare that refused to end. The walls creaked, metal and concrete shifting . . . falling.

Muffled groans alerted Taryn to her impaired hearing from the blast. Trembling, she bent to check on a young woman sprawled at her feet. Blood seeped from a head wound, and Taryn couldn't detect a pulse.

Debris rained on her. Something crashed against her head, sending her spiraling into darkness.

11:15 a.m. Monday

No one had the right to take the lives of innocent people.

Special Agent Grayson Hall always faced the challenges of his life with dogged determination. His experience with the Joint Terrorism Task Force meant his skills were needed, and he welcomed it. The bomb that exploded at IAH in a parking garage near terminal E had killed dozens and wounded countless more. The initial response team, Houston Police Department, fire department, EMTs, and FBI searched for the dead and wounded. The evidence response team labored to make the crime scene safe for investigators, conducting a postblast investigation to determine the components of what appeared to be a vehicle-borne improvised explosive device. Their findings, both electronic and physical, would lead out the investigation with the JTTF involved every step of the way. A team of FBI bomb technicians along with state and local law enforcement searched for a secondary bomb. Nothing had been found yet.

A command post had been quickly established at a hangar outside the airport on JFK Boulevard. A second post at the Houston FBI office housed the Joint Intelligence Center, and a third command post operated out of DC. Grayson worked from the FBI office, reviewing surveillance cameras. Hundreds of agents were on the case, and undoubtedly thousands would be involved before this tragedy was solved.

Those within two hundred yards of the blast were dead or would soon be. The pressure exploded their sinuses, ears, and lungs—a cruel way to die. Several victims were foreign travelers, those who believed the US was safe.

FBI agents and other Homeland Security personnel, as well as local law enforcement, were trained for disasters. But who wanted to experience it? After 9/11, every terrorist threat had the potential to be devastating, leaving too many US citizens emotional cripples. History had proven an attack on US soil could happen again.

It looked like Homeland Security had failed, and that meant Grayson had failed too.

No chatter on the wires had indicated a potential bomb threat. The FBI's Field Intelligence Group, the FIG, scrambled for missed intel. The governor was en route to Houston via helicopter, and the White House was demanding an explanation before the president spoke to the country and the world. Grayson questioned how the country's leaders would soothe the chaos in this grave situation, especially with the death toll mounting. He mentally listed US enemies who claimed responsibility, and

North Koreans and Iranians danced in the streets.

Grayson scrolled through screen after screen of heavily scrutinized security footage. The scene looked like a war zone merged with a cyclone. Agents searched for clues leading to a person or persons who might be responsible for the tragedy. He examined two segments that raised questions. Both photographs showed the guy knew where the cameras were located. Why? Unless he had something to hide. Grayson zoomed in and sent the image to the FIG.

His BlackBerry rang.

"What do you have?" Supervisory Special Agent Alan Preston, the SSA of FBI Houston, had phoned him every twenty minutes since the explosion.

"I've run info through the FIG. A couple ticketed for San Juan checked in about thirty minutes before the explosion using the names Francis Shepherd and Taryn Young. Shepherd left shortly afterward. We have Young entering a restroom, and a few moments later, Shepherd heads out and leaves in the same limo he arrived in."

"Alone?"

"Apparently. The bomb exploded five minutes after his exit."

"What do we have on them?"

"Shepherd's name is fictitious. He avoided the cameras. Wore a cap. Little for facial recognition to compile. Young works for Gated Labs

Technology, a software development company." His BlackBerry notified him of a message. "Just got a response from the FIG on the couple." Grayson blew out his exasperation. "Nothing on either of them. Continuing to search for Shepherd's identification, but we don't have a clear photo."

"I want him found and brought in for questioning. It's one thing for a man to change his mind about going away with a woman. It's another to dodge security cameras and escape a bombing."

"I don't believe in coincidences."

"Back to Young," the SSA said. "Gated Labs is high-tech. Some top-secret government contracts. Any connect?"

"Young's their top developer. Maybe the best in the country. Right now she's in a coma at Houston Northwest Medical Center."

"You and Vince get over there and find out what you can. At this point, it looks like Shepherd and Young are involved. Don't lose track of her until we see where she fits. That's your job."

Chapter 2

1:00 p.m. Monday

"Taryn Young."

A man's voice, but not Shep's.

"Miss Young, can you hear me?"

She ignored him. Special moments from her wedding poured into her mind like the bubbling champagne from the previous night—a quiet ceremony in a secluded park with only a chorus of chirping insects, an exquisite dinner at Tony's, a tender, romantic night at the St. Regis. She couldn't remember what she ate or the decor of the hotel, only the joy of being with Shep and knowing they'd share the rest of their lives together. Was it just last night they'd claimed the right of husband and wife and basked in the sweet essence of love?

Shep spoke to her in muted tones as though she were in a tunnel. That didn't make sense. He lay right beside her. She'd fallen asleep in his embrace. She attempted to touch him, but her arm wouldn't move.

More memories surfaced. Rising before dawn and fighting sleep. Shep serving her coffee in bed. An early morning limo ride to the airport. Checking in their luggage. The line through security. The explosion that shook the airport . . .

17

the screams . . . the blood. And something crashing down on her. Taryn struggled to call out to Shep. He must have escaped injury. Maybe he couldn't find her buried in the debris. She strained to hear his soothing voice.

Her eyes fluttered, and through a fog she swept aside a confusing world to focus on a man's face.

"Good, you're awake." Piercing ice-blue eyes bored into hers, as cold as his tone.

"Where am I?"

"Houston Northwest Medical Center. You were injured in the airport bombing. One of the first responders pulled you from the wreckage."

She'd need to find out a name and thank him. "How long have I been here?"

"Over two and a half hours. It's one in the afternoon, and you were brought in after ten this morning."

"Where is my husband?"

"That's what we'd like to know."

She didn't like his attitude. "I heard him talking to me." She tried to raise her head, but pain rippled across the back of her skull, forcing her onto the pillow. A steady *beep-beep* confirmed that machines monitored her vitals. An IV ushered fluids into her body. She touched her head and felt a bandage. Possibly stitches. Closing her eyes, she took a few deep breaths to manage the hammering in her head. "He has to be here in the hospital. I heard his voice—"

"What did he say?"

"I . . . I don't know."

"I need to give her something for the pain," a woman said.

Taryn turned to a woman in a white uniform, a nurse. "Please. Can you tell my husband I'd like to see him?"

"Your husband hasn't been located. I'm so sorry. Perhaps he'll be here soon." Her gentle tone might have otherwise comforted Taryn if not for her need to see Shep.

"You're wrong." She clenched her fists, fighting the confusion. "He's here. I know it."

"You're confused with all you've been through," the nurse said. "Try to stay calm. I have something to alleviate your discomfort."

"Please, don't placate me."

"Miss Young, you need to rest." The nurse took out a syringe and reached for the IV tube. "I'm going to put the pain medication into your IV and—"

"Don't give her anything." The man's voice rose. "This concerns national security."

Taryn focused on the man's cold, hard eyes. "What are you talking about?"

"Ma'am, I'm sorry about what's happened to you." A flicker of compassion swept across his face, then disappeared. "But we have questions."

A second man stood on the opposite side of the bed—thinning gray hair. Both men wore business attire. "You two don't look like doctors." She blinked and recalled the mention of national security.

The younger man flipped out a badge. "FBI. We're investigating the bombing at IAH this morning. I'm Special Agent Grayson Hall, and this is Special Agent Vince Bradshaw."

They must be questioning everyone who was injured. She remembered the dead woman on the floor of the restroom. What happened to the mother with her little girls? "How many were killed?"

"Over thirty dead."

She couldn't fathom how she'd survived. "Wounded?"

"At least that many. Terminal E has been severely damaged."

She moistened her lips, sensing an unbelievable horror numbing her head but not her heart. "I don't know anything. I was in the restroom during the explosion. That's all I remember."

"What about Francis Shepherd?"

"My husband. I told you he's here somewhere." She tried to raise her head again, but the nurse pressed her shoulders against the pillow.

"Easy, miss." Agent Bradshaw's voice reminded her of her dad's. "We understand the trauma you've been through. But we need answers."

The older man seemed more considerate.

"I have orders to administer the medication

now," the nurse said. "Do I need to page the doctor?"

"She can have it in a moment." Agent Hall's chilling gaze rested on her. "We have security footage showing the man you know as Francis Shepherd leaving the airport five minutes before the explosion. He left in a limo."

Taryn's heart pumped faster. "You have the wrong man. He was waiting for me. We were leaving for our honeymoon."

Agent Hall pulled up a photo on his Black-Berry. "Is this Francis Shepherd?"

Taryn studied it. The man looked like Shep, but his face was turned from the camera. The man in the photograph wore the same light-green shirt, jeans, and a cap. But she was well aware of what Photoshop could accomplish. "This might show his image, but you have the wrong man."

"I would be skeptical of this too," Agent Hall said. "But can you tell us where he is?"

Intense pain coupled with the agent's implication warranted tears. But she'd not give in. "He's got to be here in the hospital, and I'm sure he'll explain your concerns when we see him. He's probably getting coffee."

Agent Hall placed his phone in his jacket pocket. "Francis Shepherd doesn't exist, and he's a person of interest in today's bombing. We've informed the media of this status."

Panic clawed into Taryn's rationale. She fought

a response that wouldn't solve anything. "What do you mean he doesn't exist?"

"The name is an alias."

She blinked. "What a ridiculous accusation. I know the man I married."

"Do you?"

"Are you saying my husband is a suspect?"

"We are. Since you were traveling with him, you're also a person of interest. We've swabbed your hands for signs of bomb residue."

"You what?" What kind of nightmare had she wakened to?

He repeated his statement. "We found no evidence, but your association with Francis Shepherd certainly raises questions."

"I think you drank your lunch." Anger shot adrenaline through her body. Taryn turned to the nurse. "Please call security. I want these men removed from my room. They're impostors."

2:10 p.m. Monday

Grayson stood outside Taryn Young's room waiting for a call from the SSA while Vince went to the cafeteria for coffee. The airport had been cleared of a secondary bomb threat. But IAH was one of United's largest hubs, and it would take months to rebuild the terminal. The bomb had consisted of agricultural fertilizer and diesel fuel, likely triggered by a cell phone. Easy-to-obtain components and able to do heavy damage. The

22

driver had parked the van on level 3, abandoned the vehicle, careful to avoid security cameras, and disappeared.

Houston FBI had issued a press release stating they were assisting HPD in the investigation. The top priority was recovering the victims. The situation remained fluid, and motivation for the blast hadn't been determined. Phone numbers gave the public an opportunity to check on loved ones and supply any information or visual images that would assist in the investigation. The FBI needed all details, no matter how small.

Random, useless reports flowed in on their BlackBerries. Grayson needed facts verified by other agents. Sirens screamed. People rushed by, some crying and some shouting for answers, while medical personnel labored over the injured. Meanwhile Young slept, although she'd requested pain medication that wouldn't knock her out. The woman had continued to insist she and her husband were innocent of any crimes. However, when the hospital paged Francis Shepherd and he didn't respond, she had difficulty maintaining her composure.

"Perhaps he's one of the dead." Her voice had quivered. "He'd never have left me stranded. Have you checked all the hospitals?"

"Yes, ma'am."

"Are they still recovering those buried in rubble?"

"They are."

Young was either an expert liar, or she'd been duped. The concussion could affect her memory but not her body language, unless she'd been trained to mask her emotions. He and Vince would confiscate her personal belongings, then question her further when she wakened.

"Hate to admit it, but I think she's telling the truth." Grayson moved into the room and studied the sleeping woman's face, noting her flawless skin beneath the bruises and auburn hair. Her head injury had required stitches, and the doctor had diagnosed a concussion and prescribed overnight observation.

"Young knew exactly what she was doing. Swallowing her story could taint your excellent reputation."

"She doesn't strike me as a suicide bomber." Grayson filtered through the facts. "Why would a man marry under a fictitious name, unless he had something to hide?"

"Like another wife? Or he's part of a conspiracy?" Vince stuffed his hands into his pants pockets. "Why would he abandon her at the airport? I think she was in on it and took her chances by heading into the restroom."

"Risky. Men, women, and children died in those restrooms."

"You're letting a pretty face and green eyes cloud your judgment. Look at the FIG's report.

Her IQ is higher than yours and mine combined."

Grayson eyed his partner. Sometimes Vince's so-called experience left a bad taste in his mouth. "Hear me out. If they were part of the bombing, she got double-crossed. If he worked alone with the bombers, the marriage was part of their plan as a cover-up."

"Watch and see how Young fits into this."

Grayson regretted her incommunicable state. The nurse said she'd sleep at least an hour, which meant losing precious time before they could pose more questions. He checked his watch. He'd give her fifteen more minutes, then wake her up. Everyone in the country wanted answers to this tragedy, and now.

"I've been at this a lot longer than you have," Vince sneered. "I see things you don't."

Vince had also gotten lazy and assumed information before investigating it. "Having Shepherd's identity would go a long way in figuring this out. If he's innocent, then he should respond to the media's report and contact us." Grayson walked to the window, where afternoon sunshine streamed through the room. "I want to know why he left the airport. The death toll is rising, and our strongest lead is asleep." Frustration rolled over him that an incoherent software developer quite possibly held the only viable link to solving today's bombing. "At least we know what she was working on at Gated Labs."

"It feeds into my theory. She played a lead in designing advanced software for liquid natural gas storage at those new coastline export terminals. And the bomb's signature indicates Middle Eastern terrorism. They'd like nothing better than to take out that aspect of our economy."

Grayson agreed that Vince's statement seemed to fit. With the US launching a new LNG export business at the end of the week, the Middle East's share in oil and gas would be threatened. Even Russia, the largest exporter, was being investigated by other agents. However, Russia had just signed an agreement with the US to improve trade relations, and their involvement seemed unlikely.

"Initial findings of Young's professional background haven't connected her to this morning's tragedy. Think about this. Congress met in closed-door sessions before granting the license that gave Gated Labs exclusive permission to develop soft-ware that regulates pressure and temperatures of LNG and provides process protection," he said.

"That's a mouthful. Not sure I understand it."

Grayson nodded. "I'm in the dark about all this too, but I intend to unravel it. Anyway, Gated Labs's solution was to add a specialized firewall mechanism to prevent unauthorized access to the process control systems. Taryn Young was thoroughly vetted. When the proceedings were completed, Congress specifically requested she lead the project."

"They trusted her, even if we have our doubts." Vince lifted a brow. "The intelligent agents question her integrity."

Grayson ignored his last comment. "In the wrong hands, use of the software could cost lives and certainly billions of dollars for us and our allies. All it would take is a keystroke to raise the temps and cause a tremendous explosion." He paused to think through the implications. "But what's the connection, if any, to what happened today?" Grayson craved more information. "If this has anything to do with the software, why didn't he steal a copy instead of blowing up a chunk of the terminal? Kill her on their honeymoon?"

"Money. Always money." Vince snorted the words.

"We clearly don't have the whole picture." Grayson acknowledged the nurse who entered the room. "Do you have Ms. Young's cell phone? It's not in her purse."

The nurse started. "I used it when she was brought in—an iPhone in a red jeweled case. Since she wears a wedding ring, I called those on her favorites list to find her husband. Then I put it back in the zippered compartment."

"Were you successful in contacting anyone?"

"No. The name of Shep in her favorites simply rang. A number was listed as Mom and another as Claire, and I left voice mails on both." She searched through Young's purse and nightstand. "I don't understand why it's not here."

"Did anyone else have access to her belongings?"

"Just me." She lifted her chin.

Grayson pulled a pad and pencil from his jacket and noted the information. "We need to see all the hospital security footage since Ms. Young was brought in."

Chapter 3

2:27 p.m. Monday

Taryn climbed through her sleep stupor. She kept her head still and her eyes closed, trying to minimize the pain. Had it been just this morning when she'd greeted the predawn as Mrs. Francis Shepherd? She shoved aside the hammering in her head to think. Asking for more pain meds would prolong her inability to piece together every moment. If the FBI agents were legit, and if Shep wasn't sitting beside her bed, then she had the enormous task of proving herself and her husband innocent of the airport bombing. The mere thought of his involvement was unthinkable.

Or maybe she was afraid that if Shep didn't occupy a chair beside her bed, he could be seriously wounded . . . or dead. The tragedy at

IAH seemed unreal. She'd survived, probably because she'd been in the restroom. How bizarre that a second cup of coffee had saved her life. What about the others? The women and children who'd been in line? Was Shep buried in the debris and unable to defend himself against the FBI's accusations?

Oh, to return to those early hours when she lay cradled in his arms. The low hum of the air conditioner, the scent of the deep-red roses, and his warm caresses had set the stage for the rest of their married life. She would've sensed betrayal. Felt it in his embrace.

Moistening her lips, she braved forward. "Shep."

When no one responded, she forced her eyes open. Alone. She chewed on a fingernail, a habit Shep detested. How she longed to see him, hear him soothe away all the uncertainties stalking her since the FBI had invaded her life. Being with him was like living between the lines of poetry—beauty beyond definition.

Francis Shepherd was not a conspirator involved in a plot to blow up the airport.

The FBI agents could be reporters. False credentials could have gained them entrance into her room. Fighting the pain, she reached for the nightstand drawer. At least she wasn't cuffed to the bed. She cringed and located her purse, noting that her arm must be bruised. She'd been incredibly lucky with only a head injury. After dragging her purse onto the bed, she fished through it with both hands. No phone. A surge of panic raced through her.

Maybe it was hospital policy to confiscate cell phones, especially during a crisis such as this. A landline sat on the nightstand, and she'd memorized most of her contact list. Her mom was probably sick with worry, especially since she'd told her about the flight to San Juan. Although they were miles apart and somewhat distant in their current relationship, they cared for each other. She had to get through to her. That meant turning her head to dial and enduring blinding pain. But her mom needed to know she was okay, and maybe she could help Taryn find Shep.

She deleted her last thought and attributed it to desperation. Her mom lived in Florida. Shep didn't have her information, and her mom didn't have his. Who could help her? Their romance had been three months of seeing each other daily until he proposed. She hadn't met his friends, nor did he know any of hers—except Claire. She pressed in Claire's number. Her dear friend would be waiting to hear from her after the bombing, and the many hospital lines would be tied up with inquiries. The number rang several times. Before she could dwell further on Claire, the two men who claimed to be FBI agents walked into her room.

She was in no mood to talk to them. "Get out

unless you have identification other than your badges."

A police officer stood in the doorway. Agent Bradshaw, the older man, secured the uniformed man's attention. "Officer, would you tell Ms. Young who we are?"

"Mrs. Shepherd," Taryn said.

The officer pressed his lips together. "These men are FBI agents."

"Why are you outside my door?"

The officer's face resembled granite. "To stop anyone from entering other than medical personnel."

"Why?"

"For your own protection."

Taryn's breath caught in her chest. "My protection?" As soon as the words left her mouth, she understood. If anyone suspected her of being a part of today's bombing, her very life could be in danger. "I understand. Has my husband been here?"

The officer shook his head. "Only the FBI."

"Thank you." Concern swept through her. Time . . . she needed time to process the day's disaster.

Agent Hall handed her a business card. Was it credible? Turning to the agent, she mustered the strength to sound rational. "My phone was in my purse, but now it's missing. Have you taken it?"

"No. A nurse used it to locate an emergency

contact. Claims to have replaced it." Agent Hall studied Taryn as though she were scum. How would she approach this mess if she were in his shoes? She'd certainly listen to the suspect before passing sentence.

"I'm assuming she was unable to contact my husband. Perhaps she got through to my mom in Florida."

"Your mother responded to the nurse's voice mail. I spoke with her. She claims never to have met Francis Shepherd."

"That's true." She needed her mother, no matter how immature it sounded. Hope settled on her as though she were a child. "Is she coming?"

"The airport is closed—no flights in or out— and she isn't confident to drive this far."

Mom hadn't made arrangements to attend the wedding. She'd understood Taryn's desire for an intimate ceremony. And Taryn and Shep had planned to visit her before returning home from Puerto Rico.

In the shadows of afternoon, stress lines across Agent Hall's face displayed his obvious exhaustion. She'd failed to see how others were suffering in this tragedy, which resembled the Boston Marathon bombing. "I'm sorry. I've been wrapped up in myself and this confusion linking my husband and me to the bombing. You are as committed to finding answers as I am to proving Shep and I are not a part of today's tragedy."

Dark-blond hair fell across Agent Hall's forehead. He nodded. Emotionless.

Perhaps she could find a way to convince him of her sincerity. "You've had a rough day too. What are the casualties?"

"Currently, forty-nine confirmed dead. Over one hundred injured and fifty-five missing."

Faces from the morning flashed across her mind. Unspeakable horror. "I've tried to think of a reason why my husband would've left the airport. Had our flight been delayed?"

"No."

"Terrorist threats?"

"No."

"Was the explosion due to some malfunction at the airport?"

"Initial findings reveal a vehicle fertilizer bomb." Agent Hall pulled a chair to her bedside, and Agent Bradshaw did the same. "More than one person had to have been involved."

"Then you should be talking to *all* the wounded and those who escaped."

"Hundreds of agents are conducting interviews, Miss Young," Agent Hall said. "We are assigned to you because of our experience with the Joint Terrorism Task Force. If you're ready to help us, we have questions about your position at Gated Labs."

"What kind of questions?" She didn't like his implications. Her position was highly classified, and her newest project was the epitome of her career.

Agent Hall captured her attention. "We spoke with your supervisor about your latest project for the exportation of liquid natural gas. A little above our heads. Can you explain in simple terms your role and what the software does?"

"I'm the team leader for a software development project exclusively designed for LNG companies. The software, which we called Nehemiah, regulates the temperature of liquid natural gas, a necessary safety precaution, and includes extensive preventive measures to deter hackers. The latter is a firewall."

"So the software in itself is not a firewall?"

"Right. It's a protective mechanism."

"Is Nehemiah the firewall?"

Her patience was running thin. "No, sir. Nehemiah is the name of this specific software project that contains a firewall."

"You are fully aware of its catastrophic potential in the wrong hands."

Of course she knew the security concerns. "Your point?"

"Did Shepherd ever have access to your work files?"

"Never." Taryn recalled Shep taking her iPad. Should she tell them? Her iPhone was missing as well. A lengthy encrypted key that gave backdoor access into the software was stored

34

on it and not synced or backed up anywhere else. How could the FBI suggest such despicable things about the man she loved? "If my work files could be obtained, a hacker still couldn't—"

"Password protection means nothing." Agent Hall's eyes narrowed. "Even I know that. It's not *if* but *when*."

"In this instance, we incorporated extraordinary security measures."

"You have an extremely high IQ, Miss Young. But you're not infallible."

She swallowed hard. "I disabled the software on Friday and enabled an older version that also contained a firewall. I'm not authorized to say why."

"Your supervisor said the Nehemiah Project was fully operational."

"He lied."

Dare she state she didn't trust two members of her team—her supervisor and a woman who seemed too ambitious and yet careless? A woman whose uncle was the CEO of Gated Labs? "I planned to discuss the situation with the VP of product development today after arriving in Puerto Rico. He's been out of the country."

Agent Hall cocked his head. "Why would you leave those companies vulnerable when they're relying on the latest version of operating information and security?"

She considered telling him the truth: she'd feared Haden might compromise the software, and she wasn't sure of his hacking abilities. "The software they are using does have a firewall. Let's just say there were problems, and my decision was based upon protecting the project and ultimately the two LNG companies piloting the software."

"So you left work on Friday and didn't plan to return until a week from tomorrow? And a highly secured software project was to lay dormant until you returned?"

"Not necessarily. I know that sounds irregular—"

"And only you can re-enable the software?" Agent Hall said.

"Yes." She could reveal her suspicions, but they had nothing to do with the bombing. Agent Bradshaw shut the door. He hadn't said a word. Was he saving up for his interrogation?

"Is it normal protocol for only one person to hold the keys?" Agent Hall said.

"I'm not in a position to say anything else." She'd discovered a bug and fixed it after overhearing a conversation that threatened the reputation and future of Gated Labs. "Quite the contrary. The situation would have been rectified once I spoke to the VP."

Agent Bradshaw moved to lean over her bed. His eyes were kind, like she remembered.

"Mrs. Shepherd, we need to know the whole story. If you're innocent, you have nothing to fear."

"Then you and Agent Hall can obtain clearance and be present at a secure site when I talk to the VP of product development."

"Count on it." Agent Bradshaw shook his head and walked back to the door.

It wasn't like her to be uncooperative. "Look, I made a choice to disable the software knowing I might not have a position when I returned. The Nehemiah Project means more to me than my career."

"How noble," Agent Hall said with a huff.

"Noble?" Irritation swept through her. "Are you questioning my integrity? Because you're way out of line."

Agent Hall lifted a brow.

"Go ahead and write my response in your report."

"Did Shepherd ever ask what you were working on?" Hall said.

Taryn struggled to keep her emotions in check. "Of course he asked about my work. We were getting to know each other. When I explained the security clearance issues, he understood." Heat flooded her for so many reasons that she couldn't list them. Shep had the answers to end her fears. "I wouldn't betray Gated Labs or conduct unethical behavior." She clenched her fists. "Do you want to see the red, white, and blue tattoo on my backside?"

"I'm sure your patriotic symbol is on the hospital records," Hall said. "Perhaps you wouldn't knowingly provide information to Mr. Shepherd. Has he ever given you any reason to believe his interest in you was anything other than personal?"

"Never." Her mind slipped back to the tenderest of times. She could trace his attentiveness from the moment they met.

"Where is he employed?" Hall's voice softened and he pressed his lips together. "You do understand he didn't give you his real name."

She refused to respond to his provocation. "He owns his own business. Imports diamonds from Africa."

"Name?"

"Shepherd Gem Enterprises."

Agent Hall picked up his phone and pressed the keypad. "Shepherd Gem Enterprises does not exist. Neither are there any import businesses or diamond companies remotely resembling Shepherd Gem Enterprises."

"But I've seen his website—shepherdgem enterprises.com."

He handed her his phone. "This site is under construction."

Chapter 4

3:05 p.m. Monday

Grayson walked to the hospital parking lot with Vince at his side. He believed Taryn Young had been played. Even so, he had planted a bug in the nightstand beside her hospital bed in case Shepherd made contact.

Vince claimed she was knee-deep in a terrorist plot. The man had twenty-eight years of experience. Add seven years, and that's how long Grayson had walked the earth. Grayson wanted to believe Vince's experience partnered with wisdom, like barbecue and potato salad. But some days he wasn't in the mood to listen to Vince's war stories. Everything had to be viewed through an ego the size of Texas.

"You watch," Vince said. "She'll make a connection, and we'll lose her. If our bad guys manage to slip her out of the hospital, we're sunk. It all adds up—she hid out in the bathroom while Shepherd made his escape. She's claiming innocence, and yet we've discovered she's involved in a project with national security repercussions. To me that's a big neon sign flashing, *Terrorist*."

"I'm not convinced." Grayson unlocked his Mustang. "She could have died this morning."

"Or she could have arranged to meet another partner in the restroom. Think about what we just learned. She's up to her rear in today's mess."

Hospital cameras had filmed an unidentified man dressed in scrubs on Taryn Young's floor an hour after she arrived. His build resembled the man who called himself Francis Shepherd, but so far they had no images that facial recognition software could use. If Shepherd had been able to get to her, and she knew more about the bombing than she claimed, why didn't he kill her? Except her survival made her look guilty. Her death would indicate others were involved. Grayson wasn't ready to concede yet. If the man had slipped into her room and taken her iPhone, what did that mean?

He pulled onto a feeder road. Destination: Shepherd's high-rise condo along the waterways in The Woodlands, about twenty minutes north of the hospital. Agents had already swept it for fingerprints and DNA. So far nothing.

"Any leads on the limo Shepherd used for transportation to the airport?"

Vince scrolled through his BlackBerry. "Listed owner died four months ago. Vehicle found in Galveston about two this afternoon."

"No one commits the perfect crime. What else do we know about Shepherd?"

"Manager of the condo never met him. Everything was handled by phone or e-mail. The

40

monthly fees were an automatic draw from an account listed as Shepherd Gem Enterprises. He drove a 2014 silver BMW convertible, a confirmed lease. Again, the same company listed. He also used an e-mail account with Shepherd Gem. Unable to unlock paper trail any further." Vince seldom gave him eye contact—his gaze always darted about as though avoiding Grayson. No surprise, since neither man respected the other.

"What about the deceased limo owner?"

"A man who lived in an Alzheimer's unit in Galveston. Only relative is a nephew in Chicago who didn't attend his uncle's funeral. Both records are clean. Nothing there, farm boy."

Grayson whipped a quick look at Vince, his eyes etched with deep lines. According to the SSA, he hadn't always been so disagreeable. At one time, he'd been a highly respected agent. "Look, Vince, let's put aside our personal differences and work together on this."

"Isn't that what we're doing?" Vince jutted his chin.

"Sure it is." Grayson shoved back his ire. "So we have no photo of Shepherd or his real name."

Vince read his BlackBerry. "Got an update from the FIG. Some of those missing are confirmed dead."

What went wrong today? What had happened to the US's security measures? The media's mad scramble to find answers also meant misleading

41

information could be reported. The public deserved justice, but determining it took time and analysis of thousands of data sources. The final answers would take months.

"The situation with Shepherd and Young looks simple to me," Vince said. "They partnered with terrorists to blow up terminal E and make a chunk of change from the software."

"Possibly."

"I'm right and you know it."

Grayson let him talk while processing their findings. Young's phone was missing. Shepherd must have managed entrance to her hospital room before the FBI arrived. She claimed to have heard his voice. When Grayson told her there was no record of her marriage, she'd paled. Told him to check again.

Grayson drove to Shepherd's condo, a high-end complex with every amenity imaginable. The manager, an olive-skinned beauty, didn't appear pleased to see them.

"This is a popular place. Do I need an attorney?" she said.

"Not unless you have something to hide," Grayson said.

"I mean with what's happened and the FBI sending in a team to one of our units—" she stood, revealing a postage-stamp-size skirt—"we have legal ramifications to consider."

Grayson ignored the flick of hair over her

shoulder and the moistening of her lips. He'd experienced her type before—*Get distracted with me and forget why you're here.* "We asked you about Francis Shepherd. You can answer our questions here or at our office with your attorney." He offered his best professional smile. "Why wouldn't you want to assist us?"

She walked across the room and closed the door, the swing in her step definitely for their benefit. "I've already made a statement to the other FBI agents." She picked up an agent's card, shoving it under Grayson's nose. "This guy was rude. But go ahead. Ask the same questions and waste your time and mine."

Vince stepped into her personal space. "We have a bombing to investigate. I recommend your cooperation. The public is hot for us to make an arrest."

She blinked. "Sure. Whatever. I feel bad about the deaths, but I can't lose my job over this. We have a stellar reputation."

"Did you ever have a face-to-face with Francis Shepherd?"

"No."

"I find that difficult to believe. So he purchased his condo without seeing it?"

"The negotiations were done by phone."

"Never personally?"

"A representative from a realty company handled it all."

"I want the Realtor's name."

She swished to her desk and computer. After a few keystrokes, she stiffened. Her fingers hovered over the keyboard. "The name has been deleted from the file."

Grayson studied the woman and her shaking fingers.

"Sir, I don't know how this disappeared. No one uses this computer but me. I'll . . . I'll do my best to recall the name and then contact you. Perhaps I can find it in a backup."

"You're not helping us at all." Vince narrowed his gaze. "See if you can answer this one: Does he have a reserved parking spot?"

"Yes, but the other agent reported it empty. Are we done?" She glanced at Grayson as though she needed deliverance.

"Agent Hall can't help you." Vince stuck his face within inches of hers. "I'm in charge here."

Technically, Vince didn't have the lead, which had been a sore spot between the two. But if it offered intimidation and produced results, he could claim anything. Except this time Grayson didn't think the tough-guy facade was working.

"I've already given the payment tracking information to the FBI, along with all the information I could find about Mr. Shepherd."

"Anything you might've missed?" Vince said.

She squared her shoulders, her composure in check. Vince wouldn't get anything more from the woman. He nodded at Grayson, his cue that his partner should take over.

"Let's take a look at the condo," Vince said.

"Go ahead. I'll be there in a few minutes. I want to see the camera footage." Once Vince left, Grayson offered the woman a dazzling smile. "Sorry about my partner."

She returned an equally charming look. "That's okay. I've learned to deal with those rough-around-the-edges types."

"The truth is we're getting hammered to find who's responsible for the bombing. Hate it when the big guys pound us."

"I can only imagine."

"Especially when I'm the new guy. Sure would like to find Shepherd."

"He had a deep voice. Sexy." She sighed. "I'll pull up the footage for you." She typed, then frowned. "Agent Hall, the footage from the gate Mr. Shepherd would have used and from his parking spot are missing." She typed again. "It's all gone."

Grayson looked at the screen. The time-stamped videos had been deleted. "What about the backup program?"

"I can give you the security company's information." She reached inside a desk drawer and gave him a business card.

He phoned the FIG for their assistance. Shepherd, or whatever his name was, had the

45

cunning to cover his tracks. "Thanks for your help."

"I keep thinking I've missed a detail, but I don't think so," she said.

"Odd, he never showed up to sign papers or pick up his keys. The Realtor handled it all."

"It's not unusual for our clientele to have others handle what they feel is trivial. But there was a woman who stopped by about a week ago looking for him."

"Did she give a name?"

"Yes. I remember she said the two of them were engaged, and her first name was unusual. Had auburn hair. Attractive." She tapped her chin and reached inside her desk drawer, producing another business card. "Taryn Young. Works for Gated Labs Technology. She left a gift for him, which I kept here until he called for one of our staff to deliver it."

Like bomb pieces? "Do you know what it was?"

"No. I'm guessing a clothing article. It came from Neiman Marcus."

His BlackBerry indicated a notification from the FIG. The security company had reported a break-in. The footage from Shepherd's condo had been deleted.

4:45 p.m. Monday

Taryn would do anything to get out of the hospital. Being pumped with IVs while a police officer stood guard outside her door meant she had no control of her life—defenseless against the strong accusations hurled against her. For once in her life, she needed to step outside her introverted role and seize life before it seized her.

Media reports monopolized the TV networks. They claimed the FBI had a person of interest, and she knew it was her. Swallowing hard, she accepted the inevitable—once the doctor released her, she'd be in custody until the real bomber was found.

She must find Shep. He'd be able to explain what happened this morning. Where could he be? He'd probably stepped away from the airport to surprise her with her favorite roses.

Worrisome thoughts about his possible injury would not leave her alone. He could be in another medical facility with no ID. Or buried beneath twisted metal and concrete.

The FBI claimed he'd left in a limo. Had the driver waited for him?

Francis Shepherd wasn't his real name?

His website content had vanished?

She shivered, and the chill had nothing to do with the hospital's cold temps. They were wrong, and she'd find a way to prove her husband's innocence. But how could she when others blamed her for today's tragedy? She and Shep had far too many documented proofs to show their marriage was legitimate. A man didn't get married one day and betray his country the next.

A police officer stood in the way of her leaving. Dare she . . . ?

She focused on the IV in her arm. Couldn't be that hard to remove.

Chapter 5

5:05 p.m. Monday

Taryn stole down the hospital stairway, grasping the rail to keep her balance. She hoisted her leather bag onto her shoulder, its weight digging into her flesh. The likelihood of someone coming up or down the steps filled her with dread. Questions. Lies to cover up her identity. Blood seeped between her fingers from the inside of her arm, where she'd yanked out the IV. She pressed harder to stop the flow. Dizzying pain beat a message into her body—she'd not last long without rest. She breathed in and out to steady herself. Where were her shoes? Buried at the airport? Or another point of action from the FBI? Her capri pants and top were torn, dirty, and bloody. Barefoot and ragged, she would easily be spotted by law enforcement types.

She'd look for a taxi. Money wasn't a problem. Destination was. The FBI would have already swarmed her old apartment, but she and Shep had purchased a condo, and she'd moved in a week ago. The address wasn't on her ID.

A metal door slammed below her, and the thud of heavy footsteps came closer. She braced herself. A middle-aged man dressed in scrubs appeared. He stopped at the landing and faced her.

"Miss, do you need help? I'm a doctor."

"No, thank you. I've been treated and released."

"Were you at the airport this morning?"

"No. An automobile accident."

"I see. Did you lose your shoes?"

"They were heels, and one of them broke." How many lies must she tell? Guilt pummeled her for the things she'd done in the name of innocence.

"Do you have transportation?" He took two more steps.

"Yes. My friend is meeting me outside the parking garage." She forced a smile. "I'm okay, really."

"You should be in a wheelchair and escorted to a vehicle."

Her shoulders tightened. "None are available. Have you seen the people lining the hospital halls?"

He shook his head. "Just got called in from Galveston."

"Many need your attention. Don't worry. I'm going home to good care."

"All right. Be safe. You need to be in bed."

The doctor disappeared and Taryn sighed with relief. She'd need to hurry before he learned about the police officer in her room and realized she'd escaped from the hospital.

At the emergency exit, she bent low to push the heavy door open, using valuable energy needed to think and act with a semblance of intelligence. Once outside, she scanned the areas where cameras would be positioned. The garage brimmed with vehicles, allowing her to slip between them without being videoed by cameras. A small group of people gathered where she needed to pass. She crouched between a pickup and a Lexus and endured the agony penetrating her body. When the people finally walked by, vocalizing their fears of loved ones hurt in the bombing and vowing revenge against the bomber, tears clouded her vision. She agreed with those grieving. Whoever was responsible must be found. A flash of the carnage from the explosion pressed her on.

Across the street from the hospital, she secured a taxi and hoped the driver wouldn't comment about her bare feet. For the moment she was safe, and the thought sent determination through her. She'd prove their innocence.

5:30 p.m. Monday

Grayson slid into his Mustang and sped toward Houston Northwest Medical Center. A nagging headache settled at the base of his skull, but he shook it off. No time to fall under a demon migraine or dope himself with meds. What were they missing? He wished he had a contact at the NCTC, but the National Counterterrorism Center revealed info on a need-to-know basis, and he wasn't in that loop. His and Vince's assignment was Taryn Young and her so-called husband. Grayson accelerated up the on-ramp.

Vince snorted. "I don't look good in a body bag."

Grayson scowled and checked his speed. "Neither did the dozens who died this morning. Kids too. Elderly. Bomber didn't play favorites."

"The problem is Young saw right through you. She read a softy and took advantage of it. I'd have gotten her trust, then nailed her for information until she cratered. Instead you let her drift off to sleep."

Young's doctor had demanded she have meds, and she did Grayson little good when she couldn't string two words together. But why argue those points with Vince?

Vince pulled his BlackBerry from his jacket pocket. "Her story just doesn't check out. No application for a marriage license. Francis Shepherd doesn't exist. The only thing she aced is no priors."

Grayson swallowed his pride. Being wrong went against his gene pool. "Contact the FIG," he said. "I want to see her financial records. Cell phone history for the past year. Before the day's over, I want to talk to her employer face-to-face. Find out if her concerns about the Nehemiah Project are legit. And I want everything we can dig up about her family."

"Young's going to tell us who's behind this. Let me take over the questioning. I know how to get things done," Vince said while texting the requests.

Like Grayson didn't? "What about her background, education, and organizations?"

Vince held up a finger. "Got it right here. She graduated summa cum laude from Caltech. Obtained her PhD at MIT. Was offered a professorship there but chose her current position at Gated Labs." He paused. "Nothing at Caltech or MIT to indicate radical thinking. Of course, she could have had some Middle Eastern friends."

"Get the FIG on it. See if something turns up."

"What if we told her Shepherd was in custody, nailed her as part of the scheme?" Vince said.

"I don't think you'd get a thing. I'm working on another angle."

"Another one of your special cases? You going to rehabilitate her, too?"

Grayson wasn't in the mood for Vince's trash talk. "I'm telling you Taryn Young is no half-wit. We need to be straightforward and explain the possible charges."

"She's a woman. It's all about what feels right."

"Not for every woman. She rose in her career because of a high IQ, job performance, and knowing when to take calculated risks."

"Watch me. I'll be her daddy. Act like I believe her, then zero in for the truth." Vince's Black-Berry beeped. "This is rich. Twenty minutes after the explosion, someone wired $50,000 into your lady's account."

There went Grayson's hunch that she was inno-cent. She must have been trained in body language . . . a pro. "Where did the wire come from?"

"Singapore."

Grayson stepped on the gas, mentally organizing the facts about Young and Shepherd. Finding a connection between their financials and Singapore would set the stage for arrests.

"Hey, farm boy, slow down. We'll get a confes-sion before the day's over. Just because she made you look like an idiot doesn't mean you have to drive like a speed demon."

Grayson again checked his speed, a habit when his brain overloaded. His BlackBerry rang. The hospital's number popped up. Ah, a confession. Maybe things were going the right way for a change.

"This is Houston Northwest Medical Center concerning Taryn Young," a woman said. "Not sure whether to call you or the police."

"There's an HPD officer posted outside her door."

"Not anymore."

Grayson's senses hit tilt. His foot pressed on the gas, and he wove in and out of two lanes of traffic. "What do you mean?"

"We found him unconscious on the floor of her room."

"What kind of wound?"

"Self-defense tactic. He's now alert and in the ER."

"I want to talk to him. Now." Grayson swung toward Vince. "Do our records for Young indicate martial arts or a military background?"

He smirked. "Told you she'd escape." He whipped out his phone.

The officer came on the line, groggy—fueling Grayson's frustration.

"What happened in that hospital room?"

"Young called for help. When I stepped in, I realized she was in the bathroom. But before I could get a nurse, she kicked the door into my face, then did some kind of a snap kick to my groin."

"Anybody check the security cameras?"

"Not yet. But one of the doctors saw her in the stairwell leading to the garage. She told him someone was picking her up."

Had to be Shepherd. "We'll be there in five. Don't leak a word to the media."

"Like I'd want them to know what happened."

"Right." Grayson phoned the SSA at the

command post and reported the latest development. He whipped around freeway traffic.

"Find her, Grayson," the SSA said. "And make an arrest. The FIG will get back to you on Young and martial arts. I'll put out a BOLO."

Grayson slipped his phone into his pocket. A BOLO—a be-on-the-lookout bulletin—could bring in community support. Sure wouldn't look good on his record that he'd let a suspect escape. But she couldn't get far in her condition.

"She was probably trained in Afghanistan," Vince said. "Knows how to cut out a man's heart and fry it up for lunch."

Grayson swallowed a remark aimed at himself while fighting the hammering in his head. To think he'd believed Young was innocent.

Chapter 6

5:45 p.m. Monday

Taryn entered the rear of the high-rise building housing her and Shep's condo. Not a single police car patrolled the grounds, but what did FBI agents drive? She assumed black unmarked SUVs like in the movies, and a few of them were parked around the area.

She was tempted to take the elevator to the fourth floor, yet she couldn't risk being seen.

The taxi driver had asked if she'd been treated at the ER, and she affirmed it. Told him she'd been injured in a car accident and needed a ride home, adding one more lie to the mix. She regretted not having him drop her off at the complex adjacent to hers. Here she'd be so easy to trace. From the concern on his face, she must look battered. Even now she faced cameras at every angle. What she'd viewed as a means to keep her safe from potential criminals now posed a threat.

Every step to the fourth floor sent shooting pain up her legs and peaked at the top of her head. *Think, Taryn. Keep your mind occupied.* She mentally listed what she needed before retrieving her car. On the run as though she were a criminal . . . and she was. If Agents Hall and Bradshaw had any doubts about her guilt, the officer on the floor of the hospital room took care of that. God forgive her for how she'd over-powered him.

God? Where had He been at the airport? Spiritual answers were irrelevant when doubts paved the way for disbelief. For years she'd given God respect only on occasional Sundays, living every moment for the next breakthrough tech-nology. Although recently she'd thanked Him for bringing the perfect man into her life. Shep claimed to be a Christian. That had to be a plus in the whole big picture.

Where was her husband? In a hospital somewhere, worrying about her? Dead? Without her phone and iPad, how could she contact anyone? She didn't have a landline in her condo.

Leaving the city to get away from the chaos would give her time to think. But law enforcement officials would be covering major highways. No point involving her mom. Her home would be one of the first places the FBI looked, and they would surely tap her phone.

Taryn Young Shepherd—top ten on the FBI wanted list.

Suspected terrorist.

Slow down. Breathe in and out. You are innocent.

At the condo door, she listened for voices. Assured no one waited inside, she slipped her key into both locks, just as she'd secured them yesterday morning when Shep picked her up for their wedding. Relieved, she stepped inside and snapped on the lights.

Shock paralyzed her. Overturned chairs blocked the entrance. Her antique dining room table lay on its side against the kitchen counter. Wall decorations and pictures destroyed. Sofa cushions and pillows slashed. Contents of kitchen cabinets strewn across the floor. Broken dishes. Even the refrigerator door stood open.

Thank goodness Bentley was at the kennel. Rushing into her bedroom, she saw the same destruction repeated.

Her pulse raced. All the photographs of her and Shep were gone. She examined the broken frames where the photos had once filled her with joy. When she and Shep started dating, she'd framed a dozen or more pics. In their new home, she'd placed them in every room. She wanted to see him wherever she walked.

Pieces of glass littered the floor, and she stepped lightly in her bare feet. Panic snaked up her spine. Who had ransacked the new condo, and why had they taken only the things precious to her? The FBI had no reason to do this. Did they? And if they had, wouldn't there still be an agent posted outside?

She yanked open the dresser drawer that normally held her personal laptop. Gone. All it contained of value were photos of friends and family. Priceless to her. She was so careful to back things up at work—why hadn't she taken the time to do the same at home?

Taryn stiffened. She hadn't locked the door when she entered the condo. Hurrying back through the debris, she stepped on a piece of glass. Blood left a trail to the door. She double-bolted it and limped to the bathroom.

Urgency nipped at her heels. She used tweezers to remove the glass, but her arm was starting to bleed again where the IV had been. Flipping open a box of Band-Aids, she pressed one onto her bloody arm and another on the bottom of her foot.

She swallowed two Tylenol 3 and glanced up. The image in the mirror—hollowed eyes and a bruised face, especially around her right eye—challenged any brand of makeup. And the nurse claimed she had seven stitches along the left side of her head near the hairline. Later she'd attempt damage control.

After scrubbing blood from her hands, she pulled her hair back into a ponytail and snatched sunglasses and a baseball cap. Definitely an improvement. An extra purse lay on her closet floor, so she stuffed it with tissues, a hairbrush, a toothbrush, a tube of lipstick, and all the other items from her torn leather bag. What was she thinking, fleeing like a criminal? She fought the urge to be sick. . . . She'd taken the prescription Tylenol on an empty stomach. Or the nausea could be from all of today's stress.

She dropped the Tylenol and Band-Aids into her purse, then grabbed jeans and a shirt, tossing her torn and dirty clothes onto the bed. Every movement sapped her strength and increased the chances of the FBI beating down the door. Wrestling with each leg of her jeans brought unbidden tears. She struggled with socks and tennis shoes while straining for the sounds of voices. Whoever thought getting dressed could be so painful?

With one hand wrapped around her purse, she picked her way to the door and cracked it open to view the hallway. A familiar perky Hispanic maid pushed a cart toward her.

"No need to clean today," Taryn said in Spanish.

"*Sí*. Have a nice day." She held up clean linens and brought them to Taryn. Hoping the maid couldn't see her unsightly bruises beneath the cap and sunglasses, she took the stack and set them on the kitchen counter of what was to be her home with Shep.

"*Gracias*."

Please, forget you saw me.

Taryn limped down the hall to the stairway, silently begging the maid not to notice. She must get to her car. The FBI would have her license plate number, right? Where could she go for help to sort out this mess?

Claire. The one person she trusted to help prove her and Shep's innocence.

Taryn opened the door to the garage level. Her white Mercedes was gone.

6:15 p.m. Monday

Grayson left Young's hospital room and ended the call from the SSA. Tracing the bomb's components and conducting the thousands of interviews that went with the investigation would take days. Media hinted strongly at a Middle Eastern plot, and the public was buying it. In fact, Homeland Security considered it a viable claim. Iran praised those involved, even offered names and faces of the masterminds, wanted members of al-Qaeda.

Learning Shepherd's identity was crucial to finding out who really stood behind those involved. The one person who could provide that info now ran the streets. The FBI's media coordinator had initiated twelve digital billboards across the city that rotated every eight minutes seeking information about the bombing. Young's face circulated among them to garner public buy-in. The problem with a single person's act or a small cell meant the intel chatter was at a minimum if there was any at all.

Both sides of the corridor were lined with wounded on stretchers and chairs, a bloody blur mixed with moans for help that rose from the injured and those with them. A woman's lifeless body lay on a stretcher covered with a sheet. A man carrying a little girl grabbed a doctor. When the doctor shook him off, the man punched him in the face. More blood. Grayson stopped the scuffle, but he understood the combination of fear and fury in the presence of utter helplessness.

"They're doing the best they can," Grayson said to the man. He held him back from the doctor and captured eye contact. "Your little girl?"

He nodded. "Her arm's broken. She got knocked down at the airport."

The doctor didn't waste any time leaving the scene.

Grayson focused on the child's twisted limb. She whimpered through closed eyes and tear-stained cheeks. "How long have you waited?"

"Over seven hours. My wife's now in surgery."

"Let me see if I can speed things up."

"Please, she's suffering."

Grayson wove through the crowd to the nurses' desk. "A man's been waiting for seven hours with his little girl. Her arm appears broken, and she's in extreme pain."

The nurse buried her face in her hands. "Bring her here, and I'll see what I can do."

Grayson started back through the crowd and motioned for the man to join him. Protests erupted, and a middle-aged couple blocked the way for the man and his daughter. Grayson flipped out his badge. He didn't care if this was preferential treatment—adults could manage life's tough blows, but not a child. "FBI. Let the man through."

"Still out to save the world, farm boy? Spin-off from Billy Graham?"

Vince's smoker's voice scraped at Grayson's nerves. "Lay off."

"Our job is to find out who did this, not escort kids to the front of the line."

"I know my job."

Vince chuckled. "Did you tell the SSA the hospital stuck another patient in Young's room before a fingerprint sweep?"

Grayson glared.

"Just helping you keep track of your priorities. Saw a BOLO for Shepherd and Young. No pics of him—just your lady."

Grayson's patience was as thin as the man's who'd punched the doctor. "They won't get far."

"Unless they have a private plane." Vince pointed to the crowd. "Look around you. Nothing but misery. All hell broke loose this morning, and I don't see it letting up anytime soon. Sure glad I've got only six months until retirement. Won't miss this job at all."

Vince's retirement couldn't come soon enough. The past year had been like having his dad for a partner, the same know-it-all, condescending attitude.

"So what did your bug give us?"

"Nothing but a pathetic 'Sorry' from Young when she assaulted the officer."

"Where to now?" Vince said.

"We have the address to a condo where Young recently moved. We'll meet the team there, then go on to Gated Labs."

Grayson's BlackBerry informed him of a notification. A taxi driver reported dropping Young off at a high-rise condo less than an hour ago. He'd seen her photo on a digital billboard.

Chapter 7

6:18 p.m. Monday

How could anyone think she or Shep were responsible for the airport tragedy?

The cacophony of voices on the bus drowned Taryn's sobs—tears for all the innocent people who'd died today, for her beloved Shep, and for the things she'd done to protect herself. Embracing change had always been one of her strengths, but not when it involved horror. She'd gone from a bride to a fugitive. Her body ached, claiming the strength she desperately needed.

The whole concept of the Metro system had a learning curve, especially since she'd never used public transportation. She paid when she boarded, but she had no idea how long her money allowed her to ride.

A screen mounted in the bus displayed graphic scenes from the bombing. A woman reporter held a shaking mic while speaking about a church youth group in which three students had died in the bombing. They showed horrendous footage: missing limbs, first responders working tirelessly to pull the dead and injured from the wreckage. Taryn choked back the acid rising in her throat.

An interview with a local congresswoman called the perpetrators cowards, and she was right. "We are strong Americans, and we will unite to do whatever is necessary to find who's responsible. Here's a message to you: We stand strong. You think you put fear in us. Well, you're wrong. You've only made us more determined to preserve our way of life—our freedoms—and we are resilient."

Taryn's picture flashed as a person of interest. She slumped in the seat, hoping no one recognized her. Two phone numbers were listed for anyone who had information about her.

The interview continued. "We don't know if this is homegrown, foreign, or a combination, but know we will not rest until we find out who has done this and why. And hold them accountable."

No words could express her terror.

Hope rested in seeing Claire. She'd believe in Taryn's innocence. Claire had met Pastor Willis at the ceremony, and he'd given Taryn his card. Shep said he was a personal friend. Maybe he, too, could help her make sense of what was happening. She fumbled through her purse and pulled his card from her wallet—Pastor Willis, First Citywide Nondenominational Church of Houston. When she got to Claire's studio, she'd call him.

Or was she fishing?

If only she could clear the cobwebs from her head.

Maybe the FBI would arrest the terrorists

tonight, and all she'd face was what she had done at the hospital. They'd return her photographs and slap on a hefty fine for assaulting an officer. She'd need a good lawyer and resolve the issue at Gated Labs. Then she and Shep could honeymoon on a Puerto Rican beach. The nightmare had to end soon. But so many unanswered questions threatened what she believed to be true.

Three blocks from Claire's studio, the bus stopped. If not for the torment raging through her body, she'd have run the rest of the way. Claire was her best friend, everything Taryn was not—outgoing, vibrant, fun to be around. So creative. And her three-year-old daughter was a joy.

The sign on Claire's studio read Closed, but the knob turned. Taryn stepped inside and removed her sunglasses. Photographs covered the gallery. Claire often said, "God speaks through His children's smiles." A sign bearing *shalom* rested on the counter.

"Claire. It's me."

When no one responded, Taryn called again. She walked through the studio to the workroom, repeating Claire's name. Typical lights were on. The smell of glue and chemicals, so very much Claire, met her nostrils. She didn't hear little Zoey's giggles, though the girl usually played on Monday evenings while her mother worked late.

"Are you so engrossed that you don't hear me?" Taryn laughed, despite the horrific day. Many times Claire lost track of reality in the midst of creativity, a common joke between them.

Not a sound.

"Zoey, this is Aunt Taryn. Are you hiding from me?" She looked in all the familiar hiding places—behind the counter, under an umbrella-shaped reflector that Claire used for lighting, inside a storage closet.

Empty.

What had Claire done with her computer? Odd that she'd moved her Mac desktop and the two twenty-seven-inch screens somewhere. Her cameras were missing too. A chill crept up Taryn's spine. The phone lay upside down on the floor. The line had been cut. Fear swirled through her.

A pair of jean-covered legs jutted from the section of the workroom where Claire framed photographs. Horror repeated from the bombing.

"Oh no." Taryn rushed to her friend's side.

Claire lay in a crimson pool—her throat cut.

6:45 p.m. Monday

Grayson hadn't seen such destruction in a long time. He and Vince surveyed Young's residence, busy with agents sweeping for prints and DNA.

"Took more than one person to make this mess," a female agent said.

"Looks more like rage." Grayson stepped over the debris into the small kitchen. "Even the eggs are splattered on the floor. A stick of butter tromped on."

"We got a shoe print from the butter," she said. "I'll keep you posted."

"Wonder if they found what they were looking for." Vince bent to the hardwood floor and used his pen to sort through broken glass that looked like the remains of a crystal vase. Roses and a small puddle of water lay to the side. "Agents found blood on the floor."

"If they didn't find what they were looking for, then it wasn't here. And was it Shepherd or someone the two double-crossed?" Grayson pointed to the bedroom. "I see her clothes from the hospital. She didn't waste much time here."

"Probably meeting Shepherd for their mad dash out of the country."

Grayson reserved his opinion. He made his way to the bedroom. Even the towel bar in the bathroom had been yanked from the wall. Whatever they were looking for must have been small.

What did they think Young hid in her condo? Maybe a flash drive? Possibly a list of those involved with Nehemiah? Those who bombed the airport? Was this in support of a blackmail attempt?

He pulled data from his mental bank. The international airport had been bombed with materials that were easily obtained. Although a handful of groups claimed responsibility, the who remained a mystery. The why might be the software in Young's control, although that theory was a little out there. One scenario was she'd betrayed her country for the almighty dollar, and Shepherd chose to eliminate her instead of splitting their share. But why kill innocent people unless there were others at the airport who needed to be eliminated? Was there even a connection there?

Grayson stepped onto the balcony and closed the glass door behind him to call the SSA. The information he needed would eventually come through his BlackBerry, but he wanted it now.

As he pressed in the SSA's number, his impatience mounted with the slow trickle of information. "I'm at Young's condo. She's been here and gone, and the place is a disaster. Got anything new?"

"One of the VPs from Gated Labs was killed this morning—Ethan Formier, head of product development. A friend of Young's. He took an earlier return flight instead of his scheduled afternoon one. Follow up on that. Could be an unfortunate coincidence. Still checking the names of the dead and injured for anyone else suspicious."

"What does Gated Labs have to say?"

"They regret Formier's death. The CEO has no idea why we asked about Nehemiah because as far as he knows, there aren't any issues."

"And Young claimed she disabled it." Grayson clenched his jaw. "Said only she had the activation code. She planned to contact Ethan Formier today about the situation."

"Did she say why?"

"Refused to. Said she wasn't authorized."

"Find her and we'll get to the bottom of this. Shutting down software with advanced protective mechanisms will get her jail time. She got greedy, and now she's going to get herself killed before we have names. Formier could've been working with her."

"Or caught on to what she was doing, and that's why he arranged an earlier flight," Grayson said. "Has Formier been on your radar?"

"No. Neither do we have Shepherd's true identity. You realize all this will hit your Black-Berry in the next few minutes."

The sharp rebuke in the SSA's words halted any more questioning. "Just a bit anxious. Gated Labs knows we're on our way?"

"The CEO is waiting and has called back in those who worked with Young. Don't dismiss anyone until you get answers. Find out who's using the software and have them confirm it's fully enabled."

"Yes, sir." Extensive interviews were going on with the congressmen who'd participated in the closed-door session before issuing the export license for oil and gas companies. Leaks and payoffs could come from anywhere.

"Grayson, I want to know that Gated Labs isn't hiding anything."

Chapter 8

7:30 p.m. Monday

Grayson studied the face of Gated Labs's CEO, Brad Patterson, a forty-eight-year-old man whose face-lift pulled his lips into a permanent smile, like the Joker from *Batman*. He sat across from Grayson and Vince at a twenty-foot-long solid mahogany table in the company's boardroom, equipped with a full bar in one corner and an espresso station in the other. A wall of windows looked out from the twenty-story building onto the exclusive Galleria area.

"We appreciate your seeing us after hours. Our condolences on the loss of Ethan Formier," Grayson said.

"Thank you." Patterson nodded with a coolness that matched his arctic blast of white hair. "We lost a highly respected man. A strong leader."

"Our interest is Taryn Young. Has anyone heard from her?"

"Not to my knowledge," Patterson said. "After we received your subpoena, we faxed the FBI her employee information."

"We also need confirmation that the software project she helped complete is secure."

He folded his hands and leaned back in a dark-brown leather chair. "The Nehemiah Project. I assured your office we're in good shape." A twitch beneath Patterson's right eye gave him away.

"We need verification." Grayson removed a notepad from his jacket pocket. "Who are the companies using the software so we can double-check things?"

"It's a highly secured program."

"We're the FBI. That gives us clearance." Grayson hoped Patterson hadn't contacted his attorney. "What happened at the airport today is of national concern."

"What does the bombing have to do with who's using Nehemiah?"

Grayson shrugged. "Maybe nothing. We're looking at every angle, at anyone who has something to hide."

"I resent the implication of my company's involvement in any illegal activity." His jaw tightened.

This guy needed to climb down from his CEO throne. "No one has accused Gated Labs of any wrongdoing. We're both on the same side."

Patterson danced a pen on the highly polished table. "There's a problem."

Now they were getting somewhere. "Please explain."

"Our people are working on it."

"Elaborate for us, sir. We aren't as computer savvy as you are."

Patterson continued to tap his pen. "I was informed that Taryn Young disabled the software late Friday afternoon. She phoned the two companies and told them she had activated an earlier version. This morning both companies called customer support and wanted to know when the problem would be resolved. The situation escalated to my attention."

"We know Nehemiah is a software program that protects the process control systems that regulate underwater pipeline temperatures for natural gas," Grayson said. "We also know Congress requested Young be the lead developer. But we want to hear the history and details." Would Patterson's explanation match Young's?

"She was the head of her team, our top developer. Creative. Imaginative. I have no idea what is happening here. We have safeguards, and we're using those." He pressed his lips together as though carefully choosing each word. "The US is positioned to export natural gas. It's shipped in liquefied form, called LNG. Large companies are looking to ship the product all over the world. Nehemiah, at the moment, is the only software containing specialized hacker deterrents. If the wrong people had control of Nehemiah, they could raise the temperatures and cause a massive explosion."

"We'd like to know what companies are using it." Grayson would hate the time wasted if Patterson insisted upon another subpoena.

"A US company located in Kitimat, Canada, and one here in Houston that operates out of Corpus Christi."

"We need contact information and all dialogue between Gated Labs and the two companies." Grayson texted his request to the FBI office. "A team will be here shortly to review the information on-site. They will also need to acquire a mirror image of Taryn Young's and Ethan Formier's computers. The agents possess the necessary level of security for information classified as top secret. Mr. Patterson, as holder of the information, I think you would agree we have need-to-know."

"My opinion doesn't seem to matter here. You understand our lawyers will be notified, and we'll need a subpoena."

Grayson eyed him. "I expected no less. Thank you for your cooperation."

"Then we're done here?"

"Not yet." Grayson slid Young into the sellout category, but the airport bombing was a puzzle. "We understand Ethan Formier worked with Taryn Young."

A shadow passed over Patterson's face. "Nehemiah was her brainchild, and she worked closely with him."

"When was the last time you spoke with Mr. Formier?"

"He texted me last night and said he'd changed his flight to early this morning."

"Did he state why?"

Patterson blew out his exasperation. "Needed to discuss Nehemiah."

"We'd like to see his files." Did Patterson have something to hide, or had his lawyers advised him to be cautious?

"The subpoena?"

"We'll make sure you have it." Grayson would have said more, but there was no point in angering Patterson and closing down an interview. "How did Taryn Young get along with other employees?"

"Her supervisor was convinced she had issues."

"Formier?"

"No, her immediate supervisor, the one the FBI spoke with earlier."

"We'll want to talk to him and the rest of the team. What were your dealings with Ms. Young?"

"As I stated earlier, this comes as a shock. She's always been professional. Cooperative. Highly intelligent. Dedicated to Gated Labs, or so I thought. Ethan supported everything she did. I had no fault with her work until this hiccup."

"Anything else?"

"She's earned several awards, known worldwide for her various projects. I never knew of a problem until this morning with the software."

"I want to talk to her supervisor."

Patterson nodded and picked up his cell phone. A few moments later Grayson and Vince were introduced to Haden Rollins, a thirtysomething man who wore an Italian suit like a male model. And he knew it.

"What can you tell us about Taryn Young?" Grayson said.

"Have you arrested her yet?" Arrogance brimmed from his dark eyes. "One of our own is dead because of her."

"Pure speculation at this point," Grayson said. "For the record, I'm asking the questions here."

Vince coughed. Up to now, he'd listened while Grayson led the conversation. "We can do this here or at our office," Vince said. "You choose."

"Cooperate," Patterson said. "I want this matter resolved."

Rollins brushed his jacket sleeve. "She led the team for the Nehemiah Project. Competent, but she has a quirky personality. Paranoid, in fact. Didn't trust her team."

"I want the names of those people," Vince said.

Rollins nodded. "Friday night we discovered she'd disabled Nehemiah. Those using it were forced to use an older version."

That wasn't exactly how Young had explained it.

"I told these agents we have our best people on the problem," Patterson said. "It's only a matter of time." He pointed his pen at Vince. "When she's found, I want a full explanation."

Vince slowly stood and paced the room. He

turned to Rollins. "What did she have to say about Francis Shepherd and her marriage? We found nothing, no photos or information that connected the two."

"She's a private person. Actually, to my knowledge, she has no close friends within the workplace—"

"Except Ethan Formier, who's now dead," Patterson said. "He'd been in Mexico on a project."

"What was his business there?"

"Consulting."

"We'll want the verification," Grayson said.

"You know how to get it," Patterson said with a smirk.

Vince continued to pace the length of the conference table. "Mr. Patterson, why do I think you and Mr. Rollins aren't being completely honest with us? Do you have any idea how many people died today? How many more are injured? Unaccounted for?"

"And we have no idea if Young's role here at Gated Labs even fits," Grayson said.

Patterson stood. "I regret the loss of lives and property today."

"Sit down, Mr. Patterson. I see how caring you are," Vince said.

Vince needed to hide his tough-guy routine. Being on the same page worked better than tossing grenades. Grayson picked up the ball.

"We'd like to interview Young's team members, beginning with any she had conflicts with."

"The first would be Kinsley Stevens," Rollins said. "She's waiting in her office."

From the moment Kinsley Stevens entered the room, she gave a new definition to *sashay*—more like *seductive*. With a toss of her blonde hair, she emitted power from every inch of her body. Beauty and brains must help her maintain a high-level position within Gated Labs. Easing into a chair beside Rollins, she revealed a low-cut silk blouse and crossed her pant-covered legs.

She moistened her ruby-red lips. "Why am I here?"

Rollins focused on the young woman. "Kinsley, these two men are FBI agents investigating Taryn Young." His tone indicated irritation. "I know you're grieving Ethan, but they have a few questions."

"I see." She stared into Grayson's eyes without a blink. "I'm very concerned about Taryn and her shutdown of the software. Now the media are linking her to the bombing." She paused. "Have you located her or Mr. Shepherd?"

"We're close," Grayson said. "Tell me about your work with the Nehemiah Project."

"Taryn was the team leader."

"Why would she disable it?"

"I have no idea. Companies were already using the program. Our work was essentially complete."

"Any bugs?"

"There are always issues. How can I help the FBI?" She tilted her head. "Do you need access to my computer? I have my laptop and cell phone in my office."

This woman knew the meaning of cooperation. "Tell us about your personal relationship with Taryn Young." Grayson poised his pen.

"Off the record?"

"Sure."

She sat military straight and folded her hands. "She's a brilliant designer. The project was her baby, and she hand-selected the team. I considered myself fortunate."

"What else?"

She glanced at Rollins as though asking for permission.

"Miss Stevens," Grayson said, "do you have additional information for us?"

She nodded. "Taryn criticized everything I did. I never understood why. But the friction made it difficult in the workplace. Then she accused me of tampering with her computer."

"Did you?"

She stiffened. "Of course not. I think she wanted me fired."

"Why?"

Rollins cleared his throat. "Kinsley is highly qualified. I intended for her to be the team lead for the next project. Taryn didn't take that well."

Grayson let the information roll around in his head. If Young had provided the software to someone outside of Gated Labs, then she would have needed to keep her position secure. Getting along with her peers was important. "Were there problems with other team members?"

"You'd have to ask them," Stevens said. "We're a closemouthed group. It's a necessity with the high levels of security."

Coworkers always talked. "Oh, we will." Grayson turned to Rollins. "Please bring in the next team member."

Stevens rose, but Grayson gestured for her to wait. "Miss Stevens, Agent Bradshaw will escort you to another office while we conduct interviews."

She eased down, fury lines creased across her forehead. "Are you insinuating I haven't spoken the truth?"

Grayson met her question with cold professionalism. Rollins indicated others had problems with Taryn Young, and he intended to find out who and what. "Just like you, I have a job to do. Is there anything more you'd like to tell us?"

She rubbed her palms. "I have a photo of Francis Shepherd."

Chapter 9

7:50 p.m. Monday

Think, Taryn. Don't let emotions paralyze you.

She couldn't feel her heart beat or her feet touch the pavement. How long and how far had she walked? She hurried across the street in the midst of traffic. Horns blared. Brakes screeched. She didn't care. Claire's mutilated body stayed fixed in her mind. The blood . . . The day had been filled with so much blood.

The police needed to be contacted. Leaving Claire alone at the studio seemed heartless, but Taryn was afraid. Her fingerprints were everywhere. Why should she be surprised her name would be linked to one more brutal crime? Since her cell was missing, she had to find a pay phone. . . . When had she last seen one? Shep called them a relic of the past. She needed her husband to help her work through this nightmare.

Taryn hoped Zoey hadn't witnessed her mother's death. Or had she? Where was Zoey? The little girl must be with Lydia. That made sense. Claire could have scheduled a late-afternoon photo shoot and taken Zoey to the sitter's. Taryn pushed logic into her thoughts. But truth packed a hard punch—the poor child was now motherless.

Today's tragedies didn't involve codes and numbers that she could delete with a keystroke. Reality never responded to Shift or Backspace. Real life had to be met with strength, and hers had just run out.

An office building towered before her. But the time neared eight. As she'd feared, the doors were locked. A block down, a Starbucks was nestled in a shopping strip, its green-and-white sign glowing like a beacon. Maybe it had a pay phone. She slipped the sunglasses back on and made her way inside the café. Normally the aroma of freshly brewed coffee perked her up. But not tonight. The darkened view of her surroundings handicapped her. She wanted to be in control, and her disguise diminished her vision.

The sounds of laughter and conversation irritated her. No pay phone in sight.

She used the restroom and washed Claire's blood from her hands. Bruises continued to rise on her face. A sense of filth resonated within her, and that feeling would not dissipate until today's bomber and Claire's killer were found. Once back in the café, she scanned the tables for police officers.

"Can I help you?" A young man grinned from behind the counter. His dimples must have earned him lots of tips.

"I have an emergency, and I've lost my phone."

He pulled a phone from his pocket. "Use mine. Are you okay?"

She nodded and moved to a far table. Glancing to see that no one observed her, she pressed in 911. The police or FBI wouldn't be able to trace the call to her. How far had she sunk to avoid those who were committed to protecting the public? The operator responded.

"I want to report a murder." Her voice trembled. "Claire Levin, at her photography studio in the Galleria, near the mall. I found her in the back room a few minutes ago. The sign says Closed, but the door's unlocked. Her equipment is missing, so I assume it was a robbery."

"Where are you now?"

"I'm not sure. I . . . I couldn't stay there."

"What is your name?"

"It doesn't matter."

"What's the number you're calling from?"

The operator had her number. "I don't know."

"Stay calm, miss. Don't hang up."

Taryn disconnected the call, fighting the desire to dissolve into a puddle of emotion. A woman laughed as though her coffee held a shot of brandy. A table of teens sipped on their syrupy drinks while texting. Didn't they understand the world was falling apart?

She pressed in Shep's number, but it simply rang. She ignored a call, assuming it was the 911 operator.

Next she called Lydia. "This is Taryn. I've got to be brief."

The woman cried out her name. "Oh, the news is saying terrible things about you."

"They aren't true."

"I know, dear one. Makes me angry. I want to call the FBI and tell them they have the wrong person."

"Thanks, Lydia. Is Zoey with you?"

"She's with Claire."

How many times would terror wind a fiery trail through her body? "I just came from the studio. Someone has stolen her equipment, and . . ." Taryn's voice cracked, and she sobbed. "I hate to tell you this, but Claire is dead, and Zoey wasn't there."

Lydia broke into wailing. "What's going on? Claire is a good, kind person. Who would do such an awful thing? And where is our little girl?"

Taryn swiped beneath her eyes. "I wish I knew. Does anyone else ever keep her?"

"You know Claire only trusts you and me."

Taryn didn't say what rippled through her—the killer might have taken Zoey. Had it been a theft since Claire's equipment was missing, or was it something to do with the danger unfolding around her? "I'll find her and whoever took Claire's life."

"Where is your new husband?"

"I haven't seen him since before the explosion." Suspicions paralleled her rising panic. No. She refused to think Shep was a part of today's chaos.

"I called the police about Claire. Please don't tell them I contacted you. I'll be in touch."

"God be with you. I'm praying for this to end and bring us sweet Zoey."

Taryn ended the call. The barista studied her curiously, and she held up her finger to let him know she was nearly finished. What if he'd recognized her beneath the hat and sunglasses? As if anyone needed their eyes protected this time of evening. What if he'd already informed the police? Desperation mounted. She pulled Pastor Willis's card from her purse and pressed in his number. A respected man could provide sound counseling, help her sort through the terrifying moments since this morning. The phone rang several times. She tried again. When no one answered, her insides knotted. A pastor always had voice mail. Right? And he specifically said this number also rang into his private cell so he could be reached day or night.

She returned the phone with a polite thanks and left the coffee shop. Where could she go to think? Dusk was approaching, and predators did their best work then. Exhausted, her body throbbing in time with her pulse, she needed a safe place where she could search for more information. She loved Shep, and he loved her. Once they were together, he'd explain what really happened this morning, and she'd tell him about the break-in at their condo and poor Claire and Zoey. The FBI would be satisfied and forgive what she'd done to the police officer. Without rest, she'd soon collapse. The need to find answers drove her more strongly than clearing her and Shep's names.

Claire had told her about an Internet café four blocks from her studio. Gathering her wits, Taryn looked for street signs and pinpointed her location to backtrack. Her commitment to the truth and locating Shep deepened. Every car that drove past, every person she passed, upped the urgency in her spirit. The sign for the Internet café boasted neon red . . . the same color as blood.

Inside, she waited fifteen minutes before a computer was available. After paying ten dollars for an hour, she slid into a chair and brought the computer to life. She checked local news and cringed at her own picture. She hated the accusations.

One report listed her as a terrorist. Another as a person of interest and tied her to smuggling technology from Gated Labs to enemies of the US. Considered armed and dangerous. Her hand flew to her mouth.

No one mentioned how Nehemiah aided those exporting LNG or how she'd dedicated her efforts to protecting US infrastructure.

Taryn leaned back in the chair and stretched before focusing on the news report again. She fought the tears. Ethan was listed among the dead! How could this have happened? He was her friend and mentor. And now he was gone. He'd shared in her suspicions of Kinsley and Haden before he left for Mexico City, and he'd promised to investigate the matter. She stared at the computer screen, her heart hammering against her chest.

The death toll rose at an alarming rate. The number of injured recovered from the rubble continued to grow. More sites listed her as a bomber . . . killer . . . traitor. She clicked on the FBI's website to read their press release. Thank goodness they didn't make the horrendous claims of the media. If only she could send her mom an e-mail or call her.

She scrambled to find info about Pastor Willis. Another useless search. His church didn't exist, and the address on his card was a vacant lot. She studied the diamond Shep had placed on her left finger, promising his love and devotion. His smile said forever. Would he be horrified to learn the pastor was a fake, or did he already know? Shaking away the rising panic, she looked for proof of the things he'd told about himself. She had to learn the truth. Her fingers sped across the keyboard, seeking more answers. Even if the results shook her world.

Harris County had no listing of her and Shep's marriage license application. He was not the man she thought she'd married . . . if she were married at all.

With the last finding, she left the café but had no idea where to go. She remembered a bus stop and made her way slowly in that direction. Once there, she slid onto a bench. No one waited with her. So very hard to think when her body was one mass of bruises, and she had nowhere to turn. But she could ride the bus until she figured out the next step. Lydia would be looking for Zoey too. Perhaps she'd call the police.

The truth . . . where was it? Could Shep really be trying to save her from some unknown evil? Or was he evil personified? The thought made her physically ill. Combined with the pounding in her head, her thinking faded in and out. She wanted to give up and let the police find her. She hadn't done anything seriously wrong, but how could she prove it?

"Taryn."

She froze. Shep! She whirled around. Bolting from the bench, she flew into his arms. He held her close while she fought the urge to sink into hysteria. The familiar scent of his woodsy cologne and the strength of his arms helped make the horrors of the day fade.

"There's no need to board a bus." He stroked her hair and back. "We have to talk about the miscommunication at the airport."

She hesitated, a tug-of-war raging through her emotions. Miscommunication? "What happened this morning?"

"I got a last-minute business call. Urgent. I had to take care of it."

Her mind screamed *liar*. "You left me at the airport without a word. On our honeymoon!"

"I tried to call you after the explosion."

Shep . . . her husband, the man she loved. She'd looked for him since waking in the hospital. The FBI said he'd fed her a fictitious name. They displayed footage of him leaving the airport before the explosion. An image of Claire's body flashed. The brutal savagery of all the dead and injured. And where was Zoey? The country believed Taryn was a traitor. Still, he'd not contacted her until now . . . in the dark.

Taryn stepped back. "I want the truth."

"Don't you trust me? Babe, we have to get out of here." He grabbed her right wrist—hard. "Cops are everywhere."

In the madness of today, had she lost touch with reality? "Don't we want to go to the authorities and prove our innocence?"

A bus rolled to a stop, its brakes screeching. The driver opened the door. No one exited. "I'm running late. Y'all gettin' on?" the female bus driver said. "Haven't got all night."

Taryn tried to jerk free from Shep's hold. She opened her palm and pressed her thumbs into his wrist. He loosened control, and she stepped back.

"Trust me," he said. "You'll regret this."

"Are you threatening me?"

"Without me, you'll end up dead. You know

what I want." He reached for her, but she took another step back toward the bus.

Her worst fears had manifested and stood before her.

The bus driver called out. "Either get yourself on in here, or I'm drivin' on."

He grabbed her wrist again, and she drove a kick into his nose. Blood gushed. He doubled over and fell.

"I'll find you, you b—" he cursed. "No one can save you now."

She scrambled up the bus steps, and the door closed behind her. The bus rolled away, and contempt for the man she'd sworn to love until death settled in her.

Chapter 10

9:35 p.m. Monday

Shep's betrayal bannered across Taryn's mind. Had he committed all of today's atrocities? Sent innocent people to their deaths? Murdered Claire? Done something with Zoey? Clenching her fists, she allowed herself to accept the unthinkable. She'd been used, but for what purpose? Could it be . . . ?

Shock numbed her as the bus rumbled down the street, letting passengers on and off at various stops. She didn't want to believe what had happened. She wanted to believe that Shep hadn't threatened her but was a good man who loved her. The screen mounted inside the bus continued to report the bombing. A segment of the Houston FBI director's speech replayed . . . the number of dead and injured etched into her mind.

Special Agent Grayson Hall hadn't lied to her. His insulting questions held a vein of truth. She shivered.

She'd hurt a police officer because she believed in Shep's innocence. Her mind spun with one thought after another, all centered on hurt and betrayal. Her throat thickened, but she refused to cry. Her life had been dedicated to solving dilemmas for businesses and industries through the latest in software technology. But no amount of superior programming could reverse today.

She rode the bus through four more stops, her heart and mind torn in many directions. A huge stone church set back from the street caught her attention. Safety. Rest. Surely it would be open. The bus stopped and she exited, peering in every direction for Shep. He said she knew what he wanted. Before the question left her mind, the answer came.

The only thing she possessed that anyone would ever want was access to Nehemiah and her knowledge of other encrypted files from Gated Labs.

Once the taillights of the bus disappeared, she worked her way across a busy intersection to the church. Claire always used to say God reigned with His people, and Taryn wanted to believe her friend's words. She hoped God's house held an invisible shield to protect those who needed it.

She yanked on the main entrance door. Locked. Would the church have an alarm system? Of course it would. What was she thinking? In this world, no one could be trusted. She'd learned that valuable lesson today.

Please, God. I need rest.

She walked the perimeter of the church building, trying each door until a rear one by the children's playground surprisingly released. She stole a look over her shoulder before pulling the door open. A swing moved as though a child eased back and forth. If an alarm sounded, she'd simply escape into the night.

No sirens. Eerie quiet met her ears . . . like a low hum. She locked the door behind her and leaned against it, willing reality to lift its weight from her shoulders. She couldn't recall ever being in a church alone. But the need for rest overpowered caution. Here in the solace of those who lived by faith, she'd find a way out of today's mess.

In the shadows, she explored the hallway, finding a series of offices. A table lamp lit the desk of one of the larger ones, and she limped inside, the sting in her foot growing worse. A green leather sofa caught her attention, and she lay down, not to sleep but to close her eyes and think.

Two days ago she had readied herself for a beautiful wedding and a fairy-tale honeymoon. The problems at work with Kinsley Stevens and Haden Rollins would be easily resolved once Ethan returned from Mexico City. The overheard conversation in the break room between those two had sealed her concern about the software's vulnerability. She regretted not being more social. Making friends might have given her an edge in office activities.

Why hadn't she gone to Mr. Patterson and shared her concerns about the project on Friday? Asked for permission to disable the software? Gone ahead and revealed her doubts about his niece and Rollins? Taryn's stupid pride had been her downfall. The Nehemiah Project was her team's best work, and she feared Kinsley planned to take over her leadership role. Sleeping with Haden guaranteed it. Taryn had relied on Ethan, and he'd died in the blast. Her stomach tightened as she tried to keep from breaking into a mass of sobs.

International security implications for her team's software project were a concern from the beginning. In the wrong hands, access to the software source code could be used against the US and its allies. Could the bombing be related? How far-fetched were her suspicions? Why would anyone blow up an airport terminal for software? There had to be more, but she had a sick feeling the two were connected.

She'd told Shep that whatever project held her attention at Gated Labs came home with her. If he now had her phone along with her iPad, he would have access to the software.

The backdoor was buried deep in her iPhone, and it would take the most experienced hacker time to find and decrypt it.

Why hadn't she seen Shep's deceit in their three-month whirlwind romance? If he'd been part of a conspiracy to gain access to Gated Labs's technology, the plan had been thorough. And one person alone couldn't have put this into play. Kinsley's and Haden's names surfaced again. Was jealousy over Kinsley's connection to Brad Patterson ruling Taryn's thoughts?

She was so far from her comfort zone that she didn't recognize herself. The future looked hopeless and scary. She had to initiate proving her innocence because the world believed otherwise.

She rubbed her face as though the pounding in her head would slip into oblivion. Answers were supposed to come with the morning, but tomorrow seemed an eternity away when every law enforce-ment official in the city and state was looking for her. The search had probably gone nationwide. Not that she could blame any of them. Too many facts pointed to her supposed guilt.

Taryn forced herself to stand. Perhaps if she paced, the pieces of her jumbled mind would slide into place. She glanced at her wedding ring. It might not be real either. She hurt, not just physically, but through every fiber of her being.

Forget your feelings and focus on the bigger picture. People are dead. A child is missing. You're wanted. It can't be a coincidence Shep left you at the airport and then emerges from the dark threatening you. Something larger than her damaged heart was at stake. And she couldn't deny or hide her involvement.

She knew none of Shep's friends except the limo driver. Neither had he mentioned any names. His past was rooted in Abilene, the only child of a couple killed in a car accident when he was in college. Why hadn't she checked into his claims? She couldn't blame herself—she'd had no reason to doubt him. How clever. She nibbled on a fingernail, recalling how it annoyed him. Too bad. The events leading up to the bombing marched across her mind.

A fake wedding.

"I'll take care of everything, honey. I'll make sure our day is perfect."

She rubbed her cold arms . . . remembering.

"Drink a second cup of coffee, my precious lady. You need to wake up."

Shep had her iPad.

Their separation before the bombing.

He'd probably taken her phone too. He'd been in the hospital room, and that wasn't something she'd dreamed.

Her destroyed condo and the missing photos.

Her laptop with pictures of them gone.

Claire's murder and the missing computer and photo equipment.

Zoey's disappearance.

Ethan Formier dead in the bombing.

Shep's appearance at the bus stop.

By all rights, she should have been killed today. And if her fears were valid that his abandoning her at the airport was all about the Nehemiah Project, she could have been another body at the morgue. She shook her head, wanting to believe her injuries had taken her on a hallucinatory trip.

I've not gone mad. Somehow, someway, I'm going to find answers to all that's happened.

At the moment, she was worth more alive. Kidnapping was a strong possibility, which must have been Shep's reasoning at the bus stop. He'd meant to scare her, and it worked. She ran from the law and Shep. Who was worse? Gated Labs probably wanted her arrested or had already fired her.

She rose and limped along the wall of bookshelves, glancing at reference and history books to help whoever occupied this office form theologically sound messages. A nudging whispered to give herself up. She wanted to do the noble thing—help the FBI find those responsible for the day's tragedies and locate Zoey.

Taryn fought sleep while her body cried out for

more Tylenol 3, but she didn't want to take anything that would dull her mind. Come morning, pastors and staff would enter their offices, and a church harboring a fugitive sounded like a medieval story line. Whatever she chose for her next step, she had to figure it out now.

She shook off her weariness. The items in this pastor's office held her fingerprints. Did it really matter at this point?

A Bible lay open on a small table. She was a once-a-month believer. That's when she attended church with Claire's encouragement, or she'd not gone at all. It had been years since she studied Scripture. Her family had served faithfully in church, sending her and her brothers to every church event imaginable. But her regular attendance ended when she entered the world of science and accepted her professors' nonexistence of God. Then her father died suddenly of a heart attack, and she struggled attending church even with Claire. But today she needed to find answers outside herself—a rarity. Her world, once secure in technology and its continuous advances, had been hacked.

Her gaze dropped to the Bible. A funeral service bulletin marked Psalm 23, a passage she'd memorized as a child. Information about the deceased caught her attention.

The woman was a Holocaust survivor, a Polish Jew. Soon after she completed her education as a medical doctor, the Nazis had invaded her country. She refused an opportunity to escape because she didn't want to leave loved ones behind and was later sent to Auschwitz. While in the concentration camp, she helped others as best she could. After the liberation, she became a believer and emigrated to Houston. A Messianic Jew . . . like Claire. A quote from the woman caught Taryn's attention. "I could not blame God for the penetrating stench of death, for He was my only hope. I clung to God in worshipful desperation, and He strengthened me beyond comprehension."

Life required sacrifices in every generation. Nothing Taryn experienced had prepared her for this unfolding nightmare. So many people gone, snuffed out of life. For what? Burying her face in her hands, she reached within her soul for the faith she had found as a child.

Oh, God, I'm so scared. Forgive me for the doubts that pulled me away from You, for building a shrine to technology. I need Your wisdom. Help me. I don't know what to do.

How could she do any less than sacrifice her own freedom to find Claire's child? Taryn had no means to find Zoey. Neither could she clear her name without help. Who should she contact? A name rested in her mind—a man she hadn't regarded as a friend. Quite the opposite.

Why him, God?

98

Chapter 11

My plan was flawless.

I gave him all the necessary resources to secure information from Taryn Young and do my legwork. I even paid for a nose job after he broke it in a prison fight. Gave him her pathetic history. Her education. Wine and dine her. Sleep with her. But she had this prudish idea of marriage, so I arranged that too. His only task was to give the iPad to Breckon when he dropped off the honey-moon couple at the airport. Then eliminate her in Puerto Rico. I put the funds in her account to ensure she looks guilty of selling Gated Labs's information.

I pick up my burner phone and try him again, the fourth time in the past hour. I hate his lack of communication. He's avoiding me because he's failed. He knows he's a dead man.

The idiot thinks he can trump my ace. Thinks he can outsmart me and sell the software for a small fortune. What a fool. He has no idea what I'm capable of or who's pulling the strings—a powerful man who has no regard for life when he's motivated. Sometimes I think I'm crazy for working with a man who hates Americans, but the money is too good to pass up.

He won't ruin what's been in motion for months. Let him line up the bidders.

I've worked too long and hard for this. He'll spin this mess until he bleeds out.

The airport bomber did a great job of sidetracking law enforcement agencies. I'll congratulate him on his clever tactic and stay on his good side. I deserve to know all of his activities, although I'm not happy being left out of the loop. After all, I'm a partner in this. He will hear from me about it.

I should have researched his background more thoroughly instead of him always arranging our meetings. Never will the lure of money trump common sense again. But he can't complete the mission without me, and he knows it.

Chapter 12

10:05 p.m. Monday
At the FBI office, Grayson slipped into a chair beside Vince with a cup of coffee strong enough to stop al-Qaeda. That's what he needed. Who knew all the players in today's game? Rumors about a bidding war connected to Gated Labs held credibility, but they didn't have names of any potential buyers. Unconfirmed info indicated

North Korea, Pakistan, and Iran were among the bidders. The question driving him nuts was why bomb the airport if the bad guys had the software?

The op room was filled with special agents poring over intel. Like him, they labored over the many angles of the airport bombing according to their specialty. No one planned to leave until arrests were made. No one wanted to leave. The director of Homeland Security had elevated the threat level, and questions about how the government had allowed this to happen bellowed from the media. News reports made comparisons to other incidents, and blame scattered in a spiderweb across the globe. Grayson shoved aside media reports, which were often unreliable, to concentrate on confirmed info. His first concern was finding Young and Shepherd if they were still in the country. Now they had a photo of the man who called himself Francis Shepherd. If the man was in their system, the FIG would have an actual ID on him shortly. But Grayson's patience wore thin. Without the man's real name, Grayson fired blanks.

While waiting, he sorted through FBI updates. A woman by the name of Claire Levin had been found murdered in her photography studio. Her cell phone lay under her body, and the call history indicated she and Young talked frequently. He shook his head. If Young had been involved in the bombing, then killing a friend meant nothing.

But why would Levin's phone be under her body unless the killer wanted to implicate Young?

A woman by the name of Lydia Garza had called into the office. She claimed to be employed by Claire Levin as a babysitter for three-year-old Zoey Levin. The child was missing. An Amber Alert had been issued.

Another update caught his attention. A young woman resembling Young had entered a Starbucks six blocks from Levin's studio and used an employee's cell phone. The barista stated she was clearly shaken and upset. That supposed appearance matched the timeline for the 911 call reporting the murder. Why kill, then report the crime?

Little about this case made sense, and nothing more had surfaced from the BOLO bulletin. Background checks on Young's team brought little, except that Brad Patterson was Kinsley Stevens's uncle. Another plug for her to take over Taryn's position. Gated Labs's financial reports were sound, and their stock was up 12 percent over the previous quarter.

He blew out an exasperated sigh while arranging and rearranging facts. What had he missed that possibly linked Gated Labs and the bombing? Agents and law enforcement officials were divided on whether they were two separate incidents or somehow related.

His BlackBerry beeped with the FIG's latest findings. Francis Shepherd's real name was

Phillip Murford, an ex-con who'd done time in Arizona for several bank robberies and murder. Ex–Navy SEAL. Now they were getting somewhere. Not sure how Murford managed parole, but once released, he disappeared. Murford had lightened his hair and shortened the style, shaved a scraggly beard and mustache, and possibly gotten a nose job. But his identity was confirmed. Definitely a man who had skills and experience. The FBI finally had something concrete. An updated BOLO was going out statewide and nationwide. Based on this latest info, Murford could have killed Claire Levin, but was Young with him?

If the two were separated, as her appearance at the Starbucks indicated, she could be upset with the murder and ready to talk to authorities. All they had to do was locate her.

10:12 p.m. Monday

Taryn knew it was fruitless, but she had to know how far Shep had gone in building this elaborate scheme. Two more calls would cement Shep's fraudulent dealings in their supposed marriage. How many were involved? Had any part of their relationship been real?

The first went to Tony's Restaurant, where they'd shared dinner last night. She found the number online and reached for the pastor's desk phone.

"I dined there last evening and a particular waiter did an excellent job. His name is Winston. Is he available?"

"We don't have a waiter by that name. Is there anyone else who could assist you?"

She startled. "Oh. My husband has misplaced his credit card. The name is Francis Shepherd. Do you have his card?"

The man put her on hold. "No, ma'am. It's not here. I checked our reservations list from last night and the name isn't listed. Are you sure you have the right restaurant? This is Tony's."

"So you don't have a record of us being there?"

"Not at all. Unless it was a cash transaction."

It wasn't. "Thank you." She disconnected the call. The sophistication of what she was uncovering took her breath away.

They spent last night at the St. Regis. Shep had the room key when the limo drove them to the hotel.

"Let's take the back entrance," Shep had said and kissed her. "I don't want anyone gawking at my beautiful bride."

She called the hotel's number.

"I spent last night there, and I forgot my pearls. I think I left them in the bathroom. Room 1412."

"Ma'am, we have twelve floors. Perhaps you were at a different hotel or a different room."

More lies. "The room was registered under Mr.

and Mrs. Francis Shepherd or just my husband. It was our honeymoon, complete with champagne and roses."

"One moment, please."

Taryn's heart might give out before daylight.

"Ma'am, we don't have that name in our files. I think you have the wrong hotel. This is the St. Regis."

All physical links of her and Shep's relationship were supposedly gone. The realization seemed to strangle her. How could she deliberately have put herself in harm's way?

Taryn hung up. The same man's name surfaced again. This must be from God because Taryn saw no reason to trust anyone.

Chapter 13

10:45 p.m. Monday

Grayson scanned through an internal system, gathering more information about Phillip Murford. The man's work had been solo until now, and he had the brains to pull off the enormity of today's bombing. But did he work with others to steal the software? None of his fellow prison inmates flagged any interest. No wife or family. What about his Navy SEAL buds? Grayson made a note to do a background on all of them.

His to-do list grew. When daylight emerged, he

wanted an interview with Ethan Formier's widow. She might have insight into the case.

His BlackBerry rang. Not a number he recognized.

"Agent Grayson Hall?" a woman said.

"Speaking."

"This is Taryn Young." She sounded weak.

Grayson motioned to Vince and mouthed, *trace this call.* "Go ahead, Miss Young."

Vince moved slowly to accomplish the one task that would lead them to the person of interest.

"I need your help," she said.

He was FBI, not the Red Cross. "Are you ready to give yourself up?"

"Not yet." She drew in a breath as though in pain.

She wanted to barter? She needed a good lawyer more than the FBI's assistance. "Explain how I can help you."

"I'll speak fast. I'm innocent of today's bombing. I have no idea where Francis Shepherd is, but I'm convinced he played a part in something illegal. That's what I want to discuss with you. I have proof he used me, probably to get access to a Gated Labs project in which I was lead developer. But I can't figure out the reason for the bombing. Or if he's connected to it." Exhaustion tipped every word.

How long could this woman go on after the trauma of today? "Why contact me?"

"Because you're the only person I can trust."

Whoa. Didn't see that coming. "Why?"

"I know it doesn't make sense. But I saw sincerity in your eyes, a commitment to learn the truth. I want the truth too. But there's something more important than clearing my name."

Here it comes. . . . "Which is?"

"I found my best friend murdered in her photography studio—Claire Levin." She drew in a breath. "Claire was like a sister to me. I want her killer found. Her computer and photo equipment were missing." She sobbed, then apologized. "Claire has a daughter, a three-year-old, and I can't find her. I'm afraid something's happened to her."

Click.

Grayson laid the phone on the table, his investigative skills wrestling with Young's words. "As long as we talked, I know you got her location."

Vince shook his head.

Grayson's blood pressure inched up several points. "Why did you drag your feet?"

"Might not have been her. So she wants to bargain?"

"Not exactly."

"Why the call?"

When this case ended, Grayson would go to the SSA about ending his partnership with Vince. "Concern for Claire Levin's three-year-old daughter. I want everything on Levin and her child. Begin with phone records. Client lists. Family. Doctors. Agent Thatcher Graves is working the homicide. Talk to him."

"Slow down," Vince said. "We'll get the field plowed."

Grayson held back his fury. But his original thoughts of Taryn Young's innocence surfaced again.

10:55 p.m. Monday

Taryn's stomach growled. When had she eaten last? Didn't matter. Nothing would stay down anyway. She'd swallowed two more Tylenol 3, knowing her insides would protest and rebel. Adrenaline and the need to locate Zoey kept her going.

She'd completed her online search for Francis Shepherd. No combination of symbols or words produced anything legitimate. She couldn't hack into something that wasn't there. Who did Claire know who might have Zoey? No one marched through her thoughts. Claire had been alone in Houston except for Taryn, Lydia, and her church family.

The image of Claire in the photography studio burned in her mind while her stomach churned. They'd been so close, opposite personalities that strengthened each other. Tears dripped over her cheeks, and she whisked them away.

Right now grieving for Claire couldn't occupy

heart space because then emotions would over-rule logic. Finding Zoey had to take precedence. Later, when the path ahead was cleared of the rocks and potholes, Taryn could plan her future with the child she loved so dearly. Images of the inquisitive little girl with huge dark eyes and curly hair flashed across her mind. Squeezing her eyes shut, she could almost hear the giggles. Oh, to hear them again . . . and again. *Claire, I miss you. You were my lifeline.*

Realization stabbed her hard. Could Zoey have been taken as leverage to get her to cooperate with those who were after the software?

God gave her strength, she knew, because left on her own, she would've collapsed.

A clock ticked away on the pastor's desk. She needed to call Agent Hall back and hope the previous call hadn't been traced. Picking up the phone, her hand shook as though she'd contracted Parkinson's. Right now she'd welcome the disease over reality. The phone rang once . . . twice.

"Miss Young?" Agent Hall said. "I was hoping you'd call back."

"I have no choice but to trust someone."

"Do you know why Claire Levin was killed?"

"I'm afraid to speculate."

"Why?" Grayson said.

"I don't want to falsely accuse anyone of a horrible crime."

"What do you want me to do?"

"Meet with me alone so we can talk. Help me sort through what has happened over the past three months. The more I discover, the more fearful I become." She caught the near panic in her voice. "Will you meet with me?"

"Can I bring my partner?"

"No, sir. One more thing I wanted to tell you about Claire. With her equipment gone, our wedding pics are in someone else's hands. Also, the ones that were in my condo and my laptop are missing. I think Shep confiscated all traces of himself. Have you recovered my phone?"

"Not yet. I'll see what I can do about meeting with you privately. Where do you have in mind?"

She wanted to bolt from her resolve. Everything centered on the agent's believing her. She'd been set up by Shep, and the idea of being duped again gnawed at her conscience. Yet Zoey knew Shep. She'd go to him willingly. . . .

"Miss Young?"

"I'm sorry. My concern is for Zoey Levin." She sighed. "And all the dead and injured today. When I was in the hospital, you said Shep hadn't given me his real name. Have you identified him?"

"Yes. I can give you his information and background when we meet."

"Okay. I'm at the church on the corner of Voss and Westheimer. There's a door in the rear by the children's playground. I'll be waiting."

She ended the call and laid her head on the desk. From the hour and traffic, she estimated about thirty minutes before Agent Hall arrived. He might have lied to gain her confidence, and in a few moments the church could be surrounded by a SWAT team with every media camera in the city focused on her. Along with guns.

Great epitaph.

But she had to take this chance for Zoey's sake.

Chapter 14

11:45 p.m. Monday

A light rap at the rear church door seized Taryn's attention. The ending to *Bonnie and Clyde* filled her mind. She could do this. Help the FBI discover the truth and find Zoey. She'd written down every fact she could think of, including the problems at Gated Labs and her whirlwind romance with Shep.

The knock repeated, and she leaned her back against the door. "Who's there?"

"Special Agent Grayson Hall."

"Are you alone?"

"Yes. You have my word."

Shep had given his word too, along with pledging his love for the rest of his life. But she had to trust someone, so she opened the door. The agent stepped in, and she locked them inside, as though that could keep out a SWAT team.

"Thank you, Agent Hall." She stared at him in the shadows, hoping she'd see compassion. "I appreciate your giving me the opportunity to tell you what I've learned." They walked together down the hall, where a faint light from the pastor's office cast a golden path. She hoped it was a good omen.

"I have one hour to listen to what you have to say." He swung a look and cringed.

"I've seen my reflection in the mirror," she said. "I'm a little colorful, but I'll heal. Of course, I could leave here in a body bag."

"That's not my intention."

She believed him and told herself this wasn't another bad decision. "I'm in the second office on the right. It has a sofa and chair."

"You probably need to sit."

She led him to where she'd taken residence. Would he jam a gun into her back and slap handcuffs on her wrists? She swallowed hard. "It's very quiet. A little unsettling."

"Doubt if the building is haunted."

"Depends on what spirits are here."

He chuckled. "Good call."

"Are you wired with a team waiting outside?"

His brows narrowed. "No, and I'm taking a risk."

"Why?"

"A hunch. Against FBI protocol. Never mind my reasoning."

They sat on opposite ends of the sofa. This was a beginning to push the past several hours in the right direction.

"What do you have to tell me?" Hall said.

Her hands shook. "I've been so stupid. Now I'm angry at myself for thinking Shep cared."

"What caused you to reach out to me?"

"Putting pieces together . . . and a feeling in my spirit." That sounded lame. "Not a woman's intuition but a spiritual urge."

He nodded as if he understood. "Has Shep contacted you?"

"I saw him earlier tonight. He threatened me."

"Where? What did he say?"

She envied how he looked so relaxed. "A bus stop several blocks back. I'm sorry. I was so upset, and I don't remember which one. Finding Claire in her studio put me into a panic state. Anyway, I stopped at a couple of places to search for more information about Zoey and Shep. Everything pointed to your being right, but I didn't want to believe it. Then at the bus stop, I saw a frightening side of him. He became belligerent when I wouldn't go with him. He said I had something he wanted. That I'd end up dead without him."

"How did you get away?"

"I know self-defense, as you probably already figured out."

He nodded. "Do you mind if I record our conversation?"

"Go right ahead."

"I'll take notes too." Grayson flipped open his BlackBerry, pressed a button, and grabbed a small notepad from his jacket pocket.

"Why don't you take notes on your phone?"

He smiled, the first she'd seen. "I'm a little old-fashioned." He jotted down what she assumed was information about her. "Tell me what's happened since the day you met Francis Shepherd, whose real name is Phillip Murford." He lifted his gaze. "I'm sorry. Should have been a little more con-siderate with the news."

The alias cut through her like a knife. "Who is he?"

"A former Navy SEAL who's done time for armed robbery and murder."

"What proof do you have?" Contempt for Shep laced every word.

Grayson showed a prison pic of a man on his BlackBerry. "Here's a photo of Phillip Murford. What do you think?"

A few cosmetic changes, but the same man. She tilted her head. "The nose is wider."

"Maybe a nose job."

More events darted into her thoughts, and she pointed to Murford's picture. "I remember him complaining of a headache. Said he'd fallen playing soccer with some friends and broken his nose. That would fit." She shook her head. "I feel like such a fool. A whole lot of good my

114

IQ did when it came to judging his character."

"Emotions can deceive us."

"Make us feel like idiots. Like I should be in a straitjacket."

"Understand you're doing the right thing. We're circulating his photo on digital billboards throughout the city. We've had tremendous success using them to find suspects."

"I saw one with my pic—and the $15,000 reward for information." Exhaustion had almost overtaken her.

"How did you meet him?"

"At a party given by Gated Labs. I detest those things, but it's a part of the working environment. He introduced himself to me, and I thought he was a new employee, but he said Haden Rollins invited him. That was the weekend after Memorial Day."

"Did he and Rollins spend time together during the party?"

"No. Shep . . . Murford never left my side. We didn't talk much in the beginning. I can be incredibly shy at social functions. Total social misfit."

"You're doing fine with me."

"I'm motivated."

"Good for you."

Agent Hall could not begin to fathom what she felt—betrayed and hunted. "I thought he really knew me. For the first time, a man admired me, seemed to respect my individuality. He said and did all the things that mattered. Was attentive but didn't smother me." Details rushed through her. "He must have had access to everything about me. Suggested my favorite restaurants. Where I shopped for clothes. Understood how much I loved my Lhasa apso. He even expressed concern about Bentley's ears and how all his hair easily matted and needed special care. Why didn't I question the coincidences?" She pressed her lips together. "Of course he knew all about me. Money and technology can buy anything."

"Unfortunately you're right. What other kinds of things are you referring to, the things that mattered?"

Please, don't be playing my friend to trick me into something. "He said he preferred a shy woman who had brains, a woman committed to her career. Admired my ability to not disclose highly secured information."

"That's not too unusual."

"There's more. He claimed I was beautiful. Asked if I'd always been the center of every man's eye." She offered Grayson a sad smile. "Don't I wish. He guessed I'd been shy, had bad hair, and wore braces for years. Never dated. . . ." She drew in a deep breath. "I'm doing my best to be transparent. But this is difficult. Not my personality, and you're a stranger."

He glanced up from his note taking. "I have no

idea what you've been through, but you're doing fine. Where did he take you?"

Stupidity again slammed against her brain. "Secluded picnics. Catered dinners at his condo from my favorite restaurants. Long evening walks in the park. Rented movies." She massaged the continuous pain in her temples.

"Anyone see the two of you together?"

She thought back through their times together. "Only the limo driver, who also delivered our food—always the same man. Maybe someone paid attention at the office party. Haden. Claire and Zoey met him. But . . ."

"What?"

"I've learned he's covered his tracks for everything we did, so I imagine he has there too."

"Regarding the limo driver, later I'll put you in touch with facial recognition to see what we can find about him."

"Have you talked to Haden Rollins?" she said.

"Briefly."

"What did he say?"

He studied her. "You're exhausted. When's the last time you ate?"

So that's the game he played. Pretend to care so she'd confess to something she didn't do. She clenched her fist.

"Did you eat at the hospital?"

She'd refused a hospital tray. "A couple of strawberries this morning before being picked up for the airport." And the two cups of coffee.

"Let's check out the kitchen. See what we can find."

"I'd be stealing, and I don't think the church would have anything I'd eat. I'm vegan."

Grayson moaned. "We can look. Possibly some fruit if the church has a fridge. We can keep talking while you eat, unless vegans don't talk with their mouths full."

The hint of wit pleased her. "I can multitask."

They walked back down the hall toward the children's area and a small kitchen. "So you two dated and he proposed."

"Yes, at his condo. We'd had another catered meal."

"Do you remember the restaurant?"

"Cheesecake Factory."

"We'll see if the order can be traced and do the same for every restaurant."

"They were all on my phone's calendar. A lot of good that does now."

"Do you use iCloud?" He shook his head. "I imagine you have all the latest and greatest."

"I do, and I could log into my iCloud account later. He has my iPad and probably my iPhone. I think. The hospital and you claim not to have them." She told him how her iPad ended up in his possession.

In the kitchen, he flipped on the light and opened the fridge. He tossed her an apple, then tore off a paper towel. "Take a seat and start on this. I'll look for something more substantial."

She frowned but eased into a chair. After digging into her purse, she slapped a ten on the table. No reason to add *thief* to her list of new traits. "This should cover it."

He shook his head and grinned. "You are one unusual lady."

For the first time she noted his tan jacket over jeans and a navy shirt. When she'd seen him in the hospital, his ice-blue eyes seemed to cut through her. But now they were kind, as though he believed in her innocence. Dark-blond hair gave him an all-American look. Oddly, she liked him.

"Eat it. You look horrible." He turned to the cupboard and pulled out a jar of sunflower butter. "I suppose this is a substitute for peanut butter since so many kids are allergic to nuts." Reaching into a drawer, he handed her a spoon. "Go for it."

She took a bite of the apple, hoping her stomach cooperated. Its juicy sweetness spread through her mouth.

"How about some honey?"

"No thanks. It comes from bees."

"The vegan thing?"

She nodded.

"My preference is a triple-decker cheeseburger with lots of onions and a chocolate shake."

She laughed. How could she find humor in the middle of such a mess? "I'd starve." She also believed a vegan diet lowered her risk of cancer. But what did that matter when people were trying to kill you?

"How did you get on the vegan kick?"

She'd promised herself to hold nothing back, no matter how insignificant. "I had horrible acne as a teen. Tried everything until the change in diet cleared up my face. Even helped tame my hair."

Grayson sat across from her and pushed a button on his BlackBerry. He whipped out his notepad and pen. "What happened after the proposal?"

"He arranged everything. All I did was pick out my dress." She closed her eyes and told him what she'd learned this evening.

"Phillip Murford—"

A door slammed. Her gaze flew to Grayson.

He slipped a Glock from his jacket. "We have company," he whispered. "Did you order out for Chinese?"

Cold dread stopped her from responding.

Chapter 15

New York
12:55 a.m. Eastern, Tuesday

My phone rings, and I check caller ID. It's him. I'm aware of how he takes care of those who don't perform. The same way I do, except worse. I destroy careers or bankrupt dreams and financial portfolios. Laugh at their pathetic wailings. If someone has to disappear, I know who can make it happen and how much it will cost. My hands don't get dirty. But not the caller at the other end of the line. He kills because he's addicted to the high. Because he likes to smear blood on his hands and take the credit.

My phone rings until it rolls over to voice mail. Then it begins again. He won't give up. I finish a Scotch and answer it.

"When I call, you answer."

"Look at the time. I like to sleep."

"Where is the product?"

"Murford is bringing it in the morning."

"You want to know why that won't happen?" He curses. "Word is he's selling it to the highest bidder."

I pour another Scotch. Murford has a greedy streak. I'd seen how he operated and hired him.

Paid him well. "I have the situation under control."

"You'd better hope so."

I bristle. "You can't pull this off without me, so calm down. I—"

"You listen to me. Murford thought he had the new software, the one called Nehemiah. But Young disabled it and installed an older version. I want Nehemiah. Find your gopher. Get the job done. Understand? All I have to do is push Send, and the whole world will know you bombed IAH airport and why."

I know more than he thinks. He's powerful, but I discovered his weaknesses. "If anything happens to me, my attorney pulls a trigger. Looks like we have a stalemate."

He laughs, a high-pitched sound that scrapes at my nerves. "Your attorney is on my payroll. The plan goes into action Friday morning. That means I want the software by Thursday."

The phone clicks in my ear. I down the drink. My role is to be the go-between with Murford and the others. I still have a few tricks of my own. What he doesn't know is that I'll gain access to the old version of the software, blow up the pipeline, and make a killing in the market.

Chapter 16

12:09 a.m. Tuesday

Grayson killed the kitchen light and motioned for Taryn to stay behind him. Weapon ready, he listened. Dead silence. No footsteps. In his quest to gain her confidence, he'd allowed too long of a window before backup arrived. This was why he should have stuck to protocol, been wired, and had a surveillance team outside.

"Who's there?" he said.

"All I want is Taryn," a man said.

"Is that Murford?" Grayson whispered.

"Yes." Taryn stood so close, he could feel her breath against his neck.

"Send her out, and you'll live another day."

"Fat chance," Taryn sneered. "How's your nose? What a shame since you just had it fixed. Was it for me?"

Taryn Young didn't fit into any of the stereotypical computer geek molds. He admired her spunk . . . and he believed in her innocence.

"I want access to the Nehemiah Project," Murford said. "Give me that, and I'll forget about my nose."

She laughed. "I disabled it."

A shot whizzed past their heads. Grayson

shoved her to the floor with him. "The FBI is on their way."

"I know for a fact they're twenty minutes out. And my men are inside."

How had he gotten FBI information? They were trapped in the small kitchen. No window. No ceiling vent. He texted the SSA, but backup couldn't get there fast enough. He touched Taryn's shoulder for her to stay on the floor. Creeping across the dark room, he flipped on all four burners to the electric stove.

Grayson grabbed a roll of paper towels from the counter, tore off several strips, and laid them on three burners. On the fourth he set the rest of the roll. Then he opened a drawer, pulled out a few cloth towels, and tossed them into the mix.

Flames ignited.

"Be ready to run," he whispered. "Wait until I say you can go."

The fire alarm sounded, an ear-piercing siren guaranteed to bring the fire department.

Grayson burst into the hallway, shooting in the direction of the back door while he urged Taryn in the opposite direction, toward the front of the church. Bullets flew past them. "Move fast. I'm right behind you."

He counted two shooters. How many more waited in the shadows? He and Taryn made it into the next hallway without being shot. Faint lights from the main entrance shone both ways. He didn't see anything but furniture, and alcoves hid the unknown.

Grayson grasped Taryn's hand and pushed her against a wall. A shot sailed by, confirming his suspicions while the fire alarm sounded in his ears. He pointed to the sanctuary. From the size of the church, they'd find at least four exits there. Adrenaline pumped into his system, and he hoped the same rushed through hers. He pushed open the door, and they slipped into the dark sanctuary. An exit sign at the far left corner caught his attention.

With his hand firmly around hers, they raced to the exit. A light illuminated an exit door about forty feet away, one with a push release. A break, and they needed it as long as no surprises awaited them. Taryn slowed their pace, and he couldn't blame her with what she'd been through.

They rushed through the door. A blanket of humidity and eighty-plus temps greeted them.

"Stop right there." Phillip Murford aimed a gun at them. "You can't get away from me."

12:17 a.m. Tuesday

Hatred seeped from Taryn's pores. The blood staining his shirt had been her doing, and she wished she'd done more damage.

"Drop your weapon," Murford said.

The man she'd thought was Francis Shepherd, the man she'd believed loved her, was a *murderer*.

125

She despised him and herself for swallowing his lies. The golden arch to their future had been a pathway to hell. He had taken everything she was willing to give. But not her dignity.

"Come to daddy, Taryn." The same low tones she'd heard the night before. Then the words had filled her with desire. Now she wanted to spit on him.

"I'm not the fool from yesterday."

"Do you want me to remind you what happened at the St. Regis?"

"Not unless you want me to vomit."

He snorted. "It doesn't change a thing."

"Did you kill Claire?"

"Would I commit murder?"

"You already have. Where's Zoey?"

"How would I know?"

"Because she's missing. And I know you have her."

"Aren't you the feisty one." He tilted his head. "You have something I need."

He'd made that statement on their wedding night. She felt dirty, in a way soap and water would never wash clean. "Don't think so, Murford. Nothing I have belongs to you."

"Smart girl, you know my name. I bet you've learned I'll do whatever it takes to get the job done." He waved the gun.

"I want to talk about Zoey."

He chuckled. "I suppose we can work out a deal."

She pointed to Agent Hall. "What about him?"

"The FBI agent? You're in no position to bargain."

Sirens sounded in the distance, moving closer.

"Neither are you," Hall said.

"Taryn, I'll blow a hole right through him if—"

"Okay." Enough people had died. "I'll go with you."

"Hold on. One of those moves like I saw earlier and the agent's dead."

He'd kill Hall no matter what she did, but she could buy time. "I understand." She moved closer to him.

Murford lifted his hand to his ear, obviously to communicate with those inside the church. Hall rushed him, swung fast, and knocked the gun from his hand. It fired into Hall's left side just above his belt. Taryn dove for the weapon, its touch cold. Hall landed a punch into Murford's stomach, sending him sprawling to the ground. Murford kicked Hall's wounded side, causing him to stagger. Taryn screamed and kept her fingers secured around the gun, too frightened to use self-defense tactics.

Murford came after Hall, but the agent drove a hard right into his jaw, throwing him off-balance and giving Hall the advantage. He landed a punch to Murford's ribs, sending him backward onto the concrete.

While Hall's side dripped blood, Taryn handed

him Murford's gun. Hall jerked out the man's earbud. "Hurry, before the others find us." He gestured to a car across the street.

She was on the run again, but this time she wasn't alone.

Chapter 17

12:34 a.m. Tuesday

Grayson sped his Mustang toward the I-610 loop, fighting the agony in his side. He'd get bandaged once Taryn was safe inside FBI headquarters. A light blinked red, and he raced through the stale green. No other vehicles were in the area. Good. Innocent people wouldn't be hurt if the situation turned negative.

He pressed the SSA's number to report in, but the command post line rang busy. Was it blocked? He picked up his radio and reported to the duty agent, informing him of his wound and what had happened at the church. "On my way in," he said.

Turning his attention to Taryn, he recalled what she'd said about Murford being at the bus stop. "He's trailing you. How are they doing it?"

"I don't know." A moment later she yanked off her wedding ring, pushed the window button, and tossed it onto the street. "That's the only way he could have tracked me. I've been coherent enough to know if he did anything else." Her jaw clenched, and her fists balled. "I was too afraid to move back there. I'm sorry. When Murford shot you, I freaked. I despise that man."

"Anger can be a good thing, but don't let it control you."

"I'm working on it."

"How are you doing?"

"You're the one bleeding. I'm fine . . . a fighter."

"It shows. How is it a vegan won't visit the zoo or rodeo, but you'll level a man with martial arts?"

"Nobody's perfect."

Her quirky sense of humor must keep her sane. "Remind me not to make you mad. I read you graduated from Caltech at age seventeen with a computer science degree. Received your doctorate by age twenty-one."

"But I don't have street smarts. There's a big difference."

"What made you choose to hide out in a church?"

"God's supposed to be there, and I needed all the help I could find. The rear door was unlocked."

"Good enough reasons for me. Thanks for calling."

"I prayed first—an odd thing for me. The only two people I could trust were Claire and Ethan. And they're dead." She nibbled her lower lip. "I'm sure their deaths make you feel secure."

"We got out of the mess back there."

"Maybe this is the end of the running. Maybe now the whole world will know I'm not a killer. Do you have any idea how it feels to see your face plastered on TV with *terrorist* and *bomber* attached to your name?"

"We'll make sure the media rectifies the matter." But he knew her innocence would not hit the headlines like her alleged involvement had. "We're headed to the FBI office now." He needed to call the SSA again. A glance in the rearview mirror changed his mind. His senses sharpened. A black SUV raced toward them.

"Do you recognize the vehicle behind us?"

She whirled to take a look. "No, Agent Hall. And it's not slowing down."

"The name's Grayson. We've come too far to be formal." The SUV rode the bumper. "We may have a problem." Tossing his BlackBerry into the console, he stepped on the gas. The SUV stayed on him. A gun emerged from the vehicle's passenger window. "Duck, Taryn. They mean business." He raced ahead.

Shots fired. The rear window shattered, and the bullet exited about a foot to his right. Too close for his liking. Up ahead a truck and another SUV pulled parallel into the middle of the street.

"Sorry to ask this, but I need your eyes."

She inched up. "What's going on?"

"We're about to make a few wild turns. Hold on. Watch for any surprises." He stole a quick look at his GPS. The alley ahead to the left would take them to a one-way street—and he needed to turn the wrong way on it. The diversion might buy time.

"If you had a truck, you could crash through," she said. "Tear them apart."

Phillip Murford had met his match with this one. "I think you have a daredevil gene."

"More like a vengeful one. I want to throw a grenade."

"I have a Glock and Murford's SIG when you're ready." Two armed men appeared from the vehicles in front of them. "Hold on." He swung left and turned on two wheels. Hadn't done that since training at Quantico. Made him feel like a kid again until a shot took off the outside right mirror. He couldn't look at Taryn, or he'd risk losing control.

"Are you okay?" He zipped down the alley.

"I'm fine. Where are the police? The FBI?"

"I'm all we have at the moment." He hit a pothole, and his BlackBerry popped up and fell to the floorboard under the gas pedal. He tried to kick it with his left foot, but it wedged there. They needed speed. Now. With his toe, he maneuvered the phone until it broke free of the pedal. Grimacing at his wound, he grabbed the device and dropped it back into the console. The connection held his lifeline . . . prayer too. "Hold on to this for me."

She wrapped her fingers around it. "I'll keep it safe."

But who was going to keep them safe? *God, I hope You're watching all this because I've about run out of options.*

At the end of the alley, he turned the wrong way on a one-way street, the SUV hot after them.

"Grayson!"

A semitruck headed straight for them.

Chapter 18

12:57 a.m. Tuesday

Taryn held her breath, her hands trembling. The grille of the semitruck bared its silver teeth like a monster. Speeding closer. The horn blared. The SUV continued to ride their bumper. Computer games had never offered this kind of heart-pounding action. Neither had reality shows.

"If we live through this, I owe you," she said.

"How about a steak dinner?"

"Not Tony's."

"What?"

"Just get us away from these schizo people." Death-defying moments like what had happened over the past twelve hours made her wonder if her heart would last until Murford was stopped.

The distance between the oncoming semi and Grayson's Mustang narrowed. He whipped the car to the left, up onto a sidewalk. She jolted, her head banging against the roof of the car, while he bumped over the curb and hit a fire hydrant. Water gushed onto the street. He steered over the sidewalk and into the flow of traffic again, wheels screaming against the pavement. The sound of metal against metal told her the SUV had slammed into the front of the semi.

She rubbed her arms. "Tell me this is a nightmare so I can wake up."

"I wish." He sped through another red light, and a car laid on its horn.

Taryn couldn't blame the driver. Probably thought Grayson was high or drunk instead of running for his life with a woman wanted on both sides of the law. Closing her eyes, she willed her heart to slow its incessant pounding. She needed to think. Be logical. The way she always handled challenges. "Normally I thrive on solving problems. But not when my life depends on it. And Zoey. Where is she?" Panic rose in her voice.

"Taryn, God's with us and the little girl. He's in control."

A flicker of Claire. "My best friend used to say the same faith things. Now she's gone."

"Then she's with Jesus."

"I know, and I want to believe she's at peace. But finding her daughter is driving me crazy. I'm so afraid Murford has her."

"His insurance."

Grayson deserved the truth. "I'd tell him what he wants to save her."

"I'd expect no less. But now you have the FBI behind you."

"I'm not as trusting, but I do believe in God." Taryn gazed out the passenger window. She glanced around and saw nothing but a handful of parked cars and the lights from retail shops. "I thought we were headed to the FBI office. Isn't it on 290?"

"Need to ditch my car. Murford could have planted a tracking device while I was inside the church. And we don't have time to search for it. I'll get someone to pick it up later."

"How did he know when the FBI would arrive?"

Grayson lifted his chin. "Not sure. I'll find out. Is that the same purse you had at the hospital?"

"I changed at my condo. Nothing in there to trace me. I'm positive."

"After your experience with Murford, I bet you understand how someone can get distracted. Make a mistake."

A surge of anger swept through her. "Are you saying I should have seen through him? That I'm stupid?"

"Not at all. I'm saying you'll be better equipped in the future to deal with the dynamics of human behavior." He looked in the rearview mirror.

She needed to calm down. "Personal experience," she whispered. "Hard lesson to learn."

"I'm sorry."

"But it's the truth, and all I can hope for is to become a better person." She rubbed her forehead. "I'm touchy. Not an excuse since you saved my life and took a bullet. In case you haven't noticed, your side's bleeding."

"I feel a twinge now and then. Look, we've both seen better days, and we have to trust each other."

"Makes sense, but it sounds impossible."

He pointed ahead of them to a large retail strip. "We'll park the car there."

"Then what?"

He slid his car into a dark parking area and snatched his BlackBerry.

"Do you think there's a tracking device in there?" She'd never thought this way . . . never had to.

"I don't have any idea how that could have happened." He studied the lit area around a movie theater, his brow a mass of lines. He placed his BlackBerry in the console and stepped from the car. "This means neither of us have a phone, but too many things today haven't made sense. I'm not taking any chances. I'll find another phone to use."

"You don't know who to trust, do you?"

He gave a thin-lipped smile. "Of course I do. Let's get moving. This is just a detour."

Once she joined him, they walked hand in hand past several small closed restaurants—as though they were on a date, not wounded and running from those who wanted them dead. "How are you going to explain the blood?"

"I'm not."

Inside the theater, they moved toward the concession stand, where he produced his badge. "FBI. I need to use a phone."

The pimply-faced kid paled. "Sure, man." He pointed to a door behind him. "It's in the back."

"Show me."

The kid gulped. "You . . . you been shot? Knifed?"

"The phone."

The kid nodded like a bobblehead doll. Taryn held on to Grayson's hand and followed the kid through the door. A young girl with lip rings and violet hair swept up popcorn.

"Can we have privacy?" Grayson said.

The kid motioned to the girl, and she left her broom behind. Grayson thanked them while picking up the phone. Taryn waited with thinning patience and mounting fear of someone bursting through the door with a gun.

Grayson pressed in a number. Disconnected the call and tried again. "Great." He jabbed in the number a third time. "Can't get through. The line's tied up. At least the duty agent knows where we are . . . if we have the time." He pressed in more numbers. "Joe, I'm in a bind. Can you pick me up and another person at . . ." He rattled off an

136

address. "Thanks. The FBI knows where we are, but I'm concerned about time." He paused. "I'd appreciate it. Oh, the woman's name is Taryn." He gave her another one of his thin smiles as though to comfort her. But they weren't free from Murford yet.

"I hadn't noticed what street we're on," she said. "I'm normally better with details."

"This is what I do, and I take precautions. We have a few blocks to walk."

Weariness enveloped her. She shook her head. "What about your side? It's impossible. I—"

"*Impossible* isn't written in my book and shouldn't be in yours. Taryn, look at me." When she did, he continued. "In case we've been followed, I'm walking out of here first. If you hear me thank the kid twice, then come on out. If I mention the FBI, leave through the back door. Run and don't stop until you're six blocks down from the theater. The area is not exactly a safety zone, so be careful. Dogs run in packs. Gangs roam there, and they'd like nothing better than a pretty white girl. My uncle, Joe West, will be waiting in a blue 1974 T-Bird. Explain it all to him. He'll be looking for you."

"Are you sure?"

He dropped her hand. "As sure as I can be. Promise me you'll do what I ask."

How could she abandon him now? He'd nearly been killed for her sake.

"Promise me."

"All right."

He left her behind while he walked through the door leading into the theater lobby. Seconds ticked by. She paced. Listened at the door. Paced again.

"You might want to contact the FBI," Grayson said.

Taryn raced out the back of the theater.

Chapter 19

1:55 a.m. Tuesday

Taryn's chest ached from running, and slivers of agony shot up her legs. She wanted to look behind her, but slowing her pace might mean facing the barrel of a gun. Selfishness hammered a ruthless tune for leaving Grayson to face Murford. How could developing software to make her country a better and more prosperous place to live have caused all these tragedies?

Grayson was trained for combat and outthinking bad guys, but that didn't mean she should have deserted him. She could have helped with hand-to-hand combat, and with his wound, he needed a partner. Before yesterday, her fears had focused on the risk of presenting a new software package with too many bugs, or someone passing her up for a promotion, or Shep realizing her introverted personality was a hindrance to their relationship. Not treachery that walked with death everywhere she went. Now she ran for her life. The Nehemiah Project and the man she thought she'd married were entwined in a horrendous murdering spree.

Zoey . . . What had that wretched Murford done with her? Regret snaked through her for not probing him further about the child. He'd recover to make things worse, launch the next move to nab her, or use Zoey as bargaining power. Grayson had called it insurance to get what he wanted—but who would pay the premium?

The air smelled of rotten garbage, and the humidity carried the stench. Other odors met her nostrils—sweat and determination. She owned both. For the first time in her life, the skills she'd acquired would not help her escape those who hunted her. She had her mind and the ability to physically defend herself, but the unknown possessed more power. Everywhere she turned, the lions roared, and they were hungry.

How many blocks had she traveled? Was it two or three? Trees and shrubs grew over the uneven sidewalk, dark and menacing. A dog barked. A motorcycle whizzed by. A car slowed, blaring out rap music, and the driver shouted an obscenity. The barking grew closer, and a dog appeared in the shadows. A huge German shepherd, but oh, so lean. The breed and the man who'd betrayed her hosted irony. But she liked dogs.

"Hey, buddy. What're you doing out so early in the morning?" Her shaky voice didn't emulate the confidence she'd hoped for. Yet the dog didn't growl. She walked toward the animal, then stopped with a new realization. A friend was always a gift. Dogs were loyal, and shepherds were fiercely protective. At least the canine type.

No wagging tail greeted her. The animal sniffed, his huge nose brushing against her palm. Maybe she'd misjudged him. But it would be hard to manage a keyboard with missing fingers.

"I'm a friend." She shoved courage into her words. A nasty dog bite compounded with the wounds received in the bombing wouldn't sit well. She recalled what Claire had said about an encounter with an unfriendly dog when she and Zoey were at the park.

"Jesus loves you." Foolishness gushed forth, but what else did she have?

The dog's tail wagged.

"Thank You."

She patted his head. "Want to run with me?" The dog offered a good diversion. She stuffed her baseball cap in her purse and yanked out the ponytail holder to divert anyone who'd seen her earlier. She picked up her pace, the dog loping beside her. No collar. An angel in disguise?

Three more blocks to go, and the sidewalk seemed endless with tree roots pushing through the concrete, making each step more difficult. If she ever found the time to rest, she'd sleep for twelve hours.

Up ahead, a car parked and turned off its lights. Her heartbeat could be heard a mile away.

I'm losing my mind. I've gone without sleep until I've squished my brains.

"Okay, buddy. This is it. The driver is either Grayson's uncle or . . . never mind."

The outline of the car came into view. A T-Bird! The color was vague in the poor street lighting. She slowed to a walk. The car flashed its lights, and relief coursed through her veins. She hurried to the driver's side with the dog. An older man lowered the window.

"Joe West," he said. He had a gravelly voice and a bald head. No resemblance to Grayson. "Taryn?"

She nodded.

"Who's your skinny friend?"

She glanced at the dog. "We just met. I call him Buddy."

"Want to get in? Where's Grayson?"

"Back at the theater. He asked me to leave when we ran into trouble."

Joe revved his engine. "Climb aboard. Let's go find my nephew. Bring your pal if you want. We might be able to use him." She'd barely shut the door when he whirled his overgrown two-door car around and headed back down the street. Buddy nestled his head against her shoulder. Strangely comforting.

Joe West drove like Grayson. She'd had more wild rides tonight than in all her thirty years. St. Francis dangled from his rearview mirror. With the number of chips on the small statue, the saint had seen a lot of twists and turns.

The ride to the theater took a lot less time than hoofing it. Joe whipped the car into the rear parking area of the theater. Only two other cars were in view.

"Stay put while I see what's going on. Probably ought to get in the backseat." He reached under his seat and pulled out a gun. It looked like Grayson's. When this was over, she planned to learn more about weapons. Then again, she'd probably never want to see another gun.

"One more thing," he said. "I'm leaving the keys in the ignition. If you see someone other than Grayson or me heading out of the building, or if it goes down bad, get out of sight."

"Okay. We'll do as we're told."

He laughed, a low, pleasant sound. "You'll be the first woman I've ever met who did as I asked."

"Maybe they hadn't been through what I have during the past two days."

"The FBI may already be here." He kissed St. Francis and exited the car.

She crawled into the backseat and noted the lack of seat belts. "Buddy, it's you and me again." She patted the dog's head while he seemingly kept a vigilant eye around them. "Danger brings unusual friends, and you're one of them. I have a little dog. His name is Bentley and he's a white Lhasa apso, a bundle of hair. I bet you two would get along fine. But I warn you, he's a bit spoiled, has an attitude, and needs special grooming." She looked into the dog's huge face. "We'll need to get you on a regular bathing routine." She'd totally lost it. The German shepherd wasn't her dog.

A moment later shots rang out, yanking her to the present. Taryn swung her attention to the building. Joe, then Grayson, burst from the theater door. Grayson ran sideways, firing at two men who were after them. She leaned over to open the driver's door, then did the same with the passenger's. A few extra seconds for Grayson and Joe had to help.

Buddy growled, and she drew the animal to her. More shots.

As long as the other men didn't fire a bullet into the tires or the gas tank.

Chapter 20

2:47 a.m. Tuesday

Grayson stared out the window of his and Joe's kitchen into the blackness. In a few hours the sun would rise. Between now and then, the bad guys would remain on the loose, trying to get their hands on Taryn and eliminating anyone who got in their way. Neither the good nor the bad would rest until this was over.

Backup had arrived as he and Joe sped away, and they kept right on going. Right now he didn't want to think of what would happen to his career, all because he believed a suspect.

"Stand still so I can bandage you up," Joe said, lines deepening in his forehead. "You're one lucky hombre this doesn't need stitches. It's mostly bits of your shirt." He held up the tweezers with a bloody bit of cloth from Grayson's favorite navy-blue shirt.

"You could have sewn me up." Grayson eyed him grabbing a bottle of rubbing alcohol. "That's going to hurt worse than picking out my shirt."

"You want a bullet to hold between your teeth?"

"I might need it," Taryn said. She had a bit of green in her face.

"Don't pass out on me."

She turned away. "I'd never make it as a nurse."

"Hold on to Buddy." Grayson dreaded the alcohol burning his raw flesh.

Joe scratched his whiskered chin and nodded at Taryn. "Now's not the time to get squeamish on me. Once I disinfect this thing, I need to bandage him tight. Remember, you're the gal who'll do whatever I ask."

Eyes wide, she stepped to Joe's side. "I'm beginning to regret that statement."

The first drop of alcohol was like Joe had struck a match to his side. Tears welled in his eyes, but he'd not holler. His crusty uncle would never let him live it down.

"A mite tender, son?" Joe chuckled.

"You're enjoying this far too much." Grayson turned to Taryn, still green. "Tell me where you found your sidekick."

She told him the story of meeting Buddy on the sidewalk. "I'm sure God sent him."

Joe humphed. "I'll reserve my opinion until he's had a bath and gets a little meat on his bones. Suck it up, Grayson. This is going to hurt more. Gotta soak you in alcohol."

As if nothing to this point had threatened to flatten him. His uncle, a retired FBI agent who'd been the ASAC for Houston's violent crimes task force, was as tough as most of the cases he'd investigated. Never gave a bad guy an inch, and his gut instincts about crime were right on. Legend around the office said he was part bloodhound. But along with his reputation was a huge heart. His wife had died over twenty years ago, and the man had never shown interest in another woman.

Grayson had lived with Joe during his high school and college days. Life with his dad and brothers after Mom died would have landed Grayson in prison, full of more anger than he cared to remember. Joe showed him what it meant to be a man, a special agent for the FBI, and to have a steadfast reliance on God. From day one, the two had worked out every morning but Sunday, a habit neither man had given up. Except on stakeouts . . . or today.

"Miss Taryn, you sure have an unbelievable story," Joe said. "Of course, the media's full of crap. Whatever sells goes, and you're just too pretty to be a criminal."

"All I want is for the right people to believe me."

Grayson trusted her words, and his views had nothing to do with how she looked. He'd been duped a few times and paid the price for a so-called helpless gorgeous female who wanted the prestige of dating an FBI agent. "What about the FBI press release?"

"They're fishing," Joe said. "After reassuring the public that law enforcement officials were working around the clock to find those responsible for the bombing, they requested information on Taryn and Francis Shepherd."

"I despise being linked with him," she said.

"Have they released his real name?" Grayson groaned when Joe pulled another piece of shirt from his wound.

"Oh, I found it on my own—Phillip Murford, your typical ex-con who refused to be rehabilitated." Which meant Joe had learned more on secure sites. He handed Taryn a bandage with instructions to hold it firmly against the wound while he taped it.

"I couldn't get my call to the SSA to go through," Grayson said, relieved Joe had finished torturing him. "So I used the radio."

"Probably a good reason for that." He sent an admiring glance at the bandage. "I haven't lost the touch."

"You mean for inflicting more pain than the bullet?"

"You can handle it." He opened a kitchen cabinet and gave Grayson a prescription bottle. "Take these until they're gone." Joe flipped open a huge container of generic Tylenol and handed him three. "These too."

Grayson read the prescription. "How old's the antibiotic?"

"Old enough to do the job."

Grayson swallowed all four tablets with a glass of filtered water. Some things never changed. The meds might be five years old, but Joe would not allow anyone in his house to drink city water.

"Why don't you two rest in the living room while I find out what's going on at our friendly FBI office?"

"I suspect there's a mole there. How else would Murford have known when backup would arrive?"

"Lucky guess. Maybe."

Grayson needed a ten-minute power nap to fuel his brain. If he stretched out on his bed, he'd be out for hours. He dragged himself into the living room. Taryn trailed behind him with Buddy.

"What's with you and shepherds?" Grayson said.

"So far, this one's more loyal." Taryn's voice sounded weaker.

"You are a real sorry pair," Joe said from the kitchen. "Rather pathetic. To be superheroes, you have to attack the case with your brains in gear. I doubt this is over, so do what you can to pump some life into those pitiful bodies."

Joe always had a way of being encouraging.

"We should leave," Grayson said. "Where I live is no secret."

"The drapes are drawn and we're working with little light." Joe pointed to Buddy. "That dog will let us know if anyone approaches. From what you said, Murford needs a little while to regroup."

Grayson and Taryn eased onto opposite ends of the sofa. The middle sank to the floor, but Joe claimed he liked it that way. Every time Grayson started to nod, a thought popped into his head, and he'd jerk awake. Snippets of conversation. Research. His organizational skills competed with information he did and didn't have.

Think. What's Murford's next move? How can I be one step ahead of these guys?

Taryn stared ahead, eyes wide open. Looked like she had the same problem. "You live here too, right?"

"Yes. Two old FBI bachelors. One week I cook and he cleans. Then we swap. Joe's the better cook." He forced his eyes to stay open. "I'm thinking if neither of us can sleep, then let's talk. But not about all the near misses of tonight." A brief reprieve often caused missing pieces to slide into place, and he wanted to know more about this mystery woman.

"Give me a topic." She didn't sound convinced.

"What's the craziest story your parents ever told about you?"

She tossed him a bewildered look. "And I thought I had strange social habits. Okay. You go first."

He stood and pulled back the drape to take a peek at the street. A cat crept across the driveway. A poor squirrel was about to meet its Maker. Odd, since squirrels normally were active in the day. Grayson had always been for the underdog, and a part of him wanted to stop the game outside. Just like the case before him. "When I was six, I had this bright idea of going back outside to play after my parents put me to bed. I pulled the sheets from my mattress and tied them together, opened my bedroom window, and lowered myself." He laughed. "I hadn't calculated how many sheets I'd need, so I dangled in front of the living room window, where my parents were watching TV."

"Ouch."

"Yeah, that's what I said for about three days."

She laughed, and he enjoyed the musical ring. "Good one."

"Your turn."

When she frowned and rubbed her face, he had a clue what bothered her. "Taryn, this is a diversion. Nothing more," he said. "Something to keep our minds off what's happened, and then we'll regroup after Joe finishes talking to the SSA."

"Thanks. I do have a story. I was three, and I don't remember a single moment of what I'm about to say. But it's one of my mother's favorites. One night, they woke to me calling for them. I wasn't in my room, and they looked downstairs. My dad followed my voice to the kitchen. He snapped on the light and found me sitting on top of the fridge, where I'd eaten a whole bottle of Flintstone vitamins. Guess I couldn't get down."

Grayson laughed. "Daredevil even then."

She shrugged. "Never thought about it that way. I know I've always been interested in math and science. Computer programming came naturally. I don't have a desire to ride a motorcycle or dive off a cliff or parachute jump. What did you want to do as a kid?"

"To play professional baseball."

"Were you good?"

He waved his hand. "Depends on who I was playing against."

"Your turn for the next story."

"Can't top yours," he said. "But you mentioned *one* of your parents' favorite stories. What's another?"

She leaned her head back and closed her eyes. "After what I told you, this will come as no surprise. I was three. That seems to be my most rebellious age. My mother found me standing in her bathroom sink rummaging through her medicine cabinet. I'd eaten all of her birth control pills."

"What did she do?"

"Had my stomach pumped. I've been hormonal ever since."

He howled, allowing the mirth to relax him. "That's one I'll remember." The more he learned about Taryn, the more he liked her. She'd won numerous awards and had hit the who's who on every geek list he could find. "Who taught you hapkido?"

"Oh, you recognized it." She nodded as though appreciating his interest. "You won't find it in my records. Didn't train under my real name. I know that sounds odd, but it wasn't one of those things I wanted to incorporate into my résumé. I enrolled while in college, and I was against carrying a weapon." She paused. "I might need to rethink my decision. Anyway, I didn't compete in tourna-ments. Just trained and worked my way up to a black belt."

"What degree?"

"Third. I still train in a studio on the northwest side of town. Never had to use it until yesterday and today."

From the way she moved, she'd been at the top of her class. "What made you choose hapkido instead of the typical flashy stuff?"

"I like what it accomplishes, using an attacker's strength and power against him. It also makes use of many joint locks and pressure points."

"Glad you persevered."

"Give your sentiments to the police officer. My stunt will probably get me at least eighteen months."

"We'll wait to see how this turns out. He's fine, so don't let it bother you. I have a question, and yes, it's about you and this case." He pulled out his notepad and pen.

"Fire away." She cringed. "Poor choice of words. How about write away?"

He liked Taryn, and he hoped he didn't live to regret it. "I learned Congress met behind closed doors to decide if they'd issue an export license for companies to ship LNG." She confirmed this, and he continued. "Do you know of anyone who would be violently against the export?"

"I spent months studying the current software used to regulate temperature and pressure and the protection needed to export liquid natural gas. I understood the advanced security protection measures that are needed to ensure the US's infrastructure is safe from enemies. That said, oil and gas companies wanted this badly. Europe is a go for LNG from the East Coast, as well as countries who need the product in the west. But those who didn't want the license granted were industry and manufacturing who use natural gas here in the States. They believed it would drive up prices. If you're asking me if I know of a specific company or person who could be involved in something catastrophic, the answer is no. None of the discussions and heated arguments indicated such actions."

Grayson took copious notes. The FBI was on every angle, but then again, so was he. Terrorism was a nasty pill filled with poison that lingered long after the public pushed the event aside.

She patted Buddy's head and shook her head. "Bentley."

"What?"

"My precious little dog is at the kennel, but I guess he's okay. I made reservations for over a week." She paused. "Murford liked Bentley. Played with him. Would he have planted something to keep track of me?"

Grayson made a quick note. "He might have. Give me the name of the kennel, and I'll check it out."

"Thanks."

Joe walked into the room and sank into his recliner. His slumped shoulders and the telltale facial lines indicated bad news. "Got an update from Alan Preston."

"Bring it on."

"An anonymous tip reported to the FBI. Said you'd gone rogue and you and Taryn were working with Phillip Murford. Taryn's upset with the whole operation because she thinks Murford tried to kill her in the bombing. The caller said Taryn told Murford that when he delivered another $50,000, she'd give him the information about Nehemiah."

"Was the call traced?"

Joe snorted. "Untraceable. Since Vince wasn't with you at the church, he couldn't vouch for your innocence. Now, Alan doesn't believe the caller, but he has to take it into consideration."

For once Grayson wished Vince had been with him. "What am I supposed to do?" Grayson had neared his frustration limit.

Joe handed him his cell phone. "Call Alan. He's the SSA. Let him take your concerns to the next level."

Chapter 21

3:35 a.m. Tuesday

Taryn fought tears over the deceit that trailed through her association with Murford. Those useless displays of emotion never solved a thing. Fury best suited her, and anger she could work with. With all Murford had done . . . If he were standing before her, she'd pull the trigger on him.

Revenge made a strange bedfellow. She, Taryn Young, the woman who opposed animal cruelty and fought for their rights, now had murderous thoughts. Combine her thirst for blood with a renewal to God, and what did that make her?

This wasn't the best time to analyze herself.

She stroked Buddy's head. The dog soothed her frazzled nerves. "I'm afraid a call to your boss means an arrest for me."

"The SSA is the epitome of integrity. Both he and Joe live and breathe it," Grayson said, the phone in his hand.

"Thanks," Joe said. "Appreciate the morale boost."

Grayson nodded at his uncle and turned to Taryn. "Is there anything else you need to tell me before I make the call?"

"Not without getting online and doing a few searches." She hesitated. Like Congress, the FBI deserved all the background information she could volunteer. Chances were they already had everything documented about her life. "One more detail. When I was briefed during the closed session with Congress, I told them I regularly attended defensive and offensive hacking conferences. Some, like Black Hat, have participants who don't use their knowledge legally. Many of those conferences don't require a legal name."

"What's the difference between defensive and offensive?"

"Those who acquire defensive methods are looking to protect systems from being hacked. Those attending the offensive security conferences are looking for ways to get into a computer undetected, and that's my preference. It's more challenging and helps me find vulnerabilities in the software development process."

"How good are you?"

She shrugged. "I achieved elite hacker status. I wanted to be top of my class on both sides of the fence. You already have my career history."

Grayson handed her his notebook. "I need the name or names used for the hapkido classes and all hacker conferences."

She jotted down *Julie Harmon*. "It's the same for both instances."

Joe cleared his throat and eyed Grayson. "Make the call." Not an ounce of emotion passed over the older man's face. "Alan knows what he's doing."

"I want to get my hands on Murford and those working with him."

"Make that two of us. And I want Zoey found." Taryn refused to consider that the little girl had witnessed her mother's murder. "She's my child now, and I can't imagine her terror."

Joe pushed himself up from the recliner. "Make that *we three* want the child found—and those responsible for the chaos this week," he said. "I'll make a fresh pot of coffee while you talk to Alan."

"Joe, we need to get out of here," Grayson said. "We're sitting ducks."

"I agree," Taryn said.

Joe held up his hand. "You're safe here, or someone would already have blown in the door."

"Why are you two risking your lives to help me?" Taryn glanced from one man to the other. Both carved from the same stone. "If you live through this, your careers might end up in the sewer."

Grayson gathered his notepad and pen. "When we find who's responsible, we'll have brought all those involved to justice," he said. "And it's not just Houston's FBI working on the bombing, but the entire bureau, including agents abroad. The investigation is pooling law enforcement efforts that most of the country is not remotely aware of. Joe and I are small potatoes in the whole scheme of things. But I know the truth will surface, beginning with my call to the SSA."

"I'll grind those coffee beans," Joe said. "Grayson, when you're off the phone, you two need to figure out your priorities. Listing what you want accomplished helps us devise a plan. Right now we need caffeine flowing through our veins. How do you drink your coffee, Taryn?"

"Black and strong."

Joe gave her a thumbs-up. "Smart, pretty, and knows how to drink coffee."

She didn't add that a vegan wouldn't use dairy products.

Once Joe disappeared into the kitchen, Taryn studied Grayson. A fine man. Murford should take lessons. She wasn't sure if she supported the two agents on their decision to contact the FBI. But did she have a choice? God knew she had a difficult time trusting anyone, but she was convinced He had her back.

He pressed in a number. "This is Grayson." He smiled, something she hadn't seen too often. How sad she hadn't met him before Shep . . . Murford. Strange thought in the midst of this mess.

"I've been with Taryn Young since the agreed-upon meeting late last night," he said. "Joe patched me up. She's given me more information, and I'll send it once we're finished." He stared at her. "Fully cooperative." He explained her hacking abilities. "Although our priorities and hers are not exactly the same, I understand her concern for Claire Levin's child. Has the little girl been found?"

Taryn held her breath, but when he shook his head, she knew Zoey was still in danger.

"What are my orders?" He closed his eyes, obviously exhausted. "Yes, sir." He disconnected the call. "The boss has made it known that Taryn and I are at a hotel. Hey, Joe, Houston FBI's executive management has hired you as a post-retirement contractor and given you top-secret clearance, but I imagine you know that."

"Yep," Joe called from the kitchen.

"I need your laptop to send a secure message. Mine's at the office."

"You know where it is."

Grayson disappeared, leaving Taryn alone. She desperately wanted to hear about the conversation with the director of Houston's FBI. "Grayson, do you need any help?"

"It's my side that's bandaged, not my fingers. I'll explain more in a few minutes."

But she wanted to know now. What were they doing to find Murford? The FBI had to understand the airport bombing and the software were linked. She could see it even if she couldn't figure out why.

And Zoey?

She walked into the kitchen with Buddy trailing after her. Joe had just finished grinding coffee beans, the nutty aroma filling the room. "I'm really worried about Claire's daughter," she said. "There are so many places where they could hide a little girl."

Joe pulled three mugs from the cabinet, all black with the FBI emblem. "Those who have her will be making their move soon." Apprehension coated his words.

"I want to think they'd release a three-year-old."

Joe focused his attention on her. "Don't go there,

Taryn. False illusion. Kidnappers rarely release their victims. Too big a threat. Your friend's child could pick out the people who kidnapped her in a lineup."

She couldn't stop the tears. Her foolishness for falling for Murford was one thing, but a helpless, innocent child in danger leveled her emotions. Joe was right. If a man was part of a scheme to bomb the airport, killing innocent people, he'd have no issue eliminating anyone in his way.

4:15 a.m. Tuesday

Grayson pushed Send and joined Taryn and Joe in the living room. Joe was now working with him and Vince, not exactly protocol with his uncle's retirement. But the country's situation didn't support business as usual.

Joe handed him a cup of steaming coffee. The tantalizing smell caused his stomach to rumble.

"I heard that," Joe said. "You'll need breakfast soon."

"Wait until daylight. How do you feel about being my new partner with Vince?" Grayson said.

"Great. I'm bored with the retirement scene," Joe said. "This old man needs a little excitement. Beats game shows and crime novels. If I see one more episode of *CSI*, I'm going to puke."

Grayson took a sip, and the coffee didn't disappoint him. Joe only brewed Starbucks. "You're not surprised?"

"No, son, I'm not. Just a little odd to be a threesome with Vince. What's our assignment?"

"For right now, it's Taryn. Keeping her safe until the management has us bring her in."

"Why not now?"

"Like me, the SSA suspects a mole. Working on something that he wouldn't tell me about."

"I could help with the investigation," Taryn said.

"I'm not authorized to give you clearance," Grayson said.

She shook her head. "I don't need it." She pointed a finger. "Whatever I do, I'll take the blame."

"I'd give her anything she wanted to know," Joe said, respect brimming from his eyes.

"Thanks," she said with a smile that made Grayson's pulse race. "I want to help. Probably best I start with Shep . . . Murford. I spent three months with him. He's not so good that he didn't let something slip. I'll look for camera footage at his condo. Chances are the limo driver's in those too." She picked up a legal pad and pencil from the table and handed them to Grayson. "Since what everyone wants is out of my control, I can at least dig into online searches. I need you to tell me what's number one on the list."

Grayson tilted his head. "What do you mean 'everyone'?"

"Good and bad guys want Nehemiah. The problem is . . ."

"What?" Grayson leaned in closer.

161

"Neither my iPad nor my laptop can help them. I have a code memorized. Only a custom app on my iPhone, along with my knowledge, can give them what they want."

"The information's there?" He jotted down her words.

She nodded. "You've heard this before when I was in the hospital. But Murford was in my room, and I know that's when he swiped my phone. I can only hope he doesn't realize what's on it."

"I understand enough about computer technology to get around," Joe said. "But you're above my head. The software program is loaded on your iPhone?"

"No. That would be dangerous."

"I don't get it." Lines deepened on Joe's forehead.

"My iPhone has a key to a backdoor for Nehemiah."

"Explain it to me," Joe said.

"A backdoor is an undocumented method to access an application or system. I don't need the typical end-user log-on credentials or normal front-door method of getting into the software. The backdoor isn't documented anywhere since it serves as a point of exposure, but it is helpful during a software development process and even for ongoing support." She paused. "Understand, the old software is in place with its firewall. Hackers could be working on that aspect. They could also be hacking into the new one. But if Murford accesses the new software through my backdoor, he could install it remotely at the two companies that were using it. In short, he'd be in complete control of the LNG pipelines. It could be used to either destroy the software or plant a virus. Or it could be used for another purpose."

"Like what?"

"Like a hacker raising the temps and causing an explosion that creates lots of damage . . . property and lives."

Grayson wished he knew more about Taryn's expertise. "So all they need is access through the backdoor to accomplish whatever they're trying to do."

"Right. But I have multiple layers of encryption in the old and the new software. Nehemiah's firewall is quite sophisticated. Let's just hope they don't begin controlling Nehemiah through the backdoor."

"What are the two companies?" Grayson said. "And why don't they stop their plans until this is resolved?"

"Both are US companies: BC Moose Paw in Canada and TX-LNG in Corpus Christi. They're motivated to put their companies on the map as the first to export LNG. Unless the FBI moves fast, we're shot." She grimaced. "My choice of words isn't good."

"But you're right. Help me understand the

163

profile of a computer hacker," Grayson said. "I don't think my idea of a college student working all night in his dorm room cuts it."

"Sometimes. We're talking highly sophisticated technology. It's not difficult to be a hacker, and the root kits are inexpensive and fairly easy to understand. But the true professionals are targeted on what they're looking for. They don't make a single keystroke without weighing what it means. They use simple methods in the beginning and venture out into customizing their points of entry."

"We have a department within the FBI devoted to computer intrusion matters," Grayson said. "It's not my forte. I do know the US is losing billions to system breaches."

"What's the most common method to gain access?" Joe said.

"Social engineering amounts to approximately 41 percent of data breaches. It means using the social nature of people to obtain information. Like posting on Facebook that you're going on vacation for ten days and not taking your computer. Joe, that's not what we have here."

"I get it. High-tech stuff."

"Exactly. Then the user is in trouble if the hacker needs the information." She tilted her head. "When this is over, I'll give you a tutorial about protecting your system. Right now I believe Murford has what he needs to sabotage the software. The question is, has he found the custom app on my iPhone and secured the services of an expert hacker?"

Grayson cleared his throat. "We have no idea who the players are. We've already seen a well-organized team. Murford has a Navy SEAL's background. I imagine his people are trained in weaponry. Find the bad guys, and we find the phone."

"And Zoey," she said.

He nodded, knowing the child held priority for her. Zoey was the one way Murford could force Taryn to do whatever he wanted. That's why the SSA didn't want her out of Grayson's and Joe's sights. She swung the pendulum to help end or destroy this mission.

Chapter 22

6:35 a.m. Tuesday

Taryn had to admit, Joe could make a mean bowl of steel-cut oatmeal. He'd set out bananas, blueberries, strawberries, and granola that didn't have any of the food items she avoided. Guilt snaked through her for enjoying breakfast when the FBI didn't have answers for hurting people. Joe had spoken a glaring truth during an earlier prayer. He'd asked the Lord to bless the food to the nourishment of their bodies. She'd heard those words many times growing up, but the gravity of the situation reinforced the need to stay healthy and strong. The dog hadn't left her side, and now he lay on the floor beside her. What a gentle animal in the midst of so much uncertainty, even if he needed a bath.

She inwardly chastised the two men downing mushroom, sausage, and cheese omelets and biscuits dripping with honey and butter. Did they have any idea what they were doing to their bodies? Of course, if the health experts saw how much coffee she consumed, they'd write an article for the *American Journal of Medicine* condemning it.

Although sleep ranked at the top of her list, food helped stimulate brain cells.

Joe refilled her coffee cup. "A lot of unanswered questions are driving us nuts, but this is the big one for me."

She focused on his leathery face.

"Why was the airport bombed if Murford thought he had what he needed?"

"I don't know." She wished she had a better answer. "I'm wrestling with the same question. He could have killed me on our honeymoon and not all those people. For that matter, he had plenty of opportunities to kill me."

"Didn't he have the ability to nab your techy toys before the trip to the airport?"

She sensed a warm flush spreading through her.

How did she explain her possessiveness of the responsibility given to her, and how she felt about intimate matters? "This is a little awkward for me. . . . I never gave him the opportunity. I was always . . ." She took a sip of the coffee. "Awake. Cautious. Knew when it was time for me or him to go home. My toys stayed with me."

Joe rested his hand on her shoulder. "I'm sorry."

Embarrassment boiled her cheeks. "Thanks. I believe some things are reserved for marriage." She couldn't look at Joe or Grayson while she remembered Murford's persuasive methods.

"We haven't grasped the whole picture yet," Joe said. "Hopefully the FBI has it all figured out."

She wanted the answers now. How long would it take? "If they've solved the case, why am I on their top-ten wanted list?"

Grayson pushed his empty plate to the side. "I have a theory. Let's assume Murford works for someone else. I mean, his background doesn't show connections to anything this big. Let's say this someone has an agenda connected to LNG export. Could be a congressman leaked the info. Or someone working for Gated Labs. A manufacturing company that saw dollars escaping out the door with oil and gas prices guaranteed to rise. Or one of our country's enemies." He moistened his lips. "Ethan Formier is also dead, and it looks like a coincidence. However, I'm not a believer in those things. Were you and Formier targeted in the explosion? Or was he a victim of chance? You claim to suspect a Gated Labs employee of breaching security, and therefore you disabled the program. What happened for you to make such a critical decision, and how much was Formier aware of?"

Taryn let his words resonate through her. The situation with Ethan's death bothered her more than she wanted to admit. He'd been a respected VP, a friend, and a mentor. "Before Ethan left for his ten-day trip to Mexico, we talked about Haden Rollins and Kinsley Stevens. Company policy frowns on fraternization, but it wasn't a secret the two were seeing each other. Kinsley is Brad Patterson's niece, so that probably explains the leniency." She remembered the many times she'd walk into a meeting room and the couple would stop their conversation.

"Just before the two companies piloted the new software, I heard Kinsley and Haden talking in the break room, whispering, although they thought no one was around. Kinsley wanted my position as team leader in a big way, and Haden promised to make it happen. His words were 'I know how to discredit everything Taryn's ever done. The Nehemiah Project will go down.' I confided in Ethan. He expressed the possibility of sabotage to the project and for both of us to keep our eyes open. The next day a problem developed with the software." A rush of anger poured over her. "Ethan and I looked into it and discovered the issue came from Kinsley's computer. But she didn't have the skills to plant a bug of such magnitude. Ethan and I believed Haden had initiated the situation and blamed it on Kinsley to cover his rear."

"So you think it's more Rollins than Stevens?"

"I do." Her mind raced with Haden's capabilities. "But I don't have proof."

"What happened after that incident?"

"Ethan left for Mexico. The Friday before my so-called wedding, I overheard Kinsley and Haden." She took a deep breath. "I knew both were in the break room alone, so I listened outside the door. Haden said Nehemiah would fail while I was gone on my honeymoon. When I e-mailed Ethan, he suggested I do whatever I thought necessary to ensure the security of Nehemiah and those using the software. But to let him know what I'd done. He'd discovered something about Gated Labs that bothered him and planned to confirm it before having a face-to-face with Patterson. Ethan advised me not to cancel my wedding plans. I made the decision to disable the software and install the old one. Not Ethan."

"No one else was involved?"

"No. My word against theirs. I didn't e-mail Ethan with new access credentials because I planned to talk to him on Monday."

"We have work to do." Grayson scooted back, scraping his chair legs across the floor.

Joe pointed at Grayson. "You two make a good team. This man knows how to ask questions and access information too. I taught him most of what he knows. I'll give Quantico a little credit. But most of it comes from good genes."

Grayson laughed. "Dad would appreciate your observation."

"My brother-in-law has sand for brains. Told him so the other day."

"When?"

"Last weekend. I called him to shoot the breeze. When he criticized your and my career choice, I let him have it. As if the Marines have the market on crime fighting and protecting citizens."

"He won't change."

"Neither will I."

The varied emotions on Grayson's face told her his past must be as dysfunctional as hers. At least her parents had always supported her. Photographs of Grayson sat in every conceivable spot in Joe's living room—sports, high school graduation, college, and one with Joe in front of the FBI office. The official seal served as a backdrop for their photo. She'd once had photos too—ones that signified love and devotion. Or so she thought.

Joe stood. "Unfortunately I have a doctor's appointment at eight this morning. Nearly forgot about it, but the doc won't renew my blood pressure meds unless he sees me. I plan to stop by the FBI office on my way home. See what I can find out with my new security clearance." He winked. "Wish I had an extra computer for you. This is the best I can do." He pulled his Black-Berry from his pants pocket and handed it to Grayson. "I'll use my other phone today, and this will help you stay connected. Feels good to be doing something useful again. Right now I'm going to load the dishwasher and get a shower. You two go save the world."

"Right." Grayson carried his plate to the sink. "Since when did I become a superhero?"

"From the moment you met me," Joe said. "Hey, you'll be without a car for a while."

"We've been there before. Go get your meds."

"I can do my share," Taryn said. "I'll clean up the kitchen."

"No deal. Help Grayson stay in line."

Taryn blew him a kiss. Unlike her, but she'd grown fond of the crusty character in a very short time.

"Take care of my girl," Joe said. "She's a keeper, and Murford didn't have enough sense to realize it. Now get on out of here."

She followed Grayson into the living area and onto opposite ends of the sofa again.

He picked up the legal pad and pencil from the table before them. "They broke the mold with my uncle."

"Too bad," she said. "I like him."

Grayson's facial expression changed to stress.

"What are you thinking?" she said.

"Before we get into the computer stuff, I have a few more questions."

A lingering glance from him shadowed her, but she refused to acknowledge it. Grayson had a strange effect on her, and she hadn't processed it all.

"Tell me about Claire."

My sister-friend. "She's innocent in all this. Her only role was in taking wedding photos. Her biggest fault was being my friend."

"But Murford made himself known to her. Why take the risk?"

Holding back a swirl of emotion took a chunk of her control. A counselor would call his question therapeutic. She called it heartbreaking. "Claire's life bubbled with joy. She had an infectious laugh that made everyone around her forget life's hiccups. Makes me sick to think he planned on killing her all along."

"Does she have family? I know you're the child's guardian."

"Ex-husband, and both sets of Zoey's grandparents live in Israel. No contact with her."

"Why?"

"They're Orthodox Jews. Disowned her when she became a Christian."

He continued to write. "I get the picture. Did she like Murford?"

Taryn recalled her and Claire's near argument. "She thought he was rushing things. Wanted me to wait until after the first of the year to get married. She said we could plan a huge church wedding." She buried her face in her hands. "I told him about her concerns."

"His response?"

"He said she was only being a good friend and cautious about my welfare." She blew out another one of his many lies. "He claimed I should feel honored that she cared about my happiness."

"Did he ever say anything negative about her?"

She settled into the sofa, in the corner where she seemed to fit. Buddy placed his head in her lap, and she stroked it. The animal needed a bath, and so did she. "Hmm. He said I was lucky to have a friend like her. Brought her flowers and little gifts for Zoey. He didn't like her snapping pics when we were together, but then he asked her to take the wedding photos, even made suggestions at the so-called ceremony. He succeeded in winning her over. Like he did me."

"Are you sure no one witnessed the wedding?"

"Someone may have noticed it was happening, but we were secluded."

"What things irritated him?"

"Not being punctual. Not a problem for me. Only Claire, who had her own inner clock."

Grayson scribbled more notes. "Did he ever say anything to indicate his family's where-abouts, where he went to school, or friends?"

"He said he'd attended Texas A&M and received his master's in business, and his family had lived in Abilene. The only friend was the limo driver. Why, oh, why didn't I check him out?" She sighed. "Never mind."

"It's okay. What did Murford call his driver?"

"Buzz. It was his hair. Are you thinking a military haircut?"

"Strong possibility. Did Buzz have an accent?"

"Sounded like he was from Texas."

"Sure wish I had my iPad, but Joe's BlackBerry will do."

She understood. "Look at the bright side. We haven't been shot at since early this morning." As soon as the words sounded in the air, she regretted them.

Chapter 23

10:30 a.m. Tuesday

Grayson used Joe's BlackBerry to verify Taryn's information and type out his report to the FBI. It was tedious and boring, while her fingers danced across the laptop's keyboard. He'd been in contact with the SSA and learned that her cell phone records indicated consistent numbers used for both inbound and outbound calls. She verified one as Murford's and the second as Claire Levin's. Every bit of information she'd given about herself had been accurate.

An FBI team explored the minutes from Congress's closed, classified hearings regarding the export license for LNG. Interviews were in progress, but it took time to unscramble comments and diverse personalities. Those who'd opposed the license would be listed in the transcripts and might provide a lead to the bomber.

The other matter that needed attention was the dialogue between the two LNG companies using Gated Labs's Nehemiah software. Although he knew one was located in Kitimat, Canada, and the second in Corpus Christi, he didn't know the dynamics of the personalities in charge.

He walked to the kitchen to steal a look outside. The backyard with autumn touches of gold, orange, and purple produced color that Joe enjoyed. Flowers and bushes were planted according to the latest gardening magazine with the perfect balance of whatever the soil required. Joe had a tool belt of talents, while Grayson could kill a cactus.

"Found him." Taryn lifted her arms in more of a stretch than a victory sign. She winced and rubbed the area around her head wound.

Grayson rejoined her. "Who?"

"Buzz. I wanted to find substantial evidence to

prove he and Murford aren't the winners in this game. Those two aren't as brilliant as they'd like to think." She tilted her head, and auburn hair captured his attention. "Anyway, I have footage of him at Brown's Restaurant picking up dinner. Got the date and time, and it coincides with one of my evenings with Murford."

Grayson leaned over to see the computer screen. The camera had a clear facial shot of a square-shouldered man. "He's got quite a build for a limo driver."

"Go figure. Do you want me to ID him, or do you want to send it to the FBI?"

"Both."

She laughed, and her fingers raced over the keys. "His name is George Breckon, and he trained as a Navy SEAL. Dishonorable discharge involving the death of another SEAL. He was acquitted due to lack of evidence. Same unit as Murford." She scrolled through her information. "He's been busy. In the fall of 2012 while living in Phoenix, he was charged with assault and battery. Early 2013, he knifed and killed a man in self-defense—a bar fight. I can look deeper to tie him to Murford after their military release. Your choice."

"Go for it. It's your thing, and you obviously do it well."

Her eyes sparkled. "I'm hoping some of Murford's favorite restaurants were places the two visited before they put their plan into action." Her eyes glued to the screen while her fingers tapped at lightning speed.

"The two could have been the ones who tore apart your condo," Grayson said.

"The jerks." She narrowed her brows. "Destroyed everything I owned when they already had what they needed." Her arms lifted to the ceiling again. "Yes! Here are both of them at Tony's." She turned the laptop his way. "More evidence to send to your boss."

"Maybe you should join the FBI." Grayson hugged her shoulders.

She stiffened.

He released her as though she'd shocked him. For a moment he'd forgotten Murford's betrayal and the pain she'd gone through. "Hey, I'm sorry. Out of line."

She paled and rubbed her shoulders. "It's all right. I'm a little apprehensive. Getting over what happened will take some time." She turned her attention to the keyboard. "Even to a man who's saved my life more than once."

"I didn't mean to upset you."

She gave him a shaky smile. "I'll work on the security system backup at Murford's condo. See if pics of others are there."

Grayson mentally kicked himself for upsetting her. This woman had experienced one tragedy after another in a matter of twenty-four hours.

Despite the bruises and lack of sleep, she was gorgeous—drop-dead gorgeous, as Joe would say. Wow. Highly intelligent. Courageous . . .

He reined in his wanderings. Not the time to be thinking about a woman in that way.

As soon as the SSA gave the okay, Grayson would bring her into the office, where they'd keep her protected until arrests were made. Who was giving FBI information to bad guys?

"This one will take me a few minutes," she said. "Not sure why the security office claimed they couldn't immediately recover the condo's footage." She gave him the first eye contact since he'd touched her. "Maybe they needed to cover their behinds while they tried to retrieve it. Admitting they lost information doesn't do much for a security company's credibility."

"Makes sense. I'll send the SSA your updates." He typed a message to Alan Preston and pressed Send.

"Shouldn't Joe have been back by now?" Her voice held a ring of uneasiness.

He glanced at his watch. "You're right. His trip to the FBI office might have taken longer than he expected. What's on your mind?"

"Joe thinks we won't find Zoey alive."

"He doesn't want to build false hopes. Disappointment can destroy a person, and you've already gone through a lot of heartache."

"I understand, and I know Joe wants me to be

prepared." She didn't look his way. "Murford pretended to adore her."

"If his actions were legitimate, that's good for Zoey." Grayson had studied the worst of criminals, and many had no conscience. The adage of "the end justifies the means" fit most profiles.

"Grayson, you're trying to make me feel better, and I appreciate it. But Murford treated me the same way and left me to die in a bombing." She pointed to the drape-covered window. "I want to catch a glimpse of light in this nightmare. Claire used to tell me to put my problems in God's hands."

"My faith keeps me going when I want to quit."

"So you and your uncle are Catholic?"

Unusual question when they didn't have anything in the house pointing to Catholicism. "We're Protestant."

"What about St. Francis hanging from the rearview mirror of Joe's car?"

He couldn't help but grin. "It came with his T-Bird twenty years ago. Sentimental value, that's all."

"He kissed it before going in after you at the theater. I think he needs to hold on to dear old St. Francis."

"Joe's saved my rear more than once. What about your faith?"

"I attend Claire's church, a Messianic group."

179

"Interesting. Do you celebrate Old Testament festivals? Then add Christianity to it?"

"It's a weaving of the entire Bible, like fitting the pieces of a puzzle together. Very rich, with lots of themes carrying from the Old to the New."

He contemplated her Messianic beliefs. "Once this is over, I'd like to visit your church."

"Sure."

Strange she'd agree so quickly. "Thanks."

"Tell me, Grayson, you interviewed the people at Gated Labs. What did you think of Kinsley Stevens?"

The blonde bombshell? "Smart. Has her own agenda. What about her did you want me to see?"

"I don't trust her, especially after I caught her on my computer. Haden is definitely smarter, more conniving. Anyway, when I asked her what she was doing, she simply laughed and hit Escape before I could learn more. Told me to go to Haden, our supervisor, which I did. I was furious and didn't think about the consequences."

"What happened?"

"He accused me of being paranoid and suggested a psychiatrist who could prescribe what I needed."

"Do you still think it's more Rollins than her?" The BlackBerry rang before she answered. It was Joe.

"Get out of there now," Joe said.

Grayson was on his feet, reaching for his Glock. "What's wrong? Where are you?"

"I've been driving around trying to ditch a tail. Got a bad feeling, son. Go."

He turned to Taryn. "We've got to run."

She wrapped one hand around the laptop and coaxed Buddy with the other.

"Go out the back," Joe said. "They could be waiting for you in the front."

"Joe, are you sure about this?" he said.

"This is my fault. You wanted to leave, and I talked you out of it."

Grayson didn't waste a moment shoving Taryn and Buddy to the rear of the house. Joe's manicured backyard offered little protection except for an oak tree shading a concrete bench and ornamental shrubs and flowers. Grayson grabbed an Adirondack chair as they raced out the back. A seven-foot wood fence bordered the sides of the yard, but the rear had a brick wall separating the property from the street. They'd need to use the chair. How could he manage with his side bandaged and Taryn's head injuries?

"Where are you?" Grayson said.

"Heading toward the FBI office. I've called Alan, and he's sending two cars and HPD to the house in hopes of nabbing this guy. Alan says we're bringing you two in."

Grayson didn't have time for any more dialogue. He ended the call and stuffed the phone in his pants pocket. A spray of gunfire and shattered glass burst through the quiet neighborhood. He grabbed Taryn and pushed her to the ground, placing her body under his and covering her head.

Chapter 24

11:25 a.m. Tuesday

Taryn's chest ached from attempting to steady her trembling body. The gunfire stopped. Nothing hurt. She could think, feel, and analyze what had happened. Joe had been right, and by the grace of God, she and Grayson survived. Her arm wrapped around Buddy's head. He licked her face, and she didn't care how bad he smelled. Grayson rolled off her onto the grass.

"Are you okay?" she said.

"Yeah. What about you and Buddy?"

Taryn took another glance at the shepherd. Unharmed. No doubt frightened, as she was. "We're good." She focused on Grayson. Blood stained through his bandaged side. "You need medical help."

"I'll take care of it after we're clear of this place. I heard car doors slam. Two of them."

So had she.

He struggled to his feet, Glock in hand.

"Are they waiting for us, Grayson? Or are they sure we were in the house?"

"We're about to find out." His gaze panned the area.

"Hand me the extra gun." Rage burned in her stomach. Everyone who tried to help had been targeted.

"You don't know how to use it."

"Doesn't take much technology to pull a trigger." She'd come close to killing Murford with her bare hands. Taking a life went against all she believed and advocated, but she'd do whatever it took to block the road of the greedy and end this nightmare.

"And you'd kill us. Stick to what you do best."

"Okay. So what's the plan?" Taryn whispered as though those who wanted him dead and her in their clutches might hear. "Other than staying alive?"

He pointed to the right side of the house. "They'll come through that gate or the rear of the house." He took her hand and raced to the left side behind a gas grill. Buddy trotted beside them. The dog looked ferocious, which might help the situation.

Once there, she anticipated the screech of the gate opening. Maybe Joe kept it oiled, because nothing met her ears but the sound of neighborhood dogs. Something from the gate area had Buddy's attention, and he growled.

"I'm sure they're planning to rush us," Grayson said.

"Want me to kick in the fence behind us?"

"I'd do it, but my side's killing me."

She whirled around and kicked in two vertical boards, then two more. Her hapkido practice had been in a private studio. No one had been around . . . danger hadn't been an element. It was just a means to work off stress and work through whatever bothered her. Whatever it took when her mind flew faster than cyberspace.

The other side of the fence was clear of shooters. For now. She expected to hear a police siren, or maybe those were wishful thoughts for a quick rescue. A white car sat at the curb in front of the house. Engine running.

Grayson squeezed through the fence, and she followed. Buddy seemed to have no fear. One day she'd figure out the purpose of her angel dog—where he came from and why he'd befriended her, like Grayson. She kept tossing a look over her shoulder, expecting an armed man to aim and fire. Yet she knew Buddy would warn them.

"Stay with me." Grayson crept along the side of the brick house until they reached the front corner. He pressed in numbers and requested backup. Sliding the phone back into his pocket, he turned to her. "A driver's waiting. That means at least two more to deal with. One of them might be in the house. But my guess is they will come from behind."

She studied the driver. He held a gun in his right hand. "He looks like George Breckon. Great. Trouble in every direction. We're toast."

"Depends. I'd like to have a few answers, but I doubt he'll let me arrest him."

Breckon emerged from the car with a phone to his ear. He dropped it into his pocket and checked the clip on his gun.

"FBI. You're surrounded," Grayson shouted.

Breckon aimed in their direction, and Grayson fired.

Breckon slumped over the hood of the car and disappeared onto the pavement.

Where were the police? The FBI? Glass littered the front yard. Grayson's and Joe's homey setting looked like a demolition site. Buddy brushed against her legs. She was finished with all the tragedies.

"I'm going to bargain with them." Her gaze darted back and forth to where the danger lurked. "They want access to Nehemiah."

"Then they'd kill you."

"It would buy time."

"Listen, superwoman, neither Buddy nor I will allow it. Look, these guys will promise anything to get you out in the open. They're in the business of extracting information and eliminating the source."

An image of Zoey's sweet face and dark curls cut through her heart.

And the nightmarish disregard for human dignity.

"Backup will be here soon, and those guys know it. Right now, without a getaway vehicle, they need to get the job done or hoof it."

A siren sounded in the distance. The FBI wouldn't give an alarm. One man rushed from the front door. Murford. Why wasn't she surprised. A moment later, a second bolted from the opposite side of the house.

"Stop! FBI!" Grayson leveled his weapon.

The two dashed across the street and jumped over a fence, but not before Grayson squeezed a bullet into the second man's shoulder. Murford raced away.

A car sped down the street with two police vehicles behind it. More police cars stopped, and Grayson pointed to where the men had disappeared. Two plainclothes men and an HPD officer hurried in that direction. A female officer who looked like a defensive end made her way toward Grayson and Taryn.

Buddy growled, and Taryn attempted to relax him. He didn't have a collar, so if he took off after the officer, she'd shoot Buddy. "It's okay," Taryn whispered. "We'll be all right."

"Control that dog," the officer said.

"Yes, ma'am," Taryn said. "He's protective."

"So am I. Stand up. Sir, put your weapon down."

They obliged.

"Both of you lift your hands above your heads. Step out here where I can keep an eye on you."

"Sit, Buddy," Taryn said, and miraculously he obeyed.

"I'm FBI," Grayson said. "Can I show you my ID?"

"No thanks. I'll wait for backup."

"As soon as those men return, they'll confirm it." Grayson's voice contained an irritated edge.

"Wonderful. In the meantime, you can do what I say."

Taryn raised her hands. Grayson set his gun on the ground and complied. Breckon used to tease her about being a computer geek. Now he lay dead. Had she grown so callused in the past two days that a dead body meant nothing sacred? She shivered. Life *was* sacred.

She viewed the front of the house. Every window exposed jagged pieces of glass from the barrage of shooting. She could only imagine what the inside looked like . . . especially where she and Grayson had been sitting. Thank God for Joe's warning call. She'd done a lot of thanking Him lately. Grayson's face hardened at the home's damage. Anger seethed from every inch of him.

"I was furious when I saw my condo destroyed," she said. "I felt violated. No words can describe it . . . only reliving the same experience."

"This is more than brick and mortar," he said.

"Joe took me in when I couldn't handle living at home. He taught me how to be a man. This was my first real home in years. Guess that's why I'm still here. Whoever did this will pay."

Deadly determination she understood.

"The home is registered to Joe West," the officer said.

"My uncle. He's retired FBI."

"Where is he?"

"Meeting with agents at the office."

"Right. I'm no fool. Too much has happened the last two days for me to believe you. How were you injured?"

"Doing my job for the FBI."

"Right."

Grayson's tensed muscles showed his stress mode.

The two officers who'd gone after the shooters returned with the injured man, a Hispanic with a hard face and wiry body. Murford must have escaped. Taryn wanted to believe she was finally in good hands and stole a look at Grayson. Yes, she trusted him and Joe. But what about the other law enforcement officials? Would they lock her up? Charge her with an unspeakable crime? Not look for Zoey?

Chapter 25

12:46 p.m. Tuesday

Taryn gripped the sides of the chair opposite Houston FBI Supervisory Special Agent Alan Preston. His office alone, and all it represented, intimidated her. The man steepled his fingers while fear and innocence warred with her emotions. A bit of indignation nestled there too, for anyone who'd think she'd be part of an airport bombing or steal software from Gated Labs. Grayson sat beside her, but she wouldn't look his way. She didn't need to be rescued—only believed.

"I've heard your story from all sources," the SSA said. "Now hearing it in your words backs up Special Agent Hall."

Did she dare breathe relief? "Then you see I had nothing to do with the airport bombing."

He poured confidence into every movement, his dark-blue eyes clear. Definitely in charge. "That doesn't release you from your connection to the bombing or the accusations by Gated Labs."

Taryn released her hands from the chair. Anger was her enemy at this point, and she fought it hard. "Sir, I have spoken the truth in every answer I've given you. I figured out things, like George Breckon's identity, that you were only speculating. I accessed sites no one in your office could have found and at a speed that left your whizzes in the dust. I secured information and gave it to Special Agent Hall. What else do you want me to do? Take a polygraph? I'm not an idiot—" She almost swore but caught herself.

"I'm furious that I was used by a man who now has vital information and also attempted to kill me along with all those others at the airport. And I have no clue who wired fifty grand into my bank account or why. Sort of obvious that it's Murford, don't you think?" Her voice rose. She no longer cared what the SSA thought of her.

"He murdered my best friend. He kidnapped her daughter. He destroyed my condo. Did I mention he suggested we put the condo in my name until after we were married? He and his thugs tried to kill the only person who believes me. And I haven't begun to express how I feel about Joe West's bullet-ridden home." She told herself to control her fury, but it didn't register in her mind's data bank.

"I'd never seen the wounded man you brought in today. The only ones I recognized were George Breckon and Phillip Murford." She leaned in closer, noting his red face. "I've offered to help, and you know my reputation. Time's wasting while you're talking to me as though I'm a criminal. I was a victim along with many others at the airport, and I've been a victim ever since."

Not a trace of emotion crossed his face. "Calm down, Miss Young. You've made your point. Are you saying you have no guilt in any of this?"

Taryn pressed her lips together. "I disabled Nehemiah after expressing concerns to Ethan Formier, who is now dead. We were convinced of a security breach. He was in the process of confirming the proof. Prior to his leaving for Mexico, I inserted a backdoor program. No one knew this, not even Ethan." How many times did she need to repeat these things? "I overpowered a police officer in the hospital, and I let myself into a church because the last person out apparently hadn't locked the rear door. I used their bathroom, phone, and computer. Oh, I ate an apple and a spoonful of sunflower butter, but you'll find a ten on the kitchen counter."

He studied her for several moments, long ones, while Taryn thought back through what she'd said. Not one word would she apologize for.

"Miss Young," he said with quiet firmness, "when the case is finished, you will either be spending the rest of your life in prison, or I will personally recruit you for the FBI."

Her pulse slowed a fraction. "I can accept your conclusion."

Faint admiration met her. "I think we want the same things—Murford and whoever he's working for in custody, the software secured, answers to yesterday's bombing, and Zoey Levin found unharmed."

"You know my skill level."

He seemed to weigh her words. "We know your abilities. All right. You take orders from me, and you don't leave the office without my permission or an escort."

She nodded. He still wasn't convinced of her sincerity. "Where do I begin?"

"Once we're finished with our interview, I'm having a strategy meeting. My request is to first look for additional footage at Murford's condo and then secure information about Ethan Formier. We're attempting to obtain data from his computer at Gated Labs, but it will take time to crack the password. Our people are tracing the fifty grand from Singapore."

The SSA swung his attention to Grayson. "Finding Taryn Young's phone is top priority. The export terminal in Kitimat is launching LNG on Friday morning at the same time as TX-LNG in Corpus—regardless of not having the new software enabled and depending on the older version. Both companies plan to follow through unless given a substantial reason otherwise."

"Those companies want to be the first to export LNG," Taryn said. "It's a race to hit the history books. They won't halt the export unless you stop them. I want to help you find the evidence you need."

2:00 p.m. Tuesday

Grayson had showered at the FBI office and changed clothes, thankful he had an extra set for times like these. The FBI's nurse had taken a look at his wound and deemed Joe's patch job satisfactory. He'd gotten another BlackBerry, so he was in business again.

Taryn looked better since she'd cleaned up, but the bruises matched the dark circles under her eyes. One of the female agents, Laurel Evertson, a cryptologist who'd been in Grayson's class at Quantico, did a Kohl's run for her. Laurel searched through hundreds of messages, looking for a coded link to the bombing and the source of the bank transfer to Singapore. Another class member, Thatcher Graves, who specialized in homicide, processed Claire Levin's murder. Food had been brought in for everyone working around the clock. Even Joe had a phone and computer with his contractor status.

Then there was Buddy, the ultrathin wonder dog, who'd been housed in the auto shop. Wouldn't hurt if someone gave him a bath and flea dip. And a big meal.

The shoe print obtained at Taryn's condo matched the ones Jose Pedraza wore when he was wounded and arrested earlier. He'd been treated and questioned but could provide little substantial information. He claimed Murford hired him to do a job, and the money paid the bills. Pedraza was holding back, and Grayson intended to get some answers.

He stole another glimpse at Taryn. She blinked, and he imagined she felt the same sand and grit in her eyes. She must have sensed his attention because she focused on him.

"What's going on?" she said.

Caught, Grayson. Staring at her only invited trouble.

"I found nothing regarding Murford's condo but his coming and going," she said when he didn't immediately answer. "He knew where the cameras were located and avoided them. So did Breckon. I think the rest of it could be viewed by another analyst so I can work on Ethan's password. But not all bad news. I uncovered footage of Breckon picking up food orders at other restaurants."

He rose from his chair and bent over her shoulder. "What do you have?" He started to call her Sunset, because that's what her hair reminded him of. *Solve the case, Grayson. Then talk to her.* Two days ago, he didn't know she existed. How random.

She showed him Breckon entering and exiting restaurants with carryout. "Look at these with Breckon and Murford. According to the time stamp, these restaurants were frequented before I met them."

"Anyone else with them?"

She frowned. "A woman. I have her back. Nothing here indicates her facial features."

"Show me."

Taryn brought up the video. A tall woman. Long, dark hair. Slender. "I'd hoped Kinsley Stevens or Haden Rollins would've appeared."

"Send me what you have, and we'll see if facial recognition can do anything with it."

She leaned back in her chair. "Haden and Kinsley might've been more interested in Kinsley taking over the role of team leader than sabotaging the software." She closed her eyes. "I have to be careful I don't let exhaustion cloud my thinking and accuse innocent people." She sent the security camera information to Grayson so he could channel it up the chain of command.

"I want you to meet another agent, Thatcher Graves. He works in the violent crime squad, assigned to Claire's case."

"Okay. Maybe I can help, or does he already have all the information I gave you?"

"He does. If you remember something else, you can always approach him."

Grayson touched the small of her back and walked her to Thatcher's cubicle. He introduced the two.

"Pleasure to meet you, Miss Young," Thatcher said. "I'm sorry about your friend." His dark eyes showed his concern.

"Thank you." She paled at a photo of Claire's

body on his desk. "Do you have anything new?"

He turned the pic over. "Nothing more than you already know. Soon we'll have an arrest."

Taryn nodded. "I hope to aid in that process."

Grayson and Taryn returned to her desk. She slid into the chair, her shoulders slumped. "I'm concerned about Ethan's widow," she said. "A dear lady who supported Ethan."

"Agents interviewed her. She said he'd been in a hurry to get home from Mexico City. Told her he'd learned about disturbing issues at Gated Labs. Said heads would roll on Monday afternoon."

"Mrs. Formier had no reason to fabricate anything."

As Grayson had thought, Taryn had no new information about the widow to help them. "Mrs. Formier expressed concern about you."

"I'm not surprised." Taryn glanced at her fingers, still poised over the keyboard.

"You need sleep," Grayson said. "Are you taking the pain meds?"

"Not the prescription ones. I'm using Tylenol. Anyway, I'll rest after I make progress on accessing Ethan's files."

"We'll have Special Agent Laurel Evertson give you a hand with that."

Grayson's BlackBerry rang. The SSA. "Yes, sir. We'll be right there." He disconnected the call. "This should be interesting."

"Does it include me?"

"Yes, and Joe."

"What's going on?"

"Brad Patterson is here."

Chapter 26

2:35 p.m. Tuesday

Taryn mentally listed her priorities, and cowering to Brad Patterson missed the list. She had no intention of giving him any information until she had her hands on her iPhone.

When they found Murford, they'd find Zoey and be able to arrest the one who bombed the airport. She'd cooperate with the FBI, but not with a man who was loyal to Kinsley Stevens and wherever her ambitious greed had taken her.

She noted the men around the table—Supervisory Special Agent Alan Preston, Grayson, Joe, and Brad Patterson.

"Mr. Patterson has serious concerns about your disabling Nehemiah," the SSA said. "He claims the two companies that were using the software paid for a firewall protection program they cannot use. Obviously there are safety concerns in regulating temperature and pressure should a breach occur."

"The reputation of Gated Labs is at stake." Patterson's face resembled granite.

"They are running an earlier version and are protected," Taryn said. "I called them on Friday and enabled it to keep their infrastructure safe. When the FBI's investigation is complete, I'll gladly re-enable the software. Until then, the exposure is minimal."

Patterson raised his fist. "I want it done now or I'm filing charges."

"Go for it," she said. "Won't change my resolve."

"This will be a civil discussion, Mr. Patterson," the SSA said. "No threats or accusations, but an open discussion. National security, as well as your private interests, is at stake here."

Patterson kept his gaze focused on Taryn. "Why are you taking this ridiculous stand? Don't you know our customers are holding payment for services rendered in light of your actions?"

"Because Ethan and I suspected someone within Gated Labs was sabotaging the project."

"Who?"

"I'm researching the matter. I think the person or persons could lead the FBI to whoever bombed the airport."

"That's ludicrous. Every employee must pass a rigid security screening," Patterson said.

"Remember I developed the software for the screening, and I've never betrayed Gated Labs or revealed information, no matter how insignificant."

"You expect me to believe you? I've heard other reports about your inappropriate conduct."

She could guess who'd offered the inside scoop. "Have you opened Ethan's computer files for his research?"

When Patterson didn't comment, she knew the answer. Ethan had layers of protection in place, and it wouldn't be a simple matter to retrieve his files. If she gave in to Patterson's demands without removing the backdoor, then . . . "You understand what it means if the software gets into the wrong hands?"

Patterson huffed. "That's what your paycheck and expertise covered."

She focused on the SSA. "I'm against this, sir. Complying with Mr. Patterson's request is like feeding into the bomber's hand. I understand if you don't see a connection, but I believe it's there somewhere."

"You're lying. Miss Young, you're fired."

"Check your e-mail, Mr. Patterson. I sent you my resignation an hour ago." He probably had his niece on speed dial to take her place.

"I guarantee you won't ever work in the software industry again." Patterson whipped his attention to the SSA. His face was a sharp red contrast to his social facade. "How long until the matter is settled? I have assets to protect."

"The process will take as long as it takes," the SSA said—the man who would arrest or recruit her. "Agents will follow you to your office to continue their investigation."

"Is Taryn Young in custody or is she assisting the FBI?"

"The answer to your question hasn't been determined. In any event, she needs rest and medical attention."

"I have a dead VP and a developer who refuses to cooperate. I need answers soon or—"

"Bad idea to threaten us," the SSA said. "The FBI is in the business of solving horrendous crimes. We thrive on community support and what is best for the safety and well-being of the public. I'd think you'd want this resolved as efficiently as possible. The airport bombing was a message that we read as possibly more problems to come. We're considering Nehemiah as part of the issue, and none of us want additional lives and property destroyed. Or do you?"

Patterson crossed his arms over his chest. "My lawyer will be notified of this. If we're finished, I have work to do."

"So do we. I'd like Kinsley Stevens and Haden Rollins brought in for subsequent interviews."

Patterson stood and pounded his fist on the table. "How dare you implicate them simply because of Young's professional rivalry. They were previously questioned by Agents Hall and Bradshaw."

"Sit down, Mr. Patterson. Dramatics don't work

here either," the SSA said. "I don't take orders from you."

"Fine." Patterson eased into his chair. "Investigate everyone at Gated Labs."

The SSA gave him an emotionless stare, the same given to Taryn earlier. "We will. Thank you for your time."

Once Patterson was escorted from the room, Taryn swung her gaze to Grayson. His eyes emitted respect, and he grinned ever so slightly. Her stomach did a flip, and the response frightened her. Not now. Not in the middle of this mess. Maybe never.

"I have a suggestion." She directed her words at the SSA. "I'm sure you already have a list of prominent hackers, legal and illegal, but I'd like to give you my list of top people in that field. See if any of them are involved. If Murford is serious enough to kill for the software, then he might have engaged help."

"I thought hackers were protective of their own."

"They are. But this involves national security."

"All right. We can compare lists."

"I could contact a few to see if anyone's looking for a hacker and offer my services as bait." Taryn had to do something to stay busy. Without bidding, her mind drifted to the explosion and the carnage at the airport and the hideous moans of the injured and dying.

Claire.

Zoey.

All because of a software program designed to secure oil and gas companies' rights to export natural gas? A program she'd disabled.

The world can be so ugly.

She sat upright in the hard chair. All this time, she'd been committed to protecting the Nehemiah Project. Now that she thought about it, the move was selfish. Kinsley and Haden wanted her job. Big deal. Had her stubbornness to be at the top in her field and her loyalty to Ethan gotten in the way?

What about the LNG companies? Since they were using an older version, hackers could access it more easily . . . and the companies had a historic launch on Friday. Shouldn't she enable the software and at least do her share to keep lives and property safe?

She knew the answer. In the eyes of the world, she was a terrorist.

No more people would be hurt because of her.

Moistening her lips, she stared at the SSA. "Sir, I've decided it's in the best interests of everyone for me to enable the Nehemiah Project. Do I have your permission to call Brad Patterson?"

3:24 p.m. Tuesday

After Taryn had successfully installed Nehemiah and left the SSA's office to compile a list of hackers, Grayson sat alone with Alan Preston.

"Sir, we have a mole," Grayson said, broaching a subject sensitive to everyone at Houston's headquarters.

The SSA pushed back from his desk. "I already know who you suspect. You two have never gotten along." He frowned. "This had better be substantial."

"It is. When I left the office to meet with Taryn, I didn't tell anyone but you. Vince asked where I was going, and I said an errand. But first I had to check on something in the FIG. I left him standing in my doorway with my phone on the desk. When I returned, it had been moved. I didn't think much about it then."

"You're sure?"

"I always note where I place things. Someone knew exactly where Taryn had gone. That's a given. But someone followed me."

"Are you saying it was Vince?"

"I checked the records, and he left here shortly after I did."

"That's not enough unless you have more."

Grayson nodded. "When my car was retrieved, I asked the agent to bring me my phone. Found a bug." Grayson pulled the small device from his pocket and laid it on the SSA's desk. "It's one of ours."

The SSA examined it. "He's at the top of our list."

"Are you tailing him?"

He didn't blink. "What do you think?"

Grayson had heard a few wild tales in the FBI, but this one crept across his mind like a parasite. Now he had more reasons to despise the guy. "What clued you in?"

"His bank account." Preston shuffled papers on his desk. "You weren't the only agent to suspect a mole in this case. Vince was nowhere around when we received the call about your going rogue. The voice was disguised."

"But you don't have enough evidence to arrest him."

"Right. That's why Joe was brought in. The two used to work together."

"So Joe's aware?"

"Yes. Vince could lead us to whoever bombed the airport."

Chapter 27

3:45 p.m. Tuesday

Taryn hit Send on the e-mail to a hacker who knew all the available illegal jobs. They'd corresponded in the past, and she'd gone to dinner with him at a Black Hat conference. A total narcissist. His arrogance and money controlled him, and he didn't care who needed access to a site or about the possible grave repercussions. If anyone could point Taryn in the direction of who wanted to hack into Nehemiah, it was him. The man went by Save. Ironic, considering. She ensured her e-mail couldn't be traced. Now to see if she received a job offer for her alias, Julie Harmon.

She reached inside her purse, where a picture of Zoey was tucked away. Claire had taken it at a nearby park in August, an early-morning shot when the sun seemed to kiss the earth. . . . That was Claire's claim. Taryn swallowed a sob. Oh, how she missed her. She brushed her finger over the little girl's dark curls, then buried her face in her hands. *My sweet girl, is someone taking good care of you? Are you hungry? I'd gladly trade places with you.* Her mind replayed scenes with Claire. Gone forever. Her thoughts dwelled on Zoey—her first steps, her first words, and her adorable giggle. Taryn had to believe the FBI would find her, and she'd be okay.

Murford would not be so cruel as to extinguish the life of a child who had sat on his lap, would he? Kissed his cheek? But look what else he'd done. Reality left a bitter taste in her mouth.

Taryn clenched her fists. Hope would get her through this. Hope would build her future with Claire's daughter. Hope would fuel the FBI and others to find answers.

How would she provide for herself and Zoey? Her reputation as a software developer had been destroyed. Who would ever trust her? The media had done a tremendous job of making Taryn look like America's number one enemy. Unfortunately some journalists weren't quick to admit when they were wrong, and their accusations would stay with her forever.

Taryn stretched. Buddy probably thought she'd deserted him. Before giving in to sleep, she'd visit the dog. Let him know she loved him, appreciated his friendship. She hoped he didn't have an owner looking for him. She wanted the dog as her very own, and she didn't care if her desires were selfish. He was an angel in disguise, a protector.

The condo charged an exorbitant pet fee for Bentley, and two pets would be like a chunk of the national debt. She blew out a frustrated breath. No problem since she had no intentions of living in the same complex after their high-tech security system allowed someone to demolish her home. Plus, she no longer had employment, although her savings account had six figures. Tomorrow she'd tackle keeping Buddy in dog food . . . and pray a job arrived when Zoey was found safe.

With her mind dull and her body aching, she focused on cracking Ethan's password. Most likely a useless venture, because she and Ethan used to tease each other about the password choices of the public, who believed their files were safe. She already missed Ethan, his wit and wisdom, always challenging her to encrypt more layers into the development process.

"Protect the software" was his mantra. "Remember, the product is only as good as its developer."

She longed to reach out to his wife and family, but the SSA had asked her to wait. Taryn understood, although she wanted to grieve with Ethan's family. She paused and replayed one of her conversations with Ethan about how people were victimized by identity theft.

"Taryn, what are people thinking when they toss out personal info as word choices? Then use the same password on everything they think is protected?" Ethan had said. "They're asking for identity theft, and businesses aren't much smarter."

She'd agreed with him. "The ones who change their passwords daily are still heavy targets. Then there are the websites that will do it for them. The users follow a sequence as though hackers aren't smart enough to figure it out."

"How much effort do you put into your passwords?" Ethan's eyes twinkled.

"A lot. Totally random. Different ones for different sites. What about you?"

"Something you'd never expect."

"Try me," she'd said.

"Like hiding in plain sight?"

Taryn massaged throbbing neck muscles. Had

Ethan given her an indication of where his password was stored?

The agony in her body made it so difficult to concentrate on the many tasks before her. She craved sleep to heal and help her mind to function. But not yet. Ethan had gone to his grave with answers, and he must have recorded them where she could find them. Of course, she'd been the one to disable Nehemiah and keep the log-in credentials to herself. Tossing aside her own actions, she understood Ethan stored everything somewhere. His file would reveal findings about who was involved at Gated Labs.

Not to his wife and family.

Not to Brad Patterson or anyone on the team.

But the secret must be embedded in a file and possibly e-mails to her. She stared at the bottle of Tylenol 3 with codeine near the keyboard. Tempting. Instead she reached for a cup of coffee. Bad stuff—reminded her of church coffee.

She searched webmail for all the correspondence Ethan had sent for the past six months. This would take a while. She sorted them according to subject and then by date. The ones sent while he was in Mexico held her attention. Why hadn't she done this first? She shook her head and rolled her shoulders in hopes of clearing her mind. She couldn't give in yet. Her body had become an enemy dancing with time.

She read through Ethan's e-mails, the ones she

hadn't seen before last weekend. She'd ignored e-mails after Friday. Not like her, but getting married was the most important commitment she'd ever made. She'd never dreamed life could be so perfect—what a stupid dream. The last-minute preparations of packing for their honeymoon included finding nightwear that didn't totally humiliate her, new perfume, an outfit to wear on the plane, a new bathing suit. Taryn's throat constricted, and she reined in her emotions.

Many of the messages were a short phrase—his preferred method of handling e-mail—but when he needed to explain something, he'd detail it. She reread several until she saw one that had arrived early Saturday morning, long after she'd stopped checking:

Taryn,

Keep a heads-up on your suspicions. I'm doing a little digging here. Don't like what I see.

Document everything. Protect your project at all costs, and keep me posted.

Ethan

Later on she had received another message. At the time it might have sounded like concern from a good friend.

Taryn,

Your wedding is tomorrow. I've got to be your big brother here. Have you thought about waiting? This is sudden. Is this guy good enough for you? If he hurts you, I'll go after him myself.

I can't connect all the dots at Gated Labs. I guess you didn't make a decision about Nehemiah. We have to work together on this.

Ethan

Taryn,

Nehemiah dots are driving me crazy. The bugs that someone is planting threaten everything you and I have worked hard to accomplish. We tested for those things. My suspicions are playing out, and it's bizarre.

I know who's involved. Please send me any changes you've made to the project.

Ethan

Taryn,

My life's in danger. Be careful. Good thing you're leaving on your honeymoon. You'll be safe. Forget what I said about waiting to get married.

We'll talk when you get back.

Ethan

Taryn,

99% sure this is bigger than we thought. Get a burner phone and call me as soon as possible.
  Every thirty days life changes.

Ethan

Three hours later, when she was supposedly Mrs. Francis Shepherd:

Taryn,

Francis Shepherd isn't his real name. Please, don't marry this guy. Call me.
  I'm taking the first flight out of here in the morning.

Ethan

Tears dripped over her cheeks. She blamed her emotion on the grief of losing friends, the agonizing throb in her head, and the plethora of horrific occurrences over the past two days. Vince Bradshaw sat a few desks away from her, hunched over a computer, and she turned so he wouldn't see her pitiful lack of control.

"Hey, lady, time to rest." Joe's soothing voice interrupted her thoughts.

She stood and fell into his arms and sobbed. Yes, it was weak and unlike her. Yes, she'd be embarrassed later. But she needed another human being. She had no idea how long she wept, but with a sense of embarrassment, she stepped back and swiped beneath her eyes.

"So many good people were killed," she said. "I know none of it was my fault, but when so many believe it is . . . it's hard."

"We'll find who's responsible. Getting closer all the time."

"And Zoey. She has to be all right."

"We'll keep praying for that little girl."

"Thank you. Oh, Joe, I'm so worried about my mom. She must be miserable with all she's heard from the media."

"I'll see if we can get a personal message to her. Lady, you need a bed and no one to interrupt you for at least eight hours."

"Where could I go? Is there a cot here?"

"We have a couple of beds in the health services unit. A full-time nurse is there too. Round-the-clock protection. No one will bother you."

"I just need a few hours."

"Sure."

"Can Buddy come with me?"

"Not so sure I can arrange that. The area's not equipped for pets."

"I understand. Will you wake me with any new information or if Zoey's found?"

"Of course."

Would he really? Maybe she was an irritant to the FBI. Maybe they didn't need her skills at all.

Chapter 28

4:45 p.m. Tuesday

Grayson glanced at his watch before he and Joe entered the interview room to question Jose Pedraza. Vince chose to observe the suspect through the one-way glass. Why? Was he afraid Pedraza would recognize him? Ever since the SSA indicated Vince was under investigation, Grayson had watched his every move.

"Get this done. I need to get home," Vince said. "Aaron's out of insulin."

"Why can't he get his own medicine?" Joe said. "He's a grown man, and we have a job here."

Grayson didn't know any Aaron.

"Hey, retired agent, my personal life is none of your business."

"Suit yourself," Joe said. "People died yesterday, and it's our job to find out who's responsible." He frowned and nodded at Grayson. "You take the lead. Go with your gut."

Joe and Grayson entered the room and seated themselves at a table across from Pedraza.

Pedraza met them with a cold gaze. Grayson had tangled with Murford's men more than once in the last two days—highly trained men who'd been recruited for what? Confiscate a software program from a woman? Bring down an airport terminal?

"We have a problem, Jose, and we need your help." Grayson tossed a notebook and pen on the table.

"How do you figure?"

"We have dozens dead, a murdered mother, a missing child, and we think it's all linked to a security breach on a software program."

"And you think I have those answers?" Pedraza laughed. "Do I look like the intellectual type?"

"I think you're one smart man. And you're alive because I chose to give you a break."

"A break?" Pedraza frowned and cursed. "You shot me."

Grayson grinned. "My aim was a little off. A few inches to the right, and you'd be on a cold slab. Looks like Breckon drew the short straw."

"Thanks. Maybe I need a lawyer after all."

"You were read your Miranda rights and waived the right to a lawyer."

Pedraza stared at his hand. "I did. So let's get this done."

"As I said, you're one smart man." Grayson opened Pedraza's file and purposely took his time to leaf through it. "According to this, you have a preference for prison food and thirty minutes a day of sunlight. Or solitary confinement." When he didn't respond, Grayson closed the file. "Look, make this easy on yourself. You've had a few bad breaks and paid for them.

Now the media will have you fried if it leaks you're connected to the airport bombing. So far, you've been a lucky man. Are you going to keep your streak?"

Pedraza cocked a brow. No doubt he didn't feel the past hours had gone his way. "What are you suggesting?"

"You were in the same Navy SEAL unit as Murford and Breckon. Old buds. I wasn't in the military, but my dad retired from the Marines, and my brother will be a lifer. I understand the camaraderie."

"So how does that help me?"

"Any of the other guys you served with active in this mission?"

When Pedraza didn't respond, Grayson continued. "Tell us how to find Murford, and we'll talk to the judge."

"Lesser sentence or witness protection?" He swallowed hard, and for a split second his hands shook.

"We can let the prosecutor and judge know of your cooperation and recommend a lesser sentence or a witness security option. Depends on what you have." What did Pedraza know that scared him?

"And it better be good," Joe said. "That was my house you blasted."

Pedraza snorted. "Aren't you glad you weren't inside?"

215

"You'd better be glad I wasn't." Joe spoke just above a whisper. "Or we wouldn't be having this conversation." He leaned forward. "Let me tell you something, Pancho Villa. I'll forgive the mess you made of my house. I might even suggest a lesser sentence. But not without a solid lead to Phillip Murford and who's behind the airport bombing."

"What's an old man like you doing in the FBI?"

"They called in the best."

Go for it, Joe.

"Okay, Pedraza," Joe said. "Let's hear what you got. We'll keep you out of Murford's way, and we'll need your testimony in court." Joe did the stare down, the one he used to level on Grayson when he'd gotten into trouble.

Pedraza hesitated. Shook his head. "Murford's not who I'm concerned about."

"Who is?" Joe said.

"No idea. I said before, I'm just a low man on the food chain."

"I bet you heard a name, saw a face."

"Nope. All I know is he isn't from Houston."

"Where?"

"New York."

"What do you know about him?"

"Murford didn't like him much. Said the boss had a temper." Pedraza lifted his chin. "Took my orders from Murford. We worked by phone. You know, contract labor."

216

Joe rubbed his brow, a sign for Grayson to take over.

"What's the phone number for Murford?" Grayson shoved the notebook and pen toward Pedraza.

Joe pointed to it and Pedraza wrote a number.

"What kind of orders did Murford give you?" Grayson said.

Pedraza simply stared.

"I smell a lie," Joe said. "We need the truth."

"He contacted me for whatever he needed. In the beginning I followed Taryn Young. Took pictures. Recorded conversations. Told him where she went."

"What else?" Grayson said.

"Witness protection, right?"

Grayson leaned in. "Why are you so afraid of this man?"

Pedraza's gaze darted about the room. "Two men from our original team were killed weeks before the airport bombing."

"Why?"

"Didn't answer their phone by the second ring. It was a message to all of us."

Grayson jotted a few notes to run through the FIG later. Those hits were done recently. "What else have you done?"

Sweat formed on Pedraza's brow. "Breckon and I helped Murford tear apart Young's condo.

He was looking for a flash drive and getting all the pics of the two of them together."

"Do you know what was on the flash drive?"

"Murford called it a tiebreaker. Worth a few million or more."

"So Murford needed the flash drive to sell to someone else."

"You got it. I guess the boss needed it for something big."

"Did you take part in the airport bombing?"

"We were as shocked as the rest of the world. Don't lay that one on me."

Grayson made notes. Were the agents who explored the connection way off? "Did you murder Claire Levin?"

Pedraza narrowed his eyes. "Murford killed the woman."

"Did the little girl watch the crime?"

"Murford had me take her to the front of the studio before he took care of the woman. Then he left with the kid." No hint of regret crossed Pedraza's face.

"Did he give you an idea where he stashed the little girl?"

Pedraza shook his head. "He told us just enough to do our jobs."

At least Zoey hadn't witnessed her mother's murder. "Did the little girl go willingly with him?"

"Yes. Called him Mr. Shep."

"Anything else I haven't asked? Things we should know?"

Pedraza blinked. "I didn't kill Claire Levin. I'll swear to it."

"I believe you," Grayson said. "How many others work for Murford?"

"No one else I know of."

"Who was at the church?"

"The three of us."

Grayson would grill this guy until tomorrow if that's what it took. "Who's giving information to Murford from the FBI?"

"Do you think I'd tell you that? I'd be dead within the hour."

That confirmed a mole existed. "Give us the name and we'll make an arrest."

Pedraza stiffened. "Who said there was a mole?"

"You did, my friend."

"Nothing from me about that."

Grayson would let it rest for now, especially with Vince watching. "Whose idea to eliminate me and take Taryn Young?"

"Murford ordered both, and he had a car waiting."

"And you had no idea where he planned to take Young?"

Pedraza drummed his fingers on the table. "Told you before. I just did what I was told and collected my pay."

"We have camera footage of a woman seen

with Breckon and Murford. What do you know about her?"

"Probably Murford's girlfriend."

"I thought no one else was involved." Grayson showed her pic on his BlackBerry.

"I forgot about her," Pedraza said. "Never met her. Just heard him talking."

"How can we find her? Name?"

"You know as much as I do." He rubbed the back of his neck.

"Try again. You're smarter than that," Grayson said. "I'm ready to change your address."

Pedraza frowned. "She goes by Dina. Works in the lounge at a Marriott on the southwest side."

Grayson finally had a lead on Phillip Murford and possibly where Zoey was being held.

Chapter 29

7:00 p.m. Tuesday

Grayson pulled into the parking lot of the Southwest Marriott with Joe snoozing beside him. His uncle needed a good night's rest instead of the lifestyle of a much younger man. But Grayson wouldn't tell him that. Joe might decide to prove he still had the miles-per-hour stuff.

An accident on the interstate had stopped them for forty minutes. Then traffic crept to two lanes. An ambulance, fire trucks, HPD, and the vulture swarm of tow trucks, which didn't help his impatience—a trait he shared with his dad. Joe complained about Grayson's lead foot, but all the speed-demon remarks had been said before. Just like the speeding ticket comments. Grayson wanted to chew on somebody and spit 'em out. Not exactly the thoughts of a man who placed his trust in God.

Sleep deprivation sure made an agent testy.

Taryn's collapse had shaken him a little more than he cared to admit. How much could her body handle? Joe had initiated an escort to transport her to the health services unit, where she could rest in one of the beds there. The nurse had given her something to relax, and she'd be safe. If Grayson allowed himself to dwell on the matter, he'd admit being a twinge jealous that Joe had been there for her breakdown. Definitely an attraction, but not anything he could deal with now. He'd met the woman only hours ago, and already she'd wiggled into his heart. How incredibly unlike him—Grayson Hall, who never went beyond three dates for fear he might get captured.

Joe had made hotel reservations until the repairs on his house were finished, but Grayson didn't want to think about anything at the moment other than apprehending Murford.

"This old man is getting a little tired," Joe said as Grayson parked the car. "But don't tell your SSA."

They'd learned Dina Dancer's shift began at six o'clock. At least they'd catch her fresh before the drinking crowd stole her attention. With Breckon dead, Pedraza in custody, and a vague image of her in incriminating photos, they had leverage for the interview. Grayson and Joe exited the car and walked to the hotel's entrance.

"You're getting personally involved," Joe said.

"Nah. Just doing my job and wanting the truth to surface."

"Taryn is special. You and I felt it from the start."

As soon as Joe said her name, Grayson realized she'd gotten to him bad. Later he'd analyze his feelings. "I'm thinking Dina can lead us to not only Murford but where Zoey's being held."

"I hope you're right on both counts. Sure would like to end this tonight."

Grayson huffed. "You want to see the stats on that?"

"Not really. I might want to retire again."

"Let me refresh you," Grayson said. "The FBI interviewed over twenty-eight thousand people in the McVeigh case. Nearly a billion pieces of information. The Boston Marathon bombings were up in the thousands."

"Look at the manpower working on this. Yes, it'll take a while, but nothing will go untouched. When arrests are made, it'll be solid."

Joe wasn't claiming anything Grayson didn't already know, but his uncle put things in the right perspective. Helped Grayson calm down and zone in on his job, initiating action instead of reacting to every piece of lousy news.

Inside the hotel, they entered the shadows of the lounge area with orange-and-yellow mood lighting. A man and woman cozied up at the bar, and two couples sat at tables. No server in sight. Grayson made his way to the end of the bar and caught the bartender's attention.

"We'd like to talk to Dina Dancer." Grayson pulled out his ID. The bald man eyed them with a frown. "Can't help you there. She didn't show up tonight."

"Did she call?"

"No."

"Is not showing up for work a habit?"

"I tried her cell, but it went to voice mail. Not like her."

Grayson showed him the photo on his BlackBerry. "Is this Dina Dancer?"

The bartender examined it and shrugged. "Could be. Not sure."

"What can you tell me about her?"

"Did her job. Kept to herself."

"Anyone here she was close to?"

"She worked her shift alone."

"Just you two, huh? Did she talk a lot?"

"No. We just worked."

Grayson knew better. "We'd like her cell number and address."

"You'll have to talk to the manager about that."

Grayson showed him a pic of Murford. "Ever seen this guy?"

He studied the photo. "Can't say I have."

Grayson handed him his card. "If you see or hear from Miss Dancer or the man in the photo, please contact us."

After the hotel's manager provided Dancer's information, Grayson and Joe viewed the security camera footage from the past week. Videos showed the woman arriving to work and leaving alone. Frustration wove a mean streak through Grayson. One dead end after another.

This case would be solved by the work of hundreds of people who specialized in specific areas of crime. If he didn't get some sleep soon, he'd be one fewer set of eyes.

Grayson drove to Dancer's small home in less than ten minutes, turning several times in a middle-class subdivision where each resident had the choice of four house plans. At her address, no lights, no car in the garage, and locked doors made for a sour agent, along with his other attitude problems. After a call to headquarters for a search warrant, they were in the car again.

"What about some dinner and checking into our hotel? I'll take the foldout couch. The insurance company is picking up the tab," Joe said. "You look as old as I feel."

"My stomach's complaining, but I'll drop you off at the hotel. I'm heading to the office to check on Taryn."

Joe chuckled. "You'd turn down a hotel with your uncle for a night at the office?"

Here it comes. "I want to make sure she's okay."

He grinned. "I knew it the moment she walked into the house. The chemistry was hard to miss."

Grayson bit back a denial that Joe would see straight through. "She was married on Sunday."

"A phony wedding, right down to the preacher. And the groom murdered her best friend."

"My point. She trusted and cared for Murford enough to marry him. Although he's been exposed as a killer, her emotions must be spinning like a top. I doubt she's looking for a relationship."

"She's scared, afraid for the little girl," Joe said. "But she trusts you. I can see it in her eyes."

This was not a conversation Grayson wanted to continue. "I helped her, believed her when no one else did. Of course she'd trust me. That's it."

"What little I know of Taryn, I like," Joe said. "I've always appreciated brains and beauty. Loved your aunt and never found another woman who even came close to her. But I might be tempted with Taryn. Those green eyes and auburn hair are the looks of an angel. Whatcha think, Nephew?"

Grayson laughed to break the tension. "Thanks."

"For what?"

"Helping me get out of my nasty mood. For keeping my attention on the case and not off on some rabbit trail."

"Maybe I just want you to find a woman who makes you happy. Do you need a chaperone?"

"Once I see she's okay, I'll join you at the hotel."

"I'm coming too. Grayson, a good woman will help you forget the past. Because you've never dealt with it."

"That's God's role. While you're on the spiritual path, see what you can do with my dad."

Chapter 30

10:06 p.m. Tuesday

Taryn startled in her sleep. What had she heard? She opened her eyes to a dark room. Memories of being in the bed-rest area of the FBI's health services unit brushed across her mind. The nurse had assured her no one would bother her.

The doorknob twisted, and a small ray of light from the hall filtered in. Who was there? Why hadn't she insisted on Buddy joining her? She struggled for her foggy head to clear, the effects of the pain meds dulling her senses.

A hand clasped over her mouth. Unable to breathe, she felt panic whip through her. Murford! He'd managed to get inside the building. Overpowered the agents to get to her. She understood his plan—he'd attempt to learn what he could and then slit her throat like he'd done to Claire.

He would not win this easily. She peeled back his fingers, then snapped them. As he twisted, she jammed her elbow upward into his groin. He jumped back. Survival ruled her actions, but she couldn't see in the utter blackness.

The click of his gun stopped her.

"That's right, Miss Taryn. I have the upper hand here. All your fancy self-defense doesn't do piddly when a gun's aimed at you."

Vince.

"What's this about?"

"You and I are going to walk out of here."

"I'm not going anywhere with you."

"You have no choice. Do you want that kid to live or not?"

Her heart thudded against her chest while all the mental techniques learned in hapkido vanished. "Where?"

"You'll find out."

"If I cooperate, then Zoey will be released?"

"Yes."

She could get the edge on him, but what if that ruined her chances with Zoey? Another thought blasted against her head. If she could take him, Grayson could force him to reveal it all.

"I have Murford on speed dial. If he doesn't hear from me soon, the kid's dead."

Wouldn't having a bad guy's number on speed dial be used against him? She took a deep breath.

"I know your IQ. I have more than one burner phone."

She had no choice. At least this way Zoey had a chance. "I'm a little dizzy."

"Get over it." He stepped back from the door. "You lead the way to the entrance where you arrived."

"Why, Vince? You're an FBI agent. Did Murford offer you that much money?"

"Shut up. Not another word."

"My shoes."

"You won't need them."

She obeyed, making her way slowly down the hall toward the double doors leading to the rear parking lot.

"Hey, Agent Bradshaw," said the nurse, a kind woman who'd told Taryn all about her two sons, "Ms. Young isn't in any shape to assist you."

"The big boss needs her. Once he's finished, one of us will bring her back."

The nurse smiled and bid them good night.

Outside, the stale, hot air seemed to suck the life out of her. Vince walked beside her. She wanted to flatten him. . . .

"My car's to the left," he said.

Headlights whipped into the parking lot. Joe's T-Bird. One man emerged.

"Don't try a thing," Vince said. "I have nothing to lose here."

"Put the gun down," Joe said.

"Don't think so."

"Let Taryn go, and we'll talk about this."

Vince jammed the gun into her temple. "Move. Now."

Joe walked closer, and she sensed Vince was nervous.

"Do you really want her brains splattered?" Vince said.

"The odds aren't on your side. You shoot her, and you're done."

Taryn considered gaining the edge, but would he have a split-second advantage?

Someone knocked Vince's gun from his hand. It fired, and she fell. The person shoved him to the ground and cuffed him.

"You're under arrest," Grayson said.

"His phone," she said. "He said Zoey would be killed if I didn't go with him."

Grayson yanked two phones from Vince's pocket, his BlackBerry and a burner. "Nothing on either phone."

"You lied to me." Red-hot anger swirled through her. "You have no idea where to find Zoey."

12:30 a.m. Wednesday

Grayson and Joe viewed Vince through the one-way glass outside the interview room. They'd

229

waited before questioning him, hoping he'd think through what his charges meant to his future. Vince waved at them as if he could see them, giving his familiar sneer. He'd been where they observed him, formed the questions, and experienced the same frustration at the sight of a guilty man. FBI protocol was a game for Vince, but he'd already lost.

"You've known him longer than I have," Grayson said. "Why has he requested a lawyer and yet agreed to the interview without counsel?"

Joe studied Vince. "Everything about him spells contempt. Somewhere along the line, life jolted him, and he's blaming the FBI."

"His bank account indicates Murford paid him well. Money hits his greedy spot."

"I think there's more."

"I'm not following you."

"His son, Aaron, has type 1 diabetes and lives with Vince. The kid's nearly thirty. Way back when Vince and I worked together, his whole life was his son and his health. We can start there."

"You lead out," Grayson said. "I might get a little blood on his jacket."

"Put aside the personal stuff and concentrate on what Vince can tell us. Look how he's slouched in the chair. He's angry. Didn't think he'd get caught." He pointed to his former partner. "Or maybe he wanted to get caught, and that's why he wants to talk without his attorney."

"But then we can't use anything in court."

"Who cares, so long as we find out how to end this. I'll come across as the retired agent who saw the good and the bad in the bureau."

Joe was a legend type of agent. His tactics might have been a little off the wall, but he got results. Right now, results were what mattered. Joe stepped into the room first.

"If it isn't Batman and his sidekick farm boy. Is this the best the FBI can offer? I was expecting waterboarding."

Joe smiled while he and Grayson took seats across from Vince. "Is that any way to talk to an old friend?"

"We were never friends. The FBI isn't a country club. For the record, I don't have any friends here."

Grayson stuffed his anger and replaced it with an intense scrutiny of Vince's body language. As usual, the man attempted to gain control of a situation with caustic remarks. Hard to think of him as ever being a decent agent.

"You were a dedicated agent when you joined the bureau," Joe said. "You were an outstanding agent. Remember the cases we worked together back when? We solved some tough ones in our time. I think Aaron was still in diapers then."

"Right. I figure all I ever accomplished was sleepless nights and watching bad guys hit the streets again."

"You and I ended crime sprees, put perps in jail for a long time."

"Where're our medals?"

"Remember the serial murder case on the southeast side? We worked it for six months."

"I'm done risking my life for a government that doesn't give a lick. Never got me anywhere."

"Yes, it did. Commendations. Respect."

"You got me confused with another agent. All I ever received was lousy pay and then farm boy for a partner my last year in."

His disillusionment made him an easy target for Murford.

"What happened to turn you sour?" Joe said. "I've got a few bones to pick with the bureau too."

"None of your business." Vince leaned back in the chair.

"You're right. I should have kept in touch. Been a better partner. How's Aaron?"

"He's fine. Leave him out of this." Vince's face hardened.

Grayson made a mental note to check on Aaron's background.

Joe loosened his tie and unbuttoned the top of his shirt. "Remember when we were outnumbered on that weapons case and couldn't get backup? You and I were left to die."

A flicker of empathy touched Vince's face.

"We're just machines sent to get a job done without adequate funds and manpower."

"Don't I know it. I still wake up at night in a cold sweat with it all."

Vince nodded. "I should have got out a long time ago. Before I let it turn me into this."

"How'd you get caught up in the airport bombing?" Joe said.

Vince gave a blank look. "No deal, Joe."

"Work with me here. This doesn't look good. I want to help."

Vince clapped his hands slowly three times. "Good job, but I'm not buying it. You almost had me fooled. Nothing else from me until I talk to my lawyer."

"Once Jose Pedraza learned you were arrested, he cut a deal," Grayson said.

Vince straightened. "You're lying."

"Nope. He cooperated. Something he said was real interesting." Grayson paused. "His job was to kill you, but he got shot. He said you'd lost your value."

"Liar."

"Hmm. Pedraza spoke of a contract. . . . They just need to find you. The sad part is you're only worth two grand. Every ganger out there will be looking for Special Agent Vince Bradshaw."

"I've used those same tactics."

"We can let you talk to Pedraza. But he won't

be in custody long with the deal his lawyer worked out."

Vince glared. "You're really stupid if you think I'd believe that line of bull."

Grayson smiled. "By the way, did Murford advance you enough to take care of Aaron after you're gone?"

Vince's silence confirmed he'd been shorted.

Joe cleared his throat. "You don't do your son any good dead. You can't get his medication or clear your name."

"I want my lawyer."

Grayson stood. "I'll make sure he gets a call as soon as his office opens." He walked to the door and swung his attention to Vince. "Have you considered Murford could take out his vengeance on Aaron? I doubt a ganger cares if it's Bradshaw senior or junior as long as he collects his due."

"Are you sure this is the way you want to end your career?" Joe said as though he were talking to an old friend.

"I'm sure."

"A lawyer won't stop the charges, but a little truth could go a long way in the sentencing."

Vince blew out his scorn. He nodded at Grayson. "I told you not to mess with Taryn Young. She'll get you killed."

Chapter 31

New York
2:50 a.m. Eastern, Wednesday

I hear Breckon's dead. Pedraza and Bradshaw are in custody. Murford got away. That man's like a cat. Too bad he isn't as cunning or he wouldn't have tried to double-cross me. Three months ago I took care of his two slackers to get his attention. He's an idiot on a short leash. What he doesn't know is I have an expert hacker working on the problem. We'll get the info we need and finish this. One way or another.

Bradshaw can only point to Murford. Glad I gave Murford the agent's name, a loser looking for money.

I tap my chin. . . . What if I play desperate? Helpless? This temporary setback could put that weasel in the palm of my hand.

I dial Murford's number. He hasn't answered in the past several hours, but his ego might be ready for an adrenaline boost.

"Hey, are you seething?" Murford laughs, and I want to scratch his eyes out.

I put my kill mode in check. "Not really. You conducted business just as I expected. I'm in trouble with this. Things are spinning out of control without access to the software."

"I hear the misery. But I know you're not out of resources."

"But you can help me. We can work through our differences."

"Take it somewhere else. I'm right where I need to be."

I'll see him suffer for the trouble he's causing. "Look, you know I wouldn't be calling if a lot of money wasn't at stake."

"And I plan to collect it all."

"Your greed will get you killed."

He laughs again, and I hate the sound of it. "I'm covered, Iris," he says. "This is one time you lose."

"Don't think so. You have a private party scheduled for Friday with no hors d'oeuvres."

"You just want to be the only guest."

My blood pressure escalates. "I *am* the only guest. Look, Murford, you don't have access to Nehemiah. In fact, the old software is running. Neither do you have Taryn Young. Now you might have an idea or two, but you've exhausted balloons and party favors. I know your every move, which means your utter failures. Team members killed and arrested. You're running out of options. So I suggest we work together, and we'll both make money. I intend to sell Nehemiah, and we'll make a profit."

"What's your plan?"

I've hit his hot button. "Lure Young away from the FBI with talk about the kid. She's senseless when it comes to her. Use it. Have you gotten rid of the brat?"

"Not yet."

"Why not? She's costing you time and money. Where is she?" I know the answer, but I want to hear his response.

"Tucked away."

Right. "I know how to dispose of the body if you can't stomach it."

"I have it under control."

"Look, you nab Young, and I'll take over the situation from there."

"Not so fast. I'll get the info and let you know."

He deserves a slow death, and I hate his condescending tone. "All right. I'll wait until I hear from you. How long will it be?"

"Your boss man must be crawling up your rear."

I consider his comment . . . purposely.

"Your hesitation tells me you're crying for my help."

Leapfrog. "I'll make it worth your trouble."

I disconnect the call and hope Murford has fallen for my ploy. He knows what our boss can do and has done. A smart man would be scrambling to please.

Time to pull an ace out of the deck. I press in a number.

"Busy?" I say.

His breathless words indicate he's with a woman. "I am."

"We have to talk now."

He curses, but he'll get over it. A moment later I hear a door shut and running water. "What is it?"

"Follow Murford. See what he's up to. Understand? Time is running out."

"I'm busy."

"Not when I'm paying for the champagne."

He curses again. "I'll call when I have something."

Chapter 32

3:35 a.m. Wednesday

While Grayson talked to his SSA and made his report about Vince, Taryn waited in the break room with an escort, an agent who looked like he would rather be anywhere but with her. She refused to go back to the health services unit. Decisions needed to be made, and the process took time.

The hum of the vending machine kept her company. The room had the sterile feel of a hospital—synthetic, without emotion. The agents were far from unfeeling, but she understood the necessity to focus on logic.

She hated the cold, and this room blew air like the dead of winter. She massaged the goose bumps on her arms, all the while craving the power of Tylenol 3. She'd vowed to leave the prescription meds alone until she could finally sleep, her self-imposed deadline, and rely on over-the-counter relief. The thought of getting addicted to pain-killers was worse than her concussion and all the other aches.

She sipped on black coffee to warm her up. Caffeine bolted through her veins, and she wanted to get started with the day's work. She'd sat there too long with nothing to do, determined to prove her worth. . . .

Grayson and Joe entered the room, and her babysitter agent left. Lines formed across both men's foreheads like X-rays of stress. Grayson normally gave her immediate eye contact, but not this morning. What had he learned that had him consumed?

"What are the new developments?" she said.

"Privileged information." Grayson poured two cups of coffee.

She understood security measures. "I want to let Murford think I'll exchange Nehemiah credentials for Zoey, my iPad, and iPhone. I can give him something bogus that will allow him access through several levels and give the perception they are getting somewhere, but ultimately it will destroy the system. Wire me up or whatever you do, and let me help bring him in."

"You'd be running with big guns when all you have is a water pistol," Joe said.

"I don't care. It's an opportunity to bring these killers to justice."

Grayson sat across from her at a round table and stared into his coffee while shaking a sugar packet. "Your idea has been discussed. Understand the FBI doesn't negotiate with terrorists. Neither do we encourage civilians to be put at risk."

"But I'd be acting alone."

Grayson frowned. "We can't support your plan."

"Does it matter? I could walk out of here, and Murford would show up with reinforcements." She leaned closer. "I'm right, and you're not using me to your advantage."

"It's too dangerous."

Joe touched her arm. "Taryn, you and I talked about this. There's no guarantee Zoey is alive. The odds are against it."

His words lit a fuse inside her. "So you'll take the defensive and hope something comes up? How effective is that when you're supposed to be the offense?"

"Calm down," Grayson said as though she were a child.

She stood. "I'm perfectly calm and amazingly logical. If you don't agree, I'll go to the SSA. He'd agree my plan is superior."

"That's so intelligent." Grayson's voice rose. "You pretend to give Murford the info, he'll kill you. Very simple maneuver. He and his pals win."

"I'm not sitting by and doing nothing until you tell me this is over!"

Joe waved his arms. "A shouting match between you two won't solve a thing. We're learning more by the minute. Hundreds and thousands of agents, as well as specialty forces of Homeland Security, are working every angle of the bombing, the software theft, and Zoey's kidnapping. Some believe the software and the bombing are connected. Others do not. But in any event, we're talking about a huge task force. One overzealous woman isn't going to break this case."

"You don't know that for sure." She sensed something from the two, and she wouldn't let it rest. "Which one of you is going to tell me what has happened?"

Joe scratched his chin. "Well—"

"Joe, it's not our—"

"I'm retired, remember? What's the FBI gonna do? Send me home? Stick me in jail? Taryn steps out of here without our protection, and the first good ole boy who believes in God, the US, and fried alligator will pull the trigger. And the media will paint his face as a hero."

"I agree. But some info is confidential," Grayson said.

"What do you know?" Taryn's pulse escalated. Had they found Zoey and were afraid to tell her? "Who would I tell?"

"Telling someone is not the issue," Grayson

said. "If you aren't aware of updates, then you can't be forced to reveal something."

"If I'm tortured or killed, it would be for Nehemiah."

"It's how the information would be secured that bothers me. I'm sure Murford has a fully equipped toolbox."

She shuddered. "I'm in this mess for the duration. I deserve to know what you've learned."

"According to Pedraza, Murford killed Claire."

She swallowed the acid rising in her throat. "I suspected it was him," she said. "He's capable of anything."

"Glad we're on the same page." Grayson studied her. His clear blue eyes read concern, but was it for protocol or for her? "If you overhear something while in this building, then it stays here with you."

Learning new information always came at a price. "I want to know everything. Because I intend to help with or without your permission."

"Arguing with you uses more energy than a firefight. All right. But I don't approve of any of this."

"Thank you. I'm not trying to be difficult. I just need to do all I can . . . for all those who've died. And I don't care if I sound dramatic."

Grayson narrowed his gaze and ran his fingers through his hair. "The FBI took a call from a man who says he wants to talk to Taryn Young.

Says he knows where Zoey Levin is being held. Wants to make a deal. Came from a burner phone, and the conversation was short."

"How do I make it happen?"

"He's calling back at six."

The wall clock indicated urgency. "I don't have much time to think about this."

"Agents will be listening in, and he'll know it," Grayson said.

"Would the man be aware of Vince's arrest?"

"Depends if he's attempted to get in touch with Vince. The caller is probably Murford. He doesn't have the necessary access, and he needs it to pull off a bidding war that's supposed to happen Friday morning."

"I'm in." She followed Grayson and Joe to the operation center and watched the clock for the scheduled time.

At six, agents scurried to set up the call trace.

The phone rang and Grayson handed it to her with a nod. She needed his support.

"This is Taryn Young."

"Listen to me before you hang up."

Murford's voice nearly devastated her. All the things she wanted to say to him would have to wait. "What do you want?"

"I want to make a deal. You want Zoey, and I need access to Nehemiah."

Her knees shook, and she eased onto a chair. "How do I know she's alive?"

"I give you my word."

She clenched her fist. "Your word? Dozens of people are dead and wounded because of your word."

"I didn't bomb the terminal. In fact, I was supposed to have been blown up with it."

"You expect me to believe that? Looked like excellent timing to me."

"Doesn't matter. We both have something the other wants."

"And you expect me to believe you?" she said.

"If you're not willing to negotiate, we'll both end up dead along with Zoey."

"So you're drowning and want me to throw you a life preserver? Tell me who's the bomber."

"Doesn't matter. They're powerful, and they have plans."

She stared at Grayson. Her gaze captured his, and his smile filled her with confidence. "Let's meet and talk. For breakfast."

"Alone. I have eyes that will let me know if the FBI follows you."

She hoped those eyes were Vince's. "Deal. Tell me when and where."

Chapter 33

7:30 a.m. Wednesday

Grayson fumed over what Taryn planned to do. What made it worse was Joe and the SSA agreed with her ridiculous idea. She'd been hurt enough. How much more could she take?

Intel pouring in from various FBI departments indicated a connect in New York, but the who, why, and where hadn't been confirmed. Vince had placed four calls to a number in New York, and Pedraza claimed the real boss was located there. Now to run it down.

Would a bomber take out an airport terminal to gain access to a software program? It seemed really far-fetched, but Grayson was vested in the supposition, and the more he investigated the Nehemiah Project, the more he supported it. What had once looked like a ridiculous reason now took a different flight pattern. Although many agents asked themselves the very same questions, the answers weren't clear yet. What spurred the bomber?

A media source indicated the bomber simply wanted to make a power statement. Grayson didn't swallow the rationale. He wanted the motivation, and the why would lead them to the who. Iran's naming of the terrorists spread around the world, which indicated the bomber had feet on the ground here, people who were trained and not necessarily Middle Eastern. The media cried out for retaliation, and the world watched and listened.

For certain, having Murford in custody would mean another step toward more arrests.

A notification from the FIG diverted his attention. Definite confirmation of a bidding war taking place Friday morning at eleven Central time for some highly specialized software. Most of those taking part in it would be hard to trace. But unless Murford had expert hackers, a buy wouldn't happen. Then he'd have death warrants out for him from all over the world.

Taryn stood before him. Another store run had produced clean clothes, and she wore makeup to cover the nasty bruises. She'd combed her auburn hair over the bandage and looked . . . good. This lady, his lady, had the face of an angel. He offered a smile, but he didn't feel encouraging. These guys played for keeps. He didn't want to lose her to a bullet or a ruthless kidnapper.

"Are you wired up?" he said.

The tenderness in her eyes caused his stomach to flip. When had his wild feelings gotten this deep? *Put a lid on it, Grayson.*

"I'm ready for the rendezvous," she said. "Wearing a Kevlar vest and everything."

He rubbed the back of his neck. "Wish you had a ceramic one too. Have you been briefed on what you're walking into? This isn't a movie set. It's reality. You can back out of this and no one would blame you."

Taryn touched his arm, and he remembered when she'd recoiled from his touch. "Thank you for the concern, for believing in me when no one else did. For saving my life so many times." She shuddered. "Do you understand I have to meet with him, not only to help the FBI but to find Zoey and wipe my slate clean of what the rest of the world believes about me?"

He did understand, and once again her determination was one of the things he respected about her. "In your shoes, I'd do the same," he said. "Be careful. Murford has seen how you can defend yourself, so he'll be looking for you to try to get the best of him. That's not your job. Agents will handle apprehending him. Your role is to keep him talking, get him to confess, and exit the restaurant with him so innocent people aren't hurt. Eyes will be everywhere. Note he'll probably be in disguise."

"I know," she whispered. "And I won't go with him anywhere unless there's no other way."

He forced logic into his words so she wouldn't see the depth of his growing feelings. "Taryn, there's always another way. Putting your life in danger is your choice, but setting yourself up to be tortured and killed is another. And we both know he's capable of murder."

"I'll be careful." A flash of something came and vanished in her eyes. "I . . . I saw Buddy. He didn't want me to leave him."

"So he's a keeper?" The dog maybe, but what did she feel about *him?*

"Hope so. I should try to find his owner, but I don't really want to. He'd be a great companion for Bentley."

"I bet so too."

She shook her head. "I might have to tear Murford apart myself."

"Wait until we're finished with him."

"Thanks. All I want is five minutes. Can I check my e-mail one more time before I leave?"

He and Taryn were the masters of changing topics when conversation became uncomfortable. But this time his heart overruled logic.

"Taryn."

Her green gaze flew to him. He saw what neither of them could discuss. She sank her teeth into her lip. "We can't go there."

He wanted to take her hand, but he resisted. "But we will. I'm praying for you."

Her eyes moistened. "Us too?"

"You bet." He moved from his computer, and she slipped into the chair. The moment lost. Or was it?

Her long, slender fingers raced over the keyboard. "There's the one I'm looking for," she said. "Take a look. From Save, my old Black Hat pal."

Hey girl,

Always good to hear from you. I do have a job. Pays crazy good.
   Would need your total attention until resolved. No questions asked, and payment would arrive to your bank account. If interested, call me.

"You have a few minutes," Grayson said.
"I'll see what he offers."
He handed her a phone, one that couldn't be traced. She pressed in the number, and Grayson listened.
"Hi, this is Julie. Got your message."
"You must have remembered I don't ever sleep."
"I did. What do you have?"
"You'll need to work through me for this. The employer doesn't trust anyone. Plays for keeps."
"How serious?"
"Deadly. I don't even know the source. But I've worked for this person before."
"Okay. Doesn't matter. I need the money."
"Give me the number for the call, and I'll make the arrangements. I've been working on it but haven't gotten far. Somebody did a good job developing a firewall."

She flashed a grin at Grayson. "What kind of project?"

"Protecting process control software designed for LNG companies, and the buyer needs access ASAP."

"I'm going to be tied up until late morning with another job. Can they wait until then?"

"I'll do my best."

She gave him the number. "Thanks so much."

"Maybe the next time we meet, you won't be so quick to run off."

"You just might be right." Taryn disconnected the call. "Maybe between Save and Murford, I can provide something of value."

She already had, for him if no one else.

8:00 a.m. Wednesday

Taryn grabbed her purse and the keys to a compact rental car. She'd meet Murford at a Denny's nearby. He'd expect her to be early, and she needed time to think and pray through whatever would happen with him. She didn't dare shake or show any signs of fear. Neither could she look around the restaurant for other agents. Grayson stepped with her onto the elevator, and they rode in silence to the first floor.

Strange how her life had gone from accelerating her career through exemplary job performance to assisting in a nationwide search for terrorists who had committed unthinkable crimes. Finding Zoey alive propelled every word and action. If Taryn survived, she'd give Claire's daughter the best love-filled home in history. They'd do everything together. And just as Claire wanted, Taryn would bring Zoey up to know Jesus, love others, and learn how to make good choices. Amid the horror of the past two days, she allowed herself to dwell on the little girl making friends with Buddy, and how Bentley would probably be jealous. Oh yes, a house with a backyard and a swing set and maybe a pool. Zoey already knew how to swim. Taryn would find a job . . . possibly teaching on a college level. Any hopes of continuing to develop highly secured software had crashed.

"You're smiling," Grayson said.

She read the sign in the elevator about not discussing cases. "Honestly, I was thinking about Zoey and the life I want to give her."

"You'll be a wonderful mother."

"I've never thought about myself as a mother, but I like the sound of it."

"I hope you can make it happen. No, I pray it."

How dear of Grayson. One more time, she let the thought creep into her head. . . . If only she'd met him before the big mistake. He was a friend, and maybe when this was over, they could continue. But her trust factor with a possible relationship had hit zero.

Chapter 34

8:10 a.m. Wednesday

Grayson shoved aside his concern for Taryn. He couldn't drive to Denny's—other agents were handling it. But he wanted to be there. Instead he had to focus on the new information—the background check on Aaron Bradshaw. This guy was the motivation behind Vince's twist of allegiance.

Problem number one: Aaron Bradshaw could not hold down a job because of the severity of his diabetes. Other health complications came into play—obesity and poor circulation in his feet that often crippled him. But the most severe issue was his heart. He needed a transplant, an expensive medical procedure for a man who depended on the government and his dad to take care of rising medical costs.

Problem number two: Aaron liked to gamble, and his disability check could never pay off the figures in the report. Names of creditors meant Aaron wasn't choosy about his card-playing buddies. They were the kind who broke legs and tossed bodies into the bayou. Vince needed money, and lots of it, to bail out his son.

Now to make Aaron aware of his dad's situation, which meant he needed to be questioned.

Murford or his boss might have accessed Vince through one of Aaron's so-called friends. Possibly black-mail in exchange for Aaron's debt or the heart transplant. After discussing the possibility with the SSA, other agents were assigned to the investigation.

Grayson placed a call for Aaron Bradshaw to be picked up and learned the order had already been issued. The man was on his way to the FBI office. To keep himself busy, Grayson would summon Joe and let Vince know about questioning the younger Bradshaw. Maybe this time his old partner would crack.

8:25 a.m. Wednesday

Taryn slid into a booth at Denny's. She glanced at the other patrons and didn't recognize any of them. A young man asked what she wanted to drink.

"Coffee, please. Black." Actually, added caffeine probably wasn't the answer to her bundle of nerves.

"Bring the lady a large orange juice too. And I'll take coffee with cream."

The waiter disappeared, leaving Murford standing before her, sporting black-framed glasses, a gray suit, and an ultraconservative tie. His dark hair splayed on his forehead—what she once thought was incredibly sexy. She realized how deep her loathing was for a man

253

she'd thought she would love forever. A murderer who used people, then disposed of them.

"How nice of you to join me," she said, thankful for the wire in her bra.

He brushed back the hair from her ears, his touch making her feel like filth.

"There's nothing's there." She hoped he couldn't detect the Kevlar vest. "This is strictly you and me, just like you requested."

"I'm sorry I can't do a strip search."

She forced a smile. "I bet you are."

"What about your phone?"

She handed him her purse. "It's in the car."

He slid onto the booth bench opposite her. "First question: where did you learn self-defense?"

"My secret. Guess you and I have our share of those. Be nice or I'll show you more."

He laughed. "Have you figured out how I pulled off the dinner at Tony's and the St. Regis stay on the fourteenth floor?"

"Of course. All a big setup."

"Good call, Taryn. Ready to get Zoey back?"

"I am." She told herself she was acting, and this gig was her defining role. "What guarantees do I have she's not hurt?"

He pressed a key on his phone. "Let me see Zoey." He handed Taryn the phone.

Her precious little girl watched TV. It sounded like *Dora the Explorer*, Zoey's favorite. Her arms were wrapped around her favorite baby doll. Taryn fought the lump in her throat and the tears threatening to flow. Instead she memorized Zoey's surroundings, the burnt-orange plaid sofa where she sat. Pine-paneled walls, a fireplace behind the TV . . . A cabin.

Murford clicked off the phone. "My end's good. Now about your side of the deal." He leaned on his elbows. "I know you enabled the software."

"How?"

"I have my ways. All I want to know is how to access it. Then I need to confirm what you've given me, and we're done." Their beverages were placed before them.

"How would I get Zoey?" She took a sip of the coffee. Her trembling fingers squeezed the hot mug.

He rested his hand on her arm, like the sting of a scorpion. "No need to be afraid of me, Taryn. We're in a public place. What could I do?"

She brushed off his hand. "You could have a gun."

"And I do. In case you lie to me, I need a ticket out."

"I'm not the one prone to lying."

"But it wasn't all lies." His eyes emitted a hint of sincerity. He was such a good actor.

"You expect me to believe you?" She'd slap his face if Zoey's life didn't depend on this.

"I care about Zoey. Who wouldn't? And I don't want her hurt either. I'm not a monster, Taryn."

She'd reserve her opinion. "What did you tell her about Claire?"

His eyes softened. "That her mother was sick, and you were taking care of her."

"But you killed her?"

He leaned in. "Necessary. I only kill if there's no other way."

"Did you have my life history in front of you?"

"I had it all from the moment you were born. My poor, shy lady who didn't know how to dance."

"How convenient."

"Got me what I needed."

She raised a brow. "Not everything."

"Are you backing out on me?" he said.

"Not at all. I won't give you the info here, not without Zoey."

"We're driving to make the transfer."

"Where?"

"Not too far. A couple of hours."

Dare she try to keep him talking? Her instructions were to reassure him of her willingness to cooperate, obtain a confession, and get him outside the restaurant. Questioning him further might clue him in to the wire. "What would stop you from getting rid of me after you had the information?"

"My word."

"That's rich. I was gullible once." She wanted to use a tactic certain to cripple him for killing

Claire, but she needed him as much as he needed her.

"Now we're at the same bargaining table."

Opposite sides, but she'd not bring it up. "You told me you didn't bomb the airport. So who did?"

He shrugged. "Someone who had his own agenda. I was told to give your toys to Breckon before we left the limo. The bomber had no reason to believe I hadn't fulfilled my end."

"Middle Eastern?"

"Seems to be the popular consensus." He glanced at his watch. "Time to go."

Panic punched her hard. "I'd like to know where I'm going."

"Thought Zoey was your priority."

"She is, but I'm through playing stupid." She leaned in closer. "You know, my skills could be bought, and not just for one software program."

He eyed her and scratched his chin. "Maybe I misjudged you."

She had to make this work. "I think you did. I'm good at developing any kind of software you'd want, and my hacking skills are highly competitive. All I need is what you want to accomplish. There are buyers all over the world who'd pay for my expertise and your contacts."

"Partners?"

"Absolutely."

"What's your price?"

She caressed the side of his face and tilted her head. "Money, and lots of it. Throw in the stuff you stole from me, an apology for destroying my condo, and we can talk more." She removed her hand, repulsed at the slime seated across from her.

He took a long drink of his coffee and leaned back against the booth. "We could start all over. I find you extremely attractive. But this is a big change for you, especially when you wouldn't let me near you until we were married."

"Was it worth it?" she whispered.

Murford cursed. "You're not playing fair."

Exactly, and this conversation is disgusting. Lust for whatever he didn't have ruled his thoughts. "Let's say I'm a smarter woman, ready to bargain with whatever it takes. Except I'm not working with a team of ex-military thugs. They bore me."

He chuckled and stared out the window. "I need to process this."

"Why? Are they all dead?"

"I need to figure out if this is a smart business venture."

"How long does it take to add up dollar signs from international vendors?"

He took another drink of coffee and a peek at his watch. "What are your plans after picking up Zoey?"

Odd question, since she knew he'd already planned her death. "Driving into Mexico until I figure out my next move."

"How does the FBI feel about that?"

"They ended their protective detail when I left this morning. Their decision fell under 'we don't negotiate with terrorists.' "

"Do you expect me to believe you?"

She raised her hands. "Search me. They know I'm innocent. Got tired of hearing me ask about Zoey, and all they want is to solve the bombing."

"Are you telling me no one's looking for the kid?"

"The prez is more concerned about his image." She allowed a tear to slip over her cheek. "How he looks to his enemies means more than one little girl's life. That's why I'm ready to do whatever you need to find her. Just tell me what you want done."

"Not here. Let's go pick up Zoey. We can talk on the way."

She hadn't accomplished all she wanted, like names or places.

"What's the hesitation, Taryn?"

She gave him a nod. "Not a thing. I'm ready."

He took the bill and headed to the cashier while she scooted out of the booth. Hopefully the FBI had enough info. The many agents working this case baffled her. They could put pieces into slots and come up with viable conclusions. Of course, without the emotional pressure, she could concentrate on the algorithms to develop software that shortened the process.

Maybe she could tackle the project after arrests were made.

Taryn waited with Murford, giving him her full attention. He held open the door and pointed to a silver Explorer near the exit point of the parking lot. A stupid move on his part, unless he had a plan B. Squeezing her fingertips into her palms, she resolved to remain steady. Had to be God because otherwise she'd be a basket case.

A white car crossed in front of them, and she expected it to stop. But the driver was an older man who had both hands on the steering wheel. Would the FBI nab Murford at his SUV? Surround them as they left the parking lot? But he claimed to have a gun. Within a few feet of the vehicle, a maroon pickup shot out from the side of the restaurant and stopped in front of them. A man and a woman jumped out, guns positioned.

"FBI," the man said. "Phillip Murford, you're under arrest."

Murford shot Taryn an angry glare. "You'll pay for this."

"I already have," she said.

He reached inside his jacket, but a pop sounded, and Murford stiffened and pushed against her.

Agents fired. Taryn screamed. She fell to the pavement with Murford on top of her. Blinding pain attacked her senses. Then blackness.

Chapter 35

All Grayson knew was Taryn and Murford were down, and an ambulance was en route. He should have been there, prevented the situation from going awry. How could she be okay with the report clearly stating otherwise? Where had she been shot?

A hand rested on his shoulder. "What do you know?" Joe said.

"A sniper when agents arrested Murford. He and Taryn are headed to the hospital." His phone signaled an update. He snatched it, his eyes glued to the small screen. "Murford's in bad shape. Taryn has a head injury."

"How bad?"

"She's listed as stable."

"We need to bank on that."

Grayson attempted to swallow the wave of emotions threatening to drown him. His fragile feelings for Taryn needed to be locked away. And he certainly didn't like the idea of a woman standing in the way of him doing his job as an agent. "I'd like to head to the hospital, but the SSA wants us to interview Aaron Bradshaw first."

"Sure. Let's get it done. We'd just be in the way while they patch her up."

Grayson gazed into the leathered face. "Thanks. We have his burner phone, and they're tracing the call history through his provider. We'll have answers there soon." The potential gray areas in the next interview popped into his head. "Would you take the lead on Aaron? I think you could tie in your link to Vince. He might have heard your name mentioned."

"Sure thing."

The two walked to an interview room where Aaron waited. In view of his background, a team had been assigned to tail him until this was resolved. Grayson paused outside the one-way window and observed the man's body language. Aaron's curled lip showed his disgust at being hauled in. He cracked his knuckles and balled his fists. With his serious health issues and facing disgruntled creditors, would he cooperate?

Joe opened the door and Grayson followed. "Aaron, I'm Special Agent Joe West and this is Special Agent Grayson Hall." He stuck out his hand, but the young man refused it.

Aaron tossed a scowl at Grayson. "You're my dad's partner."

"We were. I'm sorry to report he's been arrested."

"For what?" Aaron stuck out his triple chin. He needed a class in how to hide emotions.

Joe slid into a chair across from Aaron. "He's charged with attempted murder and malicious intent to kidnap."

"You got the wrong guy." Aaron crossed his arms over his ample chest. "My dad's an FBI agent, not a ganger."

Joe laid a legal pad and a pen on the table. "We didn't make a mistake. You can try to call him." Joe pushed his phone toward Aaron.

After three tries, Aaron returned the phone. "I still don't believe it."

"We could take you to where he's being held."

He stiffened. "I don't need to see him. This is a setup for something, and I'm not playing your game. I have business to handle."

"Look," Joe said. "I used to work with your dad, and back then he was one of the best. We have no idea why he went rogue. But I bet you do."

"He's still a great agent. But he's sick of his job. Ready to retire." He rubbed his sparsely whiskered cheek. "I'm not going to say anything that would incriminate him."

"I don't blame you." Joe picked up the pen. "We think you might be able to assist us in figuring out your dad's problem. Are you willing to answer a few questions for us?"

"Would it help him? He was framed, right?"

"We think so." Not a muscle moved on Joe's face. "I hate this when it's about an old friend."

"All right. I'll do what I can."

"Where do you work?"

"Medically disabled." He shifted in the chair. "Diabetes. Heart's not good either."

"I suppose you get a disability check?"

Aaron nodded.

"Where do you live?"

"With my dad. What do you think?"

Joe's features softened as though what he planned to say next was difficult. "Aaron, do you have a gambling problem?"

"Did my dad say that?"

Joe narrowed his gaze. "What do you think?"

"If you're asking if I play cards, the answer's yes. Have to do something to keep busy. Do I have a problem with it? No. Dad's always on me about my habit, as he calls it."

"Really?" Joe pointed to his BlackBerry. "I have a report stating you've built a huge gambling debt. The fellas you owe aren't exactly pillars of the community. We have the list. How are you handling it?"

Contempt moved into Aaron's face. "I have it under control."

"Doesn't look like your disability check would begin to cover your bills. Is your dad helping you pay them off?"

"My finances or Dad's are none of your business."

"It's our business when your dad breaks the law to pay off your bills."

"Then he shouldn't have gotten caught."

"Sounds real grateful, especially when he can't pay your way while sitting in jail. For that matter, he's going to be in jail for a long time. Hard for him to send you an allowance when he's not earning any money. What about the heart replacement? Do you have someone lined up to foot the medical bills?"

Aaron fumed. "I don't appreciate the guilt thing."

Joe opened Aaron's file and leafed through it. "From this list, who do you owe?"

"Hey, those guys play for keeps. Besides, you said you had names."

"We do. But I'm sure there's one who has you running for the border."

Aaron glared and shook his head. "Not going there."

"Okay, I see you're afraid. Who are your dad's friends?"

"None he told me about."

"Nobody who comes around? Phones him?"

"I don't monitor his after-work hours."

"Looks like he should have monitored yours." Joe picked up his legal pad, where he'd written a page of his questions and Aaron's answers, or lack of. "By the way, whoever hired your dad has a contract out on him. So if he's able to post bail, he's a dead man."

Aaron's eyes widened. "You're crazy. My dad's a smart man."

"We thought so too. Looks like we're done here. Understand your gambling buds will be interviewed."

Aaron paled. "Please don't contact them."

"No choice. If you think of anything, give us a call."

"I thought you were his friend."

"I am. But right now you're the only one who can help him."

"I can't." Aaron's hands trembled. "Look at his record. And he takes care of me."

Joe huffed. "Should have thought about that long before now."

Uncle Joe had officially pulled off his gloves.

"He didn't tell me where he got the money. I assumed he borrowed it. Or had it in the bank."

"As I said, you should have thought about your choices instead of yourself."

Aaron stared at his hands, folded on the table-top. They shook. "I did hear one name mentioned."

Joe poised his pen. "I'm waiting."

"Murford. Dad met with him a few times."

Chapter 36

New York
10:35 a.m. Eastern, Wednesday
Murford's dead. I didn't order the hit, and media claim a sniper got him.

I know who arranged it. When he's finished with our business, will I end up the same? My body-guards won't be able to stop him. He's that good.

I shudder, then shove the trepidation away. I climbed this ladder to the top rung by being smart—and fearless.

What's left of Murford's people understand I mean business. So I'll let them think I'm responsible for his murder. The problem is, I don't have anyone to keep the team in line. May need to dispose of them sooner than I thought.

My contact will find out where Murford moved the kid. If she's even alive. I need her as bargaining power for Young in case my hacker doesn't come through.

I grit my teeth. I was told al-Qaeda would take credit for the airport bombing. Nothing there has changed. Then why are my nerves on edge?

I read e-mail on my phone. Save needs help to hack into the software. Wants to bring in another person whom he claims works at his caliber. I pop two Tums, reminding me I should buy stock in the company. Save's question annoys me. He claimed to have the expertise needed to access the software. He got into Houston FBI's files to find a weak link for me. Bringing in one more person spreads me thinner. But why should I stress over the details when my plan is to eliminate all those on the payroll?

I walk to my wall of windows looking out on the city. Defiance ripples through me.

Who would ever miss a couple of lowlifes who make a living from breaching computer systems?

And if it happened as soon as they completed the job, their deaths would go unnoticed by a country twisted in the upheaval of the bombing. There's no paper trail. Nothing points to me.

I have the person's number, a woman. I'll see if she measures up to my expectations.

Chapter 37

10:25 a.m. Wednesday

Taryn opened her eyes in a hospital bed to a repeat of what had happened after the airport bombing. FBI Special Agent Grayson Hall leaned over her with his incredible blue eyes, but this time they were filled with gentleness. She'd grown to rely on this man, and if she were honest, other feelings surfaced. Less than a week ago, she'd thought she was in love with Francis Shepherd. Her heart was fickle.

"Hey, superagent."

She smiled at him and nodded at Joe. "I think I have a hard head."

"Good thing you do," Grayson said. "I'm going to make sure you're fitted for a helmet."

"Is that before or after you show me how to use a gun?" Then she remembered how Murford fell on her, sending her onto the pavement. "Is he dead?"

"Yes."

"Another life wasted. Were they there to kill him or nab me?" She took a breath. "Or both?"

"His body protected you. A single sniper shot."

She moved her head and moaned.

"They have pain meds for you."

How different from the first time, when he denied her relief. "I want to talk first."

"We have plenty of time for chitchat later." Grayson's voice sounded more tender than she could ever remember.

"Chitchat?"

"Listen to the man, Taryn," Joe said. "He's wiser than he looks."

She closed her eyes and willed away the sledgehammer in her skull. "I tried to get him to provide names and places."

"You did a fine job. The SSA may recruit you yet."

With the trouble slamming against her from every direction, she doubted the SSA would offer anything but an invitation to stay away. "What about Zoey? He made a call in the restaurant, and I saw a video of her."

"Agents were able to trace her location from Murford's phone."

She wanted to sit up, question him more. "Are they on their way?"

"Yes. As soon as I hear from the team, so will you."

"How long?"

"Depends. It's a cabin on the outskirts of Huntsville State Park."

The video of Zoey had looked like a rustic setting. "Was there anything else recorded the FBI could use?"

"Honestly, I don't know. We found a consistent number to New York City."

"I don't think Murford had a reason to lie about the bombing. If anything—" A gush of pain swept across her head.

"Hey, no more talk."

"Not yet. I'm waiting for the call about the hacking job. What more can you tell me?"

Grayson frowned, but he'd get over her non-compliance. "We learned Vince has been paying his son's gambling debts, and his son needs a heart transplant. Vince had met with Murford at least once. You know, I shouldn't be telling you this."

"I can keep a secret." She closed her eyes. "I also need to figure out Ethan's password."

"Laurel's working on it."

But Agent Evertson wasn't her, and she knew Ethan's eccentric personality. "I'm sure I'll be fine after a nap."

"It's the second concussion this week," Grayson said. "You need to rest and heal."

She ignored him. "I'm in the ER. Is there an officer at the door?"

Joe laughed.

"No. Two agents," Grayson said.

"Have you warned them?"

He chuckled. "Do you plan on going somewhere?"

His words brought back the afternoon and evening of the bombing, instantly sobering her. "Why are they there? What's happened?"

"A call came in . . . threatening you. We're going to make a transport as soon as the doctor clears you."

"Back to your office?"

He shook his head. "You'll find out." His face softened. "When this is over—"

"I owe you dinner." *Please, Grayson, not yet.*

"But not Tony's."

She offered a timid smile. Did he remember everything she said? "Do you know how long I'll be here?"

Grayson glanced toward the door, then back to her. "I heard testing before you'd be dismissed. About four or five hours."

Did she dare state the overwhelming fear? Or was it the pain stomping on her courage?

"Hey, I see panic in your eyes." He took her hand, and she let him. "When you're able, take a look at your wristband. It's an assumed name."

"Thank you."

"No worries. The agents are Clint and Patti. Clint's the young guy with all the muscles, and

Patti's a redhead. Knows her stuff. They're the best, and you're safe."

"I appreciate all you've done."

"Remember, I taught him most everything he knows," Joe said.

Grayson grinned, but he didn't turn to his uncle. "Anything else bothering you?"

"I need details on the hacking job."

He nodded slowly. "Nearly forgot about that. A bank account's been set up with your alias."

"Write it down for me. My mind's mush."

He jotted the bank, name, and number on a notepad.

"You have plenty of things to do besides babysitting me," she said. "Why don't you and Joe work on what you do best. I know you'll call the moment you hear about Zoey. You don't want to make me angry. I have a reputation for being testy in hospitals."

Grayson's BlackBerry indicated a notification, capturing his attention.

As he read, she watched his face, which didn't tell her a thing. "What's going on?"

"Just following leads from the closed-door congressional meeting. It will take days."

"The conspiracy could have a wide range of participants."

"Yes, ma'am."

"Are you making fun of me?"

"Every chance I get."

She did like this man. The cell phone assigned to her rang. She caught his gaze, and he handed it to her.

"Julie Harmon?" a woman said.

"Speaking."

"I understand you have the skills I need." The voice was muffled. Now to keep the caller on the line.

"Depends. What are you looking for?"

"Let's not dance around this."

Taryn blew out her exasperation. "My expertise is accessing technological information."

"How good are you?"

"Top of the charts. Do you want a résumé?"

"Not really. You came recommended."

"I've shown him up a few times."

"Are you ready to go to work?"

"How much?"

"Fifty grand."

The same amount deposited into her banking account after the bombing.

"What's the deadline?"

"Yesterday."

"How do I contact you?"

"Through our mutual friend."

"Easy enough. How do I get the assignment?"

"Same venue. He'll give you the instructions."

"I need ten grand up front to get started."

The caller swore. "Five. I need the job done now."

"No deal."

"All right, ten. Give the account information to our friend. Keep your mouth shut or you won't live to regret it."

"Been there before, and I don't scare easily."

The call disconnected. She glanced at Grayson, who'd heard every word. "If this isn't our case, then we'll bust open a new one," he said.

But all she could think about was one more person threatening her life before she found Zoey. Grayson's eyes confirmed what she suspected and questioned about herself. Her heart had fallen prey to the man before her.

Chapter 38

12:10 p.m. Wednesday

Grayson shouted, "Yes!" Heads turned in the op room, but he waved them away. The call Taryn received had an origin in New York City, another connect to the recent intel. Agents were working on defining the location. The caller had slipped, possibly eager to secure the hacking deal.

He scooted his chair back and stared into the computer screen. According to the call Taryn received, the buyer had a time stamp on access to the software. Possibly Friday morning's launch date of exporting LNG? Did the bombing fit? He scanned through the hundreds of notations about the LNG companies in Kitimat and Corpus Christi. Although industries that used natural gas wouldn't want to see prices rise, would any of them resort to the measures seen in the past few days? The lengths had taken time, money, and superior planning. If he only had the opportunity to get into the heads of the thousands of agents working this case. Most of them probably felt the same way. Experts were running data through software designed to show stats and probability.

Murford claimed he could have been a victim at the airport. His role was to give Taryn's devices to Breckon before the departure. Pedraza said he wasn't involved either. The key rested in the hands of whoever hired Taryn to hack into her own project. His gut told him, like so many other agents on this case, that the two crimes were connected.

But his and Joe's assignment was working through this case with Taryn. She needed more than a few hours in the hospital after the week's trauma. Knowing her, she'd request a laptop before the day was over.

His mind focused on the morning's shooting, connecting the dots. He sensed Joe's eyes on him.

"Your mind is racing," Joe said. "I want to hear it."

Grayson nodded. "The bullet that killed Murford came from the rooftop of an area several hundred feet behind Denny's."

"Your point?"

Grayson grabbed his keys. "Joe, did you see the caliber of rifle used today?"

"A 7mm. Sniper or military style. I'm betting somebody saw our killer."

"Let's take a ride to Denny's."

"Our guys are there."

"But we're not," Grayson said. "There's a back way out of the strip center."

"It leads to a one-way street. I'm sure agents have questioned everyone."

"Never stopped me before."

Joe shifted his jacket. "You're so much like me it's scary. Must be why we work good together."

At Denny's, yellow tape blocked off the crime scene. Grayson whipped his Mustang to the small retail stores behind the restaurant—nail salon, pawnshop, real estate office, bakery, and shoe repair store. Although those who'd been at their businesses had already been interviewed, fresh questions could stir up something new.

Only one gal in the nail salon spoke English, and she was terrified. The pawnshop owner hadn't seen anything. The manager of the real estate office said no one got there before nine o'clock. The bakery owner offered them each coffee and a doughnut.

By the time they walked into the shoe repair shop, Grayson had about given up. A teen with Down syndrome greeted them. He wore a name tag that read *Luke*.

"Is the owner available?" Grayson said and pulled out his badge. "We're from the FBI."

Luke paled. "I'll . . . I'll get my grandpa."

An older man wearing an Astros baseball cap walked from the back of the shop. "Yes, sir, how can I help you?"

After Grayson introduced himself and Joe, he got right to the crime. "I know other agents have been here this morning after the shooting at Denny's, but I have another question for you."

"I didn't see a thing," the man said. "I was working in the back."

"There's an alley behind your shop. Did you happen to hear or see anyone right after the shooting?"

The older man shook his head. "Actually, I hadn't put in my hearing aid yet, so I can't help you."

Luke paced the area behind the counter.

"Do you have information for these agents?" the man said, his tone soft and gentle.

Luke stopped. "I was afraid I'd done something bad when the other men were here."

The older man placed a hand on Luke's shoulder. "If you know something that can help these agents, you'd be a hero."

"A hero?"

"Yes, son," Joe said.

Luke swallowed. "I was taking out the trash 'cause that's one of my jobs. I heard a shot from the roof and hid on the other side of the Dumpster.

A man jumped from the roof onto a truck bed, then got into it and raced away." Luke's eyes widened. "It was like a movie."

This could be the edge they were looking for. "Can you describe the truck?" Grayson said.

"I . . . I can do better than that." He held out his palm, where he'd written a license plate number. "I was going to show it to my grandpa later." He pointed to his shirt pocket. "Grandpa says to always carry a pen. Never know when you might need it." He pulled a cell phone from his jeans pocket. "I took a picture of the truck too."

Chapter 39

12:45 p.m. Wednesday

Taryn woke in a stupor that reminded her of a few days ago in a different hospital, where the nightmare had begun. She climbed her way through the haze to think, but not about what happened to Murford because she'd already decided his assassination was up to the FBI to figure out. Instead she prayed for Zoey, like she'd done so many times since Claire was killed.

Desperation settled on her. Lying in a hospital bed without computer access made her feel useless . . . helpless.

Her mind rested on Grayson, the kind of man heroes were made from. He'd apologized for not being at the restaurant parking lot this morning when his job assignment had been something other than her bodyguard. When had the attraction crept in? Had she betrayed her wedding vows? But she hadn't really been married. The love that embraced her girlhood dreams last Sunday afternoon had turned to loathing. She regretted Phillip Murford had lost his life, but she felt no intense grief. The emotional tie to him had died when she realized he was a liar and a killer. How could she ever heal from such deceit? Sounded like weeks in therapy, but she was alive to learn from her mistake. Her dogged determination to always rise above her circumstances held her firm—a gift from God.

Mentally shaking her confusion about what the future held, she turned her attention to unlocking Ethan's password, the one hidden in plain sight. That was her goal at this moment, but her head needed to clear, and she must manage the pain without sleep-inducing drugs.

She thought back through Ethan's last few e-mails. She'd memorized some of the key words—*dots, Nehemiah, wedding, connect, document, bugs, protect, danger,* and the puzzling phrase "Every thirty days life changes." From past conversations, she knew Ethan's wife had the passwords for their personal files. But he'd stated that his wife didn't know how he secured his business files. Where? His computer at Gated

Labs that had been mirrored by the FBI or his laptop at home? He'd never gone anywhere without his iPad, but that must have been destroyed in the bombing. She focused on Ethan's personality: fiercely loyal to family. He refused to talk to them about his projects, claimed they wouldn't understand the technical jargon and it would bore them. That meant the passwords were connected to his office, where the right people could have access.

I need a computer.

She hesitated to move, remembering the agony from her last concussion. Using the landline on her nightstand meant enduring the torment. How nice if pain meds wouldn't put her to sleep. The door in the right corner of the room was closed, and two FBI agents guarded her. She assumed the nightstand sat on the right too. Slowly she turned, moaning all the way. Pulling the phone to her, she pressed in Grayson's new number.

"This is your friendly software developer," she said.

"And you sound like you're drunk."

"If I were a drinking woman, I'd be tempted to drink a whole bottle." She closed her eyes and willed away the hammering. "Could someone bring me a laptop?"

"After you've rested."

"Grayson, please, I want to work on Ethan's password."

He sighed, and she knew it was for dramatic effect. "Do I need to remind you this is the second head trauma of the week? I'm surprised you can function."

"I do have a bedpan." Why did she say that! "Delete my last remark."

He chuckled. "You've proved my point. This is SA Hall on behalf of your medical team. Sleep until you're moved, and we'll talk about work tomorrow. If you're good, I might bring you a bunch of bananas and almond butter."

"How can I resist? Have you found Zoey?"

"I would have called."

Her spirits plummeted. "Have you arrested Murford's killer?"

"Hmm. Who are you going to tell?"

"Who do I know?"

"All right, but keep it to yourself. The media coordinator is putting together an update on the situation. So until then, this is between you and me."

"Got it."

"A hired assassin. We have a name and a BOLO for him."

How deep did this go? "Someone who worked for Murford?"

"Not Murford's caliber. International type."

She wished she could think more clearly. "How many people are involved?"

"We've all suspected Murford worked for someone else."

"So if the sniper was hired, then he knows how to stay hidden."

"Yes, Special Agent Young."

"Pass on your recommendation to the SSA."

"But that's all you're getting until I'm assured you've taken a nap."

"Yes, sir. Don't forget the bananas, almond butter, and Fritos."

"I never mentioned Fritos."

"Of course you did. See you later." She hung up the phone and tried to stay awake. Hidden in plain sight . . . What did Ethan have on his desk?

1:20 p.m. Wednesday

Grayson stuffed the last onion ring into his mouth and picked up his double cheeseburger.

"Have you ever tried mixing your food?" Joe took a long drink from his Sonic slush. They sat at a picnic table outside the fast-food restaurant.

How many times had Joe asked this? As if Grayson had any intentions of changing his eating habits. "Nope. One thing at a time so I can enjoy the whole experience."

"It all goes down the same hatch."

"It's mixed where I don't have control." Grayson took his first drink of Coke Zero.

Joe wagged a finger at him. "Control. I should have known. All these years I thought it was simply being picky."

Grayson grinned. "Truthfully, Mom got me started on it when she insisted I eat my vegetables before I tasted the food I liked. The habit stuck."

"A wise woman."

"I agree. We lost a saint." Grayson had other things to discuss, which weren't about his mother. He couldn't do a thing about her death, but he could help solve and prevent crimes. "Got a report from the agents who tailed Aaron Bradshaw after he left the office."

"What did you learn?"

"He visited a bank. Came out mad. Probably looking for funds in his dad's account to pay his gambling debts."

"What else?" Joe had indicated earlier he'd been upset with some of Aaron's responses today. "He's about the most immature thirty-year-old I've ever seen."

"He met with one of his gambling buddies, a lowlife from downtown," Grayson said. "The guy grabbed Aaron by the throat."

"Not good. Any leads to our case?"

"Nothing. Aaron's health and his gambling addiction are going to kill him if he doesn't make some changes," Grayson said. "Vince deserves whatever he gets for turning on us, but I don't see anything ahead but bitterness if Aaron's no longer on the scene."

"Glad to hear you're not holding a grudge."

"I hope I'm bigger than that. Hey, we made

headway today," Grayson said. Identifying Murford's killer brought another player into the mix.

"What do you think about our sniper? Or rather, who do you think he works for?"

"I've tried to speculate with reliable information," Grayson said. "Cameron Wallace works internationally. He's thorough and clean, and his profile is not the stereotypical assassin. No history of being a recluse or loser. Never been evaluated for mental issues. Did some postgrad work in statistics at Oxford. Left the school and entered the world as an assassin. No one ever sees where he comes from or where he goes. Of course, no one lives to tell their story."

"High-dollar killer."

"Makes me wonder if he's taken credit for assassinations he hasn't committed. But this morning he was a bit sloppy. He took a huge risk by riding in a speeding truck down that alley, but risk taking is a part of his portfolio."

"He hasn't built a reputation on being stupid."

"He's calculating, and I doubt he was hired at the last minute. I've asked the FIG to give us a dossier on his confirmed past kills." Grayson paused to put together what he did know. "Wallace must have hijacked the truck, since the vehicle was found east of town, and the driver had a bullet in his head."

"What about the driver?"

"Twenty-year-old student." Grayson pointed to his BlackBerry. "Info came in while we were talking." He pulled up another report listing every victim attributed to Wallace. The assassin's employers weren't quick to list him on their payroll. "Looks like his usual stomping ground is Europe, and he's not picky where his money comes from. Intel says he's killed in the US and Mexico too. Suspected employers have come from the Middle East, Russia, South America, and North Korea."

"Middle East," Joe said. "Like the suspected bomber."

"That makes sense. Most countries know how to hide terrorism because we'd pull aid." But Grayson wanted to delve deeper into the situation. Look for a connection. Although the Middle East had his biggest vote, he wouldn't rest until he found the answer.

Chapter 40

5:30 p.m. Wednesday

Taryn woke to the clang of meal trays. One look at the hospital's dietary special, and she turned up her nose—meat loaf, mashed potatoes, green beans with bacon, a fruit cup, and a slice of chocolate cake. That would teach her to sleep through filling out the day's menu. Okay, she

could eat the fruit and hope Grayson remembered the bananas, almond butter, and Fritos. Who
said a vegan had to neglect junk food? Iced tea
never appealed to her, so she reached for the
glass of water.

No word about Zoey. *Lord, I won't sink into
depression. I vowed to trust You.*

The pain in her head had eased. She concentrated on how to access Ethan's files and
allowed the password possibilities to float through
her mind. She reached for a pad of paper and pen
on her nightstand. The best way to see what was
in plain sight was to imagine being in his office.

On his desk sat a photo of his family. The first
letters of each of their names came to mind.
Although that idea ranked between too common
and dangerous, she jotted it down anyway, then
backward. She tried the same with Formier. With
each arrangement, she also assigned numbers
according to where the letters fell in the alphabet
and then backward. She listed the other items on
his desk—a lamp, phone, computer, notepad,
coaster, and a picture of his chocolate Lab, M&M.
Using birthdays made little sense, but she could
find out his family's and arrange and rearrange
those numbers.

She started another list—where he was married,
vacation spots, first car, name of high school,
college, grad school, and where he'd worked. . . .
All of the answers would have to come from his

wife. What else? Ethan liked to mix things up. He told jokes and loved classic movies, often reciting lines. He had a ranch in the hill country, a getaway for him and his family. A caretaker there oversaw the grounds and fed twenty head of cattle and two horses. Something there, or too obvious? She'd play with all his idiosyncrasies once she had her hands on a laptop.

She envisioned the tall, slim man with streaks of gray hair and piercing eyes. *Ethan, what did you mean by "hiding in plain sight"?*

"You don't look like you're napping to me."

She perked at the sound of Grayson's voice. He leaned against the door of the hospital room.

"I slept for hours, and now I'm working on Ethan's password." She drew in a sharp breath. "Zoey?"

He sat, shoulders slumped, and she steadied herself for the worst. "Looks like she'd been at the cabin with a woman. Clothes were found indicating so. Agents are searching the area, sweeping for fingerprints and DNA."

"If a woman has her, then I can hope Zoey is okay." A woman might show some maternal instinct that would help keep the little girl safe.

"They left in a hurry. Milk in the fridge. A box of mac and cheese on the counter."

"Good," she whispered. "You brought me hope."

He kept his chair at a proper distance. "How's the head?"

"Better than before."

"But you're frowning."

"That's because I'm hungry, and I don't have a laptop."

He peered at her supper tray. "I can see why." He set a Kroger plastic bag on the bed. "Organic bananas and almond butter and Fritos."

"Heaven has come to earth. Help yourself."

"I've eaten." Grayson pulled a single banana from the bag and handed it to her. He unscrewed the lid to the almond butter. "Want me to stir it?"

"Please, Chef Hall. And thank you." She reached for a spoon on her tray, noting he stirred the almond butter better than she did.

"Do you want it smeared over a banana?"

"Yes, please. You know my weakness."

A flash of something crossed his face, but she refused to comment.

Once her tummy was satisfied, she studied him. Tired lines fanned from his eyes. "How's Joe?"

"Good. He spent some time late this afternoon with an insurance adjuster."

She cringed. "Did they board up his windows?"

"Yesterday."

She took a long drink of her water. "Does my mom know I'm all right?"

He nodded. "We had an agent pay her a visit. Explain you are safe and not to worry."

"Thanks." She wiped the Frito crumbs from her bedding. "I've got a concern."

"A new one?"

She adored his teasing grin. "How do you sleep when cases are like spiderwebs?"

Grayson moved his chair closer, and she welcomed it, though she'd not admit that. "We can't solve this tonight. In fact, we're two small players. Tomorrow, when you're feeling better, we can explore what you can do. Right now let's talk about you, which is an amusing topic."

"I can't think of any other childhood stories. Unless you're analyzing me."

He gave her a thumbs-up. "I'm just making conversation."

She allowed herself a glimpse into his blue eyes. Again feelings rose in her she wasn't ready or willing to address. "Okay. I'll give you a little insight into what you already know. My two older brothers are incredibly talented, successful, outgoing, and good-looking. I'm the youngest. My parents wanted a girl so badly, and then they got me."

"I don't understand."

She shook her head. "I was born a total introvert—very socially backward."

"But you've always seemed comfortable with me."

She'd heard that before from a man who'd betrayed her. But it wasn't fair to compare the two. "You'd be singing another tune if you'd seen the lack of social skills in my younger days."

"Can't even imagine it." He drew in a breath. "Anyone ever tell you that your hair is the color of sunset?"

She sensed a slow blush rising from her neck.

"Hey, I've embarrassed you. Sorry."

"No problem. Anyway, I suffered through a painful adolescence and became engrossed in school. So I pursued my dream of developing software to help industries and companies do a better job."

"Good choice. Were you looking for a husband when Murford stepped onto the scene?"

"Absolutely not. Some of my high school days left a few scars." She swallowed to gain control of her emotions. "I should have known better with Murford. No one's that perfect."

"You're wiser for the next time."

She hoped so. "Now tell me about you. From the conversation at Joe's house, I gather you and your father have issues."

Grayson tossed her banana peel onto the meal tray. "Lots of issues."

"What about your mom?"

"She's dead."

"I'm so sorry."

"It was a long time ago. Her death is part of the problem." He stuffed his hands into his jeans pockets. "Are you sure you want to hear this?"

"You heard my story, and what else are we going to talk about?" She tilted her head. "I'm a good listener."

He hesitated, no doubt thinking through his decision. "Okay, here's the whole story. I had a twin who died at birth, and I was scrawny and sickly. Had asthma until I grew out of it." He paced at the foot of her bed. "Dad wasn't happy to have a wimp for a son, especially when my older brother was a replica of a Marine. When I was eight, Mom and I were driving home from Little League practice. A storm blew in, along with a twister." His brows narrowed. "Mom pulled under an overpass, and we climbed up a bank to the narrow area where the concrete bracing was built into the ground. She shoved me in, but there wasn't room for her. The tornado came through." Moistening his lips, he stared out the window. "I held her hand as long as I could."

Taryn wanted to reach for him. How horrible for a child.

"Her body was found a mile away. My dad never got over it. Still blames me. Go figure why. Anyway, our relationship is not good. Dad's now an ex-Marine, and my older brother is a lifer there. I chose to follow in Uncle Joe's career path, and that made things worse."

"How old were you when you went to live with him?"

"Fifteen. Joe's a man's man. Believes in God,

country, and the FBI." He smiled. "He's the best thing that ever happened to me."

"Sounds like a great ending."

He stared at her, and heat rose in her face again. "We make choices, Taryn. The good ones we hold on to, and the bad ones we learn from."

"And your faith has helped you deal with the problems?"

"It doesn't make the issues disappear, but it's good to know I'm not walking this life alone."

She understood what Grayson meant. Since her renewal of faith a few nights ago, she'd sensed God's presence wherever she went. Would He be there if she were killed? If she discovered Zoey had not survived?

Grayson's BlackBerry rang, and she turned to give him privacy.

"Sure. We can do it." He disconnected the call. "Pedraza's talking. He said the ones who want the software can trace you anywhere. We've got to move and figure out how they're doing it."

Chapter 41

6:15 p.m. Wednesday

Less than an hour later, Grayson walked with Taryn into a retirement center complex. Special Agents Clint and Patti were already there with Buddy.

She hugged the German shepherd as though he

were a long-lost friend. "Thank you for bringing him. Oh, he smells so good." Her eyes watered. "And he's put on a little weight. Please thank whoever's been taking care of him. I know it doesn't make sense to be so attached to a dog this soon, but I am."

Grayson felt the same way about her. He pointed to Joe. "His idea." He glanced around the small apartment equipped for a senior citizen. "Guess you won't be falling."

Joe chuckled. "This has more safety features than a hospital room."

"Very funny." Taryn stroked Buddy. "Whose idea was it to move me out of the room as a corpse?" Her humor was intact, but her face was white as a sheet.

Grayson held up a finger. "Guilty."

"The ride to the funeral home?"

"Guilty."

"And the ride here in Joe's blue beauty?"

"Me again."

She laughed and sank onto the couch. "That one's a keeper."

Grayson couldn't resist the urge to tease. "It was the first time you were quiet since we met."

"I'll get even," Taryn said. "After I take a nap and develop a good plan."

"Don't mind them," Patti said. "I have a laptop for you. We women have to stick together. Especially us redheads."

"Two questions," Taryn said. "Number one—is this arrangement permanent, or will I be returning to the FBI office?"

Grayson knew she wouldn't like the answer. "Here, until we have the situation resolved."

"In the eyes of the media, am I still a person of interest?"

Grayson rubbed his palms together. "Yes."

"When that changes, will the record show I helped with the investigation, and will the media be notified?"

"I imagine so, but the media is cruel. Your innocence isn't hot news. Your potential guilt is what the readers and listeners want."

"Okay. I figured the same. Anyway, I have a list of sites to check, and I appreciate the laptop."

He wanted to go to her side, but he needed to keep his distance. "You'll be working on accessing Formier's password, monitoring the hacker job, and behaving yourself."

"As in, I can't take advantage of the pool with all the senior citizens?"

"Not unless you dye your hair white and look eighty years old." Grayson knew she wouldn't rest until Zoey was found. But each hour that passed without signs of the little girl decreased the chances she was still alive.

Taryn's burner phone rang, and she answered it. "I thought you'd call before now."

She mouthed *Save* to Grayson.

"What's the assignment?" She wrapped a finger around an auburn strand of hair. "You what? Worked on it a while longer before calling me? I was offered big bucks for this."

Grayson studied her face. She'd make a good agent.

"So did you get in?" She laughed. "Face it. You need my nimble fingers and quick mind. What is this about?" Her gaze flew to Grayson. "So what's the problem that they can't get into the software?" She listened. "Why the deadline? Got it." She disconnected the call.

"Is it Nehemiah?" Grayson said.

"Absolutely. Friday morning at six is the deadline. So glad I enabled it. Whatever's going down happens around then. I can drag my feet, but Save has made substantial progress. I have no doubt he'll gain access very soon, but it will destroy his computer."

"Good. And it's not Friday yet," Grayson said. "More people are working on this case than you can imagine. I'm standing on those odds."

Chapter 42

New York
9:10 p.m. Eastern, Wednesday

What is wrong with these stupid people? I pace. I scream. I swear. They're supposed to be the best money can buy, and they perform like amateurs. Every member of Murford's team has been arrested or is dead except one woman. Now I don't know where they've taken Young . . . but Save and his hacker friend will have access to the software before the deadline. I have to believe it or I'll explode. When Nehemiah is mine, I want Young beaten, tortured, and killed.

My phone rings and I see it's him. His last call still burns my ears. I'm not a coward, but I regret this arrangement. If I'm not careful, he'll cheat me out of my share. I answer the phone.

"Is the bombing at IAH still fresh in your mind?" he says.

"Yes."

"Do you want to know why it happened?"

The whole world wants the answer to his question. He never says anything unless he backs it up with something . . . deadly. My opinion was he wanted to stroke his ego and show he could mastermind the explosion. "I suppose to shift attention from LNG to a national tragedy."

"Close, but not entirely accurate."

"Why then?" *Tell me so I can survive this deal gone south.*

"It's a symbol. Number one is how I feel about Americans. All of you deserve to die, and I'm committed to making it happen. But you knew my sentiments when we started this. The bombing of terminal E is what I'll do to you if this fails. Your money, your reputation, your high-rise building will crumble. You'll spend the rest of your life in solitary confinement . . . if you live past the trial. My web of people is endless. Does that inspire you, Iris?"

He ends the call before I can respond.

I'm not a quitter, and I will bulldoze this junk heap. What if he goes down first? If I shoot him in self-defense, I'll be a hero in the eyes of the free world. He claims to be in Europe, but I'm smarter than he thinks. He's not going to guard his pot of gold from anywhere but the good old US. He's in Houston, and I'm going to find him. Eliminate him before he pulls the trigger on me.

I make arrangements to get to Houston's Hobby Airport on the next flight out, then fly out of the country late tomorrow night from Dallas. Can't trust IAH with the extra security measures. He won't expect me. Either way, I win.

Chapter 43

10:45 p.m. Wednesday

At the FBI office, Grayson studied surveillance footage from the airport, before and after the bombing. Much of it he'd reviewed before. He was a single grain of sand on an investigative beach. So many agents had gone through these, but the more eyes, the better the chances of finding evidence. The photographs with Murford and Taryn had been enhanced by manipulating the angle, zoom, frame rate, and resolution. Another set of pics of the van used to house the fertilizer bomb had indicated a woman drove it into the parking garage, but she'd avoided the cameras.

The community had rallied by sending personal photographs from the bombing, sharing Facebook, Twitter, and other social media information, and anonymously phoning in information. All would be reviewed by the HPD, the FBI, or any of the dozens of local, state, and federal agencies that had joined the investigation.

He stole a look at Joe, who needed to be in bed. On Tuesday, Joe had phoned the SSA and volunteered to assist when Grayson and Taryn needed a brief reprieve—before Murford's men shot up his and Grayson's home. Now it would take a crowbar to pry Joe out of the office. But the heavy pace aged him.

"How about me dropping you off at the hotel?" Grayson said.

Joe peered at him over his bifocals. "I might have something."

Grayson stared at his uncle's computer monitor. "Is that Kinsley Stevens's Facebook page?"

"Yep. I figure if she's innocent, she posts everything. And if she's guilty, she'd have a private page." Joe clicked on photos. "Pay dirt."

Grayson viewed the screen over his uncle's shoulder. "Haden Rollins is in quite a few of them."

"Take a look at the face in the background of this happy hour scene."

"Blow it up."

Joe clicked the mouse and slapped the desk. "It's Dina Dancer, and I recognize the Marriott bar. Kinsley Stevens and Haden Rollins are part of the party."

"Blow up this other one. Looks like it was taken at the same place." Grayson examined each shadow and face. A man's outline near the bar grasped his attention. "Is that Murford and Breckon?"

"Sure looks like them," Joe said. "Do we have a family reunion here?"

"Definitely a few black sheep. Send those

photos for analysis." Grayson sat and crossed his legs. "Kinsley Stevens is no airhead. She wouldn't post pics that could potentially get her into trouble, either with a law enforcement agency or the bad guys. Makes me wonder if she was caught up in something a whole lot bigger than wanting Taryn's job and sleeping with Rollins."

Joe did a Facebook search. "His information is private except for those he invites. But I know how to get around his settings."

Grayson chuckled. "Are you taking hacking lessons from Taryn?"

"I'm old, not senile." Joe squinted at the screen. "Nothing. Rollins's page is just a place marker. Didn't the bartender at the Marriott claim he'd never seen Murford?"

"Right. And we didn't find anything on their cameras either. But it wouldn't be the first time security camera footage came up missing."

"Be interesting to ask him if he's seen any of the other people in those photos."

Grayson frowned. "But you should be in bed. I'll get another agent to go with me."

"Are you kidding? Miss the fun? How can a man sleep with questions slamming against his brain?"

Grayson stood. "All right, Captain America. We'll shake up the bartender's memory. While we're driving, I want to talk more about Haden Rollins."

• • •
11:30 p.m. Wednesday

Grayson parked his Mustang in a spot near the bar area of the Southwest Marriott. Nothing had turned up on Dina Dancer—a clear indicator of no record, at least under that name. He and Joe made their way inside, where a dozen people lounged in the small area. They sat at the farthest end of the bar, where they could face the entrance.

Grayson waved at the bartender. "Remember us?"

The bald man scowled. "What now? The last time you were here, I lost a waitress."

"This time we have a few pics for you to identify. You're in one of them."

The man tossed his bar rag. "Show me."

Grayson pulled up Kinsley Stevens's Facebook page. "We need help here, and this time we want cooperation. Unless you'd prefer an arrest for withholding information from a federal investigation."

The man took the BlackBerry and looked at the photo. "The others met here a few times. Always used the back door. I didn't ask questions. Figured they didn't want to be seen. But not her." He pointed to Kinsley. "Only remember her once."

"You must have overheard a few comments."

"Look, I gave you what you wanted. I don't need to end up in a box."

"Then you heard what they were up to."

He inhaled sharply. "They sat in the back. Huddled together. All I did was make sure their drinks were filled."

"Something spooked you."

He muttered a curse. "I have work to do."

Grayson leaned on the bar. "We'll wait."

"I have no idea what they were up to. I heard the mention of big money and working the plan."

"Anyone else ever join them?"

"No."

"When's the last time they were here?"

"Saturday night at closing. Dina served them, and they all left together."

Grayson replaced his BlackBerry. "Two of the people who were in the photo are now dead."

His eyes widened. "Look, I don't know anything."

Grayson focused on Joe. "I think we got what we came after."

Joe grinned at the bartender. "Thank you, sir. In case you haven't figured it out, don't leave town."

Once Grayson was en route to their hotel and had processed what they'd learned, he swung his attention to Joe. "You're quiet. So tell me what you're thinking."

"Nice to think an old man can still provide input."

Grayson laughed, and it felt good. "We have a connect."

"And two of them are dead. Which one of those left is pulling the strings?"

"Neither."

"Yep. I think Murford was in charge. Rollins may be living on borrowed time." Joe paused. "Our Facebook gal may be okay. But she needs to get those pics off her page."

"I'm calling her now." Grayson handed Joe his phone. "Pull up her number for me."

A few moments later, a sleepy woman answered.

"Kinsley Stevens, this is FBI Special Agent Grayson Hall. We spoke at Gated Labs and at our office."

"Why are you calling me?"

"Are you alone?"

"Yes." Her voice grew stronger.

"You have incriminating photos on your Face-book page."

"I don't understand. All I have are personal ones."

"We are familiar with the posted photos. For your safety, we suggest you remove those with Haden Rollins taken at the Southwest Marriott lounge."

"Why? That's ridiculous."

"Two of the people in those photos are dead."

She gasped. "I'll do it now."

"Understand the wrong people could have already accessed the photos."

"What should I do?" Panic rose in her words.

"Consider laying low, maybe staying with a

friend, but the FBI will need to know your whereabouts."

"Okay. Are you contacting Haden?"

"Yes." Grayson was itching to talk to the man. After thanking the woman, he had Joe find Rollins's number.

The phone rang four times and rolled over to voice mail.

He hit redial three times.

They'd make one more stop before checking into the hotel.

Chapter 44

1:30 a.m. Thursday

After agreeing to meet Joe at 7 a.m. for breakfast, Grayson unlocked his hotel room. Rollins hadn't answered his condo's door, so now they needed to see if he reported to Gated Labs in the morning. Kinsley could have lied, and Rollins was with her, but Grayson didn't think that was the case.

The bed seemed to call Grayson's name, and he'd already checked on Taryn. He wanted to spend the night on the couch at the retirement center, but job performance meant sleep and a strong focus on working through the case. He typed an e-mail to the office about tonight's findings and tried to unwind. In the darkness, his mind whirled like an EF5 tornado.

If only he could download into his brain the data from the thousands of minds working on this case. His assignment from the start had been Taryn and Murford, and life hadn't slowed since.

He snapped on the light and reached for his phone to make a few notes.

1. Who gains when oil prices go up?
2. Who loses when oil prices plummet?
3. Does anyone stand to gain in either case?

As soon as the questions were typed into his BlackBerry, the answers hit him. Oil traders. Wall Street. New York City. He checked, and agents were already on it. No great revelation there.

Calls from Vince and Murford traced to the same number in New York, a burner phone. Could an oil and gas trader stoop so low as to steal software for personal gain? And how did that theory fit into the bombing? Could the explosion have been a diversion or part one of an ultimate plan? Pretty far out there.

Why blow up a terminal to eliminate Taryn and Murford? A sniper could have easily taken care of them. Grayson could count Ethan Formier as a third person connected to the software, but his death was circumstantial. Or so some thought. No other persons had hit the radar in the investigation. Bewildering, while the public cried out for arrests.

God, I need You in this. Those responsible for

taking lives and destroying property must be brought to justice.

Grayson breathed in and out. . . . *Relax.* His mind slowly weighed the possibilities. What if the Middle Eastern signature held no credibility? Other homegrown terrorists had used fertilizer bombs, like Timothy McVeigh in Oklahoma City.

What if the signature was a deflection from the who and the motivation? He typed into his BlackBerry and read the many reports surfacing from the investigation. Specialized agents worked the same theory. They needed a link—a name, US companies, or a country that would benefit from the US not being able to export LNG. Obviously Russia didn't want their economy damaged, but they weren't that stupid.

He speculated on oil and gas traders. They were ruthless cutthroats and able to cover their tracks. He lay back on the pillow, ready to go after the complexity of the bombing from a new angle.

9:30 a.m. Thursday

Taryn woke groggy and ready to roll over and go back to sleep until she saw the clock. Twelve hours. She hadn't slept so long in years. The drapes were drawn and the room incredibly dark. Not at all like her condo, where she kept the drapes open wide for sunshine to stream through. Buddy slept on a rug beside the bed. How kind for the agents to have the dog there for her.

Like a flash flood, all the happenings since Sunday rolled over her, and a wave of panic clutched her chest. So many horrible tragedies, and none had been solved. She shuddered at the thought of the many people involved in an attempt to gain access to Nehemiah. Now Save thought he was close, but she'd designed numerous layers. Was he smart enough to see how she'd built the firewall?

I can't do this alone. But I'm not. . . . God will walk with me through this nightmare.

She climbed from the bed and opened the bedroom door. Two different agents were in the kitchen and living room area. She said good morning and turned to the shower, already imagining the warm spray relaxing her battered flesh. She'd wash her hair and be careful of the stitches, then slip into some clean clothes and grab a cup of coffee with the laptop. What a wonderful thought without fear of anything. She'd contribute something today other than another concussion.

In less than an hour, she e-mailed Grayson.

Grayson,

I feel so much better, and I'm ready to discover Ethan's password. I plan to spend half the day working on it. Then I'll delve into the hacking job. Will Special Agent Laurel Evertson contact me?

I appreciate all you've done to help me.

Please give Joe my best and thank him again for sending Buddy.

Taryn

She typed in a question about when he'd visit, but deleted it. A friend, yes. Nothing more. The only reason she'd become dependent on him was because he'd saved her life. And if she believed that, she might as well consider herself legally insane.

She fed Buddy, and one of the agents took him outside for a walk. With two cups of coffee and a bowl of dry granola and fresh fruit, she dug into the task. The agents assigned to her kept to themselves. A good thing because if they were Clint and Patti, she'd want to chat. People meant more to her now, and getting to know them mattered—from their distinct personalities to how they felt about life.

She pushed her wandering thoughts into a mental box and focused on Ethan. Her list of possible words and numbers began, and by the process of elimination, each one brought her closer to what she hoped was the answer.

When her burner phone rang, she recognized the FBI number.

"Taryn, this is Special Agent Laurel Evertson. Grayson told you about me?"

She remembered the attractive woman with short blonde hair and huge brown eyes. "Yes. I'm working on Ethan Formier's computer password and could use your help."

"Let's dig in."

"You sound excited."

"I am. Like an early Christmas present. Tell me what you have and everything you can think of about Ethan."

Taryn told Laurel about her and Ethan's close relationship and the e-mails he'd sent prior to his death. She vocalized their past conversations, talked about keywords and phrases, and toyed with letter and numerical forms. "So what would 'in plain sight' mean to a man who worked in computer security?"

"Close your eyes and envision you're in his office. Sit behind his desk. What do you see?"

"I've done this before, but here goes." She recalled an oddity about him. "Hey, I might have something. Although Ethan had sophisticated knowledge and use of technology, he still had a paper flip calendar on his desk, on the left-hand side because he was left-handed. In plain sight. 'Every thirty days life changes.'"

Laurel's keystrokes clicked through the phone. "Nothing yet. Since September is the current month, and we're assuming he wanted you to find it, I'm thinking this could be a game."

Taryn took on the challenge. She typed *September* and toyed with letters and numbers, all the while praying for a way to unlock the files. She typed the month backward in lower-case—*rebmetpes*—and assigned a number to each letter, which became *18 5 2 13 5 20 16 5 19.* Nothing.

"This is frustrating," she said. "I don't want to give up, but this is not my expertise."

Laurel laughed. "Make it fun. Would he have used the year? 2014 was too obvious, unless he wrote it backward and wove it with the month. *14 18 5 2 13 5 20 16 5 19 20.*" A moment later both realized that held nothing.

Taryn used caps with no result while Laurel used various forms.

"What if he used a capital letter instead of the number for the first letter of the month?" Laurel said. "That would make *14 18 5 2 13 5 20 16 5 S 20.*" Still didn't work.

"I'll change the *14* to an *N,* but it seems too easy." Clenching her fists, Taryn typed the password into Ethan's encrypted file. Success! Except a request for another password appeared. If this was meant for her to find, then it might be some-thing about her but not be the same code as before. What did she have in plain sight? For the next several minutes she and Laurel talked and typed in one word after another. What about her was obvious?

She closed her eyes and thought about the times she'd been at Ethan's home with his family. One of their sons loved word puzzles with keywords, and Taryn was the only person who played them with him.

Ethan's statement rang through her mind. *"Taryn, you're a unique woman."*

"With an exclamation mark," his young son said.

The descriptor became a part of her time with Ethan's family.

She shook her head. . . . Maybe. "I have an idea. Ethan's son and I used to play word games. We had our own special code, and Ethan knew it. Quite simple, actually. He might have wanted me to learn his password."

One of the first rules of using a keyword was not to repeat a letter. *Unique woman!* had two *n*'s and two *u*'s, but she'd give it a try. She and Ethan's son spelled out numbers and special characters and eliminated spaces. Grabbing a piece of paper, she listed the alphabet. Below it she wrote *uniquewoman!,* which took up the letters *a* to *l*. Beneath the original alphabet, she began with the letter *m* and assigned the letter *a,* then continued through the alphabet. After *z,* she started over with *a* through *l*. Next she used the corresponding letters of the keyword and the letter *l* for the exclamation mark. The keyword *uniquewoman!* became *GZUCGQIAYMZL.*

With a deep breath, she typed in the letters. The screen sprang to life, and the files were revealed.

"I've got it." Taryn realized she'd been holding her breath.

"Might have to recruit you," Laurel said.

"I've heard that before. Grayson's SSA said he'd either recruit me or send me to prison."

"Ouch. Now that you have the password, do you want to call Grayson?"

Oh, did she. "Sure." After reading some of Ethan's files, she contacted Grayson. "Laurel helped me with the password. I've found Ethan's research," she said. "Can you talk, or are you busy?"

"I'm at the command center near the airport. How about I wrap things up and stop by?"

"Sounds good." She ignored her quickening pulse. Her reaction to him was wrong. She needed to heal from the betrayal before allowing another man to creep inside.

"Mind if I pick up a burger and fries before we talk?"

His humor always lightened the moment. "Your poor body."

"I know, but it tastes wonderful. Do you need anything?"

"No thanks." She smiled. "I'll work on the hacker job until you get here. Grayson, I wish we'd found this earlier. Maybe the case would have been solved by now."

"Your findings bring us one step closer. Hold on a minute. I have a call coming through."

She patted Buddy, pleased she'd finally contributed something. If Grayson's call was important, she should hang up.

"I'm back." He sounded distracted.

"What's wrong? Has something happened?" Her first thought was Zoey, but she couldn't bring herself to ask the question.

"It's not Zoey." He paused. "The call was about your mother."

"What is it?"

"Your mother is being harassed by media and doesn't understand what's going on. Neither has she been able to talk to you. While your brother was visiting her, a reporter showed up and wouldn't leave, so your brother punched him."

Worry clawed at her heart. "I can call Mom, right? This is my family, Grayson."

"There are guidelines."

"Name them because I have to talk to her. I have to reassure her."

"You're bound not to discuss anything about the case or your location. And the agents there must be present during the conversation."

Fury swept through her. "They're supposed to listen to every word? You don't trust me?"

"I can't let you risk your life or your family's. If the FBI is watching your family, what do you think the other side is doing?"

"That's cruel. Mom needs me. My family doesn't deserve to suffer for this. Is nothing sacred to you?" She disconnected the call and tossed the phone on the sofa.

Chapter 45

12:04 p.m. Thursday

At Houston's Hobby Airport, I flag down a taxi to take me to the Galleria area. He'll stay at the best places, and one of the LNG companies is located in the area. He might pose as a vendor to get inside. His manipulative skills are textbook perfect, and I'm not certain if the man I met will look the same now. My nerves are raw, and I wish I had a drink.

The taxi driver stares at me through his rear-view mirror. I know I'm attractive. The blonde wig and dark-brown contacts are only one of my disguises. *Dream on, fella. This lady has standards.*

After a few personal affirmations, I'm in control and confident of my plan. While en route, I text him.

N Houston. Where do we meet?

I'm n Athens.

Liar. U R where the action is

B careful. U don't want 2 cross me

I need 2 C U

No

U got rid of Murford?

U could B next. Get the job done.

I'll B at Westin Oaks Galleria. C U soon.

If he comes to my room, I'll kill him and get away with it. He tried to attack me and I shot him. Like me, he uses different identities, but I'm smart. A new text from him snatches my attention.

Almost finished with U

I shudder, but he thrives on threats. I'll check into the hotel and meet with Rollins, the one man who's managed to survive, not getting caught or being on the receiving end of a bullet. Inside my purse, my Smith & Wesson .380 feels cold against my palm, but cold I can deal with.

I smile. My toy has a built-in laser.

Chapter 46

1:45 p.m. Thursday

Grayson drove north on I-45 toward the retirement center with Joe. Taryn had phoned her mother and honored his request. According to the agents assigned to her, the conversation brought tears. Tough mandates for him to issue, but too much was at stake.

Wasn't the first time he'd upset a woman because of protocol.

Grayson sensed the pressure of time. He, as well as others working on the complex case, understood something was scheduled to happen on Friday after six in the morning. Chatter indicated an event resembling the airport bombing. Nothing confirmed. Law enforcement officials all over the nation were on alert, especially airport security. The info leaked to media, and travelers canceled flights. Airlines screamed for the situation to end. The FIG reported that both LNG companies planned to go ahead with their pilot export tomorrow. At this point, only a credible threat could put a halt to their plans. They were bent on making history. Grayson understood business and the need to keep commitments. But what would be the price?

Three days since the explosion . . .

Earlier this morning, the FBI held another press conference to calm the public. The director congratulated citizens on responding to the billboards and offering anonymous information. He encouraged them to continue assisting the FBI and other law enforcement officials to find those responsible for the bombing. At key points during his speech, photos of the victims were shown, along with a photo of Cameron Wallace, the international assassin.

"Another person of interest is Haden Rollins from Gated Labs," the special agent in charge had said. "We would appreciate any information about this man."

A reporter asked about Taryn Young.

"She's in protective custody and cooperating with the FBI."

"Has she been charged?"

"We've found no evidence to believe she was part of the airport bombing."

"What about the top-secret files stolen from Gated Labs?"

"Again negative." The SAC ended his speech with a promise to keep the public informed. "We're talking about two separate incidents."

Grayson had breathed relief. The responses did not indicate Taryn's guilt. Neither did they fully exonerate her. Vagueness kept her alive. He'd bank on that.

"Do you feel the tension?" Joe said, breaking into Grayson's thoughts.

"Oh yeah. The clock's ticking, but no one can pinpoint what's going to happen tomorrow. If anything at all."

"It's the fear factor. The not knowing while the cowards run free. Me? I think most US citizens are mad and out for justice."

An update came through on Grayson's Black-Berry. He tossed his phone across the seat to Joe. "Read me the latest."

"FBI has surrounded a rental home on the southwest side in which confirmed reports indicate Murford, Breckon, Pedraza, and Dancer had been seen coming and going on several occasions."

Grayson palmed the steering wheel. "We should hear another update soon. I want to hear about confiscating computers, weapons, and—"

"I need to tell you something important. Your dad called me after lunch."

Grayson remembered Joe walking into the hallway with his phone. He swung a look toward his uncle and read the seriousness on his face. "What's up?"

"Ah, not good. Had a sobering doctor's appointment yesterday."

"I didn't know he was sick."

"Neither did he until he had his yearly physical last week. When he complained of having diarrhea for the past few months, tests were ordered."

Grayson's dad never spoke of personal matters, certainly not the way he'd relayed it to Joe. "How bad?"

"Colon cancer. Stage two."

Grayson stiffened, his ears humming. They got along like two pit bulls, but he didn't want to see his father suffer or die a premature death. "What's the prognosis?"

"Totally treatable. Your dad's a fighter. He'll beat this," Joe said.

"I need to see if he wants to patch things up."

"That would be wonderful. I'd like to think your dad's ready to reconnect. Go for it. Life's too short not to reach out to others."

"I'll give it my best."

"Hoped you'd say that. God's in the business of mending relationships."

Grayson pulled into the retirement center

parking area and dropped his cell phone into his jacket pocket. "You might need to take over inside. We had a few words this morning when I told her about her brother's arrest for punching a news reporter."

"As in what she could and couldn't do until this is settled?"

"Yes." Grayson parked away from the building housing Taryn. "We'll talk about Dad later. Come up with a strategy for him."

Joe clamped a hand on his shoulder. "Let's go see our pretty lady."

"Whatever she discovered from Ethan Formier's files has her interest."

Joe grabbed their Whataburger bags while Grayson scanned the area for potential problems. He loosened the top button on his shirt in the ninety-degree temps. Sounds from the pool area indicated the residents were enjoying the water.

He ignored the lift in his spirit at the thought of seeing Taryn. He had to regain her trust. When this ended, he'd discuss what he felt whenever he was with her. Why had he told her about his mother? For that matter, why had he initiated the wild kid stories? Initially it was professional, to get inside Taryn Young's head. His feelings toward her started to change that day in Joe's house. Maybe he wanted the real Taryn to get to know the real Grayson.

Inside, he found her curled up on the sofa with

319

the laptop, Buddy's head resting on her knee. Clint and Patti had arrived early and were deep in a discussion with the other two agents. Joe went straight to the coffeepot, and Grayson sat beside Taryn.

"Are you speaking to me?"

She nodded, but her attention stayed glued to the laptop screen. "After I had a good cry, I realized you were right."

"I'm glad."

"Doesn't mean I'm over it. I hurt for my family, and it's tearing me apart."

"This could all be settled soon."

For the first time, she looked at him. Her eyes were red, and she blinked. "The last thing we need is a sniper taking out my family."

He felt the wall between them. "What have you found?"

She pointed to his to-go bag. "You're probably starved."

He reached for his fries.

"When you teach me how to use a gun, I'll show you the reports on consuming animal products."

"Yes, ma'am." When he smiled, she offered one too.

"Remember the e-mails I forwarded you from Ethan?" she said.

"Yes. He warned you about Murford. Said his life was in danger and the problem with Nehemiah was bigger than he'd thought. It also sounded like he knew who was behind the problem at Gated Labs."

"Right. Once I was able to retrieve his files, it explained so much more." She pulled up the document containing the results of Ethan's research. "Take a look."

Grayson read the document, absorbing every word. He was amazed at the lengths Ethan had gone to in his personal investigation. His first entries had been made at Nehemiah's conception when Haden Rollins wanted to know why he'd not been invited to the closed sessions with Congress. Ethan had found Haden in Taryn's office right after the development team was formed and once six weeks later. He hadn't told Taryn for reasons unknown. When she found Kinsley in her office, Ethan assumed Kinsley and Haden were working together to oust Taryn from her leadership role. Later he revisited his suspicions about Kinsley and believed she was a pawn. Grayson sensed Taryn observing him.

"What do you think?" she said.

"Digesting it." He paused, focusing on the document. "Ethan believed Kinsley was simply power hungry, and that's what Joe and I concluded. On the other hand, Ethan didn't trust Haden and followed him to the airport on three separate occasions to learn he was on his way to New York City. Upon each return, he presented Ethan with an argument to replace you with

Kinsley, which wouldn't happen because of Congress's request to have you lead the project development team."

"Unless I was discredited. I worked overtime to ensure Nehemiah could not be compromised easily. Something else I need to tell you: Save thinks he's nearly there in accessing the software. Like I said before, we're okay unless he figures out what I've done."

"That's a point for our side." Grayson hated battling time. "Why would Ethan not have documented his latest findings?"

She shook her head. "Whatever he learned caused him to book an earlier flight home."

"Any chance he could have placed the information in another file?"

"This one was obviously meant for me to find, but I'll keep looking. What are you thinking?" she said. "Or should I ask, what have you learned?"

"We have photos and a witness that put Haden with Murford, Breckon, and Dancer on more than one occasion."

"What about the Hispanic man in custody?"

Grayson captured her attention. "He claims to have been a hired gun for Murford."

Taryn's eyes widened. "Is Kinsley in danger?"

"We've warned her."

"Good. What about Haden?"

"Unable to locate him. According to Gated Labs's security information, he entered his office after midnight and left twenty minutes later. Hasn't phoned in. We have a nationwide BOLO."

Taryn studied him. "Are you thinking Kinsley might have warned him?"

"Strong possibility."

"Poor Kinsley. She really cared for him, and I understand doing whatever we can for those we love. She and I finally have something in common—choosing men who use us." She tossed her sea-green gaze his way. "Can I call her?"

"I don't think it's a good idea. She could still be involved. Harboring him."

"All right. I've pushed my limit on calls today." She leaned back against the sofa. "What a mess. Now I understand Haden's role at the party where I met Murford. But I don't think Murford was the mastermind, especially since he's dead. So who's behind this?"

"The billion-dollar question. Did you make any headway on the hacking job?"

She frowned. "Save is being pressured. I worked another angle while trying to shut him down, but he has his own firewall."

"How close is he?"

"I have a false entrance that appears to be the real thing. It looks good until several steps into the program. Then a virus hoses his computer. But what if I'm wrong? What if he discovers what I've done before the FBI can make arrests?"

"I've been praying for those very arrests."

Grayson texted a message. "I want to let the SSA know there's a false front on the software that buys us time if the bad guys get confident."

"What are the agents doing about the link to New York?" She sighed. "Of course you can't tell me. I just want to know it all."

He could identify with her anxiety. "Do you recall anyone from New York visiting Gated Labs?"

"People were in and out of the office all the time, and many I never saw. What did Brad Patterson say?"

"The same. Nothing he could flag."

"I'm beginning to feel sorry for Patterson. His empire is going to crumble if the situation is not rectified soon."

"A team of agents met with them this morning. He was a little more cooperative. Planned to have a talk with his niece."

"And?"

He chuckled. "You should have been a lawyer. She identified those in the photographs but claims to know little else. When the question of working with Haden to secure your position was raised, she said it was all his idea."

"So will she go into protective custody?"

"She hasn't been threatened. At this point, she's a possible witness."

"I hope she's careful."

One more reason why he admired Taryn. She

still cared about Kinsley even though the woman wanted her job.

She reached for a flash drive on the end table beside her. "I copied Ethan's files."

"Thanks." He planned to show them to the SSA before Patterson learned about it.

"Grayson, I know thousands of people are working the case, but it seems like the web is growing instead of getting smaller."

"That's not unusual. In an investigation, every angle has to be explored. Sometimes clues and indications of guilt or involvement bring us to a wall, and we have to backtrack. The FBI must honor each person's civil rights, and search warrants or arrests can't be issued unless we have evidence supporting probable cause."

"I guess I thought you were above the law with national security at risk."

"We're simply government employees who—" His BlackBerry got his attention. "The house on the southwest side that presumably our bad guys were using? It's been stripped. All we can hope for are fingerprints or DNA."

"Murford's team is accounted for." Her eyes darkened. "Who's left but the unidentified person in New York?"

Chapter 47

2:00 p.m. Thursday

Haden Rollins sits across from me in the dining room of the hotel. He's such a pretty boy, and knows it, but he's also clever. One of the reasons I hired him. In the past, he's done his job, and I deposited money for him into his Tokyo account.

"It's only a matter of time until you're picked up," I say. "Running scared and leaving Gated Labs wasn't one of your better decisions."

His jaw tightens. "When Kinsley called, I figured my days were numbered."

"You panicked, cupcake, and now you'll pay for it."

He takes a drink of his dry martini. "I'm leaving the country when we're finished and then taking a flight overseas."

"Where?" I assume he's driving to Mexico.

He gives me his dimpled grin and leans back in an Italian suit my money paid for. "I'll call you."

"So you think you're pulling out?"

"I did my job, and now I'm wanted for questioning."

I pat his knee like he's six. "Your job is finished when I say so. At the press of a key, you're implicated in stealing top-secret files from Gated Labs."

He sends a cold smile my way. "You're delusional and not above the law. You think I won't give the FBI names? And if I don't, Special Agent Vince Bradshaw will." He smirks. "Yes, I found out Murford hired him. Told me all about it one night when he was drunk. Said you'd done backgrounds on all the agents. Exploding the LNG lines might get sticky, and you needed inside help. You gave him the name of an agent who was in a financial mess. Bingo! Special Agent Vince Bradshaw needed money and didn't mind giving inside information."

"You're an idiot. My name's not connected with his."

"Still, I've documented everything and given it to my attorney . . . in case of an emergency."

I take a sip of my Scotch. Self-confidence is why Murford lies on a cold slab. "The reason you're on *my* payroll is because I'm smarter than you and know how to cover my tracks."

"I'd be a fool to stay in Houston."

"I agree with the fool part. Stay outside the city in a cheap hotel until you find Murford's girlfriend and the Levin kid."

"You should have found them before you killed Murford."

"Call it an act of passion. I want them dead."

"I don't do murder."

I lean across the table and allow the cut of my blouse to entice him. He's never seen me without the wig and dark contacts. Not that I would ever let him crawl into my bed. "You do what I say until I end it."

Rollins stares out the window, then back at me. "I have a few ideas where they're hiding out."

"What's keeping you?"

He scowls, then gestures for the waiter.

"I'll take care of this," I say. "I want the disposal done before tomorrow morning."

"Things aren't always easy."

"But I have another job for you that's equally important. Taryn Young needs to be eliminated. I don't care how, but make it slow and painful."

He pales, and I see the scared little boy in him.

"Then Kinsley Stevens. In that order."

He stands, and I feel hatred bursting through his cells. I'll need to make sure he's out of the way soon.

I watch Rollins leave. In the lobby, two men in suits approach him, and I make my exit. He knows better than to implicate me, especially since he believes I had Murford killed. He'll be detained a few hours, but Rollins knows how to play the game. Guilt by association only holds when a crime is being committed. I know about his girlfriend's photos. Rollins should have been more on top of her business.

The nasty task of killing my nemesis needs to be over. One of my hackers secured the camera footage for his entrance into Texas. He's here, just as I thought. My heart speeds, and the adrenaline rush that hits me each day when Wall Street opens surges through my veins.

I am a very rich and powerful woman.

Chapter 48

2:50 p.m. Thursday

Taryn's mental exhaustion plus her depletion of energy equaled depression, and she struggled to fight it. Her hopes had been built on the contents of Ethan's encrypted file, but it only confirmed what had already been uncovered. Grayson sat beside her inhaling his burger. The smell of beef and grease churned her stomach. Or was it the impact of everything since the bombing?

Be logical. Work through this. Later you can process the tragedies and grief.

"Before I went to bed last night, I made a few notes," she said. "Let me see if there's a name or an event you can use." She walked into the bedroom and spotted the notepad on the nightstand. A quick inspection told her it had no value. She opened the drapes and welcomed the afternoon sunshine. The gesture made her feel better. A glimpse outside urged her to see what the rest of the world was doing. Beautiful day—sun-kissed, as her mother would say.

The senior citizens at the pool captured her

attention. From the looks on their faces, flirting didn't limit itself to the young. A much-younger woman entered the scene with a huge container of empty plastic gallon milk containers. They must all be gathered for water aerobics. Her despairing thoughts fled to what she viewed below. She laughed until tears rolled down her cheeks. "I don't believe this."

"What?" Grayson said.

She hadn't sensed him enter the room. "Take a look at this guy. He must weigh over 280 and he's in a Speedo."

Grayson stood behind her, so close she could feel his breath on her neck. His laughter soon rang through the small room. "The guy's a lady-killer. See that smile he gave the blonde?"

Mr. Speedo bent to his knees and assisted the young woman as she unloaded the plastic jugs. "A real Don Juan. Does he have any clue what he looks like?"

"Probably sees himself from thirty years ago."

"Fifty." She relaxed against him, not thinking, only enjoying a moment without stress. Her anger from this morning dissipated.

"When did this happen?" he whispered.

Her heart hammered. "Maybe when he moved into the complex and saw available women. Wanted to recapture his youth."

Grayson turned her to face him and lifted her chin. "When this is over, I want us to talk. You have little reason to trust me, and after what you've been through, I get it. But I'm not Murford, and I want the opportunity to show you I can be a friend . . . and more."

She didn't know what to say or how to protest. Her feelings skyrocketed when she was near him. One minute she felt guilty and fearful, and the next she longed for all Grayson represented.

"I'd like nothing better than to kiss you right now, but I'll wait until you tell me the time is right."

She nodded. Would her bruised heart ever allow her to love again?

3:15 p.m. Thursday

Taryn popped two extra-strength Tylenol and reached for her water bottle. Clint and Patti were in separate rooms watching out the windows. Would this ever be over? She patted Buddy's huge head resting on her knee. She appreciated his even temperament, and he seemed to sense those around her were honest people.

"Thank You," she whispered as she smiled into the dog's dark-brown eyes. Joe had promised to check on Bentley at the kennel. Once she found a new home and hopefully Buddy was hers, the two dogs would be like David and Goliath, but a kindly Goliath. Claire loved animals. So did Zoey.

Grayson's words in the bedroom lingered in her mind. This time last week, she was wildly crazy about Shep. He'd penetrated her one huge weakness—the need to be loved by a man who respected and valued her. The self-imposed wall around her heart had been breached. She needed to forgive herself for being duped by Murford and move forward with the past behind her.

Grayson stood for all those things good and right in life. But would she ever feel clean again for allowing herself to be preyed upon by an evil man? Thank goodness the decision didn't need to be made today.

Claire . . . Thinking about her friend brought a wave of emotion and a surge of prayers to keep her daughter safe. She wanted to tell Mom about Claire's death, but not until the case was solved. Zoey must be alive, and Taryn refused to give up until she was found. When Murford had showed her a video of the little girl, she looked fine. But at three years old, Zoey could be impatient and prone to tears. How much patience would her captor have?

Zoey, please be a good girl.

Taryn focused on the computer screen. Save claimed to have moved closer to obtaining access. She'd directed him toward the virus and hoped he fell for it. His unscrupulous activities in the past demonstrated his zeal for money and not the law. She didn't want to speculate on what the bad guys had in mind. Because she had a good idea . . . and more lives were at stake.

A knock at the door snatched Clint's and Patti's attention. Taryn grabbed her laptop and urged Buddy to follow her into the bedroom. The sound of casual voices relaxed her. A doctor provided by the FBI was scheduled to remove her stitches at three thirty, and she'd arrived—a tiny Asian woman who looked like a model.

Taryn sat at the kitchen table while the doctor removed the bandage and sterilized the wounded area before clipping and tweezing the stitches.

"Healing nicely," the doctor said. "And since it's along the hairline, not much of a scar. I suggest a scar cream, one you can get at Walgreens or CVS."

"I'm sure Grayson would pick it up for you," Patti said with a grin.

Taryn wasn't going there. "Or Joe."

Once the doctor finished, she pulled a folded piece of paper from her purse and handed it to Clint. "Not sure what it means, but the guard at the complex's entrance gave this to me. Said it was for Taryn Young from a friend. When he told the woman who delivered it that he didn't have a resident by that name, the woman gave him the building and apartment number." The doctor frowned. "I was told no one knew she was here."

"You're right. I doubt this is from another agent." Clint took the paper and turned to Patti. "Better call this in. I don't have a good feeling about it. They'll want to view the security camera footage and send backup."

Taryn pointed to it. "What does it say?" Every time she allowed herself to feel safe, another bomb exploded.

Clint opened the plain sheet of folded paper. Peeking over his shoulder, she saw the message was typed in large font and bolded.

Taryn, wherever you go, we'll find you. Make this easy so Zoey stays alive.

We're willing to make an exchange now. Know this: once we have confirmed access, you and Zoey are no longer assets. We suggest you act quickly. You'll be contacted soon.

She swallowed the acid rising from her stomach. Whoever was responsible seemed to know her every move, which meant Clint and Patti could be hurt. She glanced at the door, the thought of walking away pressing against her heart. "Why haven't they burst through to get me?" she said.

"Risky," Clint said. "We have agents stationed all around. HPD has their officers watching too."

Tears pooled in her eyes. What good did she contribute to the world if she could not risk all to save a child?

Chapter 49

3:45 p.m. Thursday

Grayson received the message about the need to move Taryn one more time. He was in the mood to handcuff her to a chair at the office. Were eyes watching all those entering and exiting the FBI?

"Got to pick up Taryn," he said to Joe. "They know where she's at. Left a note with the guard at the front of the retirement complex."

"What did it say?"

Grayson relayed every word while they walked to the elevator. "I'm afraid she'll try to make the swap for Zoey. Both of them would end up dead."

"We could wire her again, and you know she'd agree."

"When it comes to Zoey, she tosses caution to the wind. Taryn is desperate to save her."

"It's the mother instinct." Joe's words took Grayson back to his mother's sacrifice. He wasn't ready to have Taryn do the same thing.

Outside the building, hot September temps made it feel like they were walking into an oven.

"What you're suggesting is too dangerous," Grayson said. "We've already learned Cameron Wallace is mixed up in this. He killed Murford, and we don't know if he's still in the country. The thing is, Wallace is a professional assassin, not a kidnapper."

"Not likely he'd be after her, but I'd feel better if we knew he'd left the good old US. Better yet, apprehended." Joe turned to him in the car. "Did you have a chance to find out any of his past employers?"

"A little. The last few years have kept him in Europe. But last summer he took out six leaders of a cartel in Venezuela, putting the largest drug lord in power. Our agents tracked him down when he arrived in the States a week ago. Facial recognition showed him coming through Reynosa. Then he disappeared." Grayson, like many other agents, leaned toward a collaboration of home-grown and foreign terrorism, which meant who hired Wallace?

"The question is, does he have more hits on his list?"

"And who? Whoever's in charge in New York has a big agenda," Grayson said. "What I wouldn't give to find the link from the software to the airport bombing."

"When are you going to share your own conclusions?"

Grayson chuckled. "Soon. I have an idea brewing, but I hate being wrong. Agents are investi-gating my same thoughts, and I'm following them."

"Try me. What do you have to lose?" Joe tilted

his head and gave Grayson his full attention. "Gut instincts never failed me."

Grayson changed lanes and toyed with his hunches. "When I get to thinking about who has the most to gain from an attempt to strike fear into the American public, lots of possibilities pop up. And we have enemies all over the world taking credit for the bombing, but the software is a side note. Especially now, since the seller is dead. When I lay that alongside what could happen if access to the software got into the wrong hands, the list narrows to a small window."

"As in another country that wouldn't want us exporting LNG?"

"On the West Coast it's hard to say. On the East, it's Russia. But they're too smart to bomb an airport or implicate themselves."

"Taking us on in that capacity is ridiculous." Joe scrolled through his BlackBerry. "We'd pull aid and they'd be hurting. I know it's a possibility, but a useless venture in my opinion. My vote goes to the Middle East teamed up with someone in New York."

"Unless Russia hired someone to do their dirty work."

Joe frowned. "I still think it's the Middle East."

"Stay with me, Joe. Who has the most to gain when oil prices go up or down?"

"Oil and gas traders. You're looking at two separate theories. No connect."

"Maybe." Voicing his thoughts somehow lessened their credibility, but he wasn't ready to let it go. "I spent most of the night—what was left of it—digging into other FBI investigations. If my thoughts are in left field, why are agents on that trail?"

"I'll need more to convince me. And I promise you, I'll look into the same research, but right now I think you're fishing."

"Go back to my original statement. Oil and gas traders stand to make money regardless of pricing. Most of them care only about the almighty dollar. So an unscrupulous trader sabotages the software designed to protect our infrastructure, and that person makes millions."

"I agree a trader on the prowl makes sense. But I suggest keeping the oil trader on the front burner and ice the involvement of Russia."

Grayson let the idea slide a notch. Joe hadn't steered him wrong before. "Maybe you're right. Our assignment has always been Taryn."

"Do you have any idea how her safety was compromised?"

"Money can buy anything. I'd feel better if I had a few more puzzle pieces. Regarding the note she received, I'm afraid Zoey's not alive. Think about a three-year-old—crying, whining, hungry. Not good." He'd not admit the same thing to Taryn.

Joe nodded. "Do you want to take the chance?"

"What do you think? Taryn would walk into the

pits of hell if we asked her. I've expected a call from Clint or Patti that she's walked away from FBI protection."

"Don't you think it makes sense for us to lead the way than have her take off on her own?"

Grayson hated it when Joe was right, but the wheels began to turn. A plan formed in his mind, a way to stage Taryn that looked like she'd left the safety net of the FBI, beginning with bringing her back to the office. He shared his idea and Joe added a few details.

"It seems risky to me. But the advantage is we'd have her covered."

"I can't believe I'm suggesting it, but it beats her striking out on her own," Grayson said. "Before we get to the retirement community, would you read the latest updates? Might change our path forward."

Joe read from his BlackBerry. "A congress-man's aide confessed to leaking the information about Nehemiah to the media after Taryn was listed as a person of interest in the bombing. No evidence of the industry and manufacturing companies in the States being behind the problem at Gated Labs."

"The money behind this operation is astronomi-cal. Looks to me like several companies would need to pool funds to pull it off." It also fed into Grayson's thoughts about Russia, but he'd not bring it up again.

"Nothing from the bomb's remains point to a particular source." Joe stared out the window. "We all know the bomber would place the source elsewhere. Some sources doubt if the incident at Gated Labs is tied to the airport bombing."

"My instinct says it is."

"Oh, I know your theory. Whoa," Joe said. "We picked up Haden Rollins at the Westin Oaks. Confiscated his burner phone."

"Interesting. Hope they can crack him so we won't have to put Taryn's life in danger. But I'm probably dreaming."

4:35 p.m. Thursday

While Taryn rode to the FBI office in the backseat of Grayson's Mustang with Buddy beside her and Joe in the front, she listened to Grayson's proposal. "Yes. Wire me up. I want to get started as soon as we get to the office."

"Are you physically up to it?" Grayson said.

Her health wouldn't stop her. "Explain every detail again so I have it in my head."

"We want to make this look like you're deserting the FBI to comply with the kidnapper. We'll set up a scene outside the office to show our mutual dissatisfaction."

"I'm getting good at stepping out of my geek box." She laughed while her insides whirled.

"We might be able to get a little media support if you're wanting to go that far," Grayson said. "I could manage a leak—unofficial, of course. You'd have a rental car with a concealed tracking device. The car would have to be torn apart to find it. And you'd have a special implant for us to know where you are."

She'd seen a few movies with those things. "As in buried beneath the skin?"

"Yes."

She willed her headache to cease. "Is it also a recording device?"

"No. Taryn, this is a serious risk factor. We'll be monitoring your location and closing in on the kidnapper. Your phone has the same device. In other words, we'll have your back, but we can't stop anyone from pulling a trigger."

A flash of how the retirement center had been compromised caused a catch in her spirit. "How easy would it be to detect?"

"Difficult without specific equipment. And considering your two trips to the hospital, any lesions could be explained away. One more thing. I want to show you a photo of the man who killed Murford. He's the hired assassin, a good one. We don't believe the bad guys want you dead, but you need to be familiar with him."

Grayson handed her his BlackBerry with a photo of the man. She studied the assassin's square jaw, dark eyes, and heavy brows. "Name? Habits?"

"Cameron Wallace. Think chameleon. Known

for his disguises. The photo we have of him entering Reynosa shows him with black hair."

After committing the face to memory, she returned the phone. "So it's quite probable he changed his looks?"

"His appearance at the border could have been to throw off law enforcement." Grayson sighed. She sensed his wariness with the plan.

The only choice was also the right choice. "I'm on board. We're battling time because Save thinks he's nearly there in discovering access to the software." She hesitated. "But it will take time before he gets through the encryptions or to the point where the virus attaches to his system."

"Clarify that for me," Grayson said. "You're saying he could bypass the false front?"

"Yes, at the point where it looks like he has entrance, but it contains a virus that will shut down his system. I'm not flawless, and he could be prepared, but I don't want to take the chance. Get it arranged now, Grayson. How long will it take?"

"By the time the rental car arrives, we can put the plan in motion. Joe and I will do a quick interview with Haden, then let other agents take over there."

"Okay, what else?"

"There's a restaurant close to the office, and we'll set the argument there."

Every moment wasted ticked at Zoey's life. "Where will you and Joe be?"

"We'll be with the surveillance team. You'll always be in our sights."

The reassurance calmed her. "Thanks."

Grayson made a call. The arrangements sounded . . . clinical, and a wisp of fear settled on her. "In place," he said a few moments later. "We'll rehearse the plan while waiting on the rental."

"Is there a way to take Buddy?"

"Aw, Taryn." Joe turned to her. "If those guys care less about human life, what's an animal?"

The truth had a way of sending glass shards into open wounds. "You're right. If something happens, don't send him to the pound. Okay?"

"I'll take Buddy myself." Joe reached behind the seat and took her hand. "If I were thirty years younger, I'd be sweeping you off your feet. You're my hero, little lady."

If only she felt like one.

Chapter 50

5:05 p.m. Thursday

Grayson and Joe stood outside the interview room where Haden Rollins waited. They studied his body language, viewed his slumped shoulders.

"Look how many times he's swallowed," Joe said.

"Right." Rollins's tense facial muscles indicated

his fear. He should've known they were observing him.

With a legal pad tucked under his arm, Grayson opened the door, wishing he could monitor Taryn at the same time. "Good afternoon, Mr. Rollins."

His gaze narrowed. "If it isn't Special Agent Hall and a different sidekick."

"I'm the old guy who's experienced in nailing the guilty ones." Joe smiled. "So I'll sit back and watch while you confess to stealing Gated Labs software and setting up at least three people for murder." Joe pulled out a chair, not once losing eye contact with Rollins. "I'd like to tack on terrorism for the airport bombing, but you'll need to fill in a few blanks."

Rollins startled. "Hold it. I'm not taking the blame for all those crimes."

Grayson tossed his legal pad and pen on the table. "Why don't you begin by telling us what you are responsible for?"

"I want a lawyer."

"Sure," Grayson said. "We can pose the same questions in front of him."

Rollins crossed his arms. "Not a word from me."

"Poor Kinsley." Grayson jotted the word *lawyer* in big letters on his legal pad.

"Why? What happened?" Rollins stiffened. "Is she all right?"

Grayson raised a brow. "Didn't you hear?" He

stared at Rollins and counted to five before responding. "Her family and friends are unable to find her. We figured you'd killed her, too."

Rollins moistened his lips. "Kinsley is innocent of any of this." At the mention of her name, his voice softened.

They were onto something. "Did you use her for your own purposes?"

Rollins shook his head. "I'm not answering your questions until I talk to a lawyer."

Grayson tapped the top of the desk with his pen. "We could find her and keep her safe if you'd cooperate."

He rubbed his palms. "You mean without a lawyer?"

"With or without."

"I didn't kill anyone. That wasn't my job. I doubt the airport bombing was a part of the plan. Probably two separate situations." He scratched his chin. "But I can't figure out where it's all headed."

Grayson nodded, silently offering sincerity. "I can understand how you wouldn't want to take the blame for something you knew nothing about. Especially with so many dead. What was your job?"

He hesitated, no doubt thinking through pulling the lawyer card. "To secure Nehemiah. Taryn had this tight hold on the project, and I couldn't access it." His knuckles whitened as he clenched his fists. "I pursued Kinsley, and when I gained her confidence, I worked toward having her replace Taryn as lead developer."

"Murford hired you?"

"Thought he did."

"What do you mean?"

"Murford approached me, but I'd already been hired by someone else to keep an eye on him."

Finally they were getting somewhere. "Who?"

Rollins no longer had the pretty-boy confidence. "Four people from the original team are dead, and I figure I'm on her list too. But I don't want Kinsley to be next."

So he loved the woman, at least in his own way. "We'll do all we can to keep her from being harmed."

"She's the only thing I care about. I think this person has eyes everywhere."

"Is this person in New York City?"

He whispered yes, then shook his head. "No."

"Haden, where is this person? We have to know everything to stop the killing and investigate the possibility of a link to the airport bombing."

A streak of fear flashed across his eyes. "What about witness protection?"

First Pedraza and now Rollins. "If necessary and we recommend it."

"Could Kinsley go with me?"

"If she's still alive." Grayson stared into his eyes. "Witness protection may not be her choice."

"I couldn't blame her," Rollins said. "Especially when she finds out the truth."

Grayson jotted his request on the legal pad and circled it. "So what have you done for this person in New York?"

"I followed orders, like having Murford think he was the boss."

"What else?"

"I was an expensive gofer in a three-piece suit, and my checks were deposited into a Tokyo account." Rollins glanced away. "She's furious Murford didn't deliver the software, but I never thought he'd end up dead."

"Have you killed anyone?"

Rollins pressed his palms against the table. "No one. That's the dividing line."

"What's her plan B?"

"She hired a hacker. According to her, he should have Nehemiah working tonight. She's obsessed with gaining control of the software. Twofold plan: blow up the LNG pipes, which causes prices to rise, and sell the software to the highest bidder." He paused. "But I doubt that it all happens her way. Taryn had layers of encryption."

"What's the woman's name?"

"She's an oil and gas trader on Wall Street."

Just as Grayson and other agents had speculated. "She stands to make millions by manipulating oil and gas prices. Who is she, Haden?"

He swallowed hard. "Iris Ryan. She's staying at

the Westin, where you picked me up. At least she was. Probably gone by now."

"Why blow up the airport?"

Haden shrugged. "Not sure she lit the fuse on that one."

6:00 p.m. Thursday

Taryn had performed her best acting job with Grayson for their shouting match in the restaurant parking lot. She'd snatched the rental car keys from him and tossed him onto the ground before taking off, leaving him in feigned pain and anger. Hopefully tonight's news didn't focus on an FBI agent being deflated by a woman terrorist. Not exactly a boost for his ego.

An e-mail from Save came through just as she left the parking lot, and she forwarded it to Grayson. Save thought he'd gotten through all the layers when something changed, and it was like he was back at square one. Assuming he managed to get through the firewall and attempted to test his ability to regulate temperature and pressure of the liquid natural gas, a virus would destroy his system. Unless he discovered her virus first and figured out how to bypass it.

The deadline was tomorrow morning at six. Who would be killed once the time arrived? Taryn feared Zoey didn't have a chance either way.

Panic clawed at her, but she'd not give in to its power. She'd offer the same thing she'd done with

Murford—a partnership in developing software for whatever they demanded.

She'd not back down now. Wearing the implant injected into her upper left hip, she'd do exactly what the kidnapper wanted to deal for Zoey. She drove north on I-45 toward Huntsville because she had no clue where else to drive. Maybe the kidnapper was still close to the state park and assumed she'd head there first. Her attempt to draw him or her out could be pointless, but she sensed someone watching her every move, and it wasn't just the FBI. Could that person be the man or woman who held Zoey? Or simply paranoia? She peered into the rearview mirror for a vehicle tailing her. Nothing. So many things in her life were unsettled.

Kinsley Stevens . . . Grayson said contacting her wasn't wise, but Taryn believed differently, and the burner phone lay on the console. She couldn't change her unsociable ways of the past, but she could make amends if she didn't have tomorrow. Remembering Kinsley's cell phone number, she pressed it in. The young woman answered on the third ring.

"Kinsley, this is Taryn Young. How are you?"

She broke into sobs. "I'm so scared, and I feel so stupid."

"I know. I'm right there with you. That's why I called."

"How . . . kind of you. I'm going to be all right.

They say Haden is involved in a conspiracy to steal Nehemiah, and he's disappeared."

Taryn chose not to reveal that he was in custody. "It's hard when you love him, especially when you need the truth but fear it too."

"Exactly." Kinsley sucked in a sob. "Oh, Taryn, I don't know what to believe. He told me horrible things about you, things I realize now were lies. I did attempt to get into your computer. Haden told me you were hiding things that were valuable to the team. I feel used. Dirty."

Taryn understood the need for a perpetual shower. "Our IQs aren't attached to our hearts."

"I loved him. Still do." Kinsley's misery tugged at Taryn's own betrayal.

"I wish I could help you."

"Listening helps . . . and I am sorry."

"It's okay. Are you safe?"

"Yes. Special Agent Hall suggested I take a leave from work and not tell anyone my location but the FBI. Going crazy thinking. How are you managing?"

Taryn toyed with what to say. Her faith was new, unexplored in talking to others. "This whole mess has caused me to reach out to God."

"I thought you didn't believe in a deity, that you were an all-science person." Shock rose in Kinsley's voice.

"Oh, that was me. And finding faith is so new that it's awkward talking about it."

"I never had much use for the God thing. Impossible to trust what I can't see."

Taryn recalled what Grayson had said about his philosophy—how *impossible* wasn't a word in his book and shouldn't be in hers. "Wasn't so long ago I thought the same thing. Faith's a good healing place to start."

"Okay," Kinsley said slowly. "Are you suggesting I start going to church? Get religious?"

"Maybe just talk to Him, like you're talking to me. See if He responds."

"Odd, we're discussing God like this."

A cleansing freshness settled over Taryn. "I agree. When this is over, I'd like the opportunity to be friends—at the office and outside."

"I probably won't have a job at Gated Labs."

Taryn laughed. "I forgot. I don't have a job there either. We can stand in the unemployment line together. Drink fast-food coffee until we can afford Starbucks."

Kinsley's voice broke and she apologized for her emotions. "Thank you so much for caring enough to call. I really appreciate it. Are you going to be all right?"

She hesitated to answer.

"Taryn?"

"I hope so, but finding a little three-year-old is at the top of my list, then helping to arrest those involved with all the tragedies of the week. A big order when every law enforcement person in the country is working on the same thing."

"You've always followed through on your dreams."

"Thanks. Talk to you soon, Kinsley." Taryn ended the call, a bit shaken at her own transparency, yet peaceful.

Chapter 51

6:55 p.m. Thursday

Taryn wished the sun would stay up a few more hours, but dusk approached, and with it the hidden dangers of night. She stopped at a convenience store and gas station along I-45 past Huntsville State Park. How obvious could she be for someone tailing her?

Agents would be in disguise, and she didn't want to stare. But knowing where they were sure would go a long way in easing her fears. Rural folks in a banged-up pickup slid beside a gas pump. Two teens smoked outside the store— from their eyes, it wasn't cigarettes. A truck driver wearing shades and low-riding jeans stepped outside his semi. A middle-aged couple exited a Lexus. None looked like Grayson or Joe, or Clint or Patti, or anyone else she'd seen at the FBI office. Grabbing her purse, Taryn left the rental. She had to call Grayson.

Public restrooms gave her a bit of a phobia

after Monday, but she didn't need a full bladder while in stressed mode. After washing her hands, she made sure no one else occupied the area and keyed in his number.

"Hey. Any signs of company?" Grayson said.

"Nothing. But I need to toss this phone."

"Why?" The edge in his voice showed his concern.

"I called Kinsley. Don't say a word. It's a woman thing. I wanted to let her know I empathized with her situation." When he failed to respond, she summoned the courage to explain her actions. "She's hurting, and I couldn't go a mile farther down the road without an attempt to console her."

"The word *crusader* crosses my mind. I don't approve, but I agree. Toss the phone."

"There are others around me?"

"Yes. I saw you pull into the convenience store. Are you sure you want to risk continuing this crazy mission? No one would question your backing out."

"Quitting is not up for debate. Talk to you soon." She wanted to say more—if nothing else, to thank him for being her friend. With a grim look at her last form of communication, she powered off the phone and tossed it into the trash.

She purchased a bottle of water and a bag of mixed nuts and walked outside. The evening shadows brought a slight breeze, and she let it cool her while drinking the water. A young Hispanic gal sporting five-inch heels and a skirt the same length moved across the parking area. A man who resembled one of the characters from *Duck Dynasty* tipped the bill of his cap— not that she watched the show, but Claire did and described every detail.

A man with his little boy pumped gas.

Don't stare, Taryn. Act normal. Whatever that is.

She swung her attention to her rental car. A jean-clad man leaned against it, arms crossed and wearing a smirk. Blond shoulder-length hair swept back from his face, and he wore a diamond stud in his ear. No doubt this was the man Grayson had warned her about. The chameleon. What was the purpose of sending an assassin? Fear gripped her . . . but if his intentions were to kill her, she'd already be in a pool of blood.

Stage time. She capped her bottle of water and walked toward him. A pair of Louis Vuitton sunglasses dangled from his right hand.

"You've been expecting me," he said with no accent, not even a distinguishable hint from a part of the US.

"Wondered when you'd make your appearance." She prayed her trembling hands wouldn't give her away. "I'm ready to deal."

"Really?" He took her bag of nuts and opened them. "Love these things. Full of antioxidants to ward off disease. . . . Makes a person live longer."

354

He dipped his hand into the bag. "Do you mind if I help myself? Looks like we have something in common."

He knew where the kidnapper held Zoey, and that was in-common enough.

"I'm not vegan, though," he said with his mouth full. "Nothing like a thick rare steak." He winked.

Did he flirt with all his prey? "You know my habits. But I'm not surprised."

"What can I say? I'm good at what I do."

"So am I." She maintained a steady gaze into his dark eyes. Showing distress would be her downfall.

"We'll see. I detected one carload of your FBI friends, and I'm sure there're others. One hint of trouble, and you're dead. Understand?" He spoke through a smile as though they were old friends. Or more.

Taryn ventured closer to him. "I'm not working with the FBI or any law enforcement agency. They failed to deliver Zoey."

"I saw your dissatisfaction. Ready to take a ride?" He pointed toward a black Escalade and slipped on his sunglasses. "We'll take mine. No way to trace us." He took her hand. "Don't try anything because I'll stick a knife in you before you can swing a fist or leg."

"I want to retrieve Zoey. Nothing else."

He kissed her cheek. A brief reminder of Murford . . . only more deadly.

"Since when does a professional assassin get personal with his target?"

Wallace laughed. "When the money's good."

"For me, it's all about a little girl who needs rescuing."

"Then let's get it done, my auburn-haired beauty. Murford had good taste." He escorted her to the Escalade and opened the door. Glancing about, he pulled her close and planted a hard kiss. She recoiled, his cologne a woodsy scent that she'd never forget. "Most women enjoy this," he whispered in her ear. His hands trailed over her body, and she stiffened. "Relax. Got to make sure you're not armed." He stepped back, obviously satisfied she didn't pose a threat. He'd touched her hip where the tracking implant rested, but he hadn't lingered there.

He gestured for her to climb into his vehicle. Once she was seated, he took her purse and crammed it into a Walmart plastic bag. "Stay right here. Buckle up. I'm a fast driver." He slammed the door and took the plastic bag containing her purse to the trash.

He waved across the way as though they were . . . together.

I can handle this. She waved back just to prove she could.

Sliding into the driver's side, he yanked something out of the console and aimed it her direction.

She startled. "Are you taking my picture?"

"Not exactly. This device disables implants, like the one in your rear."

Hide your panic. God's in control, not this hired killer. The FBI wouldn't abandon her. They were watching and would follow. And they'd attempt a rescue when necessary.

He turned the air-conditioning to full blast, then dropped his keys into the cup holder. "I don't want you going to sleep," he said.

"Are you afraid your presence will bore me?"

He slapped her face. She refused to cry out or touch where her cheek and eye stung. A banner rolled across her mind with the first rule of engagement: *Don't make Cameron Wallace angry.*

"Where are we going?" she said, regaining her composure.

"Where it's quiet, secluded."

"Am I going to learn what this is about?"

"What part?" He whipped the SUV north onto I-45.

"All of it."

He flashed her a smile full of pearly white teeth as though he hadn't hit her. "I don't ask questions from those paying the bills."

"How can you plea-bargain without leverage?"

"My dossier states how many times I've been caught."

None, which was terrifying. "How were you tracking me?"

He grinned. "Pure instinct."

An animal. "Why the airport bombing?"

"Not my baby. I have a very specific job description."

If Cameron Wallace hadn't been responsible, then who was? The contact in New York?

"Are the wheels turning?" he said.

"What do you want from me?"

"You don't know?" He laughed. "Take a wild guess."

She twisted her shoulder in a desperate attempt to flirt. "Software access."

"Smart girl. But there're a few more demands."

"Enlighten me." Whoever Wallace worked for wouldn't be content with just access to Nehemiah. Would Taryn be forced to design something catastrophic?

"I'll let someone else explain it to you."

That meant she was worth more alive than dead. At least for the present. "How is the software connected to the bombing?"

"Maybe my boss will tell you."

"The one in New York?"

"Could be. What else is going on inside your pretty head of a 150 IQ?"

What didn't he know about her? "I'm thinking. I'd like to work a deal, go into partnership with whoever wants the software. I can develop any-thing your boss wants. In fact, I made the same offer to Murford."

"I know. He fell for it, but my contract has a narrower scope."

"Doesn't mean I can't work for your boss. I have top-level secret clearance."

He sneered. "The password to access the software is now in the boss's hands. Your talk is worthless."

"Do you think I'd program something that easy to get into?"

"My info said the hacker and the buyer tested it."

She shrugged. "Believe what you want. I thought we were making a deal for Zoey."

"The terms have changed."

Play the game, Taryn. Don't show your emotions. "Is she alive?"

He laughed and shook his head. "I don't know anything about a woman named Zoey."

Chapter 52

9:15 p.m. Thursday

Grayson parked a twenty-year-old Dodge pickup on the T of a country road, turned off the lights, and waited for the Escalade to pass. His nightmare had sprung to life when the driver was identified as Cameron Wallace. Taryn's implant wasn't transmitting a signal, and the thought of some scum cutting it out of her was . . . He didn't want to think about it. Agents tailed Wallace by using a series of vehicles—one would follow and turn off. Then another took its place. Wallace drove deep into the rural area east of I-45 and north of Crockett.

He remembered what Taryn said about learning self-defense through hapkido. She needed the confidence of completing something that didn't involve her IQ. Wanted to kick her way out of her self-imposed "geek" box. She had definitely kicked her way free of all restrictions . . . as long as she didn't end up on the side of the road.

Reports rolled in on various investigations. Iris Ryan had checked out of her hotel. Security cameras showed a taxi picked her up. She wore a blonde wig, jeans, and a low-cut shirt, but facial software detected her. Her real appearance was shoulder-length dark hair and blue eyes. In her professional facade, she dressed conservatively. According to the driver, he took her two blocks to the Galleria mall and dropped her off. She paid cash and waited on the sidewalk until the taxi drove away.

Agents scoured the mall, searching and checking various cameras inside and around the area. Another BOLO had been issued. Too many places to hide in this city. The SSA had requested a subpoena to search her New York office, but she'd most likely left nothing to trace her whereabouts or dealings.

"What all do we have?" Joe shifted in the passenger seat. "I mean solid stuff."

"Not so sure about solid, but here's my list: Vince refuses to talk, and his son's too selfish to cooperate. Murford's dead. Breckon's dead. Jose Pedraza is scared, but he's protecting his rear by not telling the truth. Rollins named Iris Ryan as the mastermind, and she's on the run. Kinsley Stevens was used like Taryn. Cameron Wallace is our indication that someone bigger than Iris Ryan is behind it. Probably international, and most think Iran is involved." He swung a quick look at Joe. "How's that?"

"A mess."

"Yet I think we're on the right trail with Wallace nabbing Taryn," Grayson said.

"Are you regressing to your old theory?"

"Not really." He'd voice his opinion when he had substantial proof.

"Where can we get the most bang for the buck?" Grayson rolled down the window for cooler air. "Haden Rollins. He's obviously in love with Kinsley. But he's keeping a few details to himself. I want to see all the interview transcripts."

"I'll see if the latest is available," Joe said, his eyes glued to his BlackBerry. "He sure was quick to ask for witness protection."

"Iris Ryan may have used blackmail," Grayson said. "Threatened Kinsley. But he'll need to give us more information first."

"Kinda tough to remain loyal to a boss who has a habit of eliminating those who work for her. Hey, I have a report on Rollins's latest interview." Joe whistled. "Looks like Miss Iris gave him an assignment he couldn't handle."

"My guess is it's murder."

"Right. Listen to the list—Zoey Levin, the woman with her, Kinsley Stevens, and Taryn."

"What does she have on him to make the demands?"

"He didn't answer. Nothing more without an attorney. Has to have witness protection in writing."

"Hey, text the SSA to see if Rollins will give us Dina Dancer's real name."

A moment later Joe stuck his BlackBerry back into his pocket.

"I bet he knows where Zoey's being kept," Grayson said. "Thinks he can trump his plea bargain."

Grayson's phone signaled him. "Wallace is a mile back. No headlights." He backed up a few yards and reached for night goggles. When the Escalade came into view, Grayson drove to the turnoff.

10:09 p.m. Thursday

Taryn had never been afraid of the dark. Her fears were emotional from years of rejection— the cruelty of kids because she loved math and science and was painfully shy. Great combo for a misfit. Friends were a precious commodity, and the only one during those awkward years was another socially misfit girl. Like Taryn, the other girl recognized the difference between herself and others. Neither she nor Taryn could figure out how to get past the jeers, the isolation. So they gave up and found solace in their companionship. Taryn helped her with schoolwork, and in return, she learned to value others for who they were, not for what society expected. She'd forgotten that valuable lesson once she took on professionalism to cover her shyness and lack of confidence. If only she'd understood the wonder of God's love during those agonizing years.

Claire had seen through her little-girl neediness and treasured her friendship anyway. But the years of teasing and loneliness held no comparison to riding in a vehicle with an assassin. Back then she gave up. Back then her intelligence was a deterrent. Tonight she'd use her head to find a way out of what Cameron Wallace planned for her.

Except none of her superachiever methods had worked to free her from the monster who held her captive. She had nothing left but an invisible thread between her and God. What was left but death and eternity? How would God feel about her failure during these last few days on earth? Perfectionism and over-the-top commitment to Gated Labs meant nothing when lives were at stake. *Claire said God wants all of us, not just the areas of our lives we want to give.* She had thought God helped those who helped themselves, but she didn't remember ever reading that in the Bible. Right now she was powerless. And there were things she'd reserved for herself . . . like working when she could have attended church or not listening to Claire when her friend asked if she'd prayed about marrying Murford. Her admittance of needing God a few nights ago hadn't been enough.

God, You have it all because left alone, I make one poor decision after another.

For the past several miles, Wallace had driven without headlights and made more turns than a carnival ride.

"I need a bathroom," she said.

"Hold it."

"The seat's going to get wet."

"Not my vehicle."

"Urine smells."

He cursed. "We'll have to pull over. Don't even think of trying to get away."

"I bet you don't get paid unless you deliver me."

"The key word is *alive*. I don't care how shallow your breathing is. So I'll be holding your hand."

"You've got to be kidding. Stand over me with the gun."

"Whatever." He cursed again and opened the

door, the only light except for a farmhouse in the distance. Where were the FBI agents? Had they lost Wallace when he drove with his lights off?

"I've seen your hapkido. Coming after me is a bad choice. Not only will I find you and cut out your heart, but Zoey will be dead too."

"You said you knew nothing about her." Was there no end to this evil?

"Guess you can't trust me. What's your answer?"

"I . . . I understand."

"Good. I love a cooperative woman."

I can do this. "Do you have any tissue paper?" she said.

"This model isn't upgraded."

How could she stall him? Where could she run? The hours of training . . . the instructor putting her through what-if situations that involved quick thinking and even faster reactions. Wouldn't he be more trained with a gun than in hand-to-hand combat?

She'd not come this far to let the other side win. God was with her, right?

The passenger door opened, and Wallace stepped back, his pistol in his left hand and his body shielded by the door. The keys lay in the console. Her only edge would be surprise, and her skills were based on using her attacker's strength.

"Slide those long legs of yours to the ground," he said. "Move to the right and the rear. This gun can inflict pain without killing you."

She touched her head while slowly turning in her seat.

"Hurry up. What's the problem now?"

"Look, I'm not whining. But in the last four days, I've managed two concussions, and my head hurts. I'm dizzy, not that it matters to you."

"Right. You needed a pit stop, and I'm being a gentleman. You fall, you pick yourself up. The best have tried to trick me, and they paid for it."

She slid from the seat, still holding on to her head with her left hand, the hand nearest his throat if she could act fast. To keep their location hidden, he'd have to close the door.

Her one downfall when taking advanced self-defense was timing. Too often she reacted early. Taking slow steps, she moved toward the rear of the Escalade. The door closed behind her with a click, just enough to extinguish the light. Her mind registered an image of where he'd be standing.

She whirled around, landing a punch to his throat with her left hand while knocking the gun from his hand with her right. He staggered back but quickly regained momentum and landed a sharp blow to her left arm. The bone snapped. Excruciating pain fueled her adrenaline, and she kicked his groin. He doubled over, and she squeezed back into the passenger side of the vehicle, locking the door.

She dragged herself over the console to the driver's side and locked that door. Pressing the engine to life, she slammed the Escalade into drive and sped away, leaving Wallace and gravel in her wake.

How quickly would he find his gun?

Where were the lights on this thing?

A bullet cracked the rear window and she pushed harder on the gas. But she couldn't see. Another bullet zoomed past her ear. She used her right hand to flip on the headlights. The road ahead brightened. She looked for signs of other vehicles. Nothing. On the left a barn emerged. She needed help soon with the agony in her arm. Blinking back the need to fall under a dark spell, she drove farther, ensuring miles between her and Wallace.

But Wallace had his phone. He'd make a call, and she had no idea the difference between the vehicles belonging to the FBI and those associated with Wallace. She'd have to walk for help. No choice.

Chapter 53

10:57 p.m. Thursday

Through night goggles, Grayson drove without his headlights. He could see roughly three hundred yards, but he was a safety hazard to other drivers. Wallace had taken one turn after another in an attempt to lose them. Maybe he'd succeeded because none of the FBI could figure out where he'd gone. Time and speed calculations indicated he'd slipped by them or reached his destination. Either alternative left a bitter taste in Grayson's mouth.

"Out here in the middle of nowhere, he could have pulled off the road until he saw us pass," Joe said.

"That's risky unless he has means to track us." Grayson studied the area to their right and left. "Lots of trees. Guess he could hide there beyond our vision."

"Or hold a family hostage." Joe brought up a special app on his BlackBerry system to show real-time traffic based on GPS signals and cell tower triangulation. "But that means more people he'd have to eliminate, and Wallace is known as a loner. Get in and get the job done, then slide back under a rock." He pointed to phones on the map. "These are ours. The other three are unknown."

Grayson pointed to the screen. "Let's check on this one about a mile and a half away."

Joe informed the other agents and held his phone. "I can't figure out why a professional assassin would nab Taryn. I can see how her credentials are critical for a deal tomorrow, especially with the scheduled LNG export. But Wallace is way out of his typical job."

Grayson sorted through his thoughts and

shoved ideas into place. He had to separate his feelings for Taryn from the case's facts. "Her skills are right up at the top, which she's proved with her past successes. She could develop any kind of program someone might need. The right people could force her to work on designing other projects—especially if they had Zoey."

Joe dropped his phone into his pocket. "Do you suppose they have that little girl hidden out here, or is this just a lure?"

"Hard to say. Taryn drove north because of the evidence near Huntsville State Park. Wallace followed and intercepted her at the convenience store, but he didn't turn around. Unless it was a maneuver to throw us off."

"Which brings us back to how is Wallace involved?"

"Taryn may not be the target," Grayson said. "If she'd been on his hit list, he'd have taken her out a long time ago. Who else would Iris Ryan want dead?"

"She managed to get rid of most of those who could have testified against her. But who does she want dead in addition to getting her hands on Taryn? I have no clue because none of those we've interviewed were high profile."

Joe slapped the dashboard. "We've gone too long without sleep. We keep circling the situation and running into one obstacle after another. What do you know about Iris Ryan?"

"She's the ice queen of Wall Street and an expert in all the ruthless tactics known to big business. I read where she warned the other traders she'd leave footprints on their graves and dead flowers for their widows and girl-friends."

"Sounds like 'ice queen' is a generous title. Personal life?"

"Very private. Only a few close friends, and they won't comment on their relationship. Parents deceased. No children. Been through four husbands. Each one helped spike her career. When she became more powerful than hubby, she ditched him. Her latest escort is ex-husband number four, her attorney."

"Have we talked to him yet?" Joe said.

"In progress. I imagine if anyone knows her, the ex would."

"What went on before her rise as an oil and gas trader?"

"Only child. Raised by her dad, who had her in a boarding school from the time she was six. High achiever. Best schools. Keen business sense. The problem is she doesn't care how she keeps climbing. She managed power of attorney when her father was ill. Took control of his assets and left him in a nursing home until he died."

Grayson's radio alerted him to an incoming call, and he responded.

"Spotted a black Escalade less than a mile from

your destination. Looks abandoned," the female agent said.

"Meet you there. Could be a decoy." He flipped on his lights and raced down the road.

Joe touched his shoulder. "Are you prepared to face the worst?"

Grayson clenched his jaw. For almost four days, Taryn had occupied his thoughts in one way or another. He'd gone to bat for her when others were ready to slap on the cuffs. He didn't want to think about finding her dead.

11:19 p.m. Thursday

Taryn limped along the left side of the gravel road, holding her broken arm. She'd found a flashlight in the Escalade's glove box, but she used it only when the blackness confused her. She faced oncoming traffic, but every few seconds she stole a glimpse behind her. The main road crossing ahead held an occasional vehicle, but those looked like miles away at her pace. Once she reached the crossroad, she'd find a state highway patrol car, the FBI, or someone who'd help her.

Her left arm throbbed along with the rhythm of her heartbeat. The right side of her face must be swelling because she could barely see from her right eye. When hadn't she hurt? She probably resembled a poster child for "Stay Away from Professional Assassins." No matter what she did to help the FBI, her good intentions backfired. A logical person would advise her to back off from a task that she had no skills for. But she refused to give up until Zoey and all those responsible for the mayhem were found. If she survived.

The last time she'd been afraid, Buddy had joined her. What she wouldn't give to have that beautiful German shepherd beside her. Or Grayson.

Don't go there. You're leaning on him because of your own insecurities.

Grayson, where are you? You warned me not to do this, but I insisted. His words at the retirement center flowed into her head and heart. He understood her issue with trust and spoke through her fears. She realized counseling would be needed to smooth out the speed bumps of the past three months. Did Grayson see her future along that path? Was he ready to climb aboard the train with her and Zoey? Had he given any thought to their friendship with a very needy three-year-old? God help him if he chose to take on her baggage.

To keep her mind occupied, she thought back through the evening since encountering Cameron Wallace—the things he'd said that Grayson could use. Very little, actually.

She'd barely come two miles, and dizziness wanted to overtake her. How fast would Cameron walk? Fearing she'd faint and fall on her left side, she sank to the ground. A little rest and she'd move on.

Blackness enveloped her, and she gave in to the relief from pain and her jumbled thoughts.

Chapter 54

Grayson drove toward the area where the Escalade had been spotted. Another FBI car sped behind him. A third on its way. Through his night goggles, he saw a glow from the right side of the road. A body lay on the grass. His nerves screamed alarm. He swerved and stopped behind the fallen figure, allowing the car behind him to pass.

He jerked off the night goggles and grabbed the flashlight lying on the dash. The instant the beam settled on the body, he recognized the turquoise shirt and the mass of auburn hair. His focus should be on his job, not the woman on the ground.

"Easy, Grayson," Joe said. "I'm right here with you." He grabbed his Glock.

Grayson released his seat belt, not able to get out of the car fast enough. Pulling his gun, he followed the flashlight to where she lay. "Let me know if you see that scum."

"I'll kill him and do the world a favor."

Grayson bent to Taryn's side. She lay on her back with her right arm holding her left. Her right eye was swollen and a bruise trailed down her cheek. "Taryn. Are you okay?" Her stomach rose and fell, giving him hope. "Taryn?"

"Hey," she whispered. "Is this my knight in shining armor?"

He wanted to draw her into his arms, but he might hurt her. "Just your loyal FBI agent. Where do you hurt besides the nasty bruises on your face?"

She blinked and opened her eyes. "My left arm's broken. Heard it snap."

"We can get that fixed. Anything else?"

"I'm good. Semi-good."

Her spirit hadn't been damaged. "Should I call an ambulance?"

"No. Don't want the exposure. Just drive me where I need to go."

She even sounded like an agent. "What about Wallace?"

"Left him a few miles back. He's on foot somewhere. Has his gun and phone."

That didn't make sense with the Escalade parked down the road, but he'd find out more once she was in the car and on the way to a hospital. "I'm going to help you get to the truck and avoid your left arm." He pulled his shirt over his head and tied it around her arm and neck. "Tell me when something hurts."

"Like my whole body?" She drew in a breath and reached for him with her right hand while he pulled her to her feet.

"Wallace will pay for this."

She moaned. "He already has . . . but you can add to his misery."

Grayson vowed she'd never be beaten like this again. He turned to Joe. "Do you see anything?"

"Nope. You have one tough lady there," Joe said. "I want to hear her story. Might need to put it in my memoirs."

"Joe—" her voice still a whisper—"at this rate, I'm going to write my own."

Only his Taryn could keep her humor in a raw situation. He eased her onto the seat of the old Dodge pickup. "This will be a bit of a squeeze with you in the middle. No seat belts for you."

"Grayson, be careful of my arm when you slide in, okay?"

"Sure, honey." He caught himself, but it was too late. Maybe she didn't hear.

"Grayson." She swallowed hard. "Concentrate on stopping this death spree. If you and I are to be something more, it'll have to happen later."

He felt like the tables were turned and she was Joe or the SSA. "I'm sorry."

"It's okay. Actually, it sounded good."

He chuckled and radioed the other agents about Wallace being on foot and added that he was transporting Taryn to a hospital in Huntsville. Joe joined them on the passenger side.

"Unless you intend to drive with one foot out of this truck, you'll have to touch me," she said to Grayson in a weak voice.

"Putting you in more pain is the last thing I want to do," he said.

"At this point, we're the Three Musketeers. Feel free to take over my broken arm."

Joe laughed. "Will you marry me?"

"Not today. Consummating the vows is out of the question." She gasped. "I can't believe I said that. Oh, I'm so sorry. What a crude thing to say."

"It's the battered body talking," Joe said. "We've heard a whole lot worse."

"But not from me."

"What about your tattoo?" Grayson said, remembering one of their first conversations in the hospital.

"What tattoo?"

"Uh, never mind." He hesitated before drilling her with questions. "Do you feel like talking about Wallace?"

"I have to." Her voice grew quieter. She relayed what had happened since Wallace picked her up at the convenience store. "I'd heard of devices to disengage trackers. Developed in Germany. Although he denied participating in the airport bombing, he didn't deny his link to Nehemiah."

"He gave no indication where Zoey is being held?"

She drew in a breath. "Sorry. I'm trying to be brave. I have to believe she's somewhere waiting for me. I don't think God would bring us this far and abandon us."

Joe's phone alerted him to a text. "We have an

ID on Dina Dancer, confirmed by her brother," he said. "She's Dina Pedraza, Jose's sister."

"Could she have Zoey?" Taryn said.

Grayson recalled praying for his mother and how he'd asked God to help him hold tight to her hand, even when she released it and disappeared into the whirlwind. "How will you handle it if Dina doesn't have Zoey and she's gone?"

"I don't want to think about it."

12:32 a.m. Friday

Taryn sucked in her panic. If Zoey wasn't alive? Could her death be compared to all those who'd died in the airport bombing? A statistic? Was that what Grayson meant? Or did he want her to be strong and face another possible tragedy?

She tried to put herself in his shoes. He was committed to learning the truth and finding the killers. Perhaps he could divorce himself from allowing his heart to take over, but she couldn't. She formed her words, letting them roll around in her head logically yet woven with intense emotion.

"Every person who dies needlessly deserves the responsible one to be held accountable," she said. "But I refuse to think of Zoey gone until I see her body. The reason I won't stop is because of her." She closed her eyes. "I keep seeing bodies at the airport and hospital corridors lined with the injured."

"Taryn, I'm not callous," Grayson said. "If I allow every chaotic event to affect me emotionally, then I can't do my job."

"I understand. I just want you to see where I'm coming from."

"I do. Would it be easier to relax until we can get to a hospital?"

"You mean like sitting in a dark room until someone turns the light on?" A jolt of pain raced to her shoulder. "This arm really does hurt."

Joe's gaze flew to her. "What can I do for you?"

"Be yourself." She held her breath to manage the pain. "Both of you, what else happened tonight?"

"You tell her, Grayson," Joe said.

"You can. She likes you better."

"You're younger. Better-looking."

"Guys," she said. "It hurts to laugh."

"Okay," Grayson said. "Haden Rollins came through with a name."

"The New York person?"

Grayson explained how the man confessed to what he'd done for an oil and gas trader by the name of Iris Ryan and that she'd hired a hacker to give her access. "We're looking for her."

"The BOLO thing?"

"Yes, ma'am. He indicated feelings for Kinsley Stevens. She's his biggest concern."

"Good." Taryn whispered a prayer of thanks.

Soon they'd all have answers. "Why did she have the airport bombed?"

Grayson gripped the steering wheel. "Haden doubts she initiated the bombing."

The hope from moments before died in her throat.

Chapter 55

2:13 a.m. Friday

I sit on my bed in the hotel room and call my attorney ex-husband. He hates being wakened in the middle of the night, but that's why he's paid far more than he's worth.

"I'm not asleep, Iris," he says. "The FBI issued a subpoena for your office, and they're going through every inch of your hard copy and online files."

"Why didn't you call me?"

"What good would that have done? I know you don't have anything incriminating there."

"I'm not surprised by their search. Always a step behind the masterminds of this country."

"Iris, you weren't honest about your involvement with Gated Labs or LNG."

He speaks to me like I'm an insolent child. "Excuse me?" My voice rises.

"Haden Rollins talked to the FBI. Named you as the prime mover behind the attempts to steal software from Gated Labs. There's a warrant for your arrest, and you're suspected of kidnapping a child."

Rollins would pay for his loose lips. "Build a case against him. I'll give you all you need."

"I'm not in the mood to take orders. What have you done?"

"Just business. I'm tough, but I follow the rules."

"What about the law? You're also being linked to the airport bombing in Houston."

"Your job is to represent me."

"You pulled that off? Never mind. I don't want to know."

"Right. I called you, remember? I'm not surfacing until you go to the FBI and work out a deal. I'll name the CEO, Brad Patterson, as the originator and Rollins as his accomplice. Formier ordered killings and the confiscation of top-secret files at Gated Labs. I'll claim I was sleeping with Rollins, and he confessed his part to me. I was afraid for my life and ran."

"Sure you don't want to implicate Taryn Young?" His dry tone didn't deter me.

"I'll take care of her myself."

"So that's why you're in Houston?"

"None of your business where I am or why. Call me when you have this messy thing handled." I end the call and pour myself a drink. Finishing it, I flip on the TV for the latest news. The first image I see is my photo, actually two. One is my professional shot and the other is with the blonde wig I'm wearing now. I brought a third disguise, a pixie wig with purple streaks. It looked great with green contacts and black-framed sunglasses. Each look has a different set of clothes, and those outfits are with me.

A reward's been offered for information.

I pour another drink. He hasn't called, and that's dangerous. I know he's here, so what's he doing? I pull my gun from my purse and wrap my fingers around the cold metal. It's ready for when he makes his appearance.

I call Save to make sure his work is on schedule.

Young designed a false entrance into the software, and it shut down his computer. He's behind on his commitment. Timing is everything.

Chapter 56

3:25 a.m. Friday

Taryn walked with Grayson and Joe from the treatment center of the hospital ER much sooner than she'd expected. There were perks to being escorted by the FBI. Her arm rested in a cast that extended to her fingers, and she cringed at the thought of maneuvering a keyboard. Oh, but it throbbed. When hadn't she hurt somewhere over the past four days? She'd refused an injection for pain and instead requested some non-drowsy pain medication. She hated existing on pills and injections that blocked out the real world—not her style of living.

Joe whipped out a pen from his shirt pocket. "I need something permanent to write with. Your arm is a canvas." He turned to a young woman at the receptionist desk. "Excuse me, miss. Do you have a marker?" He followed up with a smile that must have won him every female within miles when he was younger. She gave him black, green, and red markers.

Taryn offered her casted arm. "Make it good."

Joe winked and wouldn't let her see his masterpiece. She grinned at Grayson, but the look on his face shook her. They were there, his feelings for her, and he wasn't hiding them. Her face grew warm, her own vulnerability seeping through the pores of her skin.

"There you are." Joe beamed like a little boy.

Taryn took a peek and laughed. He'd written the words in green and added a touch of red. *To the girl who hacked her way into my heart.*

"That's cheesy," Grayson said. "My turn, and don't look. The artist is at work. I need the red and green markers."

"You two are incorrigible." She sealed the light moments to memory.

"Yeah, and I taught him everything he knows," Joe said. "His charm and good looks come from me."

Grayson seemed to take forever before he capped the markers and handed them to Joe. "My words will go down in infamy."

"Read it aloud, Taryn, for the full effect," Joe said.

Taryn drew in a sharp breath to keep the tears buried. " 'To my new partner, who's never let me down.' You two are going to make me cry."

"Won't be the first time." Joe wrapped his arm around her waist. "Last time I had the honors."

She shook her head to dispel the wave of emotion. "When this is over, I'm taking both of you to dinner."

"When this is over, I plan to tackle a lot of things." Grayson opened the ER door to the parking lot. It had rained, and the parking lot was a mess of puddles, as though the world were cleansed and the end was in sight.

Joe laughed. "When this is over, I'll shower our lady with fine pearls."

Taryn startled and stopped in the parking lot. "Pearls."

"What?" Grayson said.

They knew her every move. Murford had planted a tracking device . . . but what? Not her wedding ring . . . She touched her ears. "Claire gave me a pair of pearl earrings for my wedding day. When Murford saw them, he suggested I not take them off until after the honeymoon."

She yanked out one and then the other. "I think

their GPS is here." She tossed them into a puddle of water. "Now try to find me."

As they picked their way through the parking lot, Joe updated them on what was happening. Cameron Wallace had slipped under the radar and was suspected to be on foot. But his exploits around the globe had proven him highly skillful in avoiding law enforcement types. Why had he kidnapped her when his specialty was pulling the trigger? So many questions while the clock ticked closer to the 11:00 a.m. export launch of LNG. No threats had been made to the companies. No anticipated delays. Just a group of shrouded people who were intent on stopping the export with a series of bodies to prove their point.

Earlier, after Taryn had been at the convenience store, Grayson retrieved her purse and phone from the trash. A plus in the havoc of the night. She checked her cell for a message from Save. He'd texted her.

"Guys, I need to call Save." She pressed in his number, and he answered on the first ring. "Got your text. What's up?"

He cursed. "Problems and more problems. The developer has nested more layers in this program than I have time to penetrate."

"I thought you were in and testing it. I've had the flu and haven't done a thing."

"False front. When I tested the software, a virus shut me down and froze my computer. Now I'm on another laptop and working my way through this labyrinth."

"Send me what you have, and I'll see what I can do."

"Make it fast. The boss is all over me. Wants the access now."

"What did you tell her?" Taryn said.

"That I'm a hacker, a professional who needs space to think through each calculated move. Don't ask her response."

"How far are you into the system?"

"Depends on what I find. I want to be sure before I hose this laptop. I'll text you the details." Save ended the call.

Taryn ordered herself to stop trembling. "The virus worked, and now he's trying to reverse-engineer things. Wants my help."

"This will be okay," Grayson said. "Can you toss him a bone?"

"Sure. I'll wait a few minutes and text him. His boss is impatient."

Grayson opened the pickup door for her. "Iris Ryan is anything but tolerant. Joe, do we have an update on what's going on with her?"

Joe entered the passenger side and searched through his BlackBerry. "Agents report her ex-husband had nothing to state and has no idea where she is. I don't believe that for a minute. He claims she's been framed, and he's working on a statement. Nothing found in her office, but a sweep is being done of her entire building." He held up a finger. "A search warrant has also been issued for her residence."

"Anything on the other investigations?" Grayson pulled out of the hospital parking lot. One more time she was en route to the FBI office in Houston and not alone.

"Authorities are still looking for Zoey. People from Claire Levin's church are going door to door in the Huntsville State Park area, and a motorcycle club has volunteered in the search."

Taryn swallowed the sobs threatening to steal her composure. "I still think she's in the area. Murford mentioned more than once his love for fishing and a cabin there. I know the cabin was empty, and the fingerprint sweep revealed no one in your database. But I think whoever has Zoey took her to a similar site." If only the answers were a few keystrokes away. She was fishing too.

God, help us before it's too late.

"Dear lady," Joe began, "the search teams are combing every inch of that park and surrounding homes."

"Am I a fool to think when we find Zoey, we'll unlock this whole mess?"

Neither man responded.

"I'm going to think back over every conversation with Murford. No man is smart enough to guard every word."

"Maybe I can rattle something loose," Grayson

said. "Unusual phone calls? Private conversations with George Breckon?"

She concentrated on the man and his moods. "I remember a phone call in which he mentioned 'some walls were thicker than others.' Now I see he meant Nehemiah's firewall, or my refusal to sleep with him, or my reluctance to leave my techno gadgets alone with him. If he and his buds broke into my condo while I was in the hospital, why didn't he go that route before?"

"Fear of getting caught. And he thought he had the situation under control," Grayson said. "Control ranks at the top of his motivation. Along with a heavy dose of narcissism."

Taryn studied the clock on Grayson's truck. Even with all the agents and law enforcement agencies working on the bombing, the prospect of compromised software, and a missing child, how could it all be resolved before 11:00 a.m.?

"Hey, we have company," Grayson said.

Taryn whirled around. An SUV rapidly approached from the rear. "Wallace," she whispered. The highway ahead lay void of traffic . . . the perfect spot to be intercepted.

Both agents pulled their weapons.

"Taryn, get down in the seat." Grayson stepped on the gas.

"He must have watched us leave the hospital," she said. When would this be over?

She bent over in the cramped space, favoring

her left arm. The SUV crashed into their rear. Stifling a scream, she jostled and banged her head against the steering wheel. A rush of wind and sound met her, and she assumed Joe had lowered his window. An exchange of fire left her trembling and wishing she had her own gun.

"It's me they're after," she said. "I'll go with them." No one else needed to be hurt or killed.

"Fat chance," Grayson said. But his words might get him killed.

A pop sounded, and a rear tire sank to the concrete. The Dodge bounced, swerved, and leaned to the right on two wheels. She rose to see Grayson steering wildly to keep the truck on the road. She braced herself as the vehicle flipped.

Chapter 57

3:55 a.m. Friday

Taryn screamed, and the pickup ceased rolling, upside down.

Odd how life could spin and drop at the same time.

The door on Joe's side clicked open. Her mind wavered between consciousness and the safety net of blackness. A hand steadied her and then lifted her from the truck. She wouldn't say a word but listen—and pray Grayson and Joe were okay.

The scent of Cameron Wallace met her nostrils, and with it rose fear, raw and primal.

He tossed her onto the backseat of the SUV and raced off. She believed they were the only two in the vehicle and opened her eyes a slit to confirm it. She mentally checked herself for additional injuries and didn't note new ones.

"I heard you moan, Taryn," Wallace said. "Can't outrun me. I'll give you credit, though. You know how to think on your feet."

Suck it up. Play the role. Pray Joe and Grayson aren't hurt badly. She slowly sat.

"You also have a daredevil streak," he said.

The tag meant more when it came from Grayson. "Is that a compliment?"

"I'll put it in your epitaph."

She was so tired that she no longer cared about his threats. The game needed to end. But she'd not give up. She'd play until the last whistle blew. "Nothing's changed since we were together?"

"This isn't a date."

Her arm throbbed along with her head and eye. She shuddered at what he'd do in retaliation. "Okay, I get it that you killed Murford. I get it Iris Ryan wants access to the software. I get it she has a hacker working on that access. I get it she has Zoey to force me into giving her what she wants. Those things make sense. And I get it that I won't live to see many more sunrises. But why did Ryan bomb the airport?"

He chuckled. "You don't have all the facts."

"What am I missing?"

"I don't work for Iris Ryan. She and I have the same boss."

Was the FBI aware of this? "Does your boss have the little girl?"

"If you're referring to the Zoey person, that was Iris's plan."

"Will I meet the woman?"

"Before or after I kill her?"

The pieces had shifted. All this time she thought the New York connection was the mastermind linking Nehemiah and the bombing into one bizarre picture.

"A contract to kill the Ryan woman and Murford is why you're in the States?"

He glanced at her in the rearview mirror. "You sure ask a lot of questions. But yes. You're a bonus."

"Am I a third victim, or are you going to transport me to your boss?"

"Depends on your attitude."

She stared out the window, noting they were driving toward Houston on I-45. Had the FBI been able to follow them? Lights of businesses lined both sides of the highway as they drove through the Conroe area. More traffic. A state trooper passed them. How were Grayson and Joe? Neither had uttered a sound when Wallace took her from the truck. She reached for the door. Locked.

"Don't give up, do you?" Wallace said. "By the way, you look awful."

"I'll go down fighting."

"I have no doubt. You're fun, Taryn. I'll be sorry for this to end."

"Glad I've been so entertaining." But playing the witty, assertive, aggressive woman had lost its charm. Taryn Young wanted to give up. The past few days had drained the life out of her with no results. Her thoughts rested on Claire, all the dead and wounded, and Zoey.

"Lost your FBI buddies when I nabbed you the first time. Just you and me now."

"It's not over."

"I'm a calculating kind of professional." He turned left and drove north again. "Never talk to my prey. No need to. Plan the killing and do it. You've seen a side of me no other victim has. Hope you feel special."

This wasn't over yet. Did she really have a choice but to give her best a little longer? Had Zoey given up too?

4:14 a.m. Friday

In the flipped truck, Grayson opened his eyes and did a quick body assessment. Nothing hurt, except his head, and that was the hardest part of his body. He gave Joe his attention. In the shadows, blood trickled from a nasty gash on the right side of his uncle's forehead and down

391

both sides of his face. He must have hit the door. Grayson listened to his uncle's chest. Breathing. "Joe, are you okay?"

When his uncle didn't respond, Grayson released his seat belt and turned off the engine. Whoa, where was Taryn?

He'd failed to protect her.

Cameron Wallace or Iris Ryan had nabbed her.

He exited the driver's side and hurried to help Joe while pleading for his uncle to hold on to life. A semitruck stopped, and the driver waved. "I called 911."

Grayson shouted thanks and yanked on the passenger door. A low groan met him. "Stay with me, Joe. Help is on the way."

The truck driver approached, a fence-post-thin man with a tattered Astros cap. "I saw a car take off."

"I'm FBI. Don't suppose you got a license plate number?"

"Too far off. Phoned 911, though." He peered at Grayson attempting to pull Joe from the pickup. "I'll climb in on the other side and get this guy out of there. Hangin' upside down ain't good for nobody but possums."

Grayson considered the risk of taking him out of the pickup, but leaving him suspended with dripping blood couldn't be healthy. Together, they eased him out and laid him on the soft ground.

Local law enforcement arrived, and Grayson explained the situation. "I'll need your backup once we locate the SUV."

"You got it. Did you get the license plate?"

"No."

"Okay."

By the time the ambulance pulled onto the scene, Joe had regained consciousness. Except for the deep slice on his forehead, he appeared all right. His first words were concern for Taryn.

"Put a Band-Aid on my head and send those paramedics home," he said.

"You could have a concussion," Grayson said.

"Taryn's out there somewhere with more injuries than me. Get us a vehicle and let's leave this Popsicle stand."

Grayson blew out his response as the two paramedics laughed. "All right. I'll find us a ride."

The truck driver pointed behind him. "I live about two miles away. The little woman and I have us a double-wide on forty acres. Anyway, we got two extra ve-hiculars sittin' over there. Both run like racehorses. I'll call her and let you boys borrow one."

Grayson loved down-home people. "It might not return in good shape."

"Aw. That's okay. I got insurance." He pulled a cell phone from his shirt pocket and pressed in a number. "Hey, babe. I'm over here on I-45 near

393

the turnoff to home. Can you drive over? Got a couple of FBI agents who need one of our rides. Don't care which one. You choose. Thanks, babe. . . . Oh, that'd be real nice. Love you." He nodded at Grayson. "She'll be here in a few minutes, and she's bringing a couple of insulated mugs with hot coffee too."

Grayson reached out to shake his hand. "Thanks. I don't even know your name."

The man offered a firm grip. "Frank Lewis."

Joe shook his hand too. "Appreciate all you've done."

"The good Lord would have me do no less. Wish I'd gotten that there license plate for ya."

"That's all right. You've done a lot already."

Ten minutes later, Frank's wife arrived with a ten-year-old Chevy Impala, not a mark on it and all gassed up. She handed them two huge travel mugs of strong coffee that tasted heaven-made.

With Joe wearing his red badge of courage, he and Grayson sped in the direction Frank had indicated the car had gone.

"Do you suppose Rollins or Pedraza came through with information we can use?" Joe leaned his head back.

Grayson mentally kicked himself for no searching for Taryn's pain meds before leaving the crime scene. Joe had to be in pain and too stubborn to admit it. "I called while you wer getting fixed up. Pedraza said Dina lived in the Conroe area."

"Bet Taryn's there. I'll blow a few heads off if they hurt her."

Joe's knock on the head must have shaken his brains. Grayson hoped he was okay and pushed forward. "Makes sense to me that Dina would have Zoey. Right now, we—" His BlackBerry interrupted him, and he read while driving. "Pedraza has no idea if his sister has the child."

"He knows more." Joe paused. "Dad-blasted liar." He rubbed his head around the bandage.

"Are you sure you want to continue with this?"

"Yes. Just managing a little headache." He stiffened, then relaxed. "Anyway, sure would like to interrogate Pedraza and Rollins myself. The way I feel, I'd not be following any rules. Anything else?"

"Pedraza gave his sister's cell number. It's a burner, and she's not answering. Agents are en route to the address he provided."

"Makes me wonder if she's alive."

Grayson had considered the same thing. Frustration burned. He had no idea where Taryn had been taken.

"Were you unconscious when she was taken?" Joe said.

"Yep. Don't remember a thing."

When would these guys slip?

Chapter 58

4:50 a.m. Friday

Taryn rode with Wallace through heavy rain. What she'd originally thought was cleansing now splattered toward her life's end. He drove down a lane that was about a quarter mile long to a deserted house in the middle of nowhere. The headlights showed boarded windows and a small structure in bad need of paint. A dilapidated porch. No visible lights, but the covered windows could conceal what was going on inside. Wallace eased the SUV behind a barn and pulled inside. A Lincoln Town Car was parked on the right and a Honda Accord on the left. He killed the engine. The only sound was the steady rain.

"We're here," Wallace said, too chipper for her liking. "Doesn't look like much, but it serves the boss's purpose."

She blinked to adjust her eyes to the dark, but the blackness hid any sights that would give her a clue to her location. He opened his door, faint light illuminating shadows around her. A bridle looped over a nail on the wall. A bucket hung beside it. Tack for horses dominated what she could see on the barn's wall. Four stalls, two on each side. In the corner two bales of hay rested next to a pitchfork. The latter she could use in defending herself. If she seized an opportunity to grab it. He closed his door. Darkness again.

Her shirt had buttons in front. She yanked off the bottom two and clutched them in her palm. With the rain, Wallace couldn't cover his SUV tracks, and she could only pray someone would find it unusual for a vehicle to drive back into deserted property. And finding two white buttons in the middle of mud and dirt would be random.

He opened the door on her side. "You'll need to wait here until it's time for your appointment."

His face faded from view. The chameleon. What could she do to escape him?

"The boss has been asking for you, but he has a few details to work on first. Stay right here." He walked away, his feet slapping against the wet floor. A few moments later, he returned and jerked her from the vehicle. She couldn't fight what she couldn't see, and he wouldn't fall for the same trick twice. He pulled her to the right. She scuffed her feet on the barn floor . . . whatever she could think of to leave a trail. He pushed her face-first against what she realized was the Lincoln and wrapped a rope around her right wrist and then around her waist, sealing her casted arm against her.

"Does your boss have a name?" she said.

"I'll let him do the honors."

"Can you prep me for this guy?"

"You won't have any problem communicating

with him. He's the kind of man who asks the right questions and expects the right answers."

His ragged breathing seemed to singe her neck, his presence like a predator's. He gagged her with what she thought was a sweat-soaked cotton scarf or bandanna. He stepped back, and a trunk popped open. *Oh, please, not there.* Claustro-phobia plagued her, and since these people knew everything about her, they'd have this tidbit too. . . .

Wallace swept her up and dumped her into the trunk. The scent of gasoline and worn boots met her nostrils. Another rope wrapped around her ankles. "Think of this as a precursor to a coffin. Get used to it." He slammed the trunk.

She'd have air, but her instincts told her otherwise. Fighting the panic that accompanied her fear of closed spaces, she prayed for strength. This was temporary until they questioned her, a holding place designed to frighten her. And it worked.

A car engine hummed to life, but not the one she was in. Wallace was leaving in the Honda? How long would she be here? Wallace's boss needed access . . . unless Save had managed to find it. Acid rose in her throat and she forced it back down. Choking to death on her own vomit while locked in a trunk wasn't the ending she had in mind. The car left the barn, and she clung to the purr of the engine until it faded into oblivion.

God was with her, and He'd stay to the end.

She thought of Claire and how she'd wanted to prove her love. And so many others—her parents and brothers, who'd supported her even when she was the school nerd. Dear Ethan, who'd always encouraged her to stretch her mind, and how she'd only wanted to protect him by not documenting every aspect of Nehemiah. Joe, who made her laugh and see reality. The FBI, who gave her an opportunity to prove her innocence. And Grayson, the man who wanted her to trust him. The man who would have won her heart.

Soon she'd know who fought so hard to kidnap her, kill others, and do the same to her once she gave them full access to Nehemiah. If Wallace's boss didn't have Zoey, she'd refuse to cooperate and endure whatever they planned. If he did have Zoey, then God help her make the right decisions.

5:30 a.m. Friday

Grayson pulled over to the side of a country road and waited for a call back from the SSA. His BlackBerry rang. Odd—the caller was Frank Lewis. Annoyance trickled through him at even a moment's delay in finding Taryn.

"Grayson, I have an idea," Frank said. "I know this area like the back of my hand. Grew up here. I'm going to drive around to a few of my old haunts. See if I can find your friend."

"That's dangerous. You've seen what they can do."

"Not the way I look at it. I'm a God-and-country

kinda guy. Already called my two brothers. We all live right around here, and this is our territory. Those pissants ain't got a thing on us boys who know where's the best hiding places."

Grayson wanted to add that Taryn could be miles away, but Frank had a point. "Call me if you see anything suspicious. Don't be pulling out your rifles."

Frank chuckled. "Someday I'll tell you a few stories 'bout me and my brothers in our hell-raisin' days. Gotta go." He ended the call.

Grayson explained to Joe what was happening on their behalf.

"Hope those good ole boys stay safe," Joe said. "Better yet, I'd welcome them finding something solid."

"I hate the thought of being outdone." Grayson palmed the steering wheel. He'd failed all those who'd died at the airport and so many others. But worst of all, he'd failed Taryn.

Chapter 59

5:57 a.m. Friday

I've been awake for too many hours, and I need sleep. But I can't close my eyes until my path is clear. Too many people have obstructed my vision, and one by one they're paying for their lack of competency.

What's infuriating me the most is he's not responding to my texts. He knows we need to discuss critical issues and get them resolved before eleven. I have a laundry list of priorities, and he's not conducting business as partners. Neither is he keeping his part of the agreement by depositing money into my account. I'm ready to take him on, and my patience is crumbling.

I shiver, and it has nothing to do with the air-conditioning set at sixty-eight degrees. Did I get in over my head with this deal? The man's a killer and most assuredly set me up to take the fall for the Gated Labs theft and the airport bombing. However, he doesn't have enough evidence to point any fingers at me. Rollins is the obvious scapegoat for Gated Labs. I thought he was too afraid of me to break, but the media claims otherwise. My money buys a better story. Confidence wafts through me. My lawyer has me covered. That's what he's paid for.

Soon my thoughts take me to a place where fear seizes power. I'd bargained for a huge chunk of American pie, but his motives are deeper. Why else would he bomb an airport?

Wait him out.

Wait until he contacts me.

Wait in this hole of a hotel for him to summon me like I'm an employee stuck in the mail room.

This is a temporary setback. I, Iris Ryan, am at

the top of my game, and I have no place to travel but up.

His threats rumble around my brain, which is why I pack a gun. I have a permit to carry it, so all will be legal when I face charges of defending myself.

I've called Save every thirty minutes. His partner is accomplishing zilch, and I paid her front money. No matter. They'll both be dead by this time tomorrow. My tolerance for them has run thin. The deal was for this morning at 6 a.m., and they've both run out of time. I have to keep telling myself Taryn Young only thinks the software is attacker-proof. If I'd been smarter, I'd have bought her out at the beginning. But he told me it was impossible.

My bottle's empty, and I need to sober up. A shower sounds good, and I'll have my phone nearby. In the bathroom, I turn on the water and curse the threadbare towels. Definitely not the Westin. A text comes through. It's him.

6:00 is approaching. Do U have what I need?

I'm standing here naked, and I feel like he's watching me. I text my response.

Soon.

Not good enough.

Can we meet?

We will.

What does he mean? I text back and he doesn' respond. Over the months we've corresponded and met, I've seen him take the upper hand far too many times. If Save doesn't come through, I'll need to leave the country. A new identification is in my purse.

He won't win.

I take my shower. At least I have my own shampoo and conditioner, even if I have to wear the pixie wig. I dress the part and make sure my makeup is impeccable. My shoulders ache from the weariness and stress. When this is over, I'm taking a long vacation to the French Riviera.

A text comes through, and I snatch my phone.

Meet me 2.5 Miles E of I45 N on F M 1097

The map on my phone indicates the point is outside a small burg called Willis. I'll need gas. Especially if I'm driving to Oklahoma to catch a flight out of the country. Too risky to fly out of Texas. I pick up my phone to return his text.

Leaving now

I'll contact U

Chapter 60

6:35 a.m. Friday

Taryn fought the rising anxiety and difficulty breathing that accompanied her claustrophobia. She thought the problem had disappeared after a year of counseling. No longer did elevators, closed doors, planes, and small cars cause her to hyperventilate. But the scenarios in the counselor's office didn't equate to being kept prisoner in the trunk of a car. Perspiration stung her eyes and dripped down her face. Her body temp had risen along with her blood pressure.

Reactions solve nothing. Actions produce results, she thought and focused on the reality of not being alone. Hadn't she told herself she'd not endure the future by herself, no matter how short?

Her mind crept back to the three months spent with Murford and the foolishness of falling for him. Nothing clung to her heart and mind's database that she could use to pull the mess together. If only Ethan were alive. He'd be able to help Grayson and Joe end this horror. Finding Iris Ryan would help too. Oil and gas traders had a reputation for being heartless, and Ryan's hit tilt.

Taryn focused on what she knew while her body calmed. . . .

Ryan hired Murford to court Taryn and steal Nehemiah. Ryan also hired Rollins as a safeguard to get the same information through Gated Labs as an inside job, discrediting Taryn and sliding Kinsley Stevens into the leadership role. Murford thought he'd put Rollins to work, which meant Ryan had her backside covered. Murford also enlisted a team from his Navy SEAL days and a woman named Dina. The only survivor was Jose Pedraza and whoever had Zoey. Murford went to his grave with his knowledge of the child's whereabouts.

Nothing about Nehemiah registered with the airport bombing. But the link was there, and she'd not give up until she found it.

A wild card by the name of Cameron Wallace, an international assassin, stepped onto the scene. He took out Murford, kidnapped Taryn, and claimed he was supposed to kill Iris Ryan. Wallace indicated he and Ryan had the same boss, and that person was calling the shots. The spiderweb wove tighter.

The unidentified boss wanted full access to Nehemiah, and Taryn was confident the plan involved the destruction of LNG exports. Would his identity reveal the why of the bombing? Because it still made little sense.

Unless a foreign power was backing the crime, as many authorities believed. Some speculations said the Middle East. Others said Russia, the country that supplied Europe with LNG. If the export terminal exploded, the US would experience heavy delays before they'd be in a position to export again. Ryan, if she escaped the legal system, would make a killing on the market and continue to rake in money while prices soared. Taryn understood that aspect, but the unknowns were stopping the FBI from making arrests.

Think, Taryn. Anything in this world is possible.

Everything is negotiable.

7:03 a.m. Friday

Grayson and Joe now drove north on I-45 in Frank Lewis's Chevy Impala. The big car was a gas guzzler, but it ran like a dream. An anonymous tip indicated a deserted trailer house had shown signs of early morning activity. Wallace was a professional who used cunning and skill to his advantage. Highly unlikely he'd expose himself in the open, but Grayson would check out the area.

He recalled snippets of conversations with Taryn and moments when they'd been in danger. Not once had she disappointed him. Personal thoughts would have to hibernate. If he allowed himself to dwell on the high probability of finding Taryn and Zoey dead, he'd lose his edge.

If Taryn caved and gave Wallace or Ryan what they wanted, she'd need Internet connectivity to do it, but a good hot spot could accomplish that.

In short, Grayson leaned toward desperation. Other agents were shooting blanks too, while the time ticked closer to eleven.

Joe scrolled through his BlackBerry. "Agents haven't found anything yet that points to Ryan. Obviously she was careful to use a burner phone on all transactions, and those whom she hired used them too. Doesn't mean we won't find out who made the calls and when. It'll take time."

"Time. The shortage of it is driving me nuts."

"All of us. And you have a huge personal stake in finding Taryn."

Grayson chose not to respond. What could he say?

"Have you mentioned to her how you feel?"

"We've only known each other a few days. And during most of that time, I was trying to keep her alive or from a kidnapper."

"So you haven't?"

Grayson swung a look at his uncle. "I told her I wanted to talk after the case was solved."

"What did she say?"

"Joe!"

"Okay. Not my business. You're a grown man."

"Any good updates? Like finding Zoey?" Grayson said. Anything to get Joe off the subject of Taryn.

"I'm looking." He paused. "Nothing that we haven't seen before." He scrolled through his phone. "Agents haven't reported on the address where she could be held." He glanced up. "This bang on the head has me a bit crazy. Ignore anything stupid."

Grayson chuckled. "Pedraza's been protecting his sister, but he's obviously rethought another stint in prison. Did he offer any idea about the child's welfare?"

"In fact, he did. He said his sister wouldn't hurt her. The last time he saw the child, she was okay.

And his sister drove the vehicle with the bomb into the airport."

A call came through to Grayson from the SSA. "Yes, sir."

"We have information on Zoey Levin."

He didn't like the sound of the SSA's voice. "Let me have it."

"Agents found Dina Pedraza dead, single shot to the forehead. The child was not there, but food and toys indicated she'd been with the woman."

"Taryn and Zoey are probably together." Grayson tasted the bitterness of reality.

"Then find them both," the SSA said. "Alive."

Chapter 61

7:25 a.m. Friday

I despise driving. Look at some of these houses. How do people live in such squalor? I don't see a decent restaurant or hotel.

My cell notifies me of a call. Thinking it's him, I answer it on the first ring.

"This is Save. I've penetrated the firewall. The software's been tested, and it's ready to go."

My heart takes a rare leap. He's late, but there's still time to finish the deal. "And you're sure there're no unforeseen problems?"

"Positive. I'll text you with what you need

Julie is off the radar. I'm the one who hacked in."

"Great. I need it now, and once my work's done, I'll deposit a check into your account." I hang up and make another call. "Be ready. I'll text you after eleven Central time to take care of the hacker and his useless friend. You already have their information." I end the call, wishing I had champagne. The killer has worked for me before . . . discreetly, of course.

A text from Save arrives. Money is no longer the issue. It will flood in, and I'm basking in the power.

I text him the news.

Have access details

With U?

On my phone

Drive until I text U

I want 2 no where I'm going

Do U?

Do not threaten me.

I wait, but he fails to answer.

Chapter 62

7:50 a.m. Friday

If Grayson didn't find something substantial soon, he'd lose what little patience he had left. He felt inept. Stupid. His only job had been to take care of Taryn, and he'd botched it repeatedly. Those who'd planned the crimes since Monday weren't clever enough to project what law enforcement officials would do, yet every lead went south. He and Joe had backtracked and covered the same roads twice. Where had Wallace or Ryan taken Taryn?

The futility of life seized him—the lives gone in an instant, good people and bad. His dad's cancer bothered him more than he wanted to admit. The wall between him and his dad and brother had thickened over the years. They blamed him for Mom's death. No one knew that Mom had let go of his hand during the tornado. No point in telling them. They'd claim he lied. All thought he'd sent Mom into the whirling mass of wind that tossed her like a rag doll to her death. Joe had been telling him for years to forgive himself. But Grayson clung to the guilt as though he deserved condemnation.

He turned right off the interstate and into the small rural town of Willis, passing three churches.

His gaze rested on a white Mercedes and a woman pumping gas at a convenience store. Earlier this morning, agents had been made aware of a third disguise for Iris Ryan, and the woman at the gas pump held a strong resemblance to the photo. Spiked purple hair and sunglasses, along with short shorts and a pink T-shirt promoting breast cancer awareness. Grayson slowed and allowed a Honda Accord to pass, an elderly man bent over the steering wheel with a cigarette hanging from his mouth. Not Wallace. Grayson swung the car back around to the convenience store and pulled behind the Mercedes. The woman hung the handle on the pump and circled her car to leave. She did a 360 of the perimeter, climbed in, and shut the door. Perfect snapshot of the woman in the photo.

Grayson exited his car as hers sprang to life. He pulled his Glock. "Iris Ryan. Stop. FBI."

She stared at him through the exterior mirror. Emotionless. Not frightened or angry.

"Step out of your vehicle and raise your hands," Grayson said.

Ten seconds ticked by before slender legs preceded the woman, obviously for his benefit. She resembled a downtown working girl, not the Wall Street type. "Sir, what is this all about?"

Joe exited the passenger side of the car.

"Are you Iris Ryan?" Grayson said.

"Who?"

"Slowly show me your identification."

"It's in my purse on the car seat. Your partner can get it. I don't mind."

Joe moved toward the passenger side of the Mercedes. Grayson used his BlackBerry to take her photo.

"Who gave you permission to take my picture?" Her voice held a sharp edge.

"I don't need it." Grayson sent the pic to the office. "We'll visit here for a few moments while I wait for verification of your ID."

Joe held up her purse. "Ma'am, do you have a permit to carry this gun?"

"Yes, it's in my wallet with my driver's license. Be careful. It's loaded and the safety's off."

Joe removed her wallet.

"Can I put my hands down? It's tiring," she said.

"Of course." Grayson nodded. She couldn't conceal a weapon in her skimpy garb. "Shut your door and move away from the car."

Her eyes flitted in anger, but she complied.

"Joe, is she good?"

"Driver's license with name and pic. Not Ryan."

"Wonderful," the woman said. "I have no clue who Iris Ryan is, but I hope you gentlemen find her."

"We're not finished yet," Grayson said.

"I'm being detained for no reason." She arched her back like a cat. "You have nothing legally to hold me here. My attorney will be notified of this unlawful obstruction to my day."

Grayson's BlackBerry snatched his attention, and he read the response. Pulling cuffs from his pocket, he took deliberate steps toward her, satisfaction pouring through him. "Iris Ryan, you are under arrest. You have the right to remain silent, the—"

The woman's head jerked back.

A pop indicated a sniper.

Grayson instinctively crouched, the hair on the back of his neck bristling. The bullet had soared between him and Ryan. Her body slumped to the pavement. A red pool dripped down her face, her eyes wide and empty. He cuffed her and felt for a pulse.

Gone.

"Joe, are you okay?"

"Yep. Sure hope the shooter doesn't fire into one of these pumps."

Grayson cringed. "We'll all be burnt toast." He moved to the opposite side of the Mercedes and pulled out his cell. "Requesting backup. Suspect shot by sniper. Need ambulance."

Studying the area to the left, he saw that the killer could be in one of a half-dozen places—hiding behind or inside a one-story brick house that had fallen prey to neglect, a detached frame garage in disrepair, a small grove of spindly pines, or a Ford that hadn't been fired up in ten years.

Cameron Wallace had struck again.

Grayson itched to get back on the road and

check out the area where Frank had indicated unusual activity. But he and Joe were forced to wait at the crime scene until local law enforcement arrived. Joe looked weak. No wonder FBI agents were required to retire in their late fifties.

"I'm going to take a walk. Check out where our sniper came from," Grayson said.

"Not alone."

"You can cover the crime scene." Grayson walked toward the road with his gun drawn. "If we were in the sniper's sights, we'd already be with Ryan."

"Smart aleck."

Grayson gave him a sideways grin and crossed the road. The brick one-story, littered with beer cans, had long since been a home. The recent rains were too late for the burned grass, and fire-ant hills had erupted like little volcanoes. A shame some folks allowed a piece of property to deteriorate when it wouldn't have taken much to keep it looking presentable.

He explored the garage's perimeter, snapping pics of fresh boot prints that disappeared into the woods. A lack of paint, a broken window with jagged pieces of glass and kicked-in boards reminded him of someone who'd been beaten and left to bleed out. About a half mile through a thick growth of trees on a winding, muddy path, a dirt road displayed the tracks of a car. He snapped more pics. The vehicle had come from the east, stopped, turned around, and then driven back. A motorcycle would be nice about now.

While he reversed his steps over the area and stood on the same ground as Iris Ryan's sniper, he thought about what he'd learned of her past. She'd turned her bitterness into greed, and now she was dead. Grayson's father was holding on to a lot of bitterness and facing a serious diagnosis. But Grayson, too, had been carrying the bitterness torch. It wasn't his fault his mom died, but he took the blame and let it come between him and his dad.

When he stopped to explore the terrain for clues, his gaze swept over the abandoned home, reminding him of his own empty soul. Time to forgive himself, forgive his dad, and move on toward the man he was supposed to be.

And he did.

Chapter 63

8:20 a.m. Friday

Taryn's senses quickened. A car drove into the barn. A door slammed, and a single set of footsteps left the area. A click sounded and the trunk opened. Rays of sunlight streamed through the barn rafters, along with droplets of water.

Wallace stood above her wearing a sickening grin. "Hey, sunshine. Did you miss me?" He untied her ankles and pulled her from the trunk.

Needlelike prickles attacked her legs, and she fell into him. She hurt all over from one injury after another, or she'd have attempted to defend herself.

"I know I'm hard to resist, but contain yourself." Steadying her, he released the gag from her dry mouth. "Don't think about calling out. Hurting you would be an extreme pleasure. Do you under-stand?"

"Yes."

"I'm keeping your arms bound. I've seen them and your feet in action," he said. "Obeying me is the only way to survive."

"I'm not making any promises."

"Taryn, your honesty precedes you. The boss is ready to talk. Needed a few cups of coffee first."

"Where's mine?" Although frightened and with no substantial plan to free herself, relief swept through her at the idea of meeting whoever was behind the week's tragedies. Her tongue could get her into trouble, and she resolved to keep her thoughts private until she heard him or her out. Every moment benefited her with time, and her adversary would know that.

Wallace guided her to the rear of the barn and into the fresh morning. After the rain, the country-side glistened. Maybe the day would end better than the rest of the week had.

"To the rear of the house."

With Wallace at her side, she dropped the buttons she'd grasped for hours onto the spongy earth. Birds sang. In the distance, a cow mooed. Life went on . . . good and evil. The towering trees and overgrowth gave the area a tranquil appeal.

Once at the house, Wallace opened the door. It creaked like an old man settling into a chair. She stepped inside the shadowed room, where a candle lit what was once a kitchen. A window adjacent to her was boarded up. Musty smells mixed with coffee met her nostrils.

"Hi, Taryn. Did you get my note?"

Ethan?

She froze.

There had to be a mistake. Her knees trembled. Ethan Formier sat at a dust-ridden table, a gun beneath his fingers. Beside him was an iPad.

"You seem surprised." He leaned back in his chair. How many times had she seen this familiar pose? "I must admit, you've looked better."

Now she knew what Wallace meant when he said she'd have no problem communicating with his boss. She moistened her lips, anger and betrayal threatening her resolve to keep her wits. Wallace shoved her into a chair.

Keep calm. Every second alive buys time for Grayson to find you.

"You have more work to do," Ethan said to

Wallace. "Taryn and I will chat for about fifteen minutes. Return with the package then."

For Zoey's sake, she vowed to listen before losing control. Wallace left the house, leaving her alone with a monster. "What do you want?"

"Nehemiah's source code and the completion of a few other specialty projects." Ethan's menacing tone was out of character. Or was this the real Ethan, when she had grown used to his Gated Labs persona?

"Did you set me up to die in the airport blast?"

"Yes, but when you survived, I realized I could use you."

"For what?"

"For starters, to help me gain access to Nehemiah."

"I figured as much. What else?"

"Two additional software projects according to my specs."

"What kind of software?"

"The kind you're capable of developing."

"And if I refuse?" she said.

"You're not in a position to negotiate."

Taryn dug deep for courage. This man was not her respected friend. "Oh, I'm not?"

"I'll kill you if you don't cooperate. You've seen my best work, beginning with the airport."

Taryn attempted a sardonic laugh. "You will anyway. That's why Cameron Wallace is here."

"I admit to using him to his full potential."

"If I don't provide what you want, you've wasted all this time, effort, and money for nothing."

Ethan lifted a phone from his shirt pocket. "I believe you know Iris Ryan. She claimed she had the info. Said her hacker wormed his way into the software." He studied the device. "I used her to set you up. She thought Murford and Rollins would cover her rear. My hands were clean any way you look at it. Iris was a fool to trust Rollins. He didn't have the guts to get the job done." He turned the phone over in his palm. "I didn't trust her to keep her side of the bargain, so I cloned her phone. Her desire for power and money killed her." He gave Taryn a brittle smile, sending chills up her arms. He repeated a code only she knew.

Please, God, this can't be happening. "Did you clone mine too?" If he'd been successful, then he had the backdoor, which could expose everything.

"You never gave me an opportunity, but since I was your confidant, there wasn't a need."

"You did your job well," she said with all the sarcasm she could muster. "I fell right into your plan."

"From the looks of you, I see you've paid and will continue to pay. Treachery and betrayal doesn't become you, Taryn." He chuckled. "But you've been a worthy adversary." He patted a black backpack slung over his chair. "I have your iPad too."

Save had been successful, and her life was

worthless. Her destiny sat on the dirty table in front of her. "Since you have the code for Nehemiah on that phone, then all you need from me is to develop your software."

"So glad you've agreed to cooperate."

"Do you have Zoey Levin?"

"That was Iris and Murford's arrangement."

How could she believe him? "But you know where she's being held. That's why I'm here—so you can use her to manipulate me."

"Then let it be my little secret until the timing is right."

How many layers did the crimes go? "Are you going to explain to me how the airport bombing played into this?"

"How much do you want to know?"

"All of it." She leaned forward despite the rope wrapped around her waist and hands. "I have a right to understand why you've betrayed our country, sent dozens of people to their deaths, and stolen top-secret information. My life's been a disaster since Monday, and it will probably end here today. I deserve to know why."

"Whining doesn't become you. I'm in control here, and you have no rights." He took a sip of coffee. "This is not my country. I will die burying every American."

The depth of his words unleashed new fear. Up to this moment, her unanswered questions had not factored in the prospect of Ethan involved in international terrorism. She thought he was greedy, like Iris Ryan. "Why?"

"Your country stuck its nose where it didn't belong. I'm Serbian. Your country interfered in our business. My parents, four brothers, their families, and my grandmother were murdered by Albanians." He clenched his fists. "Killed with guns supplied by Americans."

Understanding gave her leverage. "Do you want others to feel your same hatred?"

"I've committed my life to it. Finding it difficult to accept the truth?" He tilted his head. "I did an excellent job. Don't you agree? How did you like those last e-mails I sent? And look how easy it was to obtain my password. Makes me look like a victim, don't you agree? No one will ever expect Ethan, even if the authorities discover I'm alive. I'll go down in history as one of America's heroes. Don't hold your breath for what's about to come."

She refused to believe the walls of her country had been breached—again. The sobering comments of Americans not grasping the threat of what lay outside their doors surfaced. He was indeed a monster. The thought of the airport bombing as a launch for yet another attack sickened her, and she was helpless to stop him. All the law enforcement with their intel and citizens committed to keeping America safe were about to be defeated. She'd experienced the horror and would never forget the blood and destruction.

"What's your real name?" she said.

"You don't like Ethan Formier? My wife does."

"She knows about your plot?" Ethan had adopted his wife's sons too. What an upstanding citizen.

He shook his head. "I'm her Ethan. Nothing else. Didn't want to risk her turning me in." He studied his phone. "She's a good woman and will go to her grave believing I died at the airport. That way she and the boys can live in the life-style I've given them and not ever experience my hand in the bombing. One of the reasons I faked my death was to protect them."

His cold bluntness meant he had no problem eliminating anyone. "Then what's your name?"

"You can call me Ethan. It comes natural for you."

"Who's paying your expenses?"

"Another one of my secrets. You're a smart woman, Taryn. You know what to ask."

In the candlelight, he no longer looked like the Ethan she respected. His eyes narrowed, and the set of his chin indicated anger . . . no, rage. She'd have to be careful. His right finger rested near the trigger of his gun. But he'd been left-handed "Are you ambidextrous?"

"Observant. I learned to use both hands Improved my golf game."

He'd be harder to overcome if he didn't favo

one hand over the other. *Stall him.* "What's happening at eleven o'clock?"

He finished his coffee. "You know the answer to that, my dear."

"Blowing up the export terminal for LNG in Corpus Christi and Canada on the West Coast."

"Well done." He chuckled, a sound she'd once welcomed. "No one will be left alive who can point a finger at me. I've plans to eliminate all those involved in Gated Labs or the bombing."

Control, Taryn. Don't look shocked or afraid. Buy time . . . and strength. "Who do you work for?"

"Think about it."

"Russia?"

"I have friends there. We share . . . let's say, similar goals."

The speculation had been one of the reasons why she'd developed Nehemiah. "I thought you wanted software developed?"

"I do—for my friends."

"What kind of projects?"

"Infrastructure designed to destroy your country."

Did he really think she'd do such a thing? Unless . . . "Where would I work?"

"Out of the country."

"I need Zoey to be set free. I do have a bargaining chip, Ethan."

"What if Wallace is taking care of her now?"

"I don't think so. She's alive until you don't need me."

Ethan swung his hand across her face, sending her sprawling to the cracked linoleum floor. She tasted blood. "That's for all the insolent remarks and the trouble you've caused me. I have your life in the palm of my hand."

"And I have the knowledge to help you reach your hideous goals. I can be just as stubborn as you."

He grabbed her chin and jerked her to her feet. "Only as long as I allow it."

At the thud of footsteps outside the back door, he bolted from his chair. Expectancy sprang to life. Could it be the FBI had found her? "It's our friend Wallace. Truly a professional. He's bringing the package."

A moment later the door squeaked open, and Wallace entered, a sleeping child in his arms.

Zoey.

Chapter 64

8:40 a.m. Friday

When the county sheriff and deputies, two FBI vehicles, and an ambulance arrived at the crime scene, Grayson phoned the SSA and left the area with Joe. Less than two and a half hours until the export launch, and like every agent and law enforcement officer committed to their job, he would not give up until those responsible were cuffed. More priorities hit his list: Taryn and Zoey found.

From the dozen or so anonymous tips that poured in from the area north of Houston, one from Frank finally held credence. At seven thirty this morning, a man and woman on motorcycles who lived in the Willis area were returning from searching for Zoey and noticed two sets of tire tracks heading down a tree-lined, mud-laden lane that led to an abandoned small house and barn. The owner lived out of state and had let it run down. Normally the couple wouldn't question the activity, due to kids partying, but there weren't any vehicles visibly parked in the open field. Not like kids, who always partied in numbers. Another oddity was the absence of beer bottles or telltale odors from a bonfire or weed.

"Did the couple ride back to the property?" Grayson said.

"He started to, but the wife talked him out of it," Frank said. "They pulled their bikes over and walked along the wooded side. Heard a car and saw a Honda Accord pull out of the old barn and head toward Willis."

In time to build a sniper nest for Iris Ryan, and he'd passed a car of that description a few minutes before the shooting. "Thanks, Frank. I'm going to owe you big-time."

"You don't owe me a thing. My friends stopped to see a feller who lives near the property. He owns woods bordering the rear of the place. The owner said he noted an SUV, a Lincoln, and a Honda driving in and out of there for the last two weeks, but the driver parked out of view of the road." Frank gave them directions.

"We're on our way." Grayson left dirt and gravel in his wake.

"You're going on your gut," Joe said.

"Seems right. Whether we find Taryn or Zoey, I feel like it's crucial we check out the spot." Urgency nipped at his heels, and he scrutinized every car and truck along the road.

"I've been in your shoes. No logic to the decision, just a sixth sense, and we follow the instinct until we hit pay dirt. Iris Ryan obviously thought she was in the right place." Joe picked up his phone. "I'm calling the SSA with this development."

The abandoned property was about three and a half miles outside of town on FM 1097 beyond Price Lake and on the outskirts of Sam Houston National Forest. Grayson fought the urge to speed. Instead he drove slowly on the country road with the windows down, always looking, always listening. Cows drank from a pond. Birds chirped their good morning. A couple of trees revealed shades of autumn. In the distance, a tractor rumbled to life. A school bus ahead flashed a signal to turn right.

A call from the SSA came in. Grayson hoped for something good since they'd just talked. "Yes, sir."

"Got an update for you," the SSA said. "Ethan Formier isn't dead."

"What do you mean?" Grayson startled. "I thought his body had been identified."

"DNA report just hit my attention, and the man with Formier's ID worked at the airport. Looks like the VP of product development at Gated Labs staged his own death."

Grayson's mind spun with the man's top security clearance. Formier had worked at his current position for over seventeen years. Taryn highly respected him. The perfect cover. "He's up to his eyeballs in this mess."

"His real name has been confirmed as Valmir Korzha, a Serbian. He's been in the US for twenty years. Fell under our radar soon after he arrived in our country. Intel shows us he took on the name of Ethan Formier, married a widow with three children, and played the role of the perfect family man. Joined a church. Supported charities. Served on the school board."

"A sleeper. He can't be happy about Taryn keeping things from him about Nehemiah."

"Right. We're working on assumptions here, but we're thinking the airport bombing was a diversion from the software theft. We've learned is parents and family were killed during the struggle when the Serbs attempted to alienate the Albanians."

"Serbs despise Americans because of our interference."

"Exactly. Could be Korzha was content living in the US until his family was killed. And that brought him out of hiding to seek revenge."

"Like making a statement at terminal E, fueling his revenge."

"By killing his alias, nothing leads back to him. High dollars are supporting his activities. We're digging deeper to find the who and what's planned. His wife is devastated, incredulous about his real identity. All of this will be presented in a briefing here in five minutes. We're holding a press conference at nine thirty and will release to the media and public all our findings on Korzha."

"Do you think the Serbian Mafia is funding him?" Grayson said.

"We have intel stating a faction inside Russia is behind this."

Enough said. "I don't suppose the export companies will postpone their launch?"

"We don't have proof of any wrongdoing, and their software is working. We've shared our concern, but it's still a go for them," the SSA said. "The two companies have stated there is little proof to link the airport bombing to them. Of course, both want to make history. Which means we have a little over two hours to wrap this up.

Korzha obviously thought he didn't need Young in the beginning and banked on her death at the airport. If his intentions are to damage our infrastructure, he'll stop at nothing. The hacker is working on the needed access, but nabbing Young ensures it."

He understood the power of torture. Not his Taryn.

The SSA cleared his throat. "I need something substantial for the two companies to alter their schedule. This is clearly a big deal for both US companies to turn on the spigot simultaneously, with lots of media attention."

"Could the file Taryn uncovered from Korzha have been a plant to draw her into a trap?" Grayson said.

"It definitely pounded a few nails in Haden Rollins's coffin. A dead man had encrypted files that pointed to the guilt of other persons in a terrorist case. With Formier's reputation, his eulogy would have read like a hero's."

"How do you think Ryan fits?"

"She was probably in just as thick. We'll see what we learn once we finish examining her files."

Grayson didn't ask how long that would take. 'So who's Wallace working for?"

"Given his reputation, I'd say Korzha. If Murford was the only assassination, he'd have left the country as soon as he completed the kill.

But Ryan's murder has his signature, which suggests she could have been running or didn't think Korzha would eliminate her. Wallace's habit is execution style, and Taryn's disappearance is his first kidnapping. The payoff must be really good."

"What's Rollins say about it?"

"Claims he never heard of Korzha. Said Formier was so straight his shoes squeaked. Neither did Pedraza recognize the name. Facing murder and possible kidnapping charges is loosening his tongue. Pedraza and his attorney have been deep in discussion. He didn't take his sister's death well. Look, Grayson, we've got to find Taryn before it's too late. Korzha and Wallace know how to get information, and if they already have access . . . you know the stakes."

"We're nearly there."

"The sheriff is offering backup. Sit tight until everything's in place. Radio the agents in the area now."

"Thanks." If he had more time to think, he could lay out all the scenarios Korzha and Wallace might use. Right now all he had was thick woods to penetrate.

Chapter 65

9:00 a.m. Friday

Some days Grayson would like to toss his BlackBerry—and he'd done that very thing a few days ago. Had it really been just the early hours of Tuesday morning when he and Taryn raced through the streets of Houston? When had his feelings for her begun?

Admiration rose when she called him from the church.

Respect hit him when she announced her determination to be a decoy.

Her courage in the middle of danger and unpredictable behavior made her more attractive.

He rubbed his eyes. The blur of days and the building of one critical issue after another were getting to him. Now he and Joe waited on the side of the road for confirmation of every man in place before pressing forward to what might be a useless venture.

"Are you going to answer that?" Joe said, his tone indicating irritation. "It's rung three times."

The caller was the SSA. "Yes, sir."

"Have you arrived at your destination?"

"We're waiting on backup. You've seen the layout with the house on the left and a barn about thirty yards to the right. But neither Korzha nor Wallace would take a chance on being surprised."

"Don't play the hero and go in alone. You've got good people there. Grayson, you're personally involved with this case. Don't let it cloud your judgment and get yourself and others killed. Taryn knew the risks when she signed on."

"Yes, sir." The SSA hadn't said anything Grayson hadn't told himself.

"Do you have any idea how many lives have been lost in this case? I refuse to lose any more on my watch. Focus on Korzha and Wallace. You're a detailer and plan to the millisecond. Get the job done."

"I will." He understood his strengths, his ability to get into a criminal's mind and keep one step ahead of their plans.

"Good luck."

Hope, the sustenance of man's fiber. A prayer lifted for all the law enforcement personnel ready to end this week of terror.

9:10 a.m. Friday

Taryn listened to Ethan explain the two software projects he wanted her to develop. Both sealed the fate of the US. His delight in crippling her country, her home, sent claws of horror through every part of her. She fought to breathe . . . think . . . pray.

Zoey slept at her feet on a filthy floor when

rodents crawled. The little girl's baby doll tucked under her arm. How could she free herself and Zoey from these two madmen? The poor child had been injected with a sleep aid that would keep her oblivious to the world for a while longer. Wallace had revealed that the woman who'd hidden her for Murford was dead—Dina Pedraza, a sister to the man in custody.

Wallace stood at the back door with a high-powered rifle.

"I'm very excited about developing new software for distinct purposes," Ethan said. "One will attack dam infrastructure. Remember our discussion several weeks ago about the concern for the US's infrastructure? Over 4,050 dams in this country are just a hair away from failing. We intend to help that problem along by eliminating a handful of the larger ones. Imagine the deaths and loss of property. Makes the airport bombing look quite small. Don't you think?" He smiled. "The second target will be the sewage system for he top five major cities. Polluted water. Disease. More deaths. Loss of fish and wildlife. People tarving. When this country's economy is snuffed ut and mass panic occurs, the US will fall. You an be a tremendous asset to us, Taryn. Other evelopers are good, but not with your tenacity nd expertise. We'll launch both projects at the me time, like we'll do with the two LNG mpanies this morning."

"Is there anything I can do to stop you from igniting this disaster?"

"And deny me the pleasure?"

"What about all the innocent lives you'll destroy?"

"No margin of concern here. The end justifies the means. Something else, too. I'll need to get into Gated Labs technology, and I'm sure you'll find a way to make that possible. It's a shame Rollins is such a wimp. I could have used him internally."

The futility of trying to talk him down from anything catastrophic hit her hard. He enjoyed what he was doing. That was the new reality. It amazed her how Ethan had fooled those at Gated Labs, his family, and her. The latter made her furious. She'd come so close to giving him Nehemiah's information before leaving the country with Murford. Nobody would ever use her like a pawn again. She'd risen to the status of leading software developer through grueling work and not compromising when the stake were high. In this instance, the stakes could no get higher . . . the lives of many innocent people including Zoey.

"So for me and Zoey to survive, I need to us my skills for the detriment of my country. Toug bargain, don't you think?"

"What are your priorities? Life or patriotis for a country that's being defeated by the san principles that made it great?" He snorted. "Your integrity bores me. Because of my generosity, you and that kid have been given an opportunity to live."

She could argue, or she could feign agreement. The US was her home, and she'd die defending it no matter what the rest of the world thought. "Ethan, you give me no choice. I see where the world's headed—technology rules the planet."

His lips curled. "You'll have the finest working environment. I've overseen the area, and you and Zoey will be able to live onsite." He smiled. "You can thank me now," he said as calmly as though he spoke about the weather.

The candle on the table flickered. "When would I begin?"

"That's a better attitude. We'll leave the country tonight."

She pretended to consider his words. At an airport, she could find a way to escape. Weren't all the airways covered? Her face was posted everywhere. "What about clothes and personal items for us?"

"I'll arrange for someone to get whatever you need. Where we're going is not a fashion spot."

Russia had much to gain by destroying the export of LNG, but controlling the infrastructure of the US? Government agencies would see what was happening and stop the grandiose scheme.

Her stomach tightened. Maybe the plan wasn't impossible.

Ethan laughed. "Even in the shadows, I see the wheels turning. You want all the answers now, but your curiosity will have to take a hiatus." He folded his arms across his chest. "Who knows? Your services could be used indefinitely. Depends on how nice you are to me."

Sleeping with the enemy. . . . A disgusting thought, but she wasn't surprised by the implication. "Can you please untie me?"

Ethan pointed to the gun on the table. He rolled up the cuff of his shirt and revealed a wicked knife. He stood and displayed a holster and another gun. "Are we on the same page? I have my own method of handling unruly and uncooperative people. Your self-defense skills are worthless when my first target is the kid."

He was right. "I understand."

He gestured around him. "This small room is the only area that's not wired to explode when entered. I have an arsenal of grenades and weaponry at my disposal. The barn will detonate in precisely twenty-five minutes. Armed helicopters will arrive to pick us up. Later on, we'll board a private plane that will take us to our destination. I've been busy while you thought was in Mexico. There's no escape and no means of rescue."

Chapter 66

Through binoculars Grayson scanned the area where Korzha and Wallace supposedly held Taryn and Zoey. A police officer on the rear side of the property confirmed the barn held three vehicles: an SUV, a Lincoln, and an Accord. Thermal imaging revealed four persons inside the boarded-up house, all in the rear.

Korzha'd had months to fine-tune his plan, and this setting was the most unlikely spot for him to hold hostages. Police officers were in the woods behind the property. Additional officers and four more FBI agents covered the mud lane leading to the house and barn. More law enforcement and FBI were on their way, including a SWAT team. Not one sound from inside the house.

Grayson handed the binoculars to Joe. "What do you see?"

Joe panned from the far left to the right. "Either a fool or a genius. And Korzha is not a fool."

"If he were to initiate a war zone in this place, what would it look like?"

"Military-trained soldiers. Weaponry. Grenades. A foolproof way to escape with hostages."

"A few land mines?" Grayson pointed to the dead grass and brush in front of the house.

437

"That's a bit much," Joe said.

"Take a few steps and prove me wrong. He had two weeks to set up the battlefield."

Joe shook his head. "You might be right, like you were about Russia's involvement."

Grayson picked up a bullhorn from the sheriff. "Valmir Korzha and Cameron Wallace, release the hostages and come out with your hands up."

"Fat chance," a male said.

"You're surrounded."

"That's what you think. If we see anyone approaching, the woman and kid are dead."

Grayson played the odds of what he'd analyzed. Korzha needed Taryn to complete his plans, or she'd already be dead.

Grayson studied the brush to the immediate right and the knee-high weeds providing coverage several feet from the barn. The area looked as deserted as the rest.

"Joe, I'm going around the barn. See if I can detect what they're doing."

"I'm with you."

A car pulled up to the scene. Grayson recognized the agents emerging—and Buddy. The German shepherd raced to Grayson's side and nestled against him. What a reminder of God' presence: the angel protector dog. Thatche Graves jogged to his side.

"Glad you're here," Grayson said. "Dealin with a couple of professionals in there."

"Thought you might need a good eye." Thatcher's dark eyes emitted sincerity. "I've always been the better shot."

Grayson grinned. He needed a boost. Buddy nearly knocked him down. "I wonder who arranged for this four-legged agent."

"I made a few calls," Joe said. "So now there's three of us going after Taryn and Zoey."

Joe didn't need to be working this hard. "I'll do this solo."

"We're partners, and I guarantee Korzha doesn't intend to stay cooped up in that old house much longer."

Grayson didn't have time to argue. He explained what he planned to the sheriff and other agents, then requested a wire cutter to cut through a barbed-wire fence separating them from the overgrown field. If Korzha and Wallace were to leave with the hostages by car, Grayson and Joe would be ready to greet them. The two men made their way behind the string of cars to the fence, bending low and avoiding exposure. Grayson clipped the wire.

"I hate snakes," Joe said, crawling through the fence opening.

"And they come in all shapes and sizes."

"Smart aleck. By the way, there's a huge ant pile on our right."

"Thanks." Grayson watched the house and barn through binoculars. Nothing was visible but the officers stationed in the woods in the distance. He hoped Buddy had an instinct for what they were about to do. "We need to hurry."

"Korzha and Wallace aren't playing hide-and-seek."

They moved fast—crouching, crawling, rushing. Buddy made his way behind Grayson and in front of Joe. Halfway between the road and the barn, Joe groaned.

"Are you all right?" Grayson said.

"Yeah. Blasted fire ants."

"Send 'em into that poor excuse for a house."

"I prefer someplace hotter."

Only Joe could find humor in the worst of situations. They had cover from the road and from the woods, and all they had to do was take out two men and free Taryn and Zoey. FBI work had never been easy, and he had no reason to think so now. Sounds from the road indicated the SWAT team was in place.

Grayson and Joe moved closer to the barn. The sound of a turbulent sky grasped his attention. Two helicopters approached, their swish of whirling blades growing louder. They weren't law enforcement. The copters circled and descended onto the field behind the house.

Grayson spoke into his mouthpiece. "Do no open fire until we see what's happening. We're circling behind them now. I'll signal when to fire." He swung a glance at Joe. The man's fac and lips were swollen. "Hey, what's wrong?"

Joe shook his head. Couldn't speak.

"Need to get you help." Grayson contacted Thatcher. "Joe's down. Looks like anaphylactic reaction to an insect or snake. Need an EpiPen." He checked Joe's breathing—shallow.

The helicopters hovered over the field. Joe grabbed Grayson's arm. "Go," he mouthed.

The pressure increased on Grayson's arm. Help was coming for Joe, but how could he leave him, the man who'd loved him unconditionally? He stared into Joe's eyes, and the message was clear. Grayson swallowed hard and nodded. He stole away with Buddy, praying for what he was leaving and what lay ahead.

The barn stood a little more than fifty yards away. He calculated his speed and the copters' mission. His thoughts turned to his dad and the cancer. Strange, when he needed to focus on disabling two helicopters without killing Taryn and Zoey. But when this was resolved, he'd call Dad. See if their relationship could be patched up.

An explosion rocked the countryside, and the barn blew splinters up and out. Grayson dove to the ground, but a flying piece of wood scraped across his thigh, anchoring itself with a nail. Probably rusty. He jerked the nail and wood from his burning flesh. Pure adrenaline and a bigger dose of God spurred him on. Buddy was uninjured.

"Good dog," he whispered. "So glad you're here."

Seeking cover behind one pile of debris after another and ignoring the pain in his thigh, he peered toward the helicopters landing near the house. He limped across the field while calling for backup to wait for his signal to open fire. The SWAT team would burst onto the scene when he gave the word.

An area between the woods and the copters exploded. . . . Within seconds, another blast erupted between the house and the road. How many more land mines were planted?

To his left, Taryn emerged from the rear of the house carrying Zoey and struggling with her left arm in a cast. She walked single file, body to body, with Wallace in front and Korzha in the rear. They moved toward the second copter. From the corner of his eye, Grayson caught sight of officers exiting the woods. One raised his rifle. Only an expert sniper needed to attempt this, and he doubted the officer was the man.

"Do not fire," Grayson shouted into the mouth-piece. "I'll give the call to take out the copter pilots." He didn't want shots fired into the engine and a resulting explosion.

The officer refused to stand down, and from Grayson's stance, he didn't have a clear shot at the pilot nearest him. Another officer rushed toward the shooter but not before he fired, missing the pilot and plunging a bullet into the engine of the copter nearest the woods. The explosion sent fragments of metal propelling in all directions. Taryn and her captors took cover beside the helicopter nearest the house. As soon as the pieces stopped flying, Korzha and Wallace used Zoey and Taryn as shields, shoving them into the remaining copter. Only time stood between Grayson and the copter exploding from the bellowing flames.

The pilot who manned the remaining copter fired repeatedly.

Gunfire split the air, most likely from Wallace, while the SWAT team rushed forward. The pilot in the hostages' copter went down.

Grayson refused to take another shot and risk the hostages' lives. Wallace climbed into the front of the copter, a skill not recorded in his profile. Korzha was the one with his pilot's license. Grayson took Wallace out, then moved around the copter to face Korzha.

"Give it up, Korzha," he said over the swirling blades.

"No thanks. My next bullet will take care of one of the hostages. Which one? You choose."

"Let's talk. What do you want?"

Korzha laughed. "I already have it. The export terminals in Corpus Christi and Kitimat will explode at eleven. Nothing you can do to stop it."

The SWAT team moved closer, but a clear shot

at Korzha was impossible. "I suggest you release them. You have the password."

"Right. And you'll shoot me down. This is a trio deal. We're leaving." He pushed Wallace's body from the cockpit with his gun aimed at Taryn. She wouldn't try to overpower him, not with Zoey and a broken arm.

Grayson calculated three seconds to take the shot, but the wound in his thigh made him dizzy, affecting his aim. Buddy barked and growled, dividing Korzha's attention. Grayson leveled a bullet into Korzha's head. The man fell back. Lifeless.

Taryn jumped from the copter. While holding Zoey with her broken arm, she grabbed the dead man's backpack.

She limped toward Grayson and Buddy amid the shouts to move away from the copter. Grayson guided her and Zoey to safety . . . hurrying them away from the death zone. Simultaneous explo-sions sent all of them to the ground. He positioned his body over Taryn and Zoey.

"Thank you," she whispered. "I knew you'd come."

Chapter 67

10:50 a.m. Friday

Taryn allowed Grayson to hold her and Zoey. Both trembled in his arms. She sobbed while clinging to Zoey, and Buddy nestled close to her. She'd stopped questioning where the dog had come from because he'd been heaven-sent. And Grayson was another gift from God.

"Hey, you're safe," he said. "Both of you."

"But I failed." She shook her head, the trauma of more lives lost sinking into her heart and mind. "He programmed a sequence of events at the export terminals in Corpus Christi and Kitimat to cause explosions at eleven. At this point, I can't stop it without using the backdoor and custom app on my iPhone. And it's not in the backpack."

Grayson motioned to Special Agent Thatcher Graves. "Call for those terminals to be evacuated immediately."

"They have to get people away from the blast zone," she said. "More will die."

Grayson squeezed her shoulder, but it did little to reassure her. "Is there anything you can do to override the command?"

"Nothing without my iPhone. The last thing he did before he disconnected was to alter the access credentials."

Zoey lifted her head from Taryn's shoulder, her dark curls framing her pale face. "Aunt Taryn, are you looking for your phone?"

"Yes, baby."

"It's in my doll. Miss Dina put it there before the bad man came." Zoey pulled the ragged and dirty doll from under her arm. "It's inside, under her dress. Miss Dina opened her up and then fixed her."

Taryn set Zoey onto the muddy lane and examined the doll. The back had been slit and glued. Inside lay the iPhone, minus her red-jeweled case. Why Dina had changed her mind would forever be a mystery, but her decision could change destiny.

"Please, let there be juice." She kissed the top of Zoey's head. Had this precious child seen Dina's murder? *Later . . . later.*

She pressed in her PIN, bringing up Nehemiah's backdoor. "How many minutes do I have?"

"Four and counting," Grayson said.

She nodded. Once inside the program, which had been set to abruptly build pressure and increase temps, she was able to access both systems simultaneously and return things to normal. A few moments later her body relaxed and she closed her eyes. "Thank You. For everything." Glancing at Grayson, she offered a shaky smile. "It's over. No fireworks on either coastline today."

He lifted her chin. "With thirty seconds to spare. You're amazing."

"My doll," Zoey whimpered.

"Don't worry, honey. I'll fix it for you," Taryn said. "Even get you a new one if you'd like."

"Okay. Where's Mama? I thought she was with you."

Taryn choked back another sob. She stole a look at Grayson, then back to Zoey. "Jesus came to get her, honey. She's in heaven with Him."

"When will I see her?"

"I'm not sure, but when you do, it will be wonderful. Until then, I'm going to take care of you."

She tilted her head and blinked back a tear. "I'm sad."

Taryn pulled the little girl close to her. "Me too. We both loved your mama very much."

Grayson's arms circled them, and she relished his strength.

"I've got you," he said. "I have both my girls."

Chapter 68

7:30 a.m. Monday

Grayson, Taryn, and Zoey walked into the stately church for Claire's celebration of life. He stole a look at his bruised and battered lady. An usher asked if she'd been in an accident.

"Sort of. I'm on the mend now."

"You have a beautiful family," he said to her and nodded at Grayson.

"Thank you, and we intend to keep it that way," she said.

Grayson felt the commitment in Taryn's words. They had a long way to go before words of love passed their lips, but this was a beginning. They both understood it.

Zoey sat in the middle of the pew. Fortunately the meaning of death was vague in her little mind. She'd been told people would be singing songs and talking about how much they loved her mommy. Time and patience would help heal all of them. The wall of terror had crumbled once Korzha had been brought down, and other arrests followed.

"Will Bentley and Buddy be all right until we get back?" Zoey said.

Taryn kissed her forehead. "They'll be fine with Uncle Joe until we return."

"Good. Uncle Joe is feeling better?"

Taryn nodded. "He just has to be careful around fire ants. I have a surprise for you. Next week, you and I are going to look for a house."

"A house?" Her brown eyes sparkled.

"With a backyard for you, Bentley, and Buddy to play."

"Mr. Grayson too? I mean, when his leg is better."

He chuckled. "Oh, I'll be making lots of visits."

Taryn caught his gaze. Her green eyes offered hope and promise. "Will you help us find the perfect home?"

"You won't mind a third wheel?"

"I'd welcome it." A slight blush filled her cheeks. "Mom said she wanted to meet you. You're her hero."

"You're the real hero. Hey, I'm really glad you were able to talk to your family and explain what happened."

"I need to arrange a visit soon." She glanced away. "Brad Patterson called me yesterday afternoon."

"Did he want to know when you were going to clean out your office?"

She gave him her attention. "Sort of. He offered me the position of VP of product development. He tossed in his apologies and a hefty raise."

Grayson gave her his best surprised look. "Well done. Are you going to take it?"

"I think so. I told him I wanted to work one day a week at home and no weekends."

"He agreed?" That didn't sound like the Brad Patterson he'd met, but Taryn had helped save Gated Labs.

"Yes." She laughed. "I also suggested the company consider an on-site day-care facility and preschool, for better employee morale."

"What did he think of your idea?"

"He's going for it. He must have been considering it before my suggestion because he talked about parents being able to share lunch with their children. Even hire an on-site nurse."

"I'll need to change my opinion of him."

She grinned. "Remember your SSA gave me an option of prison or being an FBI recruit? I'd make a poor agent—always going against the rules. And I don't want to leave my little girl for training. She needs me now. Plus, I've grown fond of the man who saved us."

"Lucky man." He would have said more, but he needed patience. "So you're taking on more responsibility?"

"I'll still be doing what I love, and that sounds good to me. I requested Kinsley to take over my leadership role on the development team, but she's resigned. Actually, Patterson said she left the city." Taryn gave him a sly look. "I bet you know all about those plans."

Grayson touched her nose. Haden Rollins and Kinsley Stevens had chosen to change their names and start all over. Grayson hoped it worked out for them.

"I'm glad you're here with us," she said.

"Before the music begins, I have something to say," Grayson said. "Congratulations on your fabulous media interview Friday afternoon. You melted those vultures. And when Zoey snuggled against you, the cameras flashed faster than the speed of light."

"For the first time in my life, I feel the path forward doesn't have to be alone."

"Not for a minute," Grayson said. "I take my protective detail seriously."

Epilogue

April—7 months later
10:00 a.m. Saturday

Taryn stole a glimpse at the clock on the microwave. Three hours until Zoey's fourth birthday party. The little girl had chosen a Hello Kitty theme, and even Buddy and Bentley wore bandannas with Hello Kitty on them. Not exactly masculine, but the two dogs would get over it.

Zoey couldn't keep still, and Taryn was stressed. The party bags hadn't been filled, and the meteorologists had threatened that the warm spring weather could bring rain. But the front and back yards sparkled with color. Joe had planted marigolds and purple petunias earlier in the week, and of course Zoey had to help.

Grayson had said he'd arrive between ten and ten thirty to pump up balloons. He'd also bring the cake—and she needed his support. They'd seen each other or spoken every day since

September. He'd promised to be her best friend, and he'd never stopped proving his devotion. She valued his advice in selecting a home, a white stucco two-story with a huge backyard, and he'd surprised Zoey with a swing set and a play-house. He'd gone with both of them to counseling . . . and two weeks ago when the adoption was finalized. Today he promised Zoey a trip to Chuck E. Cheese's after her party.

The man witnessed her ups and downs, listened to her challenges of motherhood and her triumphs, and they'd talked about everything from selecting furniture to problems in the Middle East.

In short, she loved Grayson. How very good of God to take a tragedy and weave it into a blessing. The situation with his dad had tempered slightly, and they talked often, even though the conver-sations tested Grayson's patience. The older man liked to grouse about his cancer treatment but was holding his own . . . and he adored Zoey.

Vince was in a hospital after a complete mental breakdown. Once he realized how he'd betrayed his country, he attempted suicide. And yet he still had charges to face for his actions. Grayson and Joe visited him every Sunday night.

The doorbell rang, and she hurried to answer it. Grayson stood in the doorway hosting an irresistible grin and holding a Hello Kitty birthday cake. He wore a pair of jeans like no other man on the face of the earth.

"You're a lifesaver," she said.

"I told you I'd pick up the cake."

She took it from his arms. "I'm talking about the timing. I'm stressed to the max. Why I think a four-year-old's birthday party has to be perfect is beyond me."

"Bravo." He kissed her on the cheek. "Admitting it is the first step."

She started to add that his kiss made her dizzy, but she'd save it. "I have fresh coffee, and would you believe Zoey is cleaning her room?"

"That tells me she'll need help, but I want to talk to you two together first."

Taryn crossed her arms. "Is this about our private party at Chuck E. Cheese?"

He flashed his incredible blue eyes. "It's about a party all right. I'll get the munchkin."

She poured coffee, her thoughts trailing to the party bags and the little girls from Zoey's preschool class. Motherhood was fun but exhausting.

Grayson carried Zoey into the kitchen and lowered her beside Taryn. "I've got to do this before the birthday celebration."

He bent to one knee, and Taryn smiled. He had a special gift for Miss Zoey. How considerate.

"Taryn, Zoey, I have something I want to ask you." He opened his hand and displayed two small boxes.

Taryn's heart beat triple time.

He reached for her hand. "You two are very special ladies to me. I can't imagine going through a single day without seeing or talking to you. Guess I'm saying I love you very much. I know it's only been seven months, but, Taryn, would you marry me?"

Her eyes widened. She didn't need to think twice. "Yes, oh yes. I love you, and I'll marry you. Right after the birthday party."

He laid one of the boxes on the floor and opened the other for her to see. A glittering princess-cut diamond picked up the sun rays through the window behind them.

"It's beautiful." Her eyes filled with tears. "Grayson, you shouldn't have gone to such extremes."

"My girls are worth so much more." He stood and kissed her, sending warmth and joy through every inch of her body.

Zoey tugged on his shirt. "What about me? Do I get to marry you too?"

He dropped to one knee again and took her hand. "Miss Zoey, would you let me marry Mommy Taryn and be your Daddy Grayson?" He opened the box to show a gold heart necklace that looked like two puzzle pieces.

"Ah, it fits together." Zoey clapped her hands.

"Like us," he said.

"Oh, Mr. Grayson, you shouldn't have gone to such 'tremes."

Not a muscle moved on his face. "Is that a yes?"

Zoey wrapped her arms around his neck and kissed his cheek. "Best birthday ever." She nibbled on her lip. "I think Mommy in heaven asked Jesus to give me a new mommy and daddy."

Grayson picked her up and planted another kiss on Taryn's lips. They all had a better tomorrow, and forever had a beautiful sound to it.

A Note from the Author

Dear Reader,

The idea for *Firewall* has been with me since 2007. It started as a what-if: what if a couple on their honeymoon were separated, a bomb exploded, and like Taryn, the young woman learned her husband had been using an alias? The story would not leave me alone, and the more I thought about it, the more the plot grew.

My friends at Houston FBI are amazing. They helped me with protocol and arranged phone calls with those who serve in the bomb squad and terrorism units. For their support, I'll always be grateful.

A side note: strange dogs frighten me, especially German shepherds, and I wanted a heroine who was more courageous than I in that arena. Remember what Claire told Taryn about being approached by an unfriendly dog? Claire told the dog that Jesus loved him. I say the very same thing each time I encounter a strange, unfriendly dog.

I hope you enjoyed Taryn and Grayson's story. My goal is always to entertain readers and inspire them to attempt great things!

Be blessed.

DiAnn
Expect an Adventure
DiAnn Mills
www.diannmills.com
www.facebook.com/diannmills

About the Author

DiAnn Mills is a bestselling author who believes her readers should expect an adventure. She currently has more than fifty-five books published.

Her titles have appeared on the CBA and ECPA bestseller lists; won two Christy Awards; and been finalists for the RITA, Daphne Du Maurier, Inspirational Readers' Choice, and Carol award contests. DiAnn is a founding board member of the American Christian Fiction Writers; the 2014 president of the Romance Writers of America's Faith, Hope, & Love chapter; and a member of Inspirational Writers Alive, Advanced Writers and Speakers Association, and International Thriller Writers. She speaks to various groups and teaches writing workshops around the country. DiAnn is also a craftsman mentor for the Jerry B. Jenkins Christian Writers Guild.

She and her husband live in sunny Houston, Texas. Visit her website at:
www.diannmills.com
and connect with her on

Facebook (www.facebook.com/DiAnnMills),
Twitter (@DiAnnMills),
Pinterest (www.pinterest.com/DiAnnMills),
and
Goodreads (www.goodreads.com/DiAnnMills).

Discussion Questions

1. Taryn steps too quickly into marriage with a man she believes loves her. Does Taryn, in her excitement about the relationship, ignore signs she should have heeded? Would she have seen through the deception if she'd taken more time? Have you ever been betrayed by someone you thought you could trust? Looking back at the situation, how would you have handled it differently?

2. Growing up, Taryn often felt ostracized because of her shyness and high intelligence. Have you ever been singled out because you were different? What would you say to someone who has trouble fitting in?

3. If you were in Taryn's shoes, suspected of committing a heinous act of violence, would you have run away from the hospital and the FBI? Or would you have trusted the FBI to handle things? How might things have gone for Taryn if she had stayed?

4. Grayson takes a chance when he believes Taryn's story. What convinces him she's telling the truth? Would you have trusted her? Why or why not?

5. Joe West became Grayson's mentor and gave his nephew a home when life with his dad became unbearable. Have you ever been a mentor or even taken someone into your home? What were the results? Is there someone in your life now who could use this type of guidance or hospitality?

6. In chapter 10, Taryn seeks refuge in a church and has a spiritual awakening. How do Taryn's attitude and actions change after this scene? In what ways does she succeed in clinging to God and where does she continue to rely on her own strength and wits? What lessons can you apply to your own life from her?

7. Though Taryn is afraid of dogs, a stray German shepherd becomes a huge comfort t her during this crisis. How do you feel abou dogs or other animals? Have you eve experienced a situation where somethin unexpected helped you cope with a difficul situation?

8. For years Grayson has carried guilt over his role in his mother's death, struggling to find forgiveness from his family and himself. What makes someone hold on to guilt or other emotions like that? What would you say to encourage Grayson to let go?

9. Despite Grayson's objections, Taryn repeatedly risks her life to find Zoey. Would you have done the same? Have you ever risked something big for the sake of a loved one? What was the outcome? What spiritual parallels can you draw from Taryn's sacrificial devotion to the little girl?

10. What was your reaction to the villain's motivation for the airport bombing? Does anyone ever have a right to seek revenge? If so, under what circumstances? If not, what would you suggest as an alternative? What does Romans 12:17-21 have to say about revenge?